The Tsarina's Favorite

Valtinen Erik Karille

ISBN: 978-1-969894-00-8

www.valtinen.com

Cover design by Shellie Karille

To my Mikalay, inspiration and ancestor,
who deserved a kinder legacy than being reduced to a footnote
in a tyrant's tale.

ACKNOWLEDGMENTS

This novel would not be (for better or worse) without the support and encouragement of:

Shellie Karille, my brilliant and talented wife, who not only designed the cover but continuously ensures that I do not delete every word I write immediately after writing it, and who also endures Mikhail's incessant grumpy commentary on nearly everything in our lives with absolute grace and understanding. It is due to her dedication that this book has matured into something I am proud to put out into the world.

Kiersten Thompson, my cheerleader and friend, who is loud about my storytelling in rooms I am not in and supports it in every meaningful way.

The team of Clintonville Books in Columbus, OH, with additional gratitude to Tracy Ramey, who believed in *Tsarina's Favorite* enough to host the launch party.

And, although I dedicated the book to him, the real-life Prince Mikhail Alekseevich Golitsyn, whose undeserved persecution far exceeded what I could include in a cohesive narrative and whose legacy deserves reevaluation.

I should have been afforded a change of clothing and some small allowance of hygiene before being presented to the empress. How kindly could she possibly look upon me if I did not offer her the version of me she preferred? The bedraggled, sleep-deprived, filthy cell-resident ill-fitted with the standard she demanded of court. Maybe, however, my pathetic state might inspire sympathy and mercy. Sympathy and mercy for what transgression, I had no idea, but the charge little mattered when the tsarina could perceive anything as a slight.

The other nobility avoided me and my guards as we paraded through the halls. I purposely avoided gazing into any of the mirrors that lined the walls, certain that I did not wish to see any reflection of mine in this sorry state. Maybe a good clean would be my last request, if indeed whatever my transgression was merited a last request. Surely, the empress couldn't deny me that?

When we entered the long hall of the audience chamber, my escorts paused with me. No one paid mind to our little group. Advisors and attendants swarmed around the tsarina at the far end of the hall. Courtiers occupied the edges of the cluster, creating a less dense but no less intent layer of devotees. Smaller groups in smaller clusters dispersed beyond that layer.

Alexei slipped out from his group when he saw me, careful not to draw the attention of the others. His urgent stride carried him over to us in less than ten paces, his robes flying behind him in a style more dramatic than he likely wished while trying to be covert.

"Mikhail," he whispered, his panic evident despite the lowered tone, "I thought you were in Varnasia. You look a mess!"

No one would have known that my cravat had once been of the finest Jeanvian white lace, tatted by the reclusive residents of the Great Holy fortress, Our Lady of Weeping. No one would have guessed that my shirt had been composed of the finest Nypatian linen and hand-stitched by Varnasian master tailors. The fabrics had browned by grime and body oil. Fleas and lice would have found an admirable home in my current ensemble. I denounced my brilliant blue coat as a lost cause with the gash in the shoulder from rough handling. My shoes, scuffed beyond repair, might also get tossed into a fire when I finally procured another pair.

"My apologies for not changing into a new shirt before my arrival," I shot back at my brother. "My company," I directed my eyes askance to the guards, "couldn't wait."

Alexei turned his attention to the guards. "Is there a charge?"

The guard addressed only said, "The empress requested Prince Mikhail's presence."

"It's not uncle this time," Alexei said to me. "She had him executed while you were gone."

"It could be anything."

"Not anything serious," he insisted. "She was likely in one of her moods."

Her moods. About anyone else, I might have quibbled as we all had moods, but the tsarina had power to accompany them, and that boded ill for all.

A call from the other end of the chamber echoed around the room.

"Prince Mikhail!"

Everyone's attention, not just mine, fixed all the harder

upon the tsarina. She rose from her throne, her satin skirts billowing out and shining like mirrors themselves. She caught up one side with her left hand and descended the dais almost in a hurry. The layers of assembled persons peeled away as she progressed through the crowd, the instinctive choreography of her subjects offering her an expansive corridor through the middle of the room.

Alexei retreated from my side.

"Mikhail!" The empress moved as if to embrace me and then stopped just a few steps in front of me, thinking better of it. "What a state you are in!"

"The laundering services are sorely lacking in prison, Your Majesty."

She laughed and held out her hand for me to kiss.

I stepped forward, took her hand, and bowed, kissing the back of it as silently instructed to do.

"I should have thought to get you a change of clothing. Still, I shall see to it forthwith." She waved off my guards, glanced over her shoulder, and addressed the crowd. "I shall return."

She began walking out the doorway through which I had just arrived and beckoned me to join her. I glanced at Alexei, and he glanced at me, both sets of our brows lifting in apprehension. Still, I followed, and she grabbed my arm once we were out of the main audience chamber.

"You have been gone forever," she chided me.

"Five years only."

"That's forever," she insisted. "So much has happened."

"I heard about your nephew passing. I'm so very sorry."

"I'm stuck with his wife, though."

"She's Altanian. Send her home."

"That's what she wants," the tsarina grumbled. "But I wasn't allowed to go home when my husband died. I refuse to let her either."

I refrained from offering any additional ideas, and the tsarina continued so that I would not have to devise any additional topic of conversation.

"There were riots not long ago," she continued. "I don't understand why. We're winning our campaign in the south. The Ilyichians should be happy, and yet, I fear, they are only happy when they are miserable. I have had to suppress so many demonstrations and issue countless executions. Thank The Kind and Fair that the empire is so vast, or I might run out of subjects!"

I could not speak to her direct experience, but if being a sovereign meant taking such human suffering in stride and becoming callous to it, I would never have made a good one. Even when in the military, I had not savored issuing punishments for the transgressions of my men.

"We had several more sightings of the firebird," she added when I did not comment on the state of the country. "Do you remember when I wanted the white jackdaw? I thought that was something special. Can you imagine what a coup having a firebird would be?"

"You have everything now, ma'am," I said, gesturing to the palace. "If you caught the firebird, what wish would you have it grant?"

"I would ensure that you never parted from me again," she teased. "But you won't, will you? Of course, you won't. You're back now."

Anything safe I could say would have been a lie, so I kept silent.

"And, in other good news," she continued, "my engineers finished the designs for my ice palace so I can make a marvelous tribute to The Kind and Fair this winter. The Royal Academy of Science even requested to use it to study the weather, which, of course, I'll allow. Every region of the empire will send representatives dressed in their traditional clothing to form a procession unlike any other seen before in the city. The ice palace will have everything made of ice, down to the furniture! Even with tufted upholstery and blankets. We have hundreds of sculptors lined up for the project."

The expenditure, the frivolity, the pointlessness of such an endeavor struck me as an affront to the people of the city who already despised the nobility as unconcerned with their plight. Festivities would be a distraction, but only for a short duration. Their hunger and discontent would still be there when the festivities ended.

I settled on, "That sounds like a lot of planning."

"Almost the entire time you've been gone. You spent all that time in Varnasia?"

"I went to Alfinia first, Talvia, Allemandia, then south."

"And you forgot all about me."

She directed us towards doors that led out to a courtyard and garden, the fountains bubbling, the birds singing, several people walking the gardens, laughing together over a shared joke.

Even in the fading spring, the Ilyichian chill crept into my bones.

"Never, ma'am," I assured her. Nightmares refused to let me forget her.

"I had to arrest you to ensure your return to me."

"I would have returned if I had but a little more time," I lied.

"I have had to satisfy myself with my Allemandian in your absence." She pushed a long dark ringlet strand behind her shoulder. "Long-standing though he is, he isn't you."

"I had obligations, ma'am."

"Mmmm." Her tone soured. "I heard you married again. A Varnasian wife."

"Yes."

"A Varnasian wife who worshipped the Great Holy."

"Yes."

She fell into silence, her quiet a dangerous calm that heralded a pending disaster.

We strolled through the garden, the other courtiers sliding glances at me. She noticed and nodded her head at them when they dipped into curtsies.

"It seems no one has seen the beautiful and elegant Prince Mikhail so disheveled before," she said after we passed them. The tsarina stopped us in our walk as soon as there was enough distance between us and the other strollers and turned her face up to me, her mouth tightening, her brows drawing together. "Mikhail, I have been very angry at you in your absence. You broke many a lady's heart when they heard of your marriage."

Could the tsarina be speaking about herself?

"I only intended on doing the honorable thing," I assured her, "not wound anyone. It's been eight years since Marfa passed. I need heirs."

She raised her hand and placed it on my face, brushing my cheek with her thumb. Although not an old woman, she wore her age poorly, the creases of displeasure and dissatisfaction deeper than I recalled, the creases around her mouth betraying a lifetime of scowling even if she currently schooled her face into something attempting pleasant.

"I have missed you so," she admitted. "My Allemandian's skills pale in comparison to yours."

"Skill can be acquired."

"But he can't acquire your humor or your bite."

"Give me but a few days and I can show you a dozen witty, elegant men in your court."

"They won't have your beauty."

"It is fading."

"Good thing I still want you even without it."

I shivered.

"I want you to become my lover again," she whispered.

She released me and retook my arm, directing us back to the audience chamber through the gardens.

"While you were in prison, I had rooms readied for you. And I sent for your things. You can move in immediately."

My back stiffened. When we had been lovers before, it had been occasional, casual, and done from obligation. When I escaped Ilyichia, when I escaped her, I vowed that I would never let myself be used like that again. And yet, what choice had I?

The doors that led back to the audience chamber loomed ahead of us. If I stepped through those doors and into the audience chamber with her on my arm without saying anything, I would condemn myself to a future of sexual servitude until either she or I died.

I could not allow that to happen.

Just before the doors, I stopped walking. She took another step before she realized I was not following, and she turned to me, her brows furrowed.

"Your Majesty, I...." My throat constricted. "You've been very kind," I started, easing her into this, although a stint in prison was not my definition of kind. "I appreciate everything you have done, ma'am." Words aimed at survival tumbled from my mouth. "I have missed being at court and being in your presence. I long to serve you however you see fit, but...." I held her gaze, praying that she understood my sincerity and listened to me as she had once pretended to do. "Anna, please understand. I cannot become your lover now."

"But I've done everything for you." The excited animation of her plans for my future as her bedmate collapsed into confusion. "Everything."

"I know," I assured her. I let go of her arm and took her hand with both of mine. "You've been so generous and so thoughtful to consider all my needs. But I am still grieving. I need time. I do not wish to disappoint you, but I will since I cannot be all that you would have of me."

"You will not be my lover?"

The word, though expelled in a whisper, came out clear and sure. "No."

Her mouth opened just a little. She tore her eyes away from me and blinked several times in succession. Her composure returned, if not any indication of warmth.

I ventured, "You do understand, don't you?"

"Yes, I understand." She took my arm and then turned back to the doors.

We walked through the doors together and into the audience chamber. This time, those gathered paid me more attention, and most of them wrinkled their noses at me.

"I believe you all remember Prince Mikhail Alekseevich Karilitsyn." The tsarina released my arm and turned to me, her hands folded in front of her. "Indeed, how could anyone forget him?"

Small noises came from the crowd, murmurs and rumblings of recognition passing through them like an illicit love note.

"I thought to forgive him for his transgressions," the tsarina continued, "but upon my conversation with him, I am questioning his faithfulness and therefore his worthiness of my mercy."

"I have always been faithful," I protested. "To you. To Ilyichia. I served in Ilyichia's military, ma'am. I took my state marriage vows seriously. I do not take upon such commitments with a half-heart."

"Oh yes, you just love marriage, don't you?"

"Your uncle forced me to marry Marfa. And whatever you may think, I have never stinted on service to you."

"Is that so?"

"How may I prove it?" I asked, hoping she would not re-announce her desire to have me as her lover in a crowded room.

"I have been considering this very thing." She stepped back from me and said, her voice loud enough to get the attention of all others in the room if indeed there were any others not attending yet, "All, do you see this faithful servant of mine?"

Murmurs rippled again.

"By his account, Mikhail has always been my faithful servant," she said. "And as that is so, I have treated him most poorly. He deserves not the prison, but an honored place at my side."

"I would settle for a bath and a change of clothes," I said.

"You always could make me laugh." She smiled a little too benignly. "But fear not, I have a bath and new clothing already arranged for you." She raised her voice again, not for me but for her audience. "You see my mercy? Mikhail's years of faithful service to me have not gone unnoticed. And despite his betrayal of his empress by marrying without consent, and his betrayal of the country by denouncing The Kind and Fair and following the Great Holy for that marriage—"

"Neither action affected you or the country," I protested.

"Ha! He admits his treasonous actions of his own free will," she declared.

Treason? Of course, anything she wanted to be an offense could be. But treason?

"And yet, I am merciful!" The tsarina smiled at me, eyes soft, almost kind. "I will not kill him as one who has betrayed me rightfully deserves."

The breath in my throat suspended there, suffocating me by neither entering my lungs nor being expelled. I took a step forward and guards — when had they returned? — grabbed my arms to keep me from progressing any farther.

"I shall forgive him and allow him to continue to be my

faithful servant. Is that not merciful?"

Some of the crowd cheered, although most shifted uncomfortably with the uncertainty of what such a pronouncement might mean. Her words, however generous they sounded, did not bode well for me.

"My dear Mikhail," she said as she breached the distance between us, "I do not wish to see you die, and I know you will continue to serve me in the future." She turned away and threw up a hand, inviting the room to rejoice with her as she pitched her voice. "Behold! I have a new jester!"

"*What?!*" The shout of rage and confusion bellowed out of me before I could consider the wisdom of response. The guards gripped my arms to painful throbbing points with a force that would be visible later. This couldn't be. "But I am a prince."

"Oh, didn't I tell you?" she asked, turning to look at me over her shoulder. "Not anymore. And," she returned to me and took my left hand, removing the gold wedding band from my finger, "you won't be needing this."

"Please," I begged. "That's all I have of her. Please don't take that from me."

"I think I'll have it melted down into a brooch."

"Please, Your Majesty. *Please.*"

She gestured to someone in the crowd, her thoughts completely distanced from the subject of my ring, and Alexei stepped out, sweating in his finery.

"Prince Alexei, do you wish to join your brother in his plight?"

"No, Your Majesty."

"Then?" she prompted.

My younger brother's mouth twisted into a grimace. "Prince Mikhail—"

"Just Mikhail now," the tsarina corrected.

"Mikhail," Alexei gulped. "It grieves me that you have

betrayed our empress and our country. Neither I nor the rest of our family shall have anything to do with you. You are no longer a Karilitsyn."

If blood rained down from the sky, the floor turned to wax, the heavens crashed into our mortal plane, I could not have been more stunned.

The tsarina's attention no longer on my brother, Alexei slunk back into the crowd and escaped while everyone's attention centered on me.

"You can't truly mean to do this," I said, gulping around my horror.

"But I have already done it."

I stopped fighting the arms that held mine. No physical constraint could bind me worse than my new status.

"Have my years of devotion meant nothing to you?"

"How you squawk!" She paused with that accusation and then laughed, her entire face lifting in almost girlish delight. "If you squawk so easily, Mikhail, I will make sure you have plenty of opportunity to do it for everyone." She flicked her eyes to the guards and waved her hand dismissively. "Show him to his new accommodations and ensure he makes himself fit for his next appearance."

My dry mouth prevented me from saying anything else, either in protest or my defense.

She hadn't killed me, but I wished she had.

II.

Delivered from guards to household staff, aprons replaced gold braid, and burnished glittering halls devolved into dark, cramped corridors. When deposited in a barren communal room, a servant demanded my clothing, and I did not protest. I sat near the fireplace, too stunned to care about my nudity, wiping down with a dirty rag from a basin of water whose bottom I could not see. I passed the stained, scratchy cloth over my skin dozens of times, no cleaner for the multitude of attempts at making myself so. Even the ache from sitting on the stone hearth could not pull me from my numbness. My head swam while the rest of me continued to go through the motions.

My naked ring finger finally brought tears.

Someone eventually pointed me to a straw pallet on the floor. I just nodded and retreated to it. No worse accommodation than in prison then, but I lacked the privacy to lick my wounds and indulge in self-pity. Instead, I stared at the ceiling.

Tomorrow, I told myself, reasoning with panic and misery. Tomorrow, I could think about it seriously and fully and find a solution to it. Tomorrow, I could figure out where it had all gone wrong. Tomorrow, I could worry about the future.

For now, I would just stare up at the ceiling, my wet hair plastered to my head, my nakedness covered only by a scratchy blanket, and try not to think about anything at all.

I failed miserably. My younger brother's face haunted me through the night. A grown man, of course, but all I saw was a terrified little boy who realized that even his older brother could do nothing to keep him safe. Not now. He had done what I expected him to do, and, though painful, I would never have wanted him to get pulled into any of this anyway.

But when tomorrow came, nothing happened to torment my imaginings or fulfill my fears. The day after too only saw me shelling peas and scrubbing floors in the kitchen with coarse draw-string trousers borrowed from another. Glances from those around me slid in my direction when they thought I would not notice or would not see, but each smug look burned like spitting embers from a fire.

And I kept silent.

Silence was the last bastion of dignity.

It was not humility that frightened me. The military did not skimp on physical challenges, filthy work, or menial tasks. I had put my hands to many an occupation that, outside of royal uniform, might have been consigned to serfs. I had toiled beside commoners in pursuit of a military goal. I had shared in labor and victory with all walks of life during my military career. My wealth, family name, titles, and personal achievements had cushioned the harder realities of life after I retired from the military, but few things held the power to frighten me at my age.

It was the other thing that frightened me, the word the tsarina gave me of which I had no personal knowledge beyond some court entertainment: jester.

That invited far too many possibilities for which I could not properly prepare. It implied amusement and entertainment exacted from mockery and ridicule. It was a different kind of humility than I had ever known. The humility I knew was based on necessity, and this new one was based on absurdity. So the tsarina, if she could not make me her lover, would make me absurd.

Would I be given a cap and bells? Standard in the courts throughout the continent, yes, but not often seen in Ilyichia.

Would I be made to tumble or dance or warble bawdy songs? Would the tsarina want me a wit or a dullard? And if I were to become such a thing, should I not be in communication with her others so that I might find a way to navigate the new role she had thrust upon me? I had yet to speak to anyone beyond the maids and footmen who had no idea what to do with me.

I did not have much longer to wonder. Within the week, another servant roused me from my slumber and bade me follow.

I could have disobeyed when they instructed me to follow. I could have disobeyed at any time up until now, refused to play the role assigned, attempted to flee the palace and my fate. But the servants watched, more intent and curious than any guard, and they would be the first to correct any unseemly behavior, their potential cruel glee in having the opportunity to degrade a former prince worse than any prison.

The servant conducted me to another room, not ornamental enough to be public for nobility, but slightly more ornamented than the servant rooms. Two others awaited my arrival, dressed better than the servants who had overseen my last few days. They interacted with nobles as a daily obligation. I no longer knew my precise place now, but I possessed wisdom enough to assume my lowliness. These people, servants though they may be, had charge of me.

I ran my hand over the scruffy hair growth on my face and up through my wild, unbrushed curls. I likely looked a mess, but did that matter now?

No one said anything, all of us aware of the strangeness of this arrangement.

"Put those on," the woman finally said, breaking the tension. She gestured to undergarments and white tights laid out over a bench.

Both servants pointedly looked away as I shed the trousers and replaced them with the offerings. Without a tunic or other apparent clothing to go over the tights, I shifted my anatomy to a less awkward position.

While most nobles I knew, especially those who retired from the military, turned to complacent heft in their aging comfort, my frame had lost the width and mass of muscle from daily exertions. And while nakedness did not shame me, the act of being displayed in the nude, even if it was just my top half and just in front of servants, left me wishing I had retained some of my exercise regimen and the respectable musculature it provided.

Vanity, it seemed, had not left me entirely.

The tights suggested the part of a tumbler. And without additional garments, the cold would creep into my bones unless I exerted myself.

I rubbed at a scar on my right shoulder, a token of a foolish youth who insisted he could best me in swordplay, though I had been almost twice his age at the time and thus had twice his experience. He glanced my shoulder with the blade, but the opening I had given him to do so offered me the victorious strike, permanently scarring his cheek and thoroughly disarming him so that he had no choice but to surrender.

This too had to be played like a duel. All my advantages had been stripped from me. But just because I was without weapons did not mean that I could not out-maneuver a tsarina accustomed to getting her way. I would be willing to be scratched, scarred even, if it gave me an opening to win. I prayed that I had enough energy, endurance, and fortitude still left in me.

When the silence again hung thick in the air, I asked, "Do you know what role she intends to have me play?"

The servants glanced at each other. A knowing look, but an unwilling one.

"That good?" I sighed and bowed my head. "Shall we

then?"

"We're not done," the woman said. She gestured to the bench and indicated for me to sit.

I obeyed.

The woman brought over a long-sleeved shirt and held it out for me to put my arms and head through. My arms found the sleeves without trouble, but the woman had to help me with the neck. She pushed an attached hood behind my head and pulled white gloves over my hands. She glanced at her companion when she finished.

The other servant brought over a massive white pillow and held it out in front of me.

I blinked, not comprehending what was required.

"Your arms," he explained.

I held my arms out, not certain what the aim might be. The servant found arm holes in the pillow and slipped them over my hands, up my arms, and hefted the pillow over my shoulders. My sleeves billowed out from the pillow, covered with white fabric strips. The woman came behind me to pull the pillow around and begin fastening it.

After an interminable stretch of time and my heated panic forming sweat beads on my brow, I asked, "Are the buttons that complicated?"

Another stretch of silence answered.

"No," the woman said, again unwillingly answering me but not so uncivil as to ignore me completely. "I am sewing you in."

My body assumed the stillness of prey, my shoulders and spine rigid in the heat of my horror. I tasted bile. A fever spiked as I fought not to tremble.

"I'm sorry," the woman whispered. "She said she would have my hands cut off if it came undone."

"Then," I assured her with a calm I did not feel, "please take your time and do a good job. You need your hands."

The pillow's heft and compression, growing tighter around my torso, would not allow me to remove it. This was to be my costume until the tsarina decreed otherwise.

Sweat dripped from my temples and hairline.

"What..." I struggled to choke out words. "What role am I to play?"

The man, realizing that the woman had taken the burden of this strange and tension-filled conversation, whispered, "You are going to be her chicken."

III.

I focused on the raw suede edges against the bridge of my nose and my cheeks. Pain offered visceral and immediate distraction, occupying my mind enough to keep my attention from the audience around me. The straps would cause sores and then open wounds eventually. The leather buckles, fastened behind my head, caught in my hair. Sweat soaked under the hood, through my shirt, and through the many padded layers of my costume. I couldn't put my arms down properly, and I couldn't get out of it. Despite my words to the servant and no personal wish to see her harmed, I had tried. I had to try.

After shaving, being fitted with the leather beak, and pulling the hood over my hair, I waited for the servants to turn their attentions away from me. I fought the fabric, stretching and bending in ways that might make the stitches stretch, loosen, and snap. Nothing had come of it. The tsarina had chosen a skilled seamstress for the task and had given that poor seamstress proper motivation to do the best work of her life.

"How clever you are, Your Majesty," a lady said.

I snapped back to dreadful awareness, the discomforts not enough to keep my full attention. I shifted in the basket, a clever construct designed to replicate a nest, and tried to make it as little obvious as possible. This was meant to be awkward and uncomfortable, but I had no intention of giving the tsarina the further satisfaction of seeing it.

"He always has something to say," she replied. "Why not allow him to squawk as he pleases and entertain us at the same time?"

The group laughed. Alexei, thankfully, was not among them.

If only I had to worry about discomfort alone. It was the misery, the emptiness, and the loss that tormented me. And the shame.

"Truly inspired," the first lady said.

Not just shame. Shame beyond expression.

"I've always wanted the fabled firebird for my menagerie, but alas, a firebird costume would be too stately for the nature of his crimes." The tsarina took in my costume once more. "I would have preferred real feathers, but overall, I am quite pleased with how he turned out. Real feathers can always come later."

I shut my eyes so I could not betray the extent of my hate for her.

"What's wrong, Mikhail?" the tsarina asked. "I am not accustomed to you being so silent."

When I did not think I would react on impulse, I opened my eyes and met her gaze. "What would you have of me?"

The ladies smirked behind their fans.

"First," the tsarina considered, "some kvass."

I glanced over at the array of refreshments on the marble-topped gilt console along the wall across the room. I struggled to my feet, working around the new bulk of my costume and fighting the stiffness of my legs from having been tucked in my basket nest all morning. Some of the ladies turned their faces away while others stared even more intently, waiting for me to do something particularly humiliating, as if my current predicament did not provide enough amusement.

The tsarina was of the latter group, although her stare came from an aloof observational demeanor. She studied me from her throne as I lumbered to my feet, ambled over the basket side, and began my progress to the refreshment table.

The burning gazes from the crowd added to the unbearable warmth of my costume, the fabric against my skin already soaked through. Perspiration dripped off my nose inside the beak mask.

A smaller insulated circle of women near the console table discussed me too. Though the hushed words came out with less bite, they still reached me as I hunted for the pitcher of kvass.

"I told you it was horrible," said Countess Ekaterina, a classic Ilyichian beauty with ivory skin and pale blonde hair, a woman who had once tried to capture my attention and an offer of marriage before I left for Varnasia. She doubtless counted herself fortunate now for having not succeeded.

"Doesn't it scare you?" asked a woman I did not recognize.

I tried to be surreptitious in my glance towards the small gathering. The speaker, uncharacteristically dark-skinned for an Ilyichian and extremely short for any adult, fingered the pearls around her throat. Although she had her black hair coifed in an elaborate style around her kokoshnik and she wore the latest of Ilyichian fashions, nothing could hide her foreign accent and unfavorable looks.

"I don't think he's scary, Princess Alaina," another woman said.

"Of course not," added one of the other ladies. "He's just ridiculous."

Princess Alaina. The tsarina's niece-by-law. I could see now why the tsarina, and her nephew too, had despaired over the match despite the potential political gains. From all accounts, the princess was situated to inherit the throne of Altania when her childless brother died. I had not met her or seen her before, having already emigrated to Varnasia by the time of the wedding.

"No, I didn't mean it like that," the princess said. "It

scares me that this can happen. This could be any of us if we misstep."

"You're as good as the tsarina's daughter, and, dare I say, the heir apparent of Ilyichia," a lady said. "It could never happen to you."

"And he was a prince, from one of the wealthiest and most powerful families in the empire. If it could happen to him...." The princess cast a not-so-subtle glance at me before returning her attention to her ladies. "Could you imagine being so degraded in front of your peers?"

"I would rather die," the countess said.

"He probably would too," the princess observed with another momentary glance at me.

I lowered my eyes and returned to my task of pouring kvass so that I would not have to see any others of the group look my way. Between the mockery and the pity, I could not decide which stung more.

The princess was right, of course. Mounting the scaffold to an executioner's block and facing the headsman's axe would have brought with it its own shame and embarrassment, but there would have been an end to it. A swift, sudden, immediate end. None of this indefinite torture.

I brought the glass of kvass back to the empress and stood to the side and behind her so as to keep her attention only on her current conversation. I held the glass in front of me, to the periphery of her sight, so that she would see that and nothing else.

When the conversation bounced to two of the officers in her gathering, she took the glass and asked, tone lowered so that only I could hear it, "Do you regret your decision yet?"

"What decision would that be, ma'am?" I stared at the gilt wood finial of her chair, wishing to set it on fire with her in it. "I have made so many that you hold against me."

"The one where you turned down my offer of a better

position than your current one. If you reconsidered, I might be persuaded to listen to your petition, so long as you made it worth my time."

"I would have to be a fool to do such a thing. And just because you've dressed me like a fool and given me the title, do not mistake me for one."

"Is that so?" A smile tugged at the corner of her mouth. She waved her hand and beckoned me forward, hushing the crowd around her as she did so.

"I require an entertainment," she told the group. "Mikhail, entertain us."

I stepped forward, obeying her gesture and bearing the unwanted attention of former friends and acquaintances. Portions of my soul continued to shrivel and die.

"What would you have of me?"

"I would have your humor. You're always so funny."

"He's the funniest thing of all," Sergey said, a rat-faced courtier of my age who imagined women owed him something and whose company I had never been able to tolerate.

"Clearly, you have not looked in a mirror lately," I shot back at him.

The assembled laughed, including the tsarina, and his cheeks puffed out, red and furious.

"There's my Mikhail," the tsarina said.

"But he—" the courtier spluttered.

"Did exactly as I asked," the tsarina cut him off. "Now, now, Mikhail. A joke or a tale, else you might earn yourself a beating when I am not here to defend you."

"I have only my bitterness, ma'am. You have stolen my humor from me."

"My word," she feigned surprise, "was it that easy? Very well. Something easier then. Any suggestions?"

Laughter again traveled around the grouping with various ideas being offered. Singing, dancing, juggling all given as possibilities. I paid them no mind as I waited for the tsarina's instruction. The tsarina sipped at her kvass, listening but unmoved by any of the traditional suggestions.

"I know," she said when the group found silence again. "Squawk for us!"

"Excuse me?"

"You heard me. Squawk." She leveled a malicious glare at me. "And flap your arms."

My heart refused to stop beating. My lungs refused to stop filling with air. If humiliation could kill, I should have been dead many times over by now. But I was alive and at another crossroads.

Complying would be the easiest course of action. Painful, humiliating, degrading, and ridiculous though it might be, the tsarina might leave me alone afterward if I satisfied her request. And to be forgotten sounded like the most merciful fate in my current circumstances. Complying might inspire others to seek the same torturous amusements from me in the future though, but if I failed to be as entertaining the second, third, fourth time, would they still try to provoke me?

Disobeying would be amusing to me for a whole half minute until the tsarina found another novel torment with which to burden me.

And all because I could not bring myself to become her lover again.

No one said no to the tsarina.

A deeply unsettling noise, both shrill and guttural, issued forth from my throat. My arms made wild arcs in the air at my sides to accompany the horrendous shrieks.

The tsarina threw her head back and laughed and laughed and laughed. And so too did the group around her. No one noticed when I stopped, too caught up in the hilarity to pay any attention to the object of their amusement.

The tsarina's paroxysm finally subsided, and she discarded

her empty cup before rising from her seat. She paused in front of me, taking me in again before smiling up at me. "I am never going to let you go, you realize." She reached up and patted my cheek, her palm sliding over the straps of the beak mask. "Return to your nest, Mikhail. I will see that someone comes out to feed you." She slid her hand down and patted the chest of the pillowed costume. "No one will ever want you now."

"Except you," I whispered. "What does that make you?"

"Have a good night, Mikhail," she said, her voice ice. "Tomorrow, I am fitting you with a collar."

IV.

My fitting the next day turned out not to be with a metalsmith but with the seamstress again, who sewed a constricting white boned-fabric collar around my neck. Feathers embellished this new accessory, both from above and below, lending additional verisimilitude to my costume. The white feathers from above the collar scratched my chin and face. Those from below fanned out in a heavy mantle, warm bright colors ensuring that I could not be missed in a crowd. Ribbons too dangled from the collar, small bells at the ends of them, ensuring that everyone would know I was coming from rooms away.

The collar, though not changing anything fundamentally, added discomfort to an already impossibly uncomfortable situation. The bulk of the costume already proved difficult to arrange in order to sleep, but the collar prevented any natural position. I resigned myself to sitting up to sleep, resting upon the bulk of my costume that would not enable me to rest lying down. And while being certain I would never be comfortable or rest easily again, each night my eyelids let the weight and misery of the day close them until morning.

I tried, with only a modicum of success, not to sneer at the bowls of borscht served regularly. So much of Ilyichian cuisine itself served as a punishment that anything traditional might have been met with disdain. The red lumpy liquid, almost devoid of any meat, failed to inspire anything but disgust as I circled the spoon around each bowl, hoping I might find it, if not more appetizing, at least less repellent than the last. But I ate it anyway, hunger winning out over preferences.

I eventually saw the tsarina's other jesters performing their duties when she grew tired of me and sent me to my basket nest or had me take the place beside her to pour her kvass. Most of them, of diminutive stature, tumbled or told bawdy stories. And they dressed well, not as I did with an absurd costume to denote my position, but with handsome suits and dresses that would not shame anyone should they attend an evening ball.

That was why I had not met them then, despite us all holding the same title. I would embarrass them too.

No one bothered keeping guards or servants on me now, now that I wore an unmistakable costume that would not permit me to hide or move with ease. Now that I wore a costume I could not easily remove and therefore would not get far in an escape attempt.

I took advantage of every moment of privacy to use the chamber pot too, unwilling to imagine the heights to which courtly amusement would soar if anyone realized they could ridicule me while I struggled to defecate. I only hoped the process would get easier with familiarity.

Oh, Great Holy, I did not want to get familiar with this.

My one relief came in the empty nights, waiting until I was completely alone to remove the gloves, push the hood back, and slide the straps of the beak behind my head so that I could lower it around my neck. I took every opportunity to remove the beak as it had formed terrible sores on the bridge of my nose and around my mouth. My ablutions and nightly shaves offered a small respite. I welcomed the evening chill on my face, otherwise hot with perspiration and shame. I may no longer have been Prince Mikhail, but those moments of quiet solitude free from the mask and the hood and the gloves offered me the opportunity to be a person again rather than an object of ridicule. I lived now only for those moments. And each morning, I said farewell to myself as I replaced my beak, pulled up the hood, tugged on my gloves, and resumed being the tsarina's favorite plaything.

My existence fell into a dull routine, providing merciful numbness with each tired request of amusement. At least until I did not wake early enough to replace my costume before the tsarina found me.

Prodding from a walking stick woke me. I stared up at several painted and powdered faces peering down at me, their leering expressions grotesque and unnatural. For one fleeting moment, I considered that, even in my costume, I was the least absurd in the room.

The tsarina stood at a distance from the others, the apex at a channel lined with courtiers. The tightness of the empress' lips spoke of displeasure.

"I have never seen a bird remove its beak before," one of the peering people remarked.

I fumbled for the gloves.

"Take this as your one warning, Mikhail," the tsarina said. "I will have one of your fingers cut off every time someone of my court sees you without your complete costume."

That would be impossible. Of course, I did not miss the implication that I should never be out of any part of it. The sweat on the back of my neck chilled.

"And when I run out of fingers, ma'am?"

"Then toes. Or," she mused, thinking better of her threat, "if removing fingers and toes does nothing to inspire you to change your ways, then I will have your nose sliced off that you will wear the beak willingly to cover your disfigurement."

I repositioned the straps of the beak around my neck and head, then pulled the beak up over my nose and mouth. I also pulled my hood over my hair.

"Better," the tsarina said. "It would pain me to ruin that handsome face of yours. But I will do it if I must."

Pain her, maybe, but I did not underestimate her willingness to see me lose bits of myself as a lesson to others. That's what I was now — a lesson. An example set to remind those around her that they needed her permission to live and breathe and have a life outside of her good graces.

"Fetch the kvass, Mikhail, and then keep us company while we stroll the gardens."

I obeyed, a silent servant in a chicken costume, trailing behind her group with the pitcher of kvass ready to refill their glasses.

Not even a quarter hour into our walk, Sergey tripped and spilled the contents of his glass over me, the sticky liquid soaking the feathers and padded costume. I developed a quiet endurance, having learned that silence made others lose interest in me, but I still exclaimed from the surprise of it.

The tsarina spun around to see what caused the commotion. Her gathering stopped when she did. She narrowed a glare at me, one brow lifting.

"Sergey could never hold his liquor," I explained, trying to mop up the spilled drink with my sleeve. "But now he's proven that he cannot even hold his kvass."

"It was an accident," Sergey protested.

I bit back the urge to say "was not" like I might have as a boy. But I couldn't keep my mouth shut entirely. "How relieving to know that he's as much an idiot as he appears."

The tsarina strode back to me, disregarding Sergey entirely, and threw the contents of her own glass in my face. Then she laughed.

"Sergey," she said, keeping her eyes fixed on me, "if you're going to do it, do it with intention next time and then let us know so that we can share in your amusement."

She held her empty glass out in front of me and waited.

I poured her a new glass as kvass trickled down my forehead and cheek.

"You can squawk as much as you like, Mikhail, but chickens that don't lay eggs have to provide something else." The tsarina's mouth split into a grin. "I would like to keep you around. So why don't you lay an egg for us?"

"I have no eggs to offer," I said as I wiped my face.

Her eyes flattened and her face tightened. "Do your best."

And so, swallowing down the little miserable bit of pride that still protested, I did my best.

I continued to do my best throughout the following days. Each day became a little easier in action if not in emotion. The daily exercises wore me down until I no longer recognized myself. I barely ate. And when others reminded me of my place and function, I performed like an automaton. I no longer noticed those who stopped at my basket to gawk. Even the sores that cracked and bled from the unfinished leather of my beak could not recall me from my growing apathy. Yet somehow, despite my skin thickening and my heart numbing, the torments still found my unguarded places.

The days blended into one another. I wore a significant amount of old kvass despite cleaning during the nights, the stains stark against the white padded costume, although the white had softened to a general yellow-brown.

Alone one night and absently pushing the dregs of my stew around the bowl, a voice pulled me from my wool-gathering.

"It's the chicken prince."

My back stiffened, aware that such an address could not mean anything good. Recalling the tsarina's warning, I pulled the mask back up, although I continued picking at the soup as if I had not heard.

They approached from the left, a mob of well-dressed fools with enough drink in them that I could smell it across the room. Several held wine glasses as they meandered over to me.

"How is the tsarina's pet this evening?"

"Finishing up dinner," I said.

"Since when do chickens use spoons?"

One of the querants moved forward and smacked the bowl out of my hands. The bowl hit me in the jaw, and the contents of the stew ran down my front and into my lap.

"Bawk, bawk," one of them jibed as he leered over me.

"You do that rather well." Against good sense, I looked up into his face. "I'll be sure to tell the tsarina, and she can give you a nest beside mine. I'll carry her kvass, and you can spend all of your energy trying not to make an idiot of yourself. I would find it most entertaining to see you perpetually fail."

The jiber took a step forward, but one of his companions caught him by the arm, preventing him from immediate action.

I didn't know the group of men. They were newcomers, youths — a mismatched conglomerate of sons, military upstarts, and those who married into court life. None of them would have ever been worth my notice. And they knew it.

"You have a surprising bite for a chicken," said the one who seemed to lead the group, a fair-haired man who wore a moustache and a military uniform, a young officer in Her Majesty's guards. "I think you've forgotten how a chicken acts."

"Have I? Why don't you demonstrate? I would appreciate seeing a more accurate portrayal."

"He thinks he's funny, Krintova," one of them said to the leader.

"I'm a jester now," I said. "I have to at least try."

"We can find ways for you to amuse us," Krintova said.

Two men approached me, one from either side.

Maybe I could have fought. I probably could have

successfully fought off one. Maybe two. Although my lack of energy and will to live had reduced me to nothing but a shell of myself, I did not want to try it.

"What do you want from me?" I asked.

"Get out of the basket."

I obeyed, standing and then stepping out of the nest.

One of the two men grabbed my wrists and began binding them behind my back. Once they were bound, the man lifted them, twisting my arms painfully so that he could fasten the other end of the binding around my neck. Trussed up, I could only wait to see their plan.

"Now those are proper wings!" One of them pointed to my elbows as I fought to give my wrists some release from the awkward position.

"You're already a better chicken than you were a few moments ago."

"Don't you usually look down at chickens?"

"It matters not how tall I am. Everyone looks down at me now," I assured them.

"Is that why you had to get a Varnasian wife? Was she a whore who couldn't do any better?"

That undid my self-restraint. I kicked the drunkard between his legs, and he hit the floor with a yowl and a gratifying thud.

The rest of them set upon me, bringing me down easily with my arms already bound. They bound my ankles too and attached them to my wrists, trapping me in a position from which I could not shift without pulling on something else.

The man I tried to castrate came over holding his crotch. He spat on me. Several others followed his lead.

"You haven't learned your place yet," Krintova said.

Someone from behind shoved me forward so that I fell face-first into the floor. The padding of the costume and the leather beak cushioned my fall, but I still landed eye-level with the officer's boot. He landed a kick into the bridge of my nose. Blood poured into the mask.

"I need another drink," one of them said over me.

"Should we release him?"

"Leave him," the officer said, withdrawing and leading his group with him. "He can think on his haughtiness for a night just like that."

Alone, I contemplated how best to right myself. But even with solitude, quiet, and logical effort applied to the situation, I only struggled against the costume and the bindings, unable to pry myself off the floor.

Hours passed. I dozed a little, not for long when I did manage because of how the binding pulled on the collar. Those peaceful darkened hours of quiet transformed into a nightmare as I lost feeling in my arms and legs.

The clicking of heels on tile finally offered hope as I strained my neck to glance in the sound's direction. The clicking neared.

What exactly did I shout out to get someone's attention? Help? More like they would come over to gape and laugh and walk away to find others they could show.

My debate about eliciting aid died when the clicking stopped. Then it came loud and fast as the person hurried over. My bindings loosened, my legs and then my arms, until the cord was removed from around the collar. I could barely move as my limbs regained circulation.

"Oh, merciful Kind and Fair," she breathed, "what is that?"

I found myself staring into the face of Princess Alaina sitting on the floor beside me. I turned away and tried instead to concentrate on rising. I drew my arms under my chest and pushed myself up on my forearms until I could sit back on my legs. A poor idea. I shifted instead to sitting directly on the floor and twisted my neck to try and loosen it as much as possible in the confines of the collar. I grabbed one of the formerly-white sleeves and dabbed my face inside the beak mask to clean the dried blood.

"It's blood," I told my rescuer. When she continued to stare at me, I asked slightly more defensively than the situation merited, "What? Have you never seen a chicken with a broken nose before?"

"Someone did that to you," she said.

"That doesn't matter."

"But it does!"

"The tsarina has done worse, and I'm expected to be quiet about that. So tell me, Your Highness, what does it matter what anyone else does to me?"

"It's cruel," she insisted.

"Welcome to Ilyichia." I stretched again, this time focusing on my shoulders and my back. Every joint and muscle screamed in pain. "I thought you might have been here long enough to figure that out."

"That's why I am here this early," she said. "I hate it here, and I want to go home. She's usually in a better temper in the mornings to hear petitions."

"I hope she hears you," I said, trying to be slightly more gracious to someone who had just so recently come to my aid.

"She hears me, but she never grants it. This will be my thirty-second petition in two years."

"Then I hope it is different this time."

She stared at her hands folded in her lap in an attitude of defeat.

"Thank you for your assistance," I said when she seemed disinclined to continue our conversation. "But for your sake and the sake of your petition, you may not wish to be seen speaking with me. I am not her favorite person."

"I had no idea," she said, an almost-secret smile touching the corners of her mouth.

Noises echoed outside the chamber. The princess's smile vanished as quickly as it had appeared, and she scrambled to her feet, putting as much distance as she could between us.

I retreated to use the chamber pot and to wash off as much blood and food as I could. The former was much needed, and the latter lamentably did little. I did not have time to shave though, and I returned to the chamber feeling only marginally better than when I had left it. Only petitioners had gathered when I took my place in the basket.

The tsarina arrived a short while later, a sea of bobbing heads and bowing forms preceding her. She made her way through the room and headed straight to her chair. Once there, she surveyed her gathering per usual and stopped her examination when she saw me.

"Whatever happened to you? You look appalling."

"Nothing, ma'am."

"He was beaten," Princess Alaina said at my refusal to disclose details.

The tsarina glanced at her niece-by-law and then back at me. "I warned you. Let it be a lesson to you to mind that mouth." She then returned her attention to the princess. "And what have you to say today?"

"I came to formally ask if I could return to Altania."

"No. Next!"

The princess curtsied deeply and withdrew, having been summarily dismissed. She gathered her skirts and walked to my side of the room so that she could make her escape. She sought me out with her eyes and held my gaze when she found it. She mouthed no words and made no gestures, but for that tenuous moment of connection, I understood her perfectly. I might have been in a costume and she might have been in a gown, but we were both prisoners of the tsarina and therefore exactly the same.

V.

When someone ambled into the empty chamber during the evening later that week, my body tensed up and I plotted an escape through the servant passageways. I still could not fight without the fear of dire retaliation, but I planned on taking the threat of harm more seriously. I had no desire to be trussed up again for another night.

"You're Mikhail."

I turned to the direction where the voice originated and found myself staring into a pockmarked mountain range, peaks and crags forming something akin to a face, large dark eyes the only waypoints around which I could determine other features like a nose and a beard.

"You're Mikhail," he repeated. "The prince."

"I'm Mikhail. The chicken."

The strange face formed a canyon only recognizable as a smile by the display of teeth. He clapped his fully-formed child-sized hands together. "Even better."

"I fail to see how."

"What use have most people for princes? They are dogs bred for aesthetics, not intelligence or purpose. Better to be a chicken."

"Should I not prefer to be a dog then?"

"Never." The little man's canyon smile spread. "No one would think to chain a chicken."

The corners of my mouth pulled upward — a surprise when I thought I might never have a reason to smile again. "Who are you that you are so insightful?"

The man bowed to me. "I am Drook."

"It is my pleasure to meet you, Drook," I intoned politely, unable to shed the niceties the way I had been stripped of everything else. I almost offered my hand, but refrained as it was impolite to offer a gloved hand, and I had been threatened with dismemberment should I lack any component of my costume in the presence of another. "Would that we could have met under other circumstances."

"Other circumstances are not always better circumstances."

I could not deny that observation.

"And we have met," Drook said. "Before. When you were at court."

Before, when I was a prince and he was but a lowly jester. Before, when ladies flirted with me in an attempt to become my new princess, and nobles wanted to play cards for a chance at my fortune. Before, when I had never spared him a moment to ask for his name as one polite individual to another. Or that of any of the others who amused us.

I had the good graces to blush beneath the beak for my prior indifference and superiority. I was the lowliest one here now, and as my former peers had done, I fully expected that the jesters too would expel me for not truly belonging among them.

"I was never afforded a formal introduction," I told him, gathering as much dignity as I could. "My apologies."

"Unnecessary." He buffed his nails on his coat lapel. "I like my reputation to precede me."

"Indeed," I assured him, thankful for his gracious excuse to explain my prior haughty incivility. "I heard you recite a poem about The Kind and Fair Protectors of Ilyichia the other day."

His brow lifted, and so too did the corner of his mouth. "I composed it myself."

"Masterfully done."

"Thank you."

He sat on the edge of the basket, settling in for conversation.

I asked, "Do you believe that The Kind and Fair give the tsarina magic to uphold the kingdom?"

"It's what everyone says."

"So you don't believe it?"

"I think the belief in it is traditional and in this modern age, metaphorical." He shrugged. "It's good for art, but I don't believe in actual magic."

While I too did not believe in magic, his assessment relieved me. The tsarina already wielded so much power that I shivered to think she could have more to misuse.

"How do you account for the sightings of the firebird," I persisted, "if you do not think the magic of The Kind and Fair is real?"

"Something else being mistaken for the bird of myth. Or maybe the Otherland creature is real and so too are The Kind and Fair. But magic usually goes partnered with roses, and I have never seen a rose, not even in Ilyichia. Still, I am open to being proven wrong." He canted his head at me. "You don't believe in The Kind and Fair or magic either, except that you had to make it official."

"I am a convert to the Great Holy, if that's what you mean."

"That's the reason the tsarina punished you."

"One of them." I did not want to discuss it. "I don't know that I believe in anything anymore. Or that I ever did. But I can still appreciate a well-told tale and a finely crafted poem. I need no titles or spiritual belief for that."

"I don't know much about the Great Holy, but…." He faltered. After a moment, he tried again. "If you lack spiritual conviction, why not recant?"

"Because that won't fix anything. And, at this point, she may dictate what I do, what I wear, how I am treated, but I refuse to give her sovereignty over my soul. That, if nothing else, is mine alone."

"Fair." He folded his hands on his lap and glanced around the empty hall. "Would you prefer to be alone?"

"I am always alone now."

"You don't have to be." Drook gestured towards the darkened end of the hall. "If you ever want company of an evening, you should join us. We would have invited you sooner, but none of us thought that you would want to associate with us. And then we thought, maybe it was not that you did not want to, but that you might not know that you could."

"I appreciate the invite, but I don't think I can."

"Why not?" Drook's brows battered each other. "Are you indeed a chicken chained?"

"No."

"Then I presume that it is only the confines of shame which bind you. Lose your shame and you are free."

"Oh yes, why didn't I think of just not being ashamed? The solution is so easy."

"Humph." Drook stared at me, unimpressed. "I didn't say it was easy."

"Any tips or tricks?"

"Breathe," he said. "In. And out. And in again. And out again. You'll get through it, even when you don't want to."

"If it is as you say and it is only shame that sees me trapped, then perhaps I will accept the invitation. Who offers company?"

"We offer company to each other and share meals together."

"Who does?" I asked again.

"The tsarina's jesters."

For one brief moment, all the painful isolation and fear of forever being outcast vanished. I might have been shunned and shamed by my former peers, but the jesters offered me inclusion.

"The tsarina has disgraced me. Are you sure you would not mind having me there?"

"Of course not!" Drook's eyes shone. "You are one of us now."

"He's agreed to join us!" Drook called out as he opened the door to his apartments. "I knew you would want to see him first though."

Meticulously furnished with luxurious fabrics and gilt frameworks, the rooms presented as fine as any other courtier's quarters in the palace. A woman, dressed in a modest but fashionable frock, bent over an embroidery hoop, but as the announcement echoed through the room, she glanced up from her work. And then I wasn't certain it was a woman because I had never seen a person with such a wealth of facial hair, not just on cheeks and chin but forehead and nose as well.

"Thanks be to The Kind and Fair," she said as she rose. "I've been telling Drook for weeks now that he needed to check on you."

"Klessa has been worried about you from the start," Drook explained.

"Why?" I asked.

"Because you're a prince," Klessa said. "And you have no survival skills, not in our world. I'm surprised you've held up so well."

"What choice have I?"

"You could be completely pathetic and nonsensical," Drook suggested.

"Or worse," Klessa offered, "a weeping blithering whiner who does nothing but wallow in self-pity."

"Do not hold any false assumptions about me, lady. I have done a significant amount of wallowing."

"But you're not lost to it," Klessa said as she stepped aside from the sitting area and gestured for me and Drook to find seats. "Although you are a mess." She stopped me before I passed her. "Are those spit stains?"

"I have not been afforded a change of costume yet," I said, trying not to begin a diatribe on how shamefully the tsarina treated me. "Just additions."

"And is that blood on your face?" Klessa threw her hands up in the air. "Drook, I'm holding you personally responsible for his dreadful state."

"I keep telling you," Drook said, "if the tsarina is paying attention and thinks we do too much for him, she's going to find a way to make him suffer for that too. She's been watching too closely before now."

"It's true," I agreed, coming to Drook's defense. "I was a new toy for her before. But now, so long as I am in costume and ready with her kvass, she pays little attention to me."

"Don't defend my husband," Klessa scolded me. "He should have checked on you weeks ago."

"I was waiting until she got a new baboon or something for her menagerie," Drook said.

"If only," I agreed.

Klessa finally released me and pointed to a chair. In a tone that brooked no disagreement, she instructed, "Sit, and take off your hood and beak."

"I'm not supposed to be in the company of anyone without them," I explained as I sat.

"We aren't anyone," Drook said.

"No one," I rephrased, avoiding Drook's semantics, "is supposed to see me without them."

"Perfect," Klessa announced, "because we are no one! Now, take them off."

I debated, glancing to the doorway and weighing the likelihood that anyone but the residents already here might come through. Eventually I relented, pulling back the hood and unfastening the straps to the mask.

"My wife lies," Drook said while I was busy with the beak. "Klessa is a gentleman's daughter."

"Doesn't matter though," she said with a scoff. "The moment they saw that I had my father's condition, the king gave me away as a present. I too am one step above the menagerie, and therefore, no one."

I dropped the beak into my lap and looked up at the woman with the remarkably hairy face. "I'm so sorry."

"Those are some nasty wounds." She took my chin in her hand, also extensively covered with hair, and twisted my face about so that she could get a full view. "And you have skin breakdown." She released my chin and picked up the beak mask from my lap. She examined it and ran her finger over the unfinished edges of the leather. She tossed it at Drook. "See what you can do about that. I need to address his wounds."

"You don't have to do anything," I offered, uncomfortable with the concern.

"You," she redirected her attention to me. "I don't want to hear any protest. You need to wash your hair and face. I'll show you to the basin."

Klessa started off towards another set of rooms.

I rose to follow and hurried to catch up with her.

"Thank you," I said, grateful to have anyone concerned about me at all. "But truly, it is better if the tsarina — if everyone, really — sees something awful when they see me. If anyone should look at me with anything other than disdain —"

"Drook might think he's excessively clever by waiting for the right moment, but your wounds need to be tended before they get infected. Now hush up and wash. Use mine." She pointed to a basin and ewer set out on the taller of the two marble-topped washstands.

I hushed and followed her instruction, removing my gloves. I leaned over the basin and began pouring the cool water over my head. I scrubbed my scalp and shook out the curls, having to untangle and unmat many of them. I washed my face too. At the end of the exercise, I patted my face and hair down to free them from excess water and stood, feeling almost like a new person. Or almost like my old self anew.

I caught my reflection in the mirror hanging above the washstand and stopped toweling off. Any illusion of feeling like my old self shattered. I barely recognized the gaunt, hollow-eyed man gazing back at me. A ring of livid flesh left by the beak encircled his nose and mouth, three primary areas deeply crusted with blood and lymph. Wirey hairs on his cheeks and jawline, my cheeks and jawline, stuck out at odd angles where I had missed them in shaving. Several healing cuts from the same activity blazed red against the sickly skin. I looked less like a man of two-and-forty and more like one of double my years.

When I returned to the sitting room, both Klessa and Drook pulled their attention away from their occupations. Drook grinned, but Klessa just pointed to the ottoman in front of her. I obeyed and sat facing her. She opened a jar and slathered salve on the wounds.

"Why do you care?" I glanced at Drook but returned my attention to Klessa, the question primarily for her.

"Because she insults us all when she insults any of us. And this," she slapped another dollop on one of the offensive wounds, "is an insult."

"We cannot change what she decreed," Drook said. "But none of us are alone, and you don't have to be either."

I was already alone. Nobility did not bond. It competed

and conspired and maneuvered. Even family. Even Alexei. It was only our shared parentage that made us look out for each other's interests. There was a reason I ran away to Varnasia.

"You're most welcome among us, Mikhail," Klessa said as she finished and wiped her hands on a handkerchief beside her.

"Thank you. This entire situation has sent me reeling."

"Of course it has!" Klessa tossed the handkerchief aside with disgust as if it had offended her. "I was eight years old when I was given to the Great Tsar. Maybe it was easier for me as a child, but I still lost everything I had ever known. Fortunately, the tsar was generous to me and maintained the lifestyle to which I had become accustomed. But I can scarce imagine having to go through that all over again at my age, and with a significant depletion of dignity in the process."

Depletion of dignity summed it up accurately, but a little too nicely for the harsh reality of the concept. I wore spit stains and crusted blood and old kvass, and I could do nothing about it except prepare to accumulate more.

"Maybe I am not the nonsensical blithering idiot you would both expect of someone in my position, but I fear that if I join the rest of you for evening socialization, I will make everything awkward. I am too lost and too broken."

"Piffle!" Drook spat. "Like anything that breaks, it hurts. And then it heals while you manage the pain. It's up to you whether it heals in a healthy way or in a way that makes it weaker. Spending time with us would help you heal. Properly."

Klessa poked my shoulder as if testing my sturdiness. "He'll hold up," she told Drook. "If he were going to wither, he would have done it by now."

"I suppose that's true," Drook agreed.

"Still, you *are* a prince," Klessa said disdainfully as she looked me over, "and princes rarely make decent company for anyone of actual intellect. But I would be delighted if the tsarina's witty, sarcastic chicken wished to attend our evenings instead."

The prospect of meeting the rest of the jesters overwhelmed me in the face of Klessa and Drook's concern. And if Klessa hadn't made me painfully self-aware of giving into tears, I might have indulged in a moment of such relief.

I took a deep breath and let it out. I rubbed at my knuckles. I massaged a temple. They were crazy for not wanting the prince. And I was so glad they didn't.

I raised my brows and shrugged, a child again learning how to navigate the world and interact with others. Others, this time, who wanted me because I wasn't a prince anymore.

"Maybe tomorrow?"

VI.

Drook and Klessa accompanied me to the gathering hall the next night. I half-feared that Drook would announce me to the assembled the same way he had announced me to Klessa the night before, with great pomp and expectation. But maybe it would be better to get it over all at once.

"You can take the mask and hood off," Klessa leaned in to tell me as we entered. "Gloves too. Whatever you like."

"This is where we are ourselves," Drook said, "and not the roles we are required to play."

I slid back the hood and unfastened the buckles on the beak to give my wounds a moment to breathe. I tucked the mask under the padded suit. Klessa had given me the ointment to keep in my basket nest, and Drook had taken a knife and a flame to the unfinished edges of the mask to smooth them out. There was nothing to do about the costume itself, dirty and unsightly as it was, or the collar that assaulted me with feathers and jingles at every opportunity.

Like any polite gathering, people spread across the room, gathered on chaises and chairs in small groupings, some playing cards in a corner, others at a dining table with food and drink before them. Most furniture, while as beautiful as to have a place among the rest of the palace, was rendered in miniature. Anyone unable to fit into the diminutive finery had the option of pillows on the floor, accommodations of which a few people of various heights availed themselves.

As we passed, ladies lowered their fans and men paused their conversations to see the new person in their midst, necks arching and fingers pointing. Drook brought us over to a small gathering around a low table with nearly every seat, settee, and chaise occupied around it, several others of average height occupying pillows on the ground. Klessa took an available cushion.

"All," Drook said before finding a seat himself, "Mikhail has finally decided to join us."

Drook rattled off names as he went around the gathered circle.

"Thank you for having me," I said, executing the niceties the way I would at any other party or event. "I pray I am not intruding on your conversation."

"Glad to have you!" A man whose name I had already forgotten gestured to the table laden with food and then a cushion. "Eat, converse, whatever you wish."

"We thought you might never join us," a woman said, her fan folded and forgotten with the new distraction of my company.

"I did not realize that I might be welcome."

"I have been hoping you would come," said a lady, her name something like Agra or Agara, who wore a pearl kokoshnik. "I said to my husband the other day — didn't I, dear?" She tilted her head toward the man beside her. "I said, that poor man! To have no one for company but those wretched nobles. And the tsarina worst of all. That is a punishment beyond any I can imagine. I think we're all so relieved that you've finally joined us so that we can stop worrying about you from afar."

"Fortunately, my role has been reduced to ornamental oddity and kvass-bearer, so that has significantly limited the expectation of interaction."

"Ugh, kvass," the woman said while wrinkling her nose, "I don't know how anyone can drink that stuff, especially not in the quantities she does. It's so sour."

"Doubtless," I said, "that's why her face looks like that all the time."

Several of the group snort-laughed while others grinned.

"You will fit in well with us, Mikhail," said one of the men who laughed.

"He cannot be Mikhail among us," said another. "He needs a name."

"Is there something wrong with Mikhail?" My name had served me admirably for over four decades with only brief interludes of bearing a translated version of it in other countries.

"That is a name that is your own," Klessa explained.

"You will keep that your whole life, prince or jester, and it will be used by all, friend or enemy," said the pearl kokoshnik lady. "You need another name, one just for us, to be used only by us."

This moment of acceptance among the group twisted my belly with the dreaded possibilities. I had gone through so many changes already in such a short time, and I did not relish another reminder of my pitiable state.

They tossed around a few suggestions, most of them innocuous, thankfully, and far afield from the role of chicken I had no choice in playing, but none of the nicknames caught much attention or approval.

When it seemed that all potentials had been offered and dismissed, Drook spoke up. "Mikhail rightfully pointed out that the kvass complements the tsarina's perpetual disposition. As that is so, I propose 'Kvasnik' — the server of sourness!"

"I like that!" said the first man.

Murmurs of approval spread through the group.

"And may she never know a sweet cup until her mood changes," Drook added.

Several of the group lifted their glasses in acknowledgment.

"A worthy proposal and toast," said another.

"May The Kind and Fair hear that prayer," said the pearl kokoshnik lady.

"Or the Great Holy. Mikhail converted," Drook reminded the group.

"What exactly do you believe when you convert?" asked the lady with the fan.

"I was not the most ardent pupil in my catechism. I only converted to wed, not because I found a new or better direction for my soul."

"But isn't that why the tsarina is punishing you?"

"My conversion was an excuse to punish me." I lowered my voice, resigned to the facts but not proud of them. "But it wasn't the actual cause."

Several people raised their brows, but when I said no more, several prodded.

"You cannot say that and then not tell us the rest," said a woman who had come out of her chair.

I did not know how to phrase it politely. Already warm beneath the layers of my costume, I warmed still further from embarrassment.

"You don't have to be coy with us," the pearl kokoshnik lady said. "We're adults. We can handle it."

I searched the gathering, examining their faces, all genuinely interested and not just hunting for gossip. I couldn't lower my head because of the collar, but I wanted to. I lowered my eyes instead.

"I didn't want to be trapped as her bedpartner again."

Those of the gathering, those who heard me, silenced. The noise around us from others in the room playing cards or engaging in private conversation amplified in the stunned hush of my companions.

"You said no," one of the men finally said.

"I said no."

The group settled into a new stunned silence, a mix of horror and fear and awe.

"Then Mikhail is certainly the deliverer of sourness to the tsarina," Drook announced, breaking the spell. "Kvasnik stands."

Several of the gathered company, pulling themselves from the harsh revelation, raised their glasses. Others joined in the gesture. One of them shouted for the attention of everyone in the room. The murmurs quieted, and Drook stood from his seat, his glass raised as he indicated for others who had not yet followed suit.

"Mikhail, the prince among us fools, shall be known as Kvasnik — The One Who Said No!"

"Huzzah!" shouted a member of our group.

"To Kvasnik!" Drook downed his vodka in a gulp and held the empty glass aloft.

"To Kvasnik!" the chorus of others repeated. They too emptied their glasses.

Drook glanced in my direction, and someone handed me a drink. I raised my glass just a fraction and then downed the vodka in acceptance of their gift.

"To me."

VII

I did not venture every night, certain that if I tread upon their genial company so frequently, they may no longer tolerate me. I had already been ejected and shunned from those I had once thought friends. I did not think I could bear it if I somehow misstepped and alienated myself from an even finer group of people. And yet, I could not keep away, desperate to have any conversation that kept my mind away from my own miseries.

I amused them too, not as I did with the tsarina and her courtiers, but with genuine fascination that I, someone they had only known from afar and by reputation, found their companionship pleasurable.

Most of them were not just literate but well-read, women included, and their philosophical debates bordered on the genius much the way their amusements for the tsarina bordered on the infantile. Politics, perhaps unsurprisingly, always maintained a prominent position in their discussions, and although most of the time I just wrapped my arms around the padded costume and listened, occasionally they asked for my input as someone who had possessed intimate knowledge of the highest ranks of nobility. My contributions, though less than insightful and painfully naive from my years of having to be unconcerned with most of the politics of Ilyichia, always received gratitude.

"The stones they throw down at us come from the pile upon which they sit," Drook declared one night.

"It's a never-ending supply of stones though," a man grumbled.

"That's a fantasy they've told themselves that's completely unsustainable. One day, they will topple, and it will all be because they were too stupid to see how they themselves undermined their positions. What ultimate good or service does it offer to have a title? Even the lowliest serf has greater value than the highest prince." Drook remembered himself and added in my direction, "Sorry, Kvasnik, but it's true."

I opened my eyes and raised my hands, palms to him. "No offense taken. You may be half my size, but you are double my worth. I find myself privileged to be among the true intelligentsia of Ilyichia." Trokei handed me a vodka and I downed it. "Do go on."

"Don't encourage him," Agara complained to me. "We have to hear this every night. It's fun to gripe occasionally, and I am as tired of the current situation as anyone, but every night? Who wants to play a game of cards?"

"I could do with some music," one of the group suggested instead.

"A bawdy song?"

One of the men rose from the cushions to take his place on a harpsichord bench.

"Something we can dance to," Klessa demanded as she rose from her cushion and stood in front of her husband. "Hush your lectures and work your legs as hard as your mouth."

As others partnered up, I stood from my own cushion as everyone who anticipated participating in the dancing began moving furniture out of the way to make space at the end of the room. I stepped off to the side to watch, eager to resume a quiet position again.

"You have no partner," Agara said beside me and then added with a smile in her voice, "and I just so happen to be free."

I looked at the diminutive woman and admired her

forthrightness. "There are many others here who would make a far better partner than I."

"I've always wanted to dance with a prince."

"I can make your introductions to one who still bears his titles."

"I know everyone at court." She held her hand out for me to take. "There are none as pretty as you."

"If you're sure," I said, taking it, "then I would be delighted."

"You are a little tall for my taste, but I won't hold it against you."

She led me over to the side of the makeshift dance floor, music already inspiring other couples to dance. And not in the typically courtly way. The boldness of the moves, the proximity of the bodies, the liveliness of the music reminded me of Varnasian country dances, the ones I shared with Irena when we danced in the street to musicians playing for the coins of passersby or in private in the foyer of our rented house.

Great Holy, I missed her. And thank the Powers That Be that she couldn't see what had become of me. Although she might have loved me anyway.

"None of your silly stately court dancing though," Agara warned. "You'll embarrass me if you do a minuet to a jig."

"I would never," I assured her. I let her hand go and then bowed slightly at the waist in her direction. "Might I have the honor of this dance?"

"Of course, Kvasnik. I thought you'd never ask."

It was a novel experience. None of us dancers was usual. The heights varied wildly between partners, the grace at an extreme between tumblers and storytellers, the shapes of us all so unlike any other that we simply made the best of it. By the third dance, I was laughing along with the others at the energetic abandon of the activity and the depraved lyrics sung so sweetly by our accompanist. And nothing mattered. Not

Klessa's hair or Agara's height or my bulky costume. We came as we were, and that was enough.

I ended up having to sit out a few dances due to my costume's excessive warmth. I took a place on the settee where I could continue to watch as the others enjoyed themselves.

"Kvasnik." Klessa, from behind the settee, offered me a plate heaped with delicacies from the dining table.

I took it and set it beside me. I gestured to the empty seat on the settee so that she might share the plate with me.

She disappeared for a moment and then returned, taking the offered seat. She downed a vodka and gave me another.

"It's warm," she warned.

"Still better than kvass." I downed the vodka also, indifferent to the temperature.

We both watched the dancers, picking cheese and meats off the shared plate.

"You know that's why the tsarina had to embarrass you, right?" Kless asked half a dance in. At my confusion, she continued. "There's not a woman here who doesn't want to dance with you. I suspect it's the same with your former set too." Klessa dabbed a napkin at the corner of her mouth elegantly. "The tsarina could take away your name and your wealth, but that wouldn't be enough, would it?"

"I don't understand," I admitted. "It was enough. No one from my 'former set' wishes to associate with me now."

"That's because she had to make association with you as shameful and embarrassing as she could. She couldn't take away anything that made you who you are, so she had to hide you." I went to protest, but Klessa gestured with her chin towards Agara. "I don't want to hear it. Agara is one of the most cynical and hardest to win among us, and yet, you've won her over. She blushes and titters like a child when you're mentioned. And maybe you didn't notice it, but you flashed her a smile tonight while dancing, and she just gazed at you like a Kind and Fair Protector had come in the flesh to give her special attention. While she adores her husband, I have never seen her like this." Klessa didn't let me respond before she pointed to another woman on the other side of the room who sat the dance out too. "Grigga has loudly sung your praises to all of us. She's witnessed your insolent replies to the tsarina, and she's confessed that while she admires your spirit, she has feared for your life many a time in how bold you are." Klessa leaned towards me conspiratorially. "And that's why the tsarina had to hide you, with costumes and with shame. You have everything she wants and will never have. And despite a beak and a costume, others can still see you shine. How she must hate you!"

I didn't know how to feel about Klessa's assessment. Flattered? Hopeless?

"I'm off to bed." Klessa patted her lap and then stood. "Be a dear and tell my husband."

"Of course."

"And," she added, "I'm not advocating that you do anything to put yourself in greater peril with the tsarina, but there's nothing she can do about you taking ownership of who you are, even confined to the role you must play."

I nodded, not certain that I should respond. I wasn't even certain what she was suggesting because, to my mind, I was only a pathetic former prince who was just managing to survive. I wasn't anything like what she said. All the epithets and praise while possessing my titles and fortune rang hollow, given simply because I was titled and wealthy, not because they were true.

Could Klessa be correct? Could finer attributes still be seen even without the glamorous conditions of my former status?

One too many vodkas later and only Drook remaining for company despite telling him of Klessa's departure, I had found a semi-less-uncomfortable position on an armchair, a pillow tucked behind my neck to ease and support the stiffness of the collar. I stared up at the ceiling, thoughts whirling about my current circumstances. I probably should have been more cautious about my intake, knowing how susceptible my forefathers had been to heavy drink, but did it matter? Did anything matter anymore?

The tsarina had always resented me. Even as lovers, it had never been anything but her satisfying her needs, and my relations shoving me in the back to regain her good opinion of the Karilitsyns. And, foolish me, I hadn't realized there was anything else but compliance and submission. What would have happened if I had said no then? Banishment, probably. Would that have been so bad?

But I had never considered that she just outright hated me. I had been careful never to give her reason to. But if so, at least now it was mutual.

Of course, nothing would be solved by getting sloshed, but I was willing to try it. Maybe the tsarina would prefer a staggering drink-bleary imbecile who wouldn't remember anything he had done, ridiculous or not, the next day. For the present circumstances though, my mind quieted and allowed me a moment of peace despite all. I could see how such quantities of potent drink might be alluring. If I could not change anything sober, being insensible to it offered a tempting escape.

I raised my arms above my head, stretching my shoulders in their confines. What would happen if I fell asleep here and I was not in my nest by morning? The empress had dictated my attire and my duties but not my whereabouts. She might send for me, but I couldn't be arsed to care.

Drook lounged on the chaise, halfway between sitting and reclining in the same vodka-induced torpor. Though silent, his company provided a great degree of comfort.

Thank the Great Holy for the tsarina's jesters. I never wanted to face the day now, but because of them, I became capable of doing so without wanting to die every moment.

Drook rolled to his side. The guttering candles offered dramatic lighting, forming a greater mountain range of his face than usual. The trim of his velvet suit twinkled in the darkened room. He stretched expansively with a yawn.

"How did you manage to end up here?" I asked, not the least bit subtle or sensitive to a possibly annoying question.

"Her uncle, the tsar," Drook explained. "He had an unhealthy obsession with short people. He threw a wedding and invited anyone four and a half feet or shorter to attend. Many of the attendees, like me, were already performers, and he kept some of us on. It was a fortunate opportunity for us. He paid for my wedding too. The tsarina has at least maintained the tradition of keeping us well-accommodated."

I vaguely remembered hearing about the event of the Great Tsar's jesters getting married. Many condemned it as a ribald and chaotic affair, but knowing the tellers, they fully enjoyed the raunchy abandon of the occasion.

I asked without thinking, "Do you and Klessa have any children?"

"Three, all of them grown and living their own lives now."

My throat clogged up.

"What about you?" he asked.

"I have buried three."

He breathed hard out his nose and then expelled a breath. "I cannot imagine."

"Perhaps it is a mercy." I closed my eyes and a tear slipped down my cheek. "They do not have to endure my punishment.

And I do not have to face my children's shame of me. I have found all of this difficult, but I do not think I could bear that."

Barely above a whisper, Drook asked, "And your wife?"

"Wives," I corrected. "Both dead too."

"*Blyat*," Drook muttered.

I smiled wearily at the casual but extreme profanity.

"*Blyat*," I agreed.

I should have stopped drinking, but I pried myself from the chair to find another glass of vodka on the table. I downed it before lying back in the chair again. I should have done a lot of things and hadn't. Why start now?

"Here's a hypothetical for you," Drook posed. "Tomorrow, the tsarina changes her mind. You can be reinstated and allowed to live the life that should have always been yours here in Ilyichia."

"Or?"

"Or you can leave Ilyichia again, but you leave without anything that was yours." He propped his chin on his hand. "Which would you choose?"

"I would leave Ilyichia. Without hesitation." I drew in a breath that filled me as Varnasia had once filled me with hope. Varnasia had been the pinnacle of my happiness. Even if I spent the rest of my days there as a laborer or established in some other lowly profession, it would be paradise compared to Ilyichia. Then I expelled my breath, draining my lungs as I had been drained of everything but my miserable life. "I should never have come back."

"Why did you then? Did you miss home? Family?"

"I only came back to bury my wife and child." New tears welled in the corners of my eyes. "I didn't intend to stay."

The silence lingered in the air then, Drook somewhere between respectfully quiet and confused.

Eventually, he asked, "Why didn't you leave right away?"

"They arrested me the day after the interment."

"The day after?" Drook nearly rose off the chaise, his affront and horror palpable even from my relaxed position in the chair. "Has no one any pity or sympathy left?"

"It seems not." I wiped at my eyes. "I am so tired of grieving, Drook. And it shames me to be so discontent with my lot when you and all the others I have met have risen to this position while I have fallen to it."

"It is not equitable," Drook assured me. "You have no reason for shame on that account. The tsarina has malice toward you. She barely remembers I exist."

"Be grateful."

"I am."

I stared at the handwoven rug beneath the table and chairs, examining the orderly knots on the fringe.

"Was getting married again worth it?" Drook asked hesitantly.

"I loved her," I admitted. "My first wife and I were compatible and affectionate, more than can usually be wanted from a state marriage. But when I met Irena, it inspired something I had never experienced before, something I did not think I could live without. I wouldn't change my decision about marrying her." I wiped at my eyes again, disintegrating by the moment into that weepy, pathetic prince the jesters would likely have despised me for. "And then she died, and all my titles and wealth and family connections couldn't save her." I couldn't save her or the baby. Tears resumed down my face, and I did not wipe them away. "I'm sure all think I was a fool to marry her instead of taking her as a mistress, but that hardly seemed honorable. My only mistake — indeed, my only regret — was in coming back."

"So you would consider getting married again?"

"The tsarina would love that, wouldn't she?" I snorted. "She would probably separate me from my manhood in such an event." I ran my hands through my hair. "No, things would have to be much different for me to even think about getting married again. And I would have to be an utter fool to consider it. But, now that I've said it, watch, something will happen to make me regret my words. But then, I'm better known for my looks than my intelligence."

Drook laughed and rolled onto his back again.

I glanced at the doorway and miserably contemplated returning to my basket nest. I had no desire to see what tomorrow offered. It would be the same as every other day. I would replace the beak mask and pull up my hood. I would be shunned, and mocked, and treated like dirt beneath their shoes.

"Maybe this won't be forever," Drook said from his reclined position. "Maybe she will change her mind. Or forgive you. Or perhaps a change in power will see you free."

"Maybe," I agreed. I ran my hand over my chin and decided that shaving could wait until tomorrow night since I did not trust myself with a razor. "But I don't have much hope."

He turned his head to glare at me as if he could read the direction of my thoughts. "As long as you're alive, Kvasnik, there's always hope."

VIII.

"I brought the plans as you requested, Your Majesty."

The engineer tugged at his collar and dabbed at his temple.

None of us knew for a fact that something was wrong with the ice palace construction, but we all knew that something was clearly wrong.

With a gesture from the empress, he crossed over to the table where she awaited him. He pulled out several long scrolls from under his arm and laid them to the side. He glanced at one of his party. That man came forward, bowed, and spread the first scroll out with the engineer. They set weights down along the corners, and the engineer went to the tsarina's side to begin explanation.

The delegation from the worksite milled in the back of the room. Although they were not the laborers who wore a permanent layer of dirt on their clothing, their worn coats and cloaks offered a muted palette not often seen at the palace. I alone rivaled them for the most brown in the room.

"I don't care how you do it," the tsarina said, her attention on her project, "but I want the foundation ready by the time the Talvian Ambassador comes next month."

Countess Ekaterina, presiding over the tsarina's group of ladies in the absence of Princess Alaina, took a pastry from the communal tray and then held her glass out. I withdrew from my corner to refill her cup with kvass. No one paid me mind with the attention on the tsarina's grand undertaking and its trials.

"—and we've reinforced the retaining wall on the north side six times already."

"Could you have built it upon a Kind and Fair mound?" the tsarina asked. "There are many of those along the river."

The second man opened another few scrolls and held them down by reshuffling the paperweights.

Their maneuvers reminded me of a war map, pieces sliding along the table in sequences of strategy, a defensive position here, an offensive strike there. I never realized that buildings could get a war map, reinforcement here, new construction there. Could it be used for other things that needed to be tackled, like a life, for example? Could I lay out a timeline of my life with a projection of the next few years and decide where I needed to take a defensive stance versus an offensive one to win — in this case, win back — my life from the tsarina's ownership like a country under occupation? Maybe the titles and wealth would be lost to me, but I would sacrifice all of that for the true prize of my freedom.

"You wretched thing!" Ekaterina's folded fan landed a blow against my cheek as she shot up from her chair with her glass of kvass held far out in front of her. The brown liquid dribbled over the edges. "You did that on purpose!"

A trail of drops and a large brown blemish stained her pink satin skirt. I wished I had the nerve to do it to someone intentionally. And if so, I would have chosen a better target with two pitchers full of kvass instead of simply overfilling a glass by momentary inattention.

"My apologies, my lady."

I set the pitcher down on the table and knelt to wipe up the spill with my sleeve, stained by kvass too with many such incidents of cleaning myself up.

She twitched her skirt away from me. "Don't you dare touch me."

A paperweight flew over the gathering of ladies and smashed against the wall at the other side of the room. The hideous noise brought the room to silence.

The tsarina did not have to rise from her chair to command the attention of everyone in the room.

"I cannot hear myself think," she said, staring down everyone who dared make a noise. She noticed me on the floor and raised a brow. "And what are you about, Mikhail?"

"I was cleaning up a spill, ma'am."

"He did it on purpose," the countess accused.

I did not defend myself because I didn't think it would matter.

"In this instance, I highly doubt it," the tsarina said after brief assessment. "He's always been more fond of the ladies than he should be. Just let him clean it up."

"I refuse to let him touch me," Ekaterina lamented. "He's disgusting. Just look at him!"

The tsarina took another aloof examination of me and then, as if seeing me for the first time, her eyes widened. She gestured me over, and I obeyed, presenting myself for inspection.

The engineer and his assistant both studied me from the other side of the table too. Wordless glances traveled between them and back to the other men who stood patiently waiting to hear about instruction on the ice palace.

"You are disgusting, aren't you? I suppose I will have to do something about that," she gestured to the stained costume, "before our visitor arrives." She fell into deep thought while staring at me, her mind working over what could be done with me after she had set such a precedent.

"Your Majesty?" the engineer ventured. "The collapsing wall?"

The tsarina tore her gaze away from me and flicked it over to the engineer. "We have our traditional methods of ensuring solid buildings. I don't know why you bother me with this."

"That would be murd—" the engineer protested.

"Do whatever you have to. That is the Ilyichian way. Even

I do what must be done. You see this?" She gestured to me with her eyes alone. "I had to ruin a favorite to teach everyone a lesson. We all make sacrifices."

"Are you giving us permission for immurement, ma'am?"

"By any means necessary includes immurement," the tsarina sighed. "I'm sure someone on the work force has a wife or a daughter or some other poor female relation they won't mind sacrificing for the greater glory of the country." She paused and then laughed to herself. "Maybe I should offer Princess Alaina," she said, her tone a jest but the edge one I knew as a threat. "Since she couldn't give my nephew children before he died, maybe she could finally do Ilyichia some good after all."

The ladies laughed. The engineers squirmed. And I pitied the princess who wasn't here to defend herself but probably knew what they said about her in her absence anyway.

IX.

"I like the tunic." Drook rubbed a stretch of gold braid between his fingers. "Good quality."

"It hides the stains," I admitted, not as appreciative as he was.

When the tsarina suggested doing something about my costume, I had hoped it would be to replace it with something different. Or, if not that, that I might be refitted with a new and therefore clean version of my current costume. Instead, the tsarina had a servant futilely attempt to clean it and the seamstress restuff it. Ultimately, the seamstress provided a tunic to go over the costume, making it bulkier, heavier, and tighter than before.

"You look splendid," Klessa said, smoothing down several of the collar feathers and straightening the belled ribbons. She inspected my healing wounds too. "Ready for tonight?"

"It will be the same as any other." I glanced around the ballroom at those who merited an invitation to the reception but not the dinner. They drank wine and examined their fingernails while they barely held conversations, all of them awaiting the arrival of the rest of the party. "I will be shown off, told to perform some humiliating tasks — only this time for the Talvian ambassador — and then expected to sit in my basket unless the tsarina desires some kvass."

"Has she told you to sit in the basket?"

"It's usual."

"Unless she has given you specific instructions, you can do what you like," Drook said. "It's a party and you're a jester. Mingle. Tell a dirty joke. Start an absurd rumor or two."

"Or just be your charming self and do whatever you would have without a costume," Klessa said pointedly, frowning at Drook's suggestions. "Even if you're no longer a prince in title, you are still you. You could even ask a lady sitting on the side to dance. She might say no, but...." Klessa shrugged. "Would anyone have turned you down before?"

Klessa's optimism, though appreciated, did not take into account how fragile reputation could be. I could not foresee anyone wanting to be within a few feet of me, let alone agreeing to anything more. And my dancing, even if someone should agree, would be beyond awkward in a costume not meant to offer much movement.

I glanced across the room, and Agara waved at me from her cluster of friends as we all waited for the rest of the nobles to filter in.

As if on cue, the doors above the ballroom opened and the tsarina led the throng with the ambassador at her side, his red satin sash brilliant in the reflected light. The room exploded into chatter and echoes of chatter as other brightly colored outfits piled up in the doorway and spread to the stairs, announcements made from the balcony as couples descended.

My group all bowed as the tsarina passed, and I breathed slightly more easily when she failed to notice me. Her attentions focused upon someone else tonight.

Nobles who trailed behind her did not overlook us, many of them not residents of the palace and therefore unfamiliar with our appearances. They gaped and made comments to each other, and Drook warmed to it, bowing deeply with his red tricorn hat, diverting most of the attention with the beginning of a convoluted story that would doubtless end in some filthy absurdity.

"And what are you supposed to be?" a woman wearing a badly applied wig asked of Klessa. "Some kind of lady?"

"She's more of a lady than you are." I stepped between

them. "At least she knows how to wear her hair."

The woman took several steps back. "And what, you're her personal chicken guard?"

"Clearly, you've never seen how nasty a rooster can be when defending the ladies."

The woman huffed and left us.

"You don't have to defend me." Klessa patted my shoulder. "I've been dealing with this my whole life."

"You told me to do whatever I would should I not be wearing a costume. I would never have tolerated such incivility to a lady in my presence, and I will not begin now."

"Go practice your charms on someone else, Kvasnik. I already know what a gem you are. Show others. Shine." Klessa lowered her voice. "It will drive the tsarina mad."

When she shooed me off, I wandered through the hall, identifying people who hadn't been witness to my humiliation. Most of them I knew, and I did not wish to call further attention to my new status.

"It's Mikhail," someone said loudly to my side. I debated whether I should acknowledge it or pretend that I hadn't heard it. I chose to ignore it. Moments later, ladies surrounded me, most of them from court, but they had brought other friends over, friends who did not live at the palace and therefore had not seen my disgrace.

I straightened my back and waited.

"We heard you insulted Lady Pochenka," Countess Ekaterina said.

"She was uncivil to another undeservedly," I said, "and regardless of how you see me, I still will come to a lady's defense. I would have done the same for any of you."

"Oh, we are not upset," said another.

"We thought it was marvelous. Lady Pochenka is uncivil to everyone!"

"Would you join us?" The countess gestured towards a

little circle she had formed, Princess Alaina at the center of it, her face as dour as the tsarina's.

I did not trust them, but I had no better occupation. And for a rare moment, they weren't finding novel ways to torment me.

"Lead the way and I shall follow."

Ekaterina smiled and led. The other four ladies escorted me. The countess turned to look at me over her shoulder as she introduced me into her gathering. The princess looked up and then pointedly away, fanning herself with such vigor that I thought she intended to send half the party away in a gust of wind.

They offered me a seat on a bench, and I took it, but only after I saw all of them seated first.

"What's it like being a chicken?" one of the newest ladies asked.

"Spend more time at court with all the henpecking biddies," I told her, "and you will have opportunity to witness others with far more experience than I."

Most of the group laughed.

"Is it true you were a prince?" another lady asked when no one else followed up on the initial question.

The question, although not malicious, invariably led toward a humiliating conversation at my expense. How funny, a fallen prince. Ha ha. But I wasn't just a fallen prince. I was a jester now too. I possessed a certain degree of freedom in my storytelling, as Drook had always been quick to point out. I could guide the discussion as I wished by how I framed my answers.

"Once," I told her, deliberate in my tone of confidence and sorrow. "Then an evil witch cast a spell on me and left me as you see."

Ekaterina blushed. "That's a rather romantic way to put it."

"Is it not true?" I found her eyes and gazed into them, intentional and manipulative in my connection. She had once wanted me despite whatever she had done since my return. And if Klessa was right, I could still sway her, even if not in the same capacity. "Still me, in body, mind, and spirit, in all ways of substance — and yet...."

"Is there a way to break such a spell?" A young woman gazed at me in a way I recognized and had not seen in a long time.

"Typically, it is the love of a woman true and fair which frees a prince from such a curse, but by design, no one will ever look upon me again and see someone worthwhile."

"That's not so," said one of the women. "You have such beautiful eyes."

"And a gentle way of speaking," added another.

"And I would guess that you're beautiful beneath your mask."

"Would you take the beak off and show us?"

"Please!" a chorus of ladies pleaded.

"Alas," I told them, "I cannot, as part of my curse. Should anyone see the prince I was before, I might never be free."

Their disappointment sounded in chorus too.

"I fear," I said, sounding as woeful as I could, "if no one can look beyond my trappings or the station to which they consign me, I shall never find someone to rescue me from my cruel fate."

"A cruel fate indeed!" A lady moved closer to me on the bench and reached out to pat my hand.

"However might we assist?" asked another.

I had them now wrapped up in a fairy tale of my unfair disgrace, and I bent it to serve me.

"Perhaps petitions to release me from my enchantment might remind my sorceress that she is a good and kind ruler and that I have only ever wished to serve her." I sighed with great pathos, a tragic noble figure now in the eyes of these ladies. "And perhaps, if it is not so much trouble — though I know how I must appear to you — some civility as I attempt to endure this sad state of mine with grace?"

The lady beside me took my arm. "Has anyone been so heartless as to treat you poorly?"

"I cannot blame them," I told her, refusing to look at any of the ladies who had devoted time and attention to making me feel my status with painful acuity. "My curse has been designed to encourage it."

She still clung to my arm but looked at the ladies in the group. "We must do something."

Ladies nodded their heads in agreement.

"Petition we shall," one of them assured me.

The music started, and all attention tore away from me. Conversation ceased entirely as ladies were called away by eager partners or as they went to find partners when no one asked them immediately.

"Save a dance for me," whispered the young girl who released my arm and patted my hand before she went off with what looked a steady beau.

Soon, all the ladies had been claimed except for Princess Alaina. No taller than the diminutive jesters herself and browner than any makeup would cover, no one seemed to want to claim her for a dance either.

I didn't say anything about it. Not the first dance. Or the second. Or the third.

On the fourth, when she was pointedly overlooked by men who stood to the side, I rose from the bench and approached her.

"Your Highness," I bowed, unsure how she would receive me, "might you care to dance? Despite my current circumstances, I will not shame you as a partner."

Her gaze shot up to me. Her face softened. The sheen of

tears glimmered at the corners of her eyes. But the moment passed. Her face hardened. Her eyes narrowed. A sneer twisted her mouth.

"How dare you presume that I would ever be desperate enough to accept such a degrading offer!" She huffed. "I suppose you would have me look as ridiculous as you."

I could have said something cutting, but her unexpected sharpness wounded me when I had been trying to be kind to one who had once been kind to me.

"Of course not, ma'am. I would not wish this on anyone." I bowed again. "My apologies."

I made to leave the area where the ladies had gathered since none but the ill-receptive princess remained, but the music ended, and one of the young ladies sought me out.

"Please don't go so soon," she begged. "I hoped you might ask me to dance."

Unlike the princess, she accepted my offer and held my arm like I was a prize. And other ladies followed suit, waiting for me when I returned with my prior partner so that I could take them for their turn on the floor.

"An enchanted prince," and "a prince under a spell," and "a prince in need of rescuing," several murmured through the course of the evening, partnered with words like "intriguing" and "fascinating."

Ekaterina finally caught me between partners and took my arm, pulling me aside to give me private attention.

"Some punishment," she said. "You have the ladies in love with you all over again."

"Not all of them," I demurred. "You aren't, surely."

"If you renounced the Great Holy, Mikhail," she said, blushing from her forehead to her decolletage, "she would probably forgive you. And then, maybe, once you were reinstated...."

"What if I should never be?"

"I refuse to give up hope. As you suggested, I will petition her on your behalf as many times as it takes. I know others will as well. And we will never stop."

"You have all been so unkind to me through this," I whispered. "It is painful to lose the affections of all you hold dear and to be so utterly alone. I fear that I've given up hope."

"It's just court nonsense," she said, the shine of tears forming in the corners of her eyes. She took my hands and held them in front of her. "You know how it is here! If we don't love something the tsarina loves or hate what the tsarina hates, we're all in danger." She squeezed my hands. "You must believe me. It is as you said — you are still you, no matter the silly costume she puts you in."

"It seemed to matter very much."

"Trust me." She released my hands and placed one of hers on my cheek, the leather strap of the mask beneath it. "I would be able to see the true you, no matter how you are disguised."

I never broke my gaze from hers as I took her hand. I bent over it and mimed a kiss since the mask prevented an actual one.

"A woman true and fair," I said, although I didn't believe it.

Her hand and arm turned a becoming shade of pink.

I hated her and her flimsy declaration of persistent adoration. I hated them all for being so hypocritical, for treating me so shamefully, and in the next breath pretending to be horrified at such treatment. I would have had more respect for any of them if they had hated me consistently rather than bending with the breeze of public opinion. Indeed, I had more respect for Princess Alaina not wanting to associate with me than if she had been open and receptive because those around her deemed it acceptable.

Mostly, I hated myself for the misguided desire of wanting to return to the pitiful ranks of the inconstant. I had known authenticity with Irena. And now, as one of the jesters, I had known it with them. The jesters were finer people in every capacity than any Ilyichian noble. I could never go back now.

"I never imagined the darling of the ball would be my jester," the tsarina said, approaching us accompanied by the ambassador.

"He has been so entertaining," Ekaterina said, withdrawing her hand from my grasp as if she had done something forbidden. "And he has not failed to make us laugh."

"I am delighted to hear it," the tsarina said, not delighted at all.

Ekaterina departed while I bowed politely to the tsarina and the ambassador.

"My word," the ambassador said, studying my costume. "What strange fowl you have here."

"Indeed, Ilyichia is a strange country," I responded. "Firebirds fill the sky. Princes become birds. Winter lasts all year long. Palaces are rendered in ice."

"I saw the foundations for the ice palace earlier today," the ambassador said, latching onto the only statement that made sense to him. "It should be quite a marvel of the modern world."

"Indeed, a wonder," I agreed. "All of Ilyichia is a wonder. I constantly wonder how it can be so mismanaged and still remain."

"Pay no mind to my fool," the tsarina explained. "Mikhail used to be one of my courtiers, but he displeased me. He still has not learned his lesson."

"To the contrary, I have, ma'am," I said. I turned to the ambassador. "I have learned that displeasing the tsarina is so easy to do that I caution you, Ambassador, to smile and say 'yes' to whatever she wishes, else you might join me in creating her very own flock."

"Mikhail," the tsarina said in warning as her face turned an unbecoming shade of red.

I should have kept my mouth shut. I should have submitted and let her think that she had cowed me. I should have backed off to live to fight another day. But I didn't. I had gained ground and so, stupidly, I pressed my advantage. I couldn't even blame it on drink.

"Of course, you probably don't have anything to worry about," I told the ambassador. "She only tries to humiliate the men she can't bed."

"Guards!" The word rang off every marble tile and crystal prism.

"What are you going to do?" I asked. "Strip me of my title and make me your jester?" I laughed. I couldn't stop laughing.

"Guards!" she shouted again.

Several guards materialized, and they grabbed my arms when she pointed in my direction. They forced me to my knees, but I just continued to laugh.

"Mikhail!"

I glared at her with devilish glee because I was free now. Drook was right. All I had to do was let go of my shame.

"You can degrade me, treat me like shit, and dress me up however you like," I said, "but I can take it off." I curled my lip with all the disgust she had sent my way over the past few months. "You're a bitter, angry woman because you're miserable and ugly all the time."

The tsarina stared down at me, her thoughts inward as she contemplated my fate, and then she smiled.

X.

The gathering around the bars of my cell far exceeded the capacity in the corridor, but it flattered and heartened me that I had so many who called me a friend. If nothing else, it would all be worth it just for that, to know I wasn't truly alone at the end.

A gaggle of guards sitting at the end of the hall frowned at the group outside my cell.

"We're allowed to visit!" Grigga declared as she shot a glare at them.

"You are such an idiot," Klessa despaired. "I said shine, not show off."

"It doesn't matter," I assured her.

"Of course it matters," Drook grumbled. "You're one of us."

"She was going to kill me eventually when I stopped being amusing to her. I just ensured I did not have to suffer for years of my life."

I had lived in my chicken costume for months. I could not imagine years. While still in the padded costume, I had torn off the collar. I also discarded the tunic, mask, gloves, and hood upon my arrival in the cell. What were they going to do, kill me?

I wore a scruffy beard now in the absence of an opportunity to shave.

"I don't regret it," I said.

Agara sat at the bars too, silent but glowering.

"There's nothing to be done," I said. "She is intent on having me executed, and I will welcome the release."

"You really did push her from what I heard," said Grigga.

"Intentionally," I explained. "A small punishment would have been so much worse. Ironic, no? Death is the only sentence I can live with."

Agara threw her hands up and stood. "Kvasnik, we want to fight for you, but you're not making this easy."

"Don't fight for me," I told her. "Please," I begged all of them, "please don't. None of you needs to be punished for defending me."

My friends looked at each other helplessly.

"After I am executed," I told them, "have a toast for me. Celebrate my release. And when you speak of the jester prince, I'll be there, in your stories, in your thoughts. That's enough. What a legacy — to have been regarded so dearly!"

"Do you know when it's going to be?" Agara asked.

"Soon, I imagine."

"Maybe we could break the lock," Trokei whispered.

"None of you is allowed to cause trouble on my account. Please, go back to your apartments and your daily activities. It's better if I'm by myself now. The tsarina will surely get a report of this, and I do not trust her to leave you unharmed."

"You've heard Kvasnik." Klessa stood from her stool and turned to the assembled group. "He wants to be alone, even if he is a stubborn arse for wanting it."

"I haven't slept and I need rest," I explained, not lying about my present circumstances, but definitely lying about why I needed to be alone.

The others grumbled but shifted as if to begin their departure. They filed by the bars reaching in to shake my hand, pat my shoulder or cheek, and reassure me that if I would not let them petition the tsarina, they would ensure that The Kind and Fair received an earful on my behalf.

Klessa herded them out, and I loved them all for their refusal to give up on me, even when I asked them to.

Hours later, I still didn't sleep. All my brave words meant nothing when I had the silence and space to think about the reality of execution. I presumed it would be a beheading. But what if the executioner was unskilled? What if he took multiple swings and butchered me beyond tolerance before actually landing the blow that separated my head from my neck? What if Alexei would be called in to watch, and I had to witness my brother's shame of me as the last thing I would ever see?

"Kvasnik?"

I looked up at the speaker.

Klessa stood at the bars again, this time alone.

"You didn't have to come back." I pried myself off the floor and joined her.

"You have no idea how upset we all are."

"I have an idea." I smiled a little, grateful that anyone cared.

"No, you don't, or you wouldn't have done it."

"I was raised to be a selfish prince. What else could you expect?"

"Don't try your poor jests on me."

I sighed, properly chastised.

"Have you come to blame me some more then?" I asked. "I'll sit here, and you can tell me about every fuck-up I've made. You will be here for hours since I've managed to mess up so much."

"I have no doubt of it."

I waited for her to berate me, to remind me I was an undisciplined, unchecked prince who had never had consequences before. An obnoxious noble who was accustomed to being forgiven with a smile and some smooth placating. None of it would have been true, but she didn't know that.

"Why did you do it?" she asked at length.

"Everything in court is fake," I confessed. "I had a former admirer try to convince me that she still cared about me. I had ladies fawning over me all night. And all of this after they've spent the last few months ensuring my isolation and perpetuating my humiliation. And then they expected me to believe their sudden change of heart."

"But why did you do it?"

"Because I spent the night being manipulative and false, playing to the group that might best further my interests. I loathed it, Klessa. Even if I somehow managed to win back everything I lost, I would still have to be one of them. I would still have to play that game for the rest of my life, hoping I could maintain my balance on the uncertain terrain of royal favor. After everything she's put me through, that fate seemed the more unbearable one." I sighed. "I'm so tired of lying. It was rash and ill-conceived, but I was truthful, and now I'll die for it. But for a moment, I had something no one else of court could claim — honesty."

I sat again, this time beside the bars so that Klessa could join me if she had any intention of staying beyond the answer to her question.

"You brave, stupid man."

"How neatly you sum up my life."

She sat down too and drew her legs up under her.

"Drook said it was likely some principle you decided to defend. I didn't think you would be so dumb, although I suppose I shouldn't be surprised, seeing how quickly you came to my defense. And now I have to tell him that he was right." She leveled a glare at me. "How dare you."

"Thank you for thinking I had more intelligence than I do."

"You're plenty intelligent. I think your heart is in the right place — which is the trouble.”

“What a crime that is.”

She reached between the bars and put her hand on mine. “Can I do anything?”

“Perhaps, given the circumstances, you can forgive me just this once for being raised a blithering idiot prince.” I bit my lip and looked at her. “I am terrified.”

She squeezed my hand.

“And —” My voice cracked, and I turned away when the tears started flowing. “I won’t even get to die wearing my wedding band.”

She pulled my chin back around and grabbed my arm. She yanked me to her, embracing me through the bars. All the months of misery and humiliation finally crashed into me. The tears flowed like a flood from a broken dam, and Klessa clung to me through it all.

“I’m sorry,” I finally whispered when I reached the hiccupping, snotty stage. “I know how you disdain such weakness. Please don’t despise me for it.”

“Never, Kvasnik,” Klessa said as she withdrew. She took my hands in hers and held them. “We love you.”

XI.

The lock clicking open woke me. The hinges whined when the door swung out. All my lethargy fled. There could be no mistake about the meaning of an open cell door.

Today, I would die.

Four guards greeted me, two in front and two behind. No one shackled or bound me. Perhaps they knew that they could have simply invited me to the scaffold, and I would have skipped up with a bounce in my step. We marched along, not to any of the darker private rooms below the palace as I had expected for a beheading and not to a side outer courtyard where a block might have been prepared, but through the corridors and up into the palace itself. There were not many people about: servants, a minister rushing through the halls with scrolls and books under his arms, secret lovers returning to their apartments. No one gave us attention.

Could a more public execution be planned? Or maybe, instead of the beheading given to nobles, I had misjudged, and I was to be hanged like any commoner since my title had not been reinstated. Perhaps the palace only retained silence because the majority had assembled elsewhere, awaiting me. Would I have a final moment to speak? Should I have been coming up with a speech while imprisoned? Surely the tsarina would know better than to give me another public platform to voice my impertinent grievances.

But we did not head towards courtyards, gardens, or public spaces. We climbed the central staircase, upward to halls more expansive and sumptuous in decoration than the last. My bones and muscles recognized the passageways before I did, and I nearly stumbled. Hair prickled on the back of my neck. My hands trembled, and I clasped them to keep from betraying my fear.

The guards walked through an open doorway, the room beyond illuminated by candles and the pale light filtering through uncurtained windows. They paused in formation in the center of the room. The two leading guards stepped aside, allowing a full view of the tsarina at a desk, piles of state documents in front of her.

She only looked up from her work when she finished reading the top document. She examined me briefly before shifting her attention to the guard in charge.

"Leave us now, but stay at the door."

The guards bowed and turned, the lead giving me a skeptical once-over before departing.

"Facial hair suits you," she said by way of greeting. "I might have to rescind the laws that prohibit it."

I didn't bow or speak.

"What a headache you are," she said at long last. "Do you see all of these?" She gestured to the piles of documents and letters. "These are all the petitions I have received on your behalf since the ambassador's visit."

I hated the flutter of hope that brushed my insides. "Alexei?"

She offered me an indulgent look, one she might have given a particularly stupid child. "As if a younger brother would petition on behalf of an older one when that brother's absence grants him the entire power and property of his family."

Not Alexei.

"Amazing how silent they stayed when you could still offer them amusement." She gave the piles one last look before rising from her chair. "I've had to reconsider what to do with you."

"You could exile me from the country?"

"If I wanted to," she agreed. "But I thought of something better. Follow me."

I followed her as she left the room, not seeing another choice. I gritted my teeth, remembering this walk. From the receiving room, through the sitting room, little dining room, Kilikwa dining room, drawing room, then to the monarch's corridor. To her bedroom.

I stopped outside.

"I said no," I called out, my throat hoarse but my will solid.

"You don't know what I'm offering," she said as she returned to the doorway.

"I can guess."

"How little you know me." She reached her hand out for mine. "I had a bath drawn for you."

The unexpected offer of a bath overrode my other misgivings, and she caught my hand without me pulling away. I did not resist when she led me in, my curiosity requiring the substantiation of her claim. Self-serving, perhaps, but a bath encompassed the pinnacle of all physical comforts I could request in my current state.

The metal basin rested in front of the fireplace, the steam rising from the water twisting and curling in an enticing, sensual dance. I could not remember the last time I enjoyed a proper bath. I had long given up hope of ever being clean again.

"A bath for my submission?"

"A bath because you are filthy," she said.

"What do you get from this?"

"I get to watch." She released my hand. "You have been most amusing as my chicken, but we both know that isn't what I wanted you for."

"Watching also isn't what you wanted me for."

"Do you want the bath or not?"

I refused to let her know how much I wanted it, so I asked, "Do you propose I take it in costume?"

"I planned on letting you out of it."

"For how long?"

"What if I tell you that I never expect you to wear that costume again?" She wandered around the basin and picked up an item from the low table with toiletries, towels, and folded black fabric. "I have something finer for you."

Despite my mistrust, I could not see her advantage. There had to be one. She would not offer any of this if she had no motive, and yet, I did not see a gain except for mine.

"I accept the bath," I relented.

She held up the object in her hand as she approached, a miniature set of scissors in the shape of a bird, the blades its beak, the fingerholds its legs. Embroidery scissors.

"They are accustomed to undoing mistakes." She crossed behind me and began working on the stitches that kept the costume fastened. "You see, I am not so much the villain you think I am."

I nearly scoffed at her calling my deliberate humiliation a mistake, but I clamped my mouth shut. I would wait until I was out of the costume. I would wait until I luxuriated in a bath. I would wait, but only until I could make a viable attempt at escape.

My shoulders relaxed as she cut the stitches. The weight of the costume shifted and then fell away. The stench overpowered my relief, and I gagged as it assaulted me. I picked at the undershirt plastered to my torso by sweat and body oil, crust falling away as I pried it up. I tore it off only when I ensured it would not take skin with it. My tights and shoes too joined the pile of discarded clothing destined, I hoped, for a fire.

Although wishing to revel in my freedom, my filth tainted any fleeting notion of celebration. I launched myself into the bathing tub, submerging my head and resurfacing only to wipe water and hair from my face, careful around the sores from the beak mask. I leaned back against the basin and stretched.

"You look terrible," the tsarina said as she took a chair that afforded her an unobstructed view of the basin.

"I wonder why."

"It didn't have to be like this."

Refusing to dignify her statement with a response, I turned my attention to the table beside the basin to review the offerings. I lifted a small bottle, hand-blown, with only a third of the contents left. Her own toiletries.

"Couldn't find anything less dignified for me to use?" I asked.

"I wanted you to smell like me."

I set the bottle down and retrieved one of the towels instead, determined to scour myself until I bled in my bid for cleanliness rather than resort to using her items. While she said nothing, pretending to ignore her required more concentration than anticipated as I rubbed my skin raw. I had never successfully ignored the possessiveness of her gaze, although I succeeded in hiding the shivers it inspired.

"Do I get to shave?"

"As if I would trust you with a razor right now."

I grabbed one of the small towels, wet it, and laid it over my eyes. I slid down into the water up to my chin and marinated.

"Aren't you going to ask about what I have planned for you?"

"And ruin the fleeting pleasure of a bath? Not likely."

Maybe I should want to know what my future held. Maybe, if she told me, I could find a way out of whatever nefarious plan she had. But the future would come no matter what it held for me, and I could not endanger my fragile momentary delight for a miserable inevitability.

I only contemplated leaving the basin when the water chilled beyond tolerance. Even then, I delayed, unwilling to abandon my place of relative safety for an ominous unknown. When I finally rose from the water, the tsarina too rose from her seat, retrieving the final towel before I did, which she held out for me.

I tore it from her hands and began drying off.

"You said watch, not touch," I reminded her.

"So I did."

I toweled my hair off last, dismayed at its length and tempted to try the embroidery scissors on it.

"Your clothes," she said, gesturing to the pile of black fabric now revealed with the removal of the towel.

"Mourning for my own death?" I didn't dislike the color, but it boded ill given my situation. The clothes were little more than suggestions of a shirt and trousers, threadbare, patched, and more mending than material. "Couldn't find anything worse?"

"I can always have you sewn back into your chicken costume."

I heaved a sigh and began dressing to cover up the visceral fear of her doing just that. If it had been an endurance test, perhaps I could have done it again, another few months, and then freedom and a forever farewell to Ilyichia. But the only sure end to such torment would have been to outlive her, and I could not spend years trapped in a costume I could not remove. For all my resilience, that would break me.

She crossed over to the door that led out to her balcony and pulled on a blue summer cloak and white kidskin gloves. She gestured towards another cloak waiting for me.

"Don't want me to die of cold?" It wasn't cold enough outside to kill me, not yet, but my clothes were thin and I was disinclined to be civil. "Wouldn't that spare you from having to issue the order yourself?"

"You'll die when I see fit and not before." She gestured at the cloak and gloves again. "Put them on. I don't want you losing any fingers that I did not order to have cut off myself."

I pulled the sumptuous cloak on, enjoying the softness of it as I secured it around my shoulders. Fiery embroidery in the design of a firebird trailing feathers trimmed the edges. The black kidskin gloves that accompanied it fit like a tailor used my measurements.

"They were Pytor's," she explained. She looked me over approvingly. "You can use them for the game I have planned."

"I will not play any game with you," I told her. "You would never leave it up to chance with me. Therefore, it is a game I cannot win. "

"You're clever." She stepped out onto the balcony and moved across it towards the stairs on the far side. "You might surprise me."

I shivered. Summer it may be, but Ilyichia always burned with cold. My longing for the warm, lush climes of Varnasia twisted in my spleen.

I followed out of uncertainty. Could I just walk back out to the guards and ask them to take me to my cell again? Or would I have enough time to climb the hedge walls from the balcony and make an escape over the other side?

"I hate games," I grumbled.

I trailed her, mostly because I was certain that I would get caught if I attempted to escape. A small courtyard greeted us at the bottom of the stairs, dark from the immensely tall hedges and barren of any decorative flora. A closed door offered the only additional feature of interest.

"You might like this one, since you have a chance to win your life and your freedom," she said as she opened the door and led me into another courtyard, this one overflowing with color.

Roses overwhelmed all else in the alcove.

Drook told me that roses were linked with magic. Not that I believed in magic, but the roses served a dire warning of my situation. Could The Kind and Fair truly give the tsarina magic to uphold the empire?

Most of the roses were white here, although other colors lived on the periphery. The white marble basin used for offerings and currently serving as a birdbath formed the focal point between bushes. I had never left an offering for The Kind and Fair or the Great Holy, but the setup looked much the same for both entities. And in my disappointing life, I had never seen much proof to believe in the existence of one or the other.

I surveyed the courtyard, taking note of another door on the far side of the roses if I needed to plan for escape.

"Your life and your freedom, Mikhail," she repeated.

"I know you too well. I have no chance."

"Slim, you're correct, but there is." She moved to the basin and removed a glove, twirling the tip of a finger in the water. "Or should I just have you stuffed back into a costume and remove your tongue since it's not serving me?"

She would do it too.

"I propose a test of faith." She stopped swirling the water and gazed into the mirror of it once the ripples faded away. "My Kind and Fair against your Great Holy."

If I had to rely on the Great Holy or The Kind and Fair to provide my freedom, it was as I told her. I could not win. Even with offerings I could not give. Even with belief I did not have.

"How do you propose to test them?"

"The Kind and Fair protect Ilyichia, but I will give your Great Holy an opportunity to sway me." She grasped one of the blooms on the nearest bush and twisted it off the stem. "Pray, Mikhail. Ask that the Great Holy guides your steps to freedom. I will then release you. If you can leave the palace grounds before my guards catch you, then you are free, and the Great Holy presides. If you cannot, you are mine again."

I knelt in an attitude of prayer, although I could not pray. I had spent weeks praying to any higher power that deigned to listen for Irena and the baby before they died. Nothing answered.

The tsarina turned away, devoting her attention to her ritual. I watched her instead of attending to my own futile prayers, uncertain how she went about asking favors from The Kind and Fair.

"Please hear me," she murmured during her rite. "Please hear the petition of one who has long worshipped you. My bird will fly from the nest within moments. See that he returns."

She pressed one of the thorns from the flower stem into the tip of her finger until a drop of blood welled up. She pressed the blood to the broken stem on the bush and then stained one of the white petals of the rose with what remained. She dipped her bleeding finger into the basin of water before she thrust the blood-stained rose at me.

"Take it and you may go. May your Great Holy look kindly upon you, for no one else will if you fail."

A fool's bargain. The threat heated my bones. But I had no better choice.

I found my feet and took the rose she held out. Although the broken stem bore no thorns, I did not want to touch it. The bloodstain boded ill. Something worse than I had known awaited me if I failed, and I could not imagine worse than the past months.

"Go, Mikhail." She pointed to the other door. "You have no time to waste. I will inform my guards of your flight in a quarter hour. Use it wisely."

As she instructed, I fled.

I had no expectation of escape, but I would not make recapture easy. The black clothing, cloak, gloves, and boots served a better camouflage than anything else I might have accessed. Did she plan it that way? And if so, why would she help me?

This game possessed all the trappings of a fair opportunity, but the prickled hairs on the back of my neck warned me otherwise. The nervous energy that built up in anticipation of a future certainly worse than death drove me through the forest. I discarded the rose at my earliest awareness of anything but the distance between me and the palace. The pale flower lay on the forest floor, innocent and luminous.

I diverted my journey to the east, toward the densest forest, anticipating the movements of the pursuing palace guards. Perhaps I should have continued on the fastest path to the border of the park, but that would be the first route explored. Although I trusted in my own abilities far more than those of the guards, I was a possession the tsarina would never allow to depart with ease, and the guards would be searching for me as if their lives depended upon it. And for all I knew, they may.

My heart beat twice as fast with each uncertain moment. The blood rushed through my veins. Sweat poured off my brow. I tried to muffle my labored breathing. As if the forest knew of my plight and conspired in my downfall, all other sounds halted. No birds sang to each other. No rabbits explored the bases of trees or bushes. Only the leaves crunched beneath my boots, announcing to all of my position. I surveyed the trees in my vicinity to see which might offer the best cover should I need to climb instead and wait out any approaching search party.

I took another few paces and froze. I heard no sound and spied no movement, but there was something, a sensation, a fear, that breathed down my neck like a predator. I sheltered behind the nearest tree. When silence convinced me of my paranoia, I peered around the tree to assess my surroundings.

The burning heat of an attack flayed my back. I stumbled forward and fell, catching my toe on a root and slamming into the ground with a force that would leave me bruised for weeks. I clawed at the creature that had struck such a blow, struggling to my knees as the wild feathered thing continued to tear my back apart. I slammed my back against the trunk of the tree, landing an impact to dislodge the creature that clung to me. It threw me again to the ground. My back burned all the more, strips of fabric and skin ripped away. I fought to rise, but my feet refused to hold me. They too were on fire. My entire body was ablaze in invisible flames.

Against all self-preservation, I screamed with the pain and blinding heat. Something ripped my face open. Blood filled my mouth. My hands lost sensation, and I could not find the footing to flee.

One thought lingered before I blacked out. Somehow, the tsarina had won.

XII.

Someone moaned.

After the third time, I had to consider the possibility that it came from me. But I had burned to death out in the forest. I had been attacked, torn apart, and consumed by flame. The dead did not groan in pain. So, was I alive or dead?

Unless this was some strange afterlife where both could simultaneously be true. Would such an afterlife belong to the domain of The Kind and Fair or the Great Holy? I did not know enough about either religion to have any enlightened perspective and, in the absence of that, I disbelieved in the afterlife entirely.

My body, distant though my limbs might be, registered the ache of an unyielding floor beneath me. My swollen tongue filled my mouth. I rolled onto my side. My head swam with the movement, and I heaved. Blood and bile splattered the ground, droplets flying back at me.

I couldn't be dead and still produce such undignified bodily responses. But I should have been dead. I had been engulfed in fire out in the cold. And I was sure, before much longer, I would wish to be dead. Again.

Everything pinched and pulled. My legs constricted as if running for days. My numb feet no longer registered socks or boots. My hands refused to function. And my back. If I were told that someone had slit my back open and torn my ribs out from behind, I would have believed it.

I just wanted to sleep. Sleep would cure the pain. And a sweet, forever sleep would ensure that I never suffered again.

"I would caution you not to go in," a man said.

"I had no intention," a woman replied.

I tried to locate the source of the conversation, my eyes nearly swollen shut and bleary in the dimness of the room. As I propped myself up to a sitting position, my head spun again. Another round of heaved fluids forced me to my elbows, and the undignified dry retching after shook my body like a toddler having a tantrum.

I trembled with pain and exhaustion and the knowledge that my visitor couldn't be any of my jester friends this time. The crushing weight of my spectacular failure caused another heave of my belly.

What would she do now? How could anything be worse than what she had already done? Even death offered more solace than her former decree.

"I wish to observe my new prize," she said.

I was an old problem, not a new prize.

"Would you like us to stay with you?"

"That will be unnecessary."

The echoes of boots drifted away and all again returned to silence.

After a prolonged quiet, the empress harrumphed.

"I'm disappointed," she said. "I thought you would be raging at me by now. I suppose I shouldn't have raised my hopes. The guards tell me you gave them almost no challenge at all."

I could barely form thoughts. How could I rally enough to scratch her with words?

I fought to push myself upright and find her so that I could address her properly. As I did so, my hands came into view. I now wore black feathered gloves with long hooked talons. The black feathers extended up the backs of my fingers, hands, and arms. I groaned, not with pain but with frustration. What ridiculous costume had the tsarina chosen for me this time?

"That's why you haven't protested," she said. "You haven't seen."

Another bird outfit then. Worse than before if she expected my fury.

I took long, measured breaths. I refused to break in front of her. I could nurse wounds later and address my much-abused pride in solitude. But now, I needed to stay together.

I hastily assessed the situation: a black feathered suit this time. And she had shoved me back into the loathsome beak mask. The sores on my nose and around my mouth from prior wear barely registered in the wake of my other pains. My suit, though fluffed with feathers, was not padded.

My head throbbed. Still, I managed to keep my panic in check. "What do you intend to do with me?"

"Why, my dear, I intend to keep you as my beloved pet."

"More nest sitting? More public squawking?" I snorted and pushed myself onto my knees. "Your court has already seen it, ma'am." I turned to the doorway where she stood behind the barred window. I had long been empty of shame and horror. She had wrung it all out of me. "I fear we are all bored."

"Fear not," she said, a smile creeping into her voice. "I found a way to make it more exciting. If not for the court, at least for me."

I narrowed my eyes at her. I did not see how much worse it could get.

"Then do it and leave. Surely, you have better things to do than waste your time on me."

"It is done," she said. "I was rather hoping you would have figured that out by now. As I said, disappointing. I wanted your arms to become your wings, but alas, I am as subject to the magic of The Kind and Fair as any of us."

Wings? Magic?

My nausea welled up as I turned my head. If the tsarina

had not mentioned wings, I would have doubted my senses. Black feathered appendages loomed over the equally feathered crest of my shoulder. I reached to touch one of the alien limbs. Despite the lightness of the touch, it radiated down my back.

It couldn't be.

I withdrew my hand as if the wing burned. My back still did.

They were part of me. And if the wings were part of me.... If everything was a part of me….

Another wave of nausea passed over me.

The tsarina's low chuckle echoed off the walls.

"What have you done to me?" I stared up at her, too stunned for the tears I would shed later.

"I won our game." The tsarina's mouth twisted into a triumphant smirk. "You told my ladies that an evil witch cast a spell on you. If I am to be accused, I may as well do the deed. And so I, through The Kind and Fair, gave you ugliness you cannot remove."

"I'm...." Numb horror sent tremors down my limbs. I needed to discover the extent of my terrible circumstances, but I couldn't bear to do it in front of her. "You've made me...."

"I couldn't get an actual firebird," she lamented, "so I had to make one myself."

My chest convulsed. My throat tightened. I nearly stopped breathing. I couldn't break. I couldn't. Not now. Not in front of her. Later. I would do it later. Whatever else, I couldn't give her my moment of breaking. She had taken everything else from me, and I refused to give her that final satisfaction.

"I told you I could not win," I snarled. "Your victory is hollow."

"If your Great Holy had been powerful enough, it would not have been impossible."

"All this," I surveyed my hands and arms, "because I did not wish to become a lover after becoming a widower?"

"All this," she repeated, "because you forgot that you cannot say no to me."

"And you imagine, after everything you have put me through, I will submit to you now?"

"Now, my dear, you have no choice. I made an example of you, and once my point was made, I no longer needed you."

"Have you not already punished me?"

"Punished you, yes, but it did not achieve what I intended. Now, I will have you however I like, and no one will turn you into a martyr."

"Others will still look for me."

"No one is looking for you," she assured me. "Former Prince Mikhail's execution was announced yesterday. If I choose to starve you, or chain you to my dais, or blind you, or muzzle you for the rest of your life, no one will say anything. You are a part of my menagerie now."

The heat of panic chilled. No one would rescue me. No one would come to my aid. My friends in my time of trial would not know that I needed their support and company more than ever. Trapped. In body. In will. In every meaningful way.

The impulse to scream burned my lungs, but I refused to do it. She wanted to see me panic, and I would not give it to her.

"Only your exterior has transformed," she continued, "but it's remarkable how such a shallow change can make all the difference, isn't it?"

"Why?" I asked, a pitiful, breathless question as I considered the bleak, miserable future ahead of me. "Why me?"

"It's not personal." She paused as she made to turn from the window, reconsidering her words. "That's not true. It is personal. Extremely personal. You betrayed me. But, my dear, do not flatter yourself that you are all that important in the scheme of things. You aren't, and you never were. That's why."

I stared at the door long after she abandoned it, trembling with fatigue, sick with fear and fury. I did not dare look down again, terrified of seeing the evidence of what I had become. So long as I did not look, did not feel, did not explore, I could pretend. I could pretend this was just another prison cell. I could pretend that I was waiting for Klessa or Drook or Agara or anyone to come visit me. I could pretend that I wore a costume that could be removed.

I practiced breathing as Drook had once suggested as a way to abandon shame, hoping it would bring a moment of calm. Even the simple exercise came with difficulty. I closed my eyes to concentrate.

Breathe in. Hold. Breathe out. Hold. Breathe in. Breathe out. In. Out.

The tremors vanished after a time. My fury cooled. My heart slowed its frantic beating. I opened my eyes again, not wanting to face the inconceivable truth but ready to try.

I raised my hands and arms for inspection. Gloves were standard uniform for most of my life. From the coldness of Ilyichia inspiring such protection, to the military requiring the formality of dress, to the ballroom demanding that dancing partners not touch hands directly, gloves featured as everyday attire. And these horrible, long, black feathered things embellished with realistic-looking talons were nothing other than gloves too, I lied to myself. I would wear these gloves, scaled, gnarled, and feathered though they were.

Wild black feathers framed my vision from above, taking the place of my hair. But it was just a hood like before.

I had already worn a stiff, scratchy collar and horrible

padded costume for months without reprieve. The sleek black feathers on my neck, chest, and torso, though adding a little bulk, did not offer the same cumbersome and uncomfortable conditions as my prior costume. Further inspection ensured, much to my relief, that my manhood remained intact and undisturbed, though hidden too by a sheath of feathers.

I did not know how to reconcile the wings on my back. Heavy and awkward now that the pain had subsided, I flexed my shoulders. The wings responded with stiffness when I tried to shift or spread them. A line of golden red primary feathers edged both wings, matching the tail feathers I saw when I twisted to get a better view.

My feet nearly caused me to heave again when I finally worked up the courage to examine them. Like my hands, they had become scaly, taloned things, the black feathers mostly stopping at the ankles. But I could not rationalize the appearance of my feet with simply wearing convincing shoes. Each foot had been divided into three long toes tipped with talons, with a fourth clawed toe on my heel. And that's where the ability to reconcile it with just another costume ended.

Magic. The tsarina possessed magic.

I hadn't found the courage to touch my face. I could see it, or at least I could see the beak, and I tried desperately to ignore it. And although I struggled with thirst, I could not bring myself to go over to the water pail by the door and drink from it. If I did, I would have to look at my reflection first, if only from perverse curiosity. By drinking, I would have to use the beak since I could not just pull it down or off until I was finished. I could not bear to do that, afraid that admission of necessity would shatter the tenuous hold on my faculties.

I kept breathing. In. Out. In. Out.

Had the tsarina planned this from the beginning?

Everything I had already endured now appeared like preparation. If I had fallen prey to this from the start, I may not have retained sanity.

Or, worse, had I done this to myself?

At her party, I had teased about being an enchanted prince under a spell. It framed my experience in a way that would win the ladies. How could I have guessed that the tsarina might have the power to make it come true?

If Irena were alive, none of this would have ever happened. If Irena were alive, I would be with her in Varnasia, and Ilyichia would be but a distant nightmare consigned to my past. If Irena were alive....

But she wasn't.

When we first met, she did not know I was a prince. Her uncle, who made our introduction, told me later that she asked him to introduce her to the handsome Ilyichian idiot whose attempts at speaking Varnasian could only be described as comical. I would have given up everything for her. I tossed my religion to the wayside. I kept my titles quiet. We rented a villa in a remote village. We had been happy. Life had been simple and easy. Would that it could have always been. But I did not know if Irena's devotion could have outlasted this new phase, even if it was the truest love I had ever known. I didn't think anyone's could. Not now. Not like this. Not Alexei. Not Irena. Not Klessa or Drook or Agara or Grigga. They had loved a man. Granted, a foolish, flawed man, but still a man despite the humiliation.

What was I now?

I staggered to my feet. I tested my footing, unsure with the talons but finding balance. I avoided the drying vomit as I staggered over to the water pail. I lifted it from the ground and held it for several prolonged moments during which I debated the wisdom of this. And then I looked down into it. Something hideous stared back at me with its black scaled and feathered face. The beak, sharp-edged and rigid, suggested something carnivorous. But the monster had my green eyes, and those eyes filled with tears.

I bent my head and set the beak within the water. It drank. I drank. The monster and I drank together. And when we were done, I set the pail down and breathed.

In. Out.

I was so tired. I had lost so much and endured even more. And I couldn't fight against magic.

In. Out.

I turned and looked at the pathetic cell to which I had been relegated as the newest member of the tsarina's menagerie. I couldn't live like this.

In.

The former Prince Mikhail had been executed anyway. No one would miss me.

Out.

I stared at my hands again, the hooked razor talons offering me a new sense of hope. I tested one against the toughened skin of my wrist and broke through the surface with only a little trouble.

In.

It was time to give up.

Out.

XIII.

Bits of down circled above me. Several drifted back to the blankets and pillows. Small and white, they couldn't be my feathers. They had to have come from the bedding.

The concept of bedding startled me into wakefulness.

I was dead. Again. I had to be dead this time. I had to be.

I hadn't enjoyed pillows and blankets since before the tsarina arrested me the first time. Could this be the afterlife? I closed my eyes again and let myself believe it for a moment. I deserved a moment of rest before I faced my circumstances.

With the sunshine warming my face and the bedding enfolding me in peaceful safety, I could almost believe that this was Varnasia, my place of pinnacle happiness. Maybe Irena would realize that I was awake and cuddle behind me, wrapping her arm over my shoulder. Maybe she would kiss the place behind my ear that made me melt and nuzzle her nose into my hair. Or maybe, if I rolled over, Irena would be there still dozing. Maybe I could catch her while she slept and admire the bow of her lips and the fan of her lashes. Maybe I could wake her with stolen kisses and lay my head on her chest and tell her about my nightmares. She would stroke my face and run her hands through my hair and promise me sweet distraction from the horrors that plagued my slumber. I might say something sweet and romantic in Varnasian, and she would laugh because I had mistakenly said something that sounded anything but sweet and romantic. And then all need for words would disappear if we took full advantage of the morning.

Irena didn't embrace me, and I didn't roll over.

She wouldn't be there.

The wings on my back remained. I could not imagine an afterlife so cruel as to make me wear my last shape for an eternity. So I had to be alive.

I fought the blankets with one arm. A bandaged wrist greeted me, the white linen stark against the black feathers and skin, the blood seepage starker still against both.

Rustling skirts moved across the room and stopped behind me.

I twisted my shoulders to see who kept me company.

The glittering molded plaster ceiling decorated with ornate tableaux of shepherds, putti, and domestic animals filled my vision. I remembered this ceiling well, although the tsarina had never been averse to coupling against corridor walls or on dining room tables when the mood struck her.

She laid her hand on my forehead and then replaced her hand with a cool, damp cloth. Her braided hair fell over her shoulder, strands loose and wild from the bulk, wisps around her face.

I tore the cloth away and flung it somewhere. I pushed her arm aside and rolled back to my initial position so that I wouldn't have to look at her.

"I never thought you would try it," she said. "Thank The Kind and Fair that you didn't succeed."

I attempted to say something cutting and found that I couldn't, issuing only a pathetic noise of surprise instead.

"You're muzzled," she explained. "But only because I didn't want you to give yourself away by talking in your sleep. I can take it off now if you'll behave yourself."

I refused to turn back to her. I buried my face in the pillows and pulled the blanket up to cover the rest of me, beak, muzzle, and all.

"You're so stubborn," she griped. "I'm trying to take care of you."

I did not re-emerge from the blankets. Maybe I should want the muzzle removed, but I didn't care because I had nothing to say to her. No. That wasn't true. I had plenty to say to her. I was just certain that I shouldn't say it.

"Fine," she said. Her skirts rustled again as she moved away from me. "When you're done sulking, maybe we can talk like adults."

I shut my eyes and swallowed the hate that threatened to consume me. I was too tired for hate. Unfortunately, hate without fire deteriorated into despair, and I fought tears instead. And somehow, having her see me weep seemed an even greater failure than not being successful in my attempt on my life.

When skirts rustled again, this time to leave the room, I breathed a sigh of relief. I waited to ensure she was not coming back before I threw the blankets off and forced myself up to sitting with my elbows. Tendrils of black feathers clung to the sheets. I did not get much farther though since I overestimated my energy and ended up winding myself before I could rise.

I had been afforded a well-appointed sleeping cot at the far wall across from the tsarina's bed. The blankets and pillows, clean and white until I had shed on them, were of the softest goose down. A stool for company and a small table sat off to the side to provide me with anything I might need. A book and a bowl of water occupied the table.

I retrieved the small gilt-spined red leather-bound book, left opened and placed pages down, to examine what had occupied the tsarina while I slept. The exterior read, *The Collected Works and Writings of Ilya: A Discourse on The Kind and Fair.* The few lines I read offered confusing philosophical conundrums that I had no mind to tackle just now.

I wished I could still visit the other jesters. But if I could, what might they say of me now? What might they have already said of me now, not knowing who I was?

Whatever had the tsarina said to get a cot set up for me in her own room? Probably nothing more than "do it," but I would dearly have loved to hear the servants theorize about the intention. Would any of them guess the truth? Not the truth of me being Mikhail. The truth of her intention of making me, in my horrible avian guise, her lover. If anyone dared to suggest it, they might lose something dear to them, but the idea had to have crossed someone's mind.

I pulled a leg up and folded my arms atop it, resting my head on my arms afterward. My wrists didn't throb the way I thought they should after such wounds, but maybe I was too numb to everything to register them. My only spike of emotion came from the frustration of having endured so much so far for the sake of my moral compass only to end up without a choice. And this time, as something worse than ever.

I might have fallen asleep again because when next I opened my eyes, the tsarina strode through the doorway, a servant carrying a tray behind her. I instinctively shifted from my position and put the wall at my back to better observe. The servant caught my movement and stopped walking, the color draining from her face.

The tsarina waited a half minute before stepping forward, grabbing the book and the bowl from the side table, and then turning to the servant as if to dare her to refuse to come nearer now that she had proven that she had no fear. The servant moused forward and set the tray down, scuttling back a distance with her completed assignment.

The tsarina dismissed her with a glare, and when we were alone again, the tsarina set the bowl and book down on the nearest dresser. She returned to my side and settled on the stool.

As she surveyed the food offerings on the tray, she asked, "Are you feeling any better?"

"Not at all," and "I never expect to again," and "Are you

delusional?" fought for response. But I hadn't even attempted to remove the muzzle. I shook my head and looked away.

"You haven't eaten in days, my dear."

Now I was her dear. I wanted to laugh, but that sounded like too much effort.

"I felled the deer myself yesterday." She lifted a bite of meat on a two-tonged fork and waved it in front of me. "It's fresh."

It smelled divine.

She put the fork back down on the tray and beckoned me forward.

Hunger weakened me. I slid toward the edge of the bed and bent my head down so that she could remove the muzzle. I was too tired to fight, but I wasn't too tired to hate myself for my weakness.

She set the discarded muzzle on the table when it fell away. I stared at the bit of padded leather and then glared at her.

"I was only looking after you," she said.

She lifted the fork again and offered me the bite. I took it and hated myself for taking it.

"If you behave, I will see that you enjoy everything that you should have already been enjoying."

"Except as a monster."

"I didn't want to do it," she said. "But no one likes a powerful woman, and I needed a lesson to be learned."

Power was one thing, but unnecessary cruelty was another.

"Then give me back my wedding band."

"Firebirds don't wear wedding bands." She skewered another bit of meat off the tray. "But I can indulge you in everything else now. As a lesson, I needed to be harsh so that everyone could see what happened to those who displeased me. But since you are now a beloved pet, I can spoil you."

"Did I not get my point across?" I held out my bandaged wrists. "I would rather be dead."

"Let's get your strength back," she said, ignoring my bandages and my gesture. "And then we can see about everything else."

"I want my body back."

"That was rash, wasn't it?" Her face fell into an expression of deep contrition, not a look she often wore. "You have said such horrible things to me, embarrassed me in ways I never wish to recall."

I said horrible things to her? I embarrassed her? After how she treated me these past months?

"I should never have done it," she said at last.

"Undo it then."

"Alas, my dear, I am unable. I set it in motion, but it is cast by The Kind and Fair."

"Convenient."

"For all that you think me heartless, there is a way out."

Like her challenge between The Kind and Fair and the Great Holy, probably. Chances slim to impossible. But still. A way out. Any way out.

"Which is?"

"You cannot tell anyone that you were ever human. If you do not savor living the rest of your life as a bird, I suggest you stay silent and play your role as my pet."

"That's not an objective. What great task must I accomplish?"

"No great task at all. Indeed, it's like the children's stories. Someone has to tell you that they love you."

"Love me?" Dizziness struck me. "*Like this?!*"

"It's always been so easy for you. After all, isn't this what you told everyone at the party? All those ladies could not tear themselves away!"

Despite what the tsarina claimed, I wasn't an easy man to love, never had been. I didn't know my father. My mother tolerated me as her eldest, but no more. Alexei might have loved me once, but not now. Marfa respected me but did not love me, and I had never expected her to. State marriages rarely involved love, even if she and I had managed to make it work for all those years. There had been mistresses and women who wanted me, the tsarina among them, because I was wealthy, and handsome, and eligible. But it had never been about me. Irena alone had been the person who wanted me, loved me, took me for all that I was. But with only two scant years together, would she too have grown discontent when I did not live up to her idea of me?

Drook and Klessa and my unlikely friends alone had shown me that I wasn't wholly without merit, for they had loved me even without the trappings that others had once desired me for. Even older, set in my ways, prickly and disillusioned by life, they had claimed me as a friend. But I did not think that would be enough.

There would never be another Irena. I wasn't good enough or talented enough or kind enough or soft enough or tolerant enough or whatever it was that made people lovable. I could twist myself into knots trying to be something someone would want, and I would never be enough. Who I was, beyond wealth and titles, beyond feathers and a face, didn't matter to anyone. And if it had, I would still be found wanting.

"I can help you," she offered, "if you let me help you."

"Help how?" I asked. "No one is going to want me."

"That's not true." She abandoned the stool for the edge of my cot and took my hand, my clawed, feathered hand, in hers. "You forget, my dear." She leaned forward and pressed a soft kiss on my cheek. "I have always wanted you."

XIV.

"Do you want us to remove that thing from your room yet?"

"I don't trust anyone to look after it properly," she said.

I burrowed deeper into the blankets. I probably should have been listening to their plans for me, but no outcome could be anything but depressing in my present circumstances.

The guards wanted the strange, mythical animal in the menagerie where I could be viewed by all and do no harm. And the tsarina wanted me near to her so that I would not be viewed by anyone while I fulfilled my true purpose in her bed.

"It did not take capture well," the tsarina said. "I would like it to be docile when I finally introduce it to court."

I almost lost what little food I had in me. I wasn't the fallen Prince Mikhail this time, but if I returned to court, I would be subject to a different kind of humiliation. I uncovered myself and sat, unable to pretend ignorance.

When she came in, she paused. "Oh, you're awake."

"You're bringing me back to court?"

"I have to," she said, taking her place on the stool. "You know how gossip spreads. Everyone will grow suspicious if I do not show you off. Who captures a firebird and then doesn't display it?"

I almost pointed out that she hadn't caught a firebird either, not a real one, but I did not think that observation would help.

"I know it will be difficult," she said. "But no one will dare harm you or hurt you this time." She took one of my hands in hers. "I will be beside you every moment. You won't face anything alone."

I would be beside her, but I would face everything alone. She offered no comfort. No one else might dare to hurt or harm me, but that did not apply to the tsarina herself, who would always find ways to wound.

"And maybe," she said as if she were a coquettish girl and not my empress, "perhaps, if you need comfort, I could provide that for you too. After."

I could agree, but then everything I had already suffered would have been for naught. I could tell her no yet again and suffer punishments anew. I had one other choice, the most reckless but the only one that offered me neither immediate hardship nor a future of sexual submission. If I could pull it off.

"This has all been so devastating," I told her. "I think I might need a great deal of comfort. After."

"I have missed you so much." Her dark eyes met mine, and a small smile touched the corners of her mouth. Then it fell. "Why didn't you just agree to begin with? You could have spared yourself all of this!"

"Grief."

"My poor dear." She stood and extracted her hands from mine. "I have obligations this afternoon. Be sure to eat and rest."

I nodded obediently.

"I need you strong and healthy." She paused at the doorway, her hope radiant. "I will see you later."

In my solitude, I launched myself from the cot and bolted to the balcony door. I retraced the path down to the gardens and into the palace park. My heart crashed against my ribs. I was doing this. Again.

This time, without guards in pursuit, I had a chance of escape. I didn't know where I would go beyond leaving the grounds. I didn't have a hope of regaining my humanity. But I couldn't stay. Not after everything. Not with the promise of display. And not with the certainty of being forced into the tsarina's bed.

Maybe, probably, I would fail again. But I had to try. I would never stop trying.

Being marched through the audience chamber while the tsarina heard petitions ruined her day at least. My right wing throbbed, but watching the tsarina's face cycle through confusion to rage to hurt made up for it just a little. And she couldn't say anything about her reaction either, which also helped ease the burden of my failure.

I also spoiled her plans for introducing me back into court as her firebird. That brought me some joy too. With everyone hurrying out of the way of a massive mythic bird-creature, leashed though it may be, the tsarina could have no hope of presenting me with any pomp and grandeur later on.

A guard, followed by others as backup, led me in on a rope with my wings bound together and my wrists tied behind my back. A humbling position, but certainly not the worst I had endured of late. And strangely, though my condition and status had degraded from prince-in-costume to a menagerie creature with permanent beak and feathers, it was almost easier now not being the former Prince Mikhail. I didn't have anyone to know me or feel shamed by me. I didn't have to carry the burden of being stripped of my name as punishment. I didn't have to bear the repulsion of former friends. Because, as far as anyone but the tsarina knew, I was just a wild creature newly captured. If someone poured kvass on me now, it was because they were a mean-spirited person who hated and harmed anything that came their way, not because it was me. It also meant that I had the luxury of pretending complete ignorance and disinterest as any other animal did in tedious human affairs.

"What is all this?" the tsarina asked, interrupting the man speaking.

The main guard brought me up to the tsarina, and I, contrary as ever, did not follow obediently. I had to be jerked along several times as I gave everything else my attention except the empress, ready to vent her displeasure.

"We found it out in the park, Your Majesty," the guard holding my lead said. "It must have found a way out of your quarters."

"You found it outside?" Her voice trembled. Her hands gripped the chair like she might tear the arms off.

"It fought re-capture with more strength than anyone imagined it possessed and took down five of us before it was subdued."

"'Took down,'" she repeated. "Killed?"

"No, Your Majesty, but severely wounded. Nikov won't be able to use his legs for at least a few months, and Yonen has a punctured lung. Things might have turned out differently had Krintova not landed the shot that enabled us to take advantage."

The tsarina stood from the chair, tension rippling off in huge, heavy waves. She did not have a thought to spare for me with her eyes trained on the guards.

"Krintova shot my firebird?"

"Only in the wing, Your Majesty." The guard who had broken my nose stepped out from behind me and bowed. "I knew of its great importance to you."

"*Only* the wing?"

Krintova glanced first at his fellow guards, then at the crowd around us. Realizing he had little support from any quarter, he returned his attention to the tsarina. "It would have killed us."

"I wish it had," she said, her voice icy and dispassionate. "A firebird is worth a hundred of you. You are under arrest for wounding my prize."

Two guards materialized from the right and took position on either side of Krintova. They put their hands on his shoulders and arms, not as they had done with me, with force and malice, but with sympathetic gentleness.

"I helped ensure that it found its way back to you!" he called when he realized his situation.

"Pray my firebird is not gravely injured or you shall be also." She gestured for the two guards and prisoner to leave.

My personal captor continued, "Although it is not violent now, I would like to move it to the menagerie to ensure there are no repeats of this incident."

"For now, yes," she agreed. She heaved a sigh as she resumed her seat, her face drained of all animation. Even her dour expression sagged. "I am so very disappointed."

XV.

They passed me from one set of hands to another, each new set taking the rope-lead with a little less zeal and a wealth of apprehension. No one wanted to be near a creature who had, as the entire palace had now heard, maimed and nearly killed several of the armed guards who patrolled the park, even if I had gone docile on the leash.

Could anyone figure out that I was intelligent and had thus deduced the futility of fighting when injured and bound in such a way? No one put it together. And while the tsarina knew, she would not say. She could not say, not if she wanted all to think that she possessed a firebird and that her former jester was truly dead. And, even more personal to her, did she want everyone aware of the power she wielded via The Kind and Fair? Many had said that the tsarina was a sorceress, although mostly as a descriptor of her unchecked power, but no one had seen the truth of it, or had witnessed enough to give others proof. Unless they too were like me, put in an impossible situation where disclosure would ruin any hope of their freedom.

The menagerie was a broad term to describe many of the enclosures, exhibits, pavilions, and aviaries where the Great One, successors, and other palace residents stored and maintained creatures from foreign dignitaries, personal hunting expeditions, and courtier gifts. The only thing it told me was that I would be put somewhere outside of the palace and with greater precautions so that I would not be able to flee again.

My guard settled on a pavilion out in the park, not far

from the palace. Secluded and shielded by a line of trees, I would be completely alone. Peacocks might once have occupied it, which might have been why they brought another massive bird to it. With no gates or cages — doubtless because the peacocks had been allowed to roam freely — it only possessed a half-roof to keep out the elements and old straw laid out on the ground. A private bench occupied the wall across from the shelter in the event anyone should want to observe the tsarina's bird. My attendants led me to the stone wall that circled the shelter. My last remaining guard from the transfer held the lead while one of the last attendants to receive me bound my ankles, a small length of rope between them so that I could still move, but not enough to let me run off with ease. They secured that rope to a metal ring in the wall, much like jesses in falconry. Then they backed away to see if they had neglected anything, the guard eager to drop my lead after prolonged exposure.

Another came to join the two assigned to my relocation. This one, a stout man likely not much older than I, came armed with a bolt of fabric and a leather bag. He set his burdens down at the edge of the shelter and observed for a long moment, a mix of awe and wariness. After an awkward period of watching me, he held his hand out in front of him to see if I would fight. When I simply stepped backward, he scooped up his leather bag and fabric and pressed his advance.

"I'm not here to hurt you," he coaxed. "I need to look at that wing of yours."

If I continued to back away, my companions would assume I would lash out as any cornered wild creature and try to pin me. If I moved forward at the reassurance of aid, then my companions might guess that I could understand them. So I didn't move.

"Can't have our firebird wounded now, can we? Not after all the time it took for the tsarina to finally get you. You're doing so good," he assured me as he reached to unbind my wings.

I twitched them away.

He glanced over his shoulder and eyed the guard and attendant to see if either of them might be useful in holding me should I struggle. The disappointment in his face as he turned back to address me again almost made me smile. An impulse I quickly had to squash lest I give myself away.

Except I had a beak now. Could I smile at all? Probably in no way that would translate to a person not expecting such a thing from such a creature.

The man set down the leather bag and fabric. He rolled up his sleeves, even in the chill, in preparation for a difficult time.

"Gentle," he cooed at me. "I'm here to help."

With only a little difficulty, less because I gave it to him intentionally and more because he exercised excessive caution, he finally snagged the bindings.

I didn't want to fight aid, even if I wanted to make myself everyone's problem for the rest of my natural existence, so I held still. The man found the place in my wing and probed at it. I yelped, and he caught me by the shoulder.

"Hold there," he said, releasing me. "I'll be but a moment."

Not having wings in my natural shape, I did not know how they correlated to my old anatomy. Were the wings part of my shoulder blades or my ribs or my spine, or a combination? And now that I had a bullet hole in one of them, I could not determine where the wound might have been on a human body. If by some miracle I escaped this fate, would I have a scar on my back from this?

He grabbed the fabric with his free hand and began wrapping my wing, undoing the bindings as he replaced them with the softer material.

"I don't have an Aba large enough for you," he told me as

he worked. "We might have to have one made so you don't hurt yourself. Just be still now."

As he passed the fabric under a wing, he paused. Then he turned his attention to the two useless people at the enclosure entrance.

"It has arms," he said to them.

"I know," answered the guard. "We bound them too. The thing is unnatural."

"I suppose firebirds, and other Otherland creatures, are, by definition, unnatural. Or perhaps supernatural."

The man gave me another long examination and passed the back of his hand over his brow. Then he resumed binding my wings until only a small patch around the wound remained visible. With the main task done, the man dug around in his bag and extracted a tool that I did not want anywhere near me.

"I didn't see a bullet," he said to me, as if I could understand, which I did, but he didn't know that. "But I need to clean it. You're doing so well."

Despite my apprehension, I set myself to endure. I almost vomited from the pain, but he was deft with his tool and eventually produced a squashed round to show me.

"I'm glad I looked." He spun it in his fingers. "I don't know how this will affect your flight —"

I couldn't fly. I had already tried it. But I appreciated his concern.

"—but we can only do our best, right?"

He might have had a fainting spell if I answered him, so I just looked away.

He tossed the spent bullet into his bag with the tool and retrieved ointment of which he slathered obscene amounts on my wound.

"We can't have our firebird getting an infection now," he soothed as he bandaged up the tender area.

"Are you sure it's a firebird?" the attendant asked.

"I thought the firebird was supposed to be red and gold," the guard said. "This one is just black. I don't know that a few bright feathers count as a firebird."

"Those are all legends," the man said. "Tell me, have you ever seen another such creature? I certainly haven't, and I see them all!"

If this man attended all of tsarina's creatures, then I supposed I could safely assume that she was not hiding hordes of other enchanted princes somewhere on palace grounds. Somehow, knowing I was the only one did not flatter me.

"Maybe, somewhere, there's still a firebird that looks like the creatures of yore," he continued as he tied off the fabric. "Maybe deep in the Otherlands. I cannot imagine that Otherland creatures that live in the Mundane Lands look much like their legendary counterparts, if only for survival. How else might this one have eluded us for so long?"

"I suppose that's true," observed the guard.

"Maybe," said the attendant with more skepticism.

"If the tsarina calls it a firebird," said the man rolling his sleeves down to denote the completion of his work, "I will too. And unless one comes along that looks more like what we expect, there will be nothing to sway my opinion." He paused. "Unless the tsarina decides to change her mind."

He was a survivalist too then, having the sense not to contradict the tsarina. That was likely why he had charge of her strange pets.

After closing his bag, he took another long look at me. He swept his hand up my shoulder, causing strange discomfort by brushing the feathers in the wrong direction. I side-stepped him, pulling my shoulder away.

"You have a good bloom to your coat. I don't think your beak needs any coping, but I would like to look."

He reached over and caught the beak, forcing me to face him. I didn't fight because I wanted this to be over. He opened the beak and then paused. He did not let me go, but he met my eyes meaningfully.

"You are not built like a bird," he said.

"What was that?" the guard shouted.

"It has teeth," the man shouted so that they could hear them. Then he returned his attention to me. "Human teeth," he said for my benefit alone. He resumed his examination. When he finally released me, he lowered his voice. "Do you speak?"

I didn't know the mechanics of my nose and mouth becoming a beak. I had not touched it or examined it because then it truly would be part of me. The tsarina had told me I was still a man but in a costume I could not remove, and in that, I had been content to take her at her word. So long as I could still function and eat and communicate, I did not need to examine how any of it was accomplished. I just hadn't realized that my anatomy, or inconsistent anatomy, might give me away.

In answer, I just stared blankly at him. He doubted me, but he took a step back.

"Now, those talons of yours need attention." He retrieved a new tool, this one designed, I assumed, to trim claws. My fingers bent, and the tools snapped one by one. "There. Much less dangerous for everyone now." He dropped the tool back in the bag. "I'll be back to see how your wound is healing."

"Is there a reason you talk to the dumb animals like they can understand you?" the attendant asked as the man trudged out of the enclosure, the guard following.

"They are more intelligent than you think," came the reply.

The guard shot one last wary look at me before leaving completely.

Little did they know.

My wing healed slowly, and I grew impatient with having both wings and arms bound. My shoulders ached from the position, and I lost feeling in my arms even though the bindings on my wrists did not impede my circulation. The man who had done the work checked on me, bringing my daily meals consisting of pails of water and plates of raw meat, and offering the only company I currently enjoyed. Several people peeked into the enclosure over the days, but none of them trusted my restraints enough to venture further.

On the fourth day, several guards accompanied my caretaker. He approached alone, but a complement of guards meant I was going somewhere. He set his bag down and fell into the routine of checking my wing.

"It's healing nicely," he said to his entire audience, but he meant it for me. He returned to his bag and dug around, pulling out bands of leather. "I had anklets and jesses made," he said as he grabbed two of the larger bands and a stretch of leather cording, "so we can get those nasty ropes off you."

My body froze up. Of course, I looked like a bird of prey. They were going to treat me like one. Even if I would never be used for falconry, I would be subject to all the restraints of it. I had harmed several guards. No one would let me go about unbound now.

"Why don't you let us muzzle it first?"

Maybe I should want to be muzzled because this was going to happen whether I fought it or not. The urge to beg the caretaker not to do it came on so forcefully that I almost slipped. I managed to catch myself, the wisdom of silence prevailing since I dared not let any of the guards hear lest they find new interest in me.

My caretaker locked eyes with me. "Do they need to muzzle you?"

I maintained eye contact while he ventured to his knees to undo the rope bindings on my ankles. The moment he touched the ropes, I lunged at him. I had no intention of harming him, but the surprise gave him a jolt, and he launched himself back several feet away to keep out of my radius.

The guards didn't need to be asked to intervene. They wrestled me to the ground so that I could not struggle. They fit the muzzle over my beak and fastened it behind my head before addressing the ropes on my ankles.

"Gentle with it," the caretaker said as he dusted himself off. "I am unhurt. I startled it. It was my fault. I sometimes forget these things are wild, especially when it's taken aid with minimal resistance."

Even prone, I breathed a sigh of relief. He didn't know, and I had successfully disabused him of the idea of my sentience.

The guards kept my shoulders and legs down while the caretaker unfastened the rope that kept me in the enclosure, and then pulled the rope from my legs. He muttered a curse and ended up putting ointment on them before fastening the anklets. And then the process was repeated with my wrists.

Were falconry anklets on wrists still technically anklets, since in the history of mankind, there had never been a bird with human arms and hands before?

The leather bands on my wrists, although still bound, offered a slightly wider range of movement and did not rub on the healing wounds from my talons. They didn't let me up right away though, and I strained to see what caused the delay.

"The bewits are larger than the bells," one of those holding me down said.

"The tsarina wanted them, especially with the history of wandering," the caretaker said as he fiddled again with my ankles. "Even if they are not proportional."

The weight and noise told me exactly what was happening.

Falconry bells. I hadn't worn bells as a jester, not traditional bells anyway, although there had been a few on the feathered mantle of my collar. But I would wear them now. I supposed, if I had the option, ankles were less annoying than a collar.

Something fitted around my neck moments later.

Blyat.

I couldn't figure out how they fastened it, although with my hands bound, it hardly mattered, as I couldn't get at it anyway.

Everyone rose and then released me, the pressure of hands and knees easing until I could shift without being forced back to the ground. I struggled to my knees and waited. The tension in the air spoke of more to come.

One of the guards stepped forward and attached a chain lead to my new collar. Then he tugged. I took the hint and rose. Progress was slow with the jesses since they were for birds being carried on a falconer's arm, not one forced to walk. And again, I was marched in through the palace, up the stairs, and back through the wing to the tsarina's quarters.

Of course, she wanted me where she had kept me before. In her bedroom.

I shivered, not with cold, but with apprehension.

She was not there to greet me in her study. And my escorts took me through the same rooms as the tsarina had led me last time: the receiving room, sitting room, little dining room, Kilikwa dining room, drawing room, then through the monarch's corridor and to her bedroom. She did not greet me there either.

The cot had been removed.

They fastened the lead to the foot of her bed.

"Is that all?" a guard asked.

"She said to leave it," answered another.

Scanning the faces of the escorts, the caretaker was not among them. Did he know what the tsarina wanted me for?

Did any of them? Had that rumor already started circulating? I wished I could tell someone. The jesters knew that had been the case before, but now, when I was beyond recognition, would they still suspect?

"Then we have done our job," said the first and turned to go.

The other guards turned with him and left me, filing out of the room a bit too eagerly.

I tested my bonds. I tugged on the chain. I tried yet again to reach my hands down to my ankles to undo them with no more success than the first time I tried it. The tinkling bells annoyed me beyond reason. Maybe that's why the tsarina had requested them, knowing they would drive me half-mad. Maybe I already was. Maybe I should want to be by the time she joined me.

I huddled up against the bed and closed my eyes.

Breathe in. Breathe out.

I practiced my breathing, trying to ease my frantically beating heart and to stop my spinning mind. I sought calm, even if my situation did not enable it. After all, what could I do? I had tried so many desperate things and ended up right back in her power, each time worse than before. I would be too tired to fight soon. Should I have just agreed from the start? How much more would I hate myself if I just let the inevitable happen?

"You look marvelous," she said from the doorway.

I took another deep breath and looked up at her. I couldn't respond, not with the muzzle, but I was tired and had no wish to banter with her. I just stared. That took all the energy I had.

She passed me on the way to her dressing room and disappeared for a few moments. She returned, still in her day dress but without her gloves. She eyed me.

"I wish things could have been different," she said, "but

you have left me no choice."

She stood over me and sank to the floor beside me. From there, she found my sheath of feathers. I squirmed and fumbled, fighting against her. I positioned my legs in front of me and forced several strikes with my knees to move her hands. Pressed back against the headboard as she clutched at me, I doubled over with the painful grasp on my anatomy and the tiny feathers around it. She took the opportunity to force me to the ground. Unable to go anywhere else as I recovered, she climbed over me and sat atop my legs, preventing any additional strikes or intervention from them. With her weight on me, and my hands and wings bound, I could not find leverage to roll or dislodge her.

"I hope your principles bring you comfort in moments like this," she cooed at me.

She removed her hands from my body, affording me a moment to breathe, and set about arranging her skirts.

"I hoped this would be more challenging," she remarked as she began to renew her work. "But your little guard at the gate still responds even when you don't want it to, doesn't it?"

I shuddered.

"I love the noises you make." She stroked my face with her fingertip, gentle and appreciative, tracing the beak and the muzzle that kept it shut. "And the sound of the bells as your legs shake only makes me want this more."

My legs jerked with a particularly effective maneuver of her hands as if to illustrate the sound she liked so much.

"Just like that!" She laughed. "I didn't expect you to be ready for me so soon."

I struggled to shift her off me, leveraging my body against the floor to free my legs or find the strength in my belly to sit. She grabbed at larger, sensitive feathers and shoved me back down. I struck my head against the tile. Tiny lights flickered through my vision, and when I turned my head to clear it, blood pooled from beneath me.

I tried to beg her to stop. I tried to plead with her that this was an action too low and too base for her. But it wasn't. It wasn't beneath her at all. And when she mounted me, I could do nothing about it. I breathed. I tried to breathe. I struggled with even that as she forced every ounce of strength out of me until I broke.

She continued even then, even as I shrank beneath her. I shivered and made myself small. And when she was done, she slid herself off me and stood, wiping her hands on a handkerchief she pulled from the folds of her skirts.

"I didn't want it that way," she said as if it made a difference. "I tried to give you everything, and you turned me down. Why have you made me do this to you?" When I did not acknowledge her, she huffed. "You're going back to your pen soon. But I will have you brought back. Don't ever make me do it like that again."

When the doors shut behind her, the tears started. Every indignity, every humiliation, every pain and discomfort and struggle over the past few months, everything, had been for nothing.

XVI.

Once brought back to my enclosure, I struck my head
against the wall with persistent determination. It was a messy,
ineffective, and crude method of trying to kill myself, but I had
exhausted my options. I had played every card of my hand and
lost. Not just lost. I had lost spectacularly. The caretaker found
me trying to bash my brains out. He dragged me from the wall
and called for aid. I was too weak to fight.

While he cleaned me up, others tied my jesses to a bolt set
into a boulder that was then set into the ground, where I could
not repeat my attempt. The next day, although they removed
the muzzle, they fitted me with a falconry hood. Silenced by
my circumstances, collared by the tsarina's will, and now
blinded by a precautionary measure, my days existed in the chill
of the outdoors, in darkness, and in fear of the next time I
would be brought to the tsarina.

I didn't know what I was anymore. Not a prince. Not a
jester. Not a man. Not even a bird. I was lower than any
creature of the menagerie, a depth to which I never imagined
one could fall. Did that make me a monster?

Each day, the caretaker came by, but I didn't stir for him.
Not even when he removed the hood to check on my head
wound. Not even when he unbound my wings. I just sat there,
defeated. I barely ate or drank. I withdrew from every other
action or indication of awareness. Even without a muzzle, I
kept silent and still for unknown stretches of time. I did little
more than sit or sleep now. Perhaps the caretaker thought I
sustained damage from my foolishness. I would let him think

that. I would let everyone think that if my disinclination to react discouraged them from visiting the famed firebird. I hoped the tsarina heard about it. Maybe she would have no more use for me if she thought me mentally compromised too.

I grew accustomed to silence and darkness. I never wandered more than a step or two from my tether in the ground. If I somehow got loose, I would never have known, and I wouldn't have cared. This wasn't a life, and mine had become too cheap to fight for.

The rustle of skirts one afternoon perked my attention as my body stiffened with horrible expectation. I did not move or otherwise shift from my curled-up position on the ground. If it were the tsarina, she would have ample access without having to fight for it this time, and I could remain blissfully distant from my body. If it were anyone else, I would not give them the satisfaction of a reaction.

But the skirts did not venture close to me. They stopped just inside the enclosure, and I guessed that the person had taken a seat on the bench. When the skirts stopped filling the space with their swishes, only then could the muffled sniffling be heard. A lady was crying. Why not? And why not my enclosure? After all, misery had dogged my footsteps for so long and finally taken a firm foothold in a tortured shape destined to be misused. Why shouldn't everyone with tears to shed come here? It was private enough, at least if they didn't mind a hooded, silent Otherland creature keeping them company.

She sniffled and hiccupped for a long stretch of time, ignoring me. Eventually, tears dried and hiccups stopped, and only her skirts could be heard. And then they rustled again, this time louder as she approached.

"I don't know if you're the firebird," she said. "The tsarina says you are. I know it's too much to hope for, but if you could, grant me a wish?"

It was Princess Alaina. Although she spoke low and secretively, the faint Altanian accent betrayed her to my sightless eyes.

I probably could have lived up to my reputation as the firebird and stopped her there. I could have told her what her wish was — to go home — and she would have gaped and gasped and would have run to tell everyone else in the palace that I truly was the firebird. And then I would be treated to months of everyone, nobles and staff and groundkeepers alike, lining up to see if I would grant their deepest longings and secret desires.

I didn't say anything. I had more than my fill of being displayed.

"I want, more than anything, to go home."

She should have added quantifiers like "while still young" or "with my pride intact" since I well knew the treachery of the court and the empress who ruled over it.

She added, as if she could hear my thoughts, "Alive. And soon, preferably."

Smart lady.

When I still did not respond, she harrumphed, and something hit me in the shoulder.

"Are you dead?" she asked. It wasn't a question of concern, but of petulant discontent at my lack of response.

I rolled farther away from her, putting my back to her to indicate that she, and thus her question, meant nothing to me, and she was dismissed.

"I should have known better," she sighed. "A creature as ugly as you could never be the firebird."

Yes, precisely. So please, leave me alone.

"You're just a stupid misshapen monster," she paused and added under her breath, "but I'm desperate."

She visited several more times. Sometimes she came to sit on the bench quietly for hours. Sometimes she moved near my shelter and watched me. Through it all, I remained hooded, but now I could recognize her perfume, so even when she said nothing, I knew it was she who kept me company. Having discovered how private my enclosure was, doubtless she too took comfort in being away from the glittering, farcical spectacle of court life.

I missed my friends, those jesters who had made my days bearable, and wished it were Drook or Klessa who visited me now. They might have inspired me to care a little more about my days or have more hope about the course of my life, but they couldn't know me now. And it was probably just as well. I would never want them to suffer for their association with me.

I didn't think Princess Alaina would benefit from the association either, but at least her company came only because I was a silent creature in a private enclosure in an otherwise noisy place without privacy. She did not visit me because of who I had been when I simply wore a costume. And for the tsarina, there would be a difference.

Sometimes the princess read aloud, which was a nice change from the days of silence or the casual verbal abuse she sprinkled into anything she said to me directly. Sometimes it was Ilyichian, and I could get lost in the text. Other times, it was Altanian, and I settled in to listen to the cadence of her speech and occasionally pick out a word or two that I thought I knew. Altanian was not a language I had any confidence in speaking or writing, but then again, I was not confident in any language other than Ilyichian, despite my best efforts. But it still flowed beautifully from someone whose familiarity with it extended from childhood.

Most of the time, she picked poetry, usually on the side of

sentimental if not outright maudlin, although the occasional philosophical discourse joined the selections. I instinctively slipped into listening and absorbing appreciatively as I had done with my jester friends during their nightly gatherings. Especially in this trying time, I found solace in the beauty of the sentiments, wisdom in well-turned phrases, and hope in others' daunting experiences, even if they were but fictions to inspire and amuse.

> "'and when love be true,
> not form or face or silver shines warmer through,
> not the snowy Kind and Fair brilliance of old
> nor the fear fire that blazes but dies in the cold.'"

A fanciful, idealistic poem from a vapid poet with no life experience or hardships endured. Wouldn't it be nice if love did not depend upon appearance or wealth? But that wasn't life. If it were, I might have a hope, but I had already realized that the tsarina dangled a futile method of escape as a way to keep me compliant, not as a way to be rid of her forever. Did it matter then if anyone knew about me?

The princess closed the book with a soft thwump and then sat there in silence for a long time.

"Firebird," she said when her reveries were over, "if you can't get me home, can you do anything else to help me? Please?"

It didn't matter if I spoke to her, did it? Not when I was certain that the tsarina's promise of a way out was false. Even if it wasn't, it was impossible. By design. But I didn't ever want to be Mikhail again, not like this, in bird shape, degraded beyond even what I had imagined were my lowest points. Perhaps the tsarina had truly done me a favor then in announcing to all that she had me executed. I didn't want to be Mikhail like this, and I didn't have to be. I could be the firebird. Or at least a pathetic imitation of one. And why shouldn't an Otherland creature have the power of speech?

"Useless!" she declared while I was still considering my options. "I hate you," the princess added. "You refuse to grant wishes. You have no responsibilities or obligations. You don't have to keep company with odious people that you secretly loathe."

I had to keep company with her, so I did not think her assessment entirely fair.

"You can just sleep all day. You have your meals brought to you. No one cares about what you wear or don't wear. You aren't under supervision every moment of your life. You don't know how well you have it."

No, of course not, because I only existed now in bindings so that I could fulfill the tsarina's needs when she felt so inclined.

"The tsarina has talked about having a cage made so that you can live inside during the winter. I suppose you'll have a taste of it then." She groaned. "Oh, to be a dumb animal and not care."

She fell into silence again, and I decided that she didn't deserve me speaking to her. She was a spoiled, indulged, naive, petulant child in a woman's body who lashed out at the only creature who could not lash back in kind.

"I hate it here," she said, this time her voice low and husky as if she had been crying. "I'm surrounded by people who resent me." When she started sniffling, that confirmed the tears. "I never knew I could be so alone in the company of others until I came to Ilyichia. I'm more alone now than ever." Her voice dropped to a whisper. "I don't want to be so lonely all the time."

Princess Alaina and I had locked eyes once, after her failed petition, after she advocated for me, after she had come to my rescue. And we had been worlds apart in that audience chamber, separated by arbitrary titles and social standing, but at our cores, we were identical: two isolated people owned by the tsarina. I had cared about her in that moment, wishing I had any ability to protect her from the malice of our owner. And, despite all, she had cared about me too.

Somewhere in this spoiled, indulged, naive, and petulant child, kindness and empathy existed, even if she never wanted anyone to see them. They made my decision for me.

"You wouldn't have to be so alone," I whispered, "if you were but a little kinder to one who has never done you ill."

A long silence followed.

"Did you—? That's impossible."

I awkwardly sat up, better at using my wings for leverage now with familiarity and the return of their strength since no one had seen fit to allow me the use of my hands yet. I turned in her direction to acknowledge that, yes, I was addressing her. And yes, I could.

Skirts rustled as she approached me. She did not stop very near, likely at the edge of the shelter, but her voice shook. "You... You can understand me."

"I wish I did not," I told her.

"How was I to know?"

"If the tsarina kicks you, do you kick her dogs in retaliation, just because you can?"

"No, of course not!" Her voice betrayed her deep offense.

"Then why me?"

"I.... I don't know."

"Is it because there might be consequences for cruelty towards the things the tsarina cares about?"

"I heard that you harmed several of the soldiers. One even died. Cruelty towards you is not without potential consequences."

No one had told me that one of the guards had died. That might explain why no one else had come to torment me —

fear of being harmed too. Small mercies.

"That was in self-defense." Not that it did any good. "And now I am bound and blinded and rendered helpless. Do you like to torment helpless things?"

"I didn't realize that's what I was doing," she said. "I'm just frustrated and angry, and no one listens to me, and I don't have anywhere else to go."

"While I am sorry to hear that you are unhappy in your circumstances, I do not deserve the words you hear from others."

That silenced her.

"Like you," I told her after a moment, "I have no choice in being here."

"No, I don't suppose you do."

After another long stretch of silence during which she was likely figuring out how to make her escape from this awkward development, she asked, "Do you possess the power to send me home?"

"If I had that power, I would send you home with such speed, others might get carried along with you."

"Have I made myself that much of a nuisance to you?" she asked, an undercurrent of amusement in her voice.

"Indeed," I assured her. "I thought such was your aim."

"I am sorry. I never intended to cause hurt or distress."

"On the grounds that you apologized, I am willing to fulfill your second wish. I am not much of a companion kept like this, but if you can keep a civil tongue, you do not have to be alone."

"I would like that," she confessed. "Although, if that means I must flatter you instead, I am incapable of doing it sufficiently. You appear an evil, ugly creature, and I admit, I am frightened by all of this."

"There is nothing to be done about how I appear to you. But between us, you have been the evil one to malign me so.

You may come and sit or read as you wish. I am under no obligation to give you my thoughts or my words."

"I assume that you would ask me not to share this secret with others. No one has even whispered the suggestion that you speak, and I cannot imagine that it would benefit you if others found out. The tsarina would probably have my head if she learned that you spoke to me before her."

"Very likely," I agreed.

"I was going in now for dinner. Should I come tomorrow?"

"Whenever you wish. If you are in want of company, I probably am too."

"I'll bring books. They help in passing the time. Do you have any preference on which I read to you?"

"No." Then I reconsidered. "But please, nothing sad."

XVII.

I didn't struggle when my escorts brought me back to the palace. I stumbled enough from clumsiness with my jesses and sightlessness from the hood for it to be seen as potential intentional delay. The pulling on the lead told me nothing but which direction was forward. I took several hard hits on loose gravel and stairs. Eventually, two of my escorts grabbed an arm each and caught me before I went down the next few times. We made painfully slow progress in this fashion. And like before, when we arrived at her room, they affixed the lead to the end of the bed and left me.

Hours passed. I huddled on the tile floor and tried to sleep. Servants worked and cleaned in the rooms adjacent to the bedroom. The bedroom door opened once, but the maid gave a strangled little gasp, likely when she saw me, and then several others joined her. No one approached, and the door closed again not long after, staying closed this time.

When the tsarina finally made her appearance, it was with many of her ladies in tow. The chatter died immediately when one of them pointed me out.

"Why do you keep that thing here?" one of the ladies asked. "It could hurt you."

"Don't be fools," the tsarina scolded them. "Like any creature, it needs to be shown who is its master. It is learning."

"It's a horrible thing," another, probably Ekaterina, said. "When the guards brought it into the audience hall that time, I thought I might faint!"

So much for Ekaterina's declaration that she could see me through any disguise.

"When did that happen?" This time, the one asking sounded like Princess Alaina.

"A few weeks ago," the tsarina answered, "before I had the chance to properly introduce it to court. Just as well. It still fought confinement."

"You should count yourself fortunate that you did not see," Ekaterina said. "It's almost as ugly as an Altanian!"

Others laughed, although the princess probably did not.

"Ugly or not, I am told it is doing much better and finally settling into its new home," the tsarina continued. "I thought it might be time again to bring it indoors occasionally, to get it accustomed to the environment, especially in preparation for winter. I would like to be able to show my firebird off, but I need it to submit to me before it is ready for wider audiences."

"You plan on handling it, ma'am?"

"I plan on its obedience, however that is achieved."

"Why would you want to keep something so awful and strange near you?"

"Because it amuses me to do so. I do not plan on letting my firebird go after it took so long to obtain. Now, enough about that thing. Come, ladies."

The gaggle wandered into the dressing room, the laughter and chatter fading with their withdrawal.

As long as the ladies remained, I could breathe. She wouldn't do anything while they were there lest they suspect her true designs on me.

I settled back against the floor and did not bother straining to hear the chatter. I did not think any of their discourse would be helpful or pertinent.

A servant brought evening chocolate. Then another served other offerings. The ladies only began filtering back out to the bedroom once the tsarina yawned.

"Have a lovely night," one of the ladies told her.

"Will you be able to sleep well with that thing so close?"

"That sounds like a punishment!"

"It knows better than to give me any trouble," the tsarina assured them. "And if it does, it will learn not to."

"We only worry about you," Ekaterina assured her.

"Go now," the tsarina told them, almost sweetly. "I will see you all tomorrow. Pietrodillo has assured me that he has another fantastic routine for us."

I recognized Drook's public name and wished I could get a message to him somehow. I didn't know what I would say though. I couldn't tell him I was alive and well, because though alive, I was not well. Could I send a message conveying my distress? I very much might have appreciated rescuing or a merciful death, but then truly it would damn me, if not because the tsarina assured me anonymity was my only way out, then because I did not want anyone to know me like this as Mikhail. Pride ever my downfall, I could not imagine the depth of my shame if even they should know the true extent of my debasement.

"Good night," echoed from several ladies as their skirts and slippers and voices faded down the corridor and the doors clicked shut behind them.

The tsarina made several more movements around the room before approaching the bed. She tapped me with her foot between the wings. I rolled onto my back as much as the wings would allow to face her direction, even though I was still hooded and could not see.

"Are you going to behave tonight, my dear?" She waited a moment, and when I didn't respond, she hummed through pursed lips in dismay. "Nothing to say? I can see you're not muzzled."

"I have nothing to say," I confirmed.

"Very well. We can make this quick then."

She climbed over me and sat. She began working in silence, and when my body responded, she took up her position and worked me until she was spent. My ankles jingled, and I could not prevent the occasional grunt or whimper, but all of it got lost in her vocalizations. And then she climbed off me.

"So much easier than last time," she said, "though not nearly as much fun. Where's your wit, my dear?"

It ran away, I almost said, because I cannot. But I didn't say anything. I just rolled over onto my side again and breathed.

In. Out. In. Out.

Why did breathing have to be so difficult? And why couldn't I stop when I wanted to?

Eventually, she left my side and climbed into her bed.

Long after I thought she had fallen asleep, she whispered into the dark, "I wish you had said 'yes' from the beginning. None of this would have had to happen."

"None of this had to happen even then," I whispered back.

"It'll get easier, my dear." She shifted in the bed, the swish of sheets and blankets and the groaning of boards suggested she sat upright. "Just do as I wish, and you will be happy again."

I didn't know how she could make such a promise since she had never possessed the ability to make me happy. And that was the problem, right there. I had never been happy with her, not then as a lover, never as a prospective wife, and not now — and she couldn't stand it.

"I promise, my dear. Things will be different. You'll see."

"Yes," I agreed. "We will see."

"Does the tsarina often keep you in her room?"

The princess didn't seem to have the capacity for niceties

when next she found me in my enclosure. A weight dropped on the bench — I guessed an assortment of books — and then she approached the shelter.

"I came out the other day to read to you and you weren't here," she explained. "And then I saw you up in her room the other night. Have you been there all this time?"

Although I did not mind being out of the cold, taking meals and being available to the tsarina's needs in her bedroom for a several-day stretch had not been the change of environment I had wished for.

"She finds my presence…" I didn't know how to phrase it. "Exciting," I finally decided upon. I shifted in my sitting position, my tail feathers bending in odd ways since sitting like a person wasn't natural for a bird, and yet I was not built enough like a bird to perch.

"No one would dare say anything explicit," the princess said, "but the servants have remarked upon stray black feather remnants on her night gowns. Might you know anything about that?"

"How the tsarina chooses to amuse herself has little to do with the agreement or compliance of those around her."

"Oh, Great Holy, it's true then."

To Mikhail, she had used an invocation to The Kind and Fair. But in private, with a creature who was not supposed to be able to speak, she called upon the Great Holy. No one else here invoked the Great Holy, and I warmed to her for even that small show of accidental solidarity.

"For your own safety," I warned, "say nothing."

"I would never." She paused, a question poised at the end of her teeth, while she debated if she should push it out or not. "Is it okay for you then, in there? She must dote on you and look after you, no? I worried about you for a moment, but she has to look after you better inside than out here, right?"

I wanted to laugh. I wanted to cry. I wanted to shake the

princess with hands I no longer had access to and ask her to look at how I was kept. I wanted to scream in her face about the nightmare of my current existence. I wanted to show her the self-inflicted wounds and ask her if she thought I was being cared for to any extent. But I didn't. I swallowed down my bitterness. She was naive and hopeful, and that, although wildly frustrating, remained a precious commodity in a world that seemed designed to torment me for the rest of my days.

"No," I said.

"But she—"

"Please," I asked as humbly as I could. "I do not wish to speak of it."

"Of course," she said, realizing how insensitive her questions might appear. "I brought books, unless you'd rather talk about something else."

Half of me wanted to have her relay the gossip of court, the things that circulated around me but no longer involved me, things I could listen to now without taking things to heart, and maybe hear about Alexei and how he fared as head of our branch of the Karilitsyns. I wanted her to tell me of my friends, the jesters, their troubles and triumphs, but I didn't know how to ask specifically about them without giving away that I knew them fairly well, though they had never visited the strange Otherland bird.

"You were with the group of women who helped the tsarina retire for the evening the other night?" I knew the answer since she had mentioned seeing me in the tsarina's room, but as of yet, I had to pretend ignorance about knowing who she was since she had never visited me while I could see her.

"That's when I saw you there."

"She mentioned Pietrodillo giving a performance. He doesn't sound Ilyichian. Who is he?" It was Drook, but I had to pretend ignorance on that too.

"One of her jesters," the princess explained. "And he's ethnically Varnasian, I think?"

"Was he any good?"

"He's her finest. Clever and funny. The entire continent knows him! Maybe, if she plans to bring you inside, you will get to see him sometime."

"That will be the only nice thing of coming in for the winter," I mused aloud. "Perhaps I will get to experience some degree of cheer."

"The tsarina just lost one of her favorites," the princess said, "and has been in a dour mood for such a long time now that everyone has tried to bolster her spirits."

"So that she doesn't further retaliate," I said.

"Unfortunately, yes."

I considered all of the tsarina's favorites. She never had many, and those she did, she never fully released. Maybe it was her Allemandian lover, or maybe it was some young officer that she had more recently set her sights on.

"How did she lose a favorite?"

"She had him executed for... for... for a few things, I think?"

Was the princess referring to me? I hardly ever counted as a favorite. Unless she meant a favorite to torment.

"That doesn't sound like he was highly prized."

"It's complicated." The princess paused and then sighed. "We all hoped that catching a firebird would lift her spirits, but she's been even worse, if that's possible. No one dares even look at her with a cross thought lest she call you upon it and accuse you of foul intentions towards her."

"All the better then that I am hooded, else she might have my head too."

"Are you that expressive?"

I didn't think I was, not with a beak freezing most of the expressions on my face from nose to chin, but eyes could say enough, couldn't they?

"I have a lot of cross thoughts," I explained. Before she could say anything else along the lines of my discontent, I asked, "What were you doing up in the tsarina's rooms?"

"The tsarina occasionally likes to have her ladies get her ready to retire."

"Oh, you're one of her ladies then." I added to nettle her, "I didn't think serfs could read."

"I am not a serf!"

"My apologies," I couldn't help barbing her, knowing the flimsiness of titles, "but I cannot imagine that anyone of actual substance would have nothing better to do than visit me."

"Nonsense," she assured me. "Have you forgotten? I'm only using you to get home."

XVIII.

"I'm bored," the tsarina lamented.

I said nothing.

"I expected my firebird to keep me better amused," she said.

Again, I said nothing.

She swung herself out of bed by the rustling of bedsheets and blankets. Then she toed my hood. "Are you awake?"

"Call a jester if you require entertainment," I said, pulling away from her. "That is no longer my title."

"Not this early in the morning."

"Is it morning? You've kept me blinded for weeks. I no longer have a sense of time." I did keep time, of course, by visits and routines, but I didn't need to let her know that.

"Is that what's bothering you?" She heaved a sigh and sat down beside me. "If you didn't have to go and do something as ridiculous as hurt yourself — again! — I would never have had you wear it. But I can't trust you!"

I wished the hood were the only thing that bothered me. How far could I get into a list of irritants, complaints, frustrations, and miseries before she struck me or kicked me? How much of a morning would we have before she took me in her hands and mounted me?

"How are you healing?" she asked when she realized I wasn't going to respond to her.

"You don't care, so please do us both the courtesy of not pretending."

"You don't understand. It seems you never did." Her fingers brushed over one of my wings in the wrong direction of the feathers, and I shivered. "I have always cared about you — even when you didn't care about me."

It took all my willpower not to rebuke her or call her out on her abhorrent behavior.

She lifted my head and then set it down, by the shape and firmness beneath it, in her lap. The braces on the hood loosened one by one. Then light assaulted me when the hood came off. I turned my face to shield my eyes, but the beak prevented it, and so I scrunched my eyes all the harder.

She ran her fingers through feathers in place of hair, gentle in her motions as she found several injuries.

"They are healing nicely." Her fingers brushed over the wounds. "Some scabbing, but that's to be expected. Head wounds always bleed so much, even when they are but little."

"When do I get my arms back?"

"I haven't decided."

"The muscles are going to atrophy since I can't use them, if they haven't already."

"You need to re-earn my trust. You've broken it so many times. Maybe I'll only let you have them back once they're completely useless."

I didn't have the energy to persuade her otherwise. She would do what she wanted when she wanted to do it. My resistance gave her thrill, and so if I stopped resisting, she would grow bored. She already had if I could go by her morning declaration.

"I'll release them just for the time you're with me," she said after a moment, "to give you something to look forward to when you come visit." She stroked my head again. "Don't make me regret it, my dear."

It wasn't like I could run away with my ankles kept in bands and jesses, but with my arms unbound, I might have a chance to undo them. Still, what would that accomplish? I was tired and weak and kept weaker by the restraints and the limited meals. Even with free legs, I did not think I would have any greater chance at escape now than before. And if there were no chance, I would not dare risk losing something else that I did not realize I could lose until she took it from me.

"Sit up," she instructed as she pushed me out of her lap.

When I righted myself and put my back to her, she untied the bindings between wrist bands. My arms and wrists barely registered their new freedom, but my shoulders screamed in pain as my arms fell to my sides and released the muscles in my back. I could barely wiggle my fingers, and it took a monumental effort to set my wrists on my thighs. Long leather straps dangled from each wide leather band. I did not miss the width of the leather bands either, wide enough to prevent me from making another assault on my own wrists.

The tsarina placed her hands on my shoulders and began rubbing.

I almost jerked away from her. Almost. I managed to bear her touch only because any perceived rejection now would cause her to retaliate. But I didn't want her touching me, not when she had been the cause of my suffering. She wanted to be my solace now, my comfort. Her kindness was almost worse than her cruelty. And for all the disgust and revulsion I had for her, I had to endure it if I wanted any small measure of freedom in my current degraded state.

"You're so tense, my dear," she said as she focused on muscles that had spent the last few weeks building up knots.

Her thumbs worked between and under the feathers, traveling up my neck into what should have been my hair. She tilted my head from side to side to stretch muscle and tendon. Then she slid her hands back down and rubbed at the muscles between my wings.

"Why a bird?" I asked, proud of how unemotional I sounded about it.

"Why not?"

"Don't play coy. You dressed me like a chicken first and then gave me real feathers. Why?"

She dropped her hands and moved away from me. Then she stood and began unbraiding her hair. "You had the audacity to fly away from Ilyichia — from *me* — and nest with a Varnasian whore that took your fancy."

"She was not a whore," I whispered. "She was a gentleman's daughter, and I married her."

"Yes, ever the noble one, aren't you?" She knelt in front of me. "I heard about your other mistresses too. Did your uncle introduce you to the one you took in Alfinia? I heard she bore a child that could have been yours — a head full of dark ringlets and skin like milk. Did you know that? I did. I heard about everything."

I didn't know anything about a possible child. Could the tsarina be lying to me, just to hurt me? That seemed a likely possibility, but maybe it wasn't a lie. I had been involved with a woman in Alfinia — which I thought I had kept sufficiently quiet — and a child was a possibility too.

"You flew from one woman to another, never caring who you hurt in the process."

"I never wanted to hurt anyone," I said.

"But you did anyway. And then you returned. So I made you a bird. The most ridiculous one I could think of, so that no one else would be swayed by your charms. So that I wouldn't be swayed again." She reached out and put her hand on my cheek. "And it didn't work."

The touch from anyone else might have been sweet and soft and warm, but I well knew the cruelty that lay hidden in her palm, the tenderness of muscles that could turn sour in moments, the possession that permeated her bones. She conflated obedience and ownership with love. I did not think she could truly love anyone, not now, not after so long of hating those who would not give her what she wanted, I among them.

"And this form?"

"In this form, no one but me would want you." She stroked her thumb over my cheek. "You are the only thing I would have asked for from the firebird, and so now, I get both in one." She smiled, truly smiled, devoid of bitterness and hate, a rare expression that I had once appreciated my first round of being her lover but now found unspeakably sad. "You are my perfect companion."

Her perfect companion. That sounded like a forever kind of thing. I had already guessed that her offer of a way out was false, so I didn't despair any more than I already had. But even like this, I would have preferred a forever anywhere else but at her side.

But, smiling, contented, she was in a place where I could ask things of her. Not all things. I couldn't ask to have my ankles unbound. After the removal of the hood and the release of my arms, she would shrink if I asked for more of my restraints to be removed. But other things, yes. I just couldn't phrase them like asks.

"I have such a poor diet," I said. "I may not be with you long."

"That can be fixed, my dear. Just behave, and then everything gets better."

"Will I always be chained?" I looked meaningfully at the leash tied to the bed.

"Show me I can trust you, and that will go away too."

I didn't know how to do that because she couldn't trust me. I would always be looking for the way out. But I nodded as if I understood.

She slid her hand from my face, down my neck, and over my chest appreciatively, finally resting it over my heart.

"You are not alone," she told me. "I know this is difficult, but it doesn't need to be. You have me, have always had me.

Rely on me. Need me. And I will prove to you how much I care about you."

The lies issued forth so convincingly that she likely did not think them lies at all. Somehow, she had rationalized all of it, and I, lowly creature as I was, should forgive her entirely because she claimed to do it from a place of caring.

"What do I look like now?" The question, though originating from my throat, surprised even me. "I know I am ugly," I said, heading off any vague description she might use to placate me. "You and all others have made no secret of it. But I haven't seen. Not everything. Not all at once."

Her hand slid off of me entirely and fell back onto her lap. "You don't want to."

Maybe I shouldn't want to, but now I had to know.

I had guessed at much since I could see a beak and feathers and could extrapolate from there. But I hadn't touched my face, at first too afraid of what the truth would be beneath my fingers and then unable to raise my hands to my face at all. I could look down and see a full torso of feathers, legs of feathers, feet of feathers and scales. I could feel the weight of wings pulling muscles in my back. Like the mosaic floors of Varnasia, I could see the tiles, but I had not yet stood back far enough to see the whole.

I reached out, trembling as much from weakness as with hesitance. The leather strips that dangled from the band brushed her wrist. I laid my horrible, clawed hand on top of the one she had withdrawn.

Her eyes traveled down to our hands. A fleeting expression of guilt passed her face. She glanced back up to me, her brows knitted.

"Please," I asked.

She took the hand that lay on top of hers and stood. With her other, she unclasped the chain lead from the bed. She dropped the leash and tugged on my hand. I shifted my legs to position them beneath me, and then I stood. I stared down at her, through feathers and over a beak.

"Are you sure you want to do this?" she asked.

I wasn't sure. By the moment I turned more cowardly. But I had to know. I had managed rather well when stuffed into a costume not to look at myself beyond absolute necessity, but that had been a costume. I knew what I looked like outside of it. I didn't know who or what I had become now.

I nodded, words nowhere to be found.

She led me patiently through the bed surround, through the room, and into her dressing room, the ankle bells noting each step. She dropped my hand just inside the doorway and went to the window to draw back the curtains. Morning light flooded the room. I stood stark against the sea of glimmering satins and pastel accessories. She returned to my side and took my hand again, leading me forward to her golden-framed pier mirror.

She didn't drop my hand when I stumbled. She clung to it as if offering her strength while I did this impossible thing. But I just stared at the creature that stared back at me from the glass. My logic alone recognized it as my reflection, although every other aspect of my personhood said, no, absolutely not, this is not you. I couldn't correlate any of the creature's attributes with mine. Little wonder no one would recognize me if I could not see myself in this Otherland monstrosity.

I dropped her hand when I took another step forward, more fascinated than horrified, my shock still leading the motions rather than my horror repelling me. I reached out and touched the glass, my talons following the movement of the creature's talons as they tapped along the surface. I stretched a shoulder, twisting it in the socket to loosen the arm, and the creature did too. Skin not covered by feathers had gained a scaled texture, black and gray in gradient, going darker as feathers took over. I tilted my face from side to side to better see myself. Even my eyes, the creature's eyes, reflected only a dim light of what had once been.

I raised my clawed hand to my chest and stroked down to keep the feathers smooth, every rib a prominent bump along the way. Somehow, this was me. This.

I had never blamed anyone for exercising caution around a man-sized bird known to have caused harm. A creature of the Otherlands, in all its strange, monstrous glory, would give anyone pause. And somehow, even retaining all my faculties and higher reasoning, knowing that this monster of legend was me, I wanted to flee from it too.

She came up beside me and put her hand on my arm.

"You truly have murdered me," I said, proud of my detachment, grateful for my calm. "There is none of me in this."

"That's where you're wrong," she whispered. "You are all here. All of you. There's just one difference — I'm the only one who can see it."

To anyone else, her sentiment might have seemed sweet, loving even, but she didn't know who I was. Or she didn't want to know. She had an idea of me, an old and outdated image of a former lover that she clung to beyond any new knowledge or circumstance. I wasn't her idea, couldn't be her idea. Not without giving up most of the pieces that made me who I truly was. There was no space in her daydream for a grieving widower, an unwilling lover, or a world-weary man. She rejected all parts of me that she couldn't own or control — most notably, the part of me that did not want her.

"Come back to bed," she said after an eternity of me staring at my reflection. When she managed to tear me away, she wrapped herself around my arm and led me back into the bedroom. "I have ideas on how to distract you and solve my boredom in the process."

XIX.

"You're back!"

I recalled myself from distant thoughts and looked up at my companion.

Alaina took a step backward and clutched her books to her chest.

We stared at each other.

"You're not wearing the hood today," she stated.

"I am aware."

"Yes. Of course." She took a deep breath and regained her step toward me. "You are just as ugly as I expected," she announced to cover up her initial fear.

I could have been gracious and let it slide, but this was supposed to be my first time seeing her too, so I sized her up visibly, wanting her to squirm a little under my assessment. Her looks had been much maligned in my, mostly for her dark complexion and the larger nose associated with traditional Altanian features. Although not a beauty in Ilyichia, and probably not in Altania either, I could not bring myself to further insult her on something she had likely heard from everyone else many times.

"And you are scrawnier than I imagined," I said. "I have perched on twigs more substantial than you."

Her mouth fell open, and her hold on the books relaxed. "Whatever do you mean?"

"You look little more than a child," I teased. "I am surprised that such a little body can contain such a huge opinion of itself."

"And you're still a contrary creature," she said.

A small grin played at the corners of her mouth. Mischief twinkled in her eyes. All this time we had been talking, I had apparently missed much by not being able to see her. How often had she smiled while we talked?

"I fail to see why I should behave any differently, in or out of a hood."

"Not that you would ever know it, considering you thought me a serf the other day," she said haughtily, "but I am a princess."

"A princess," I repeated, a degree of patronization tinting my words as I played ignorance. "It sounds important. What is that?"

"It's like a tsarina." A fallen smile and reddened cheeks betrayed her fluster at having to explain a concept so fundamental to court life. "It means I am superior to you."

And I had been a prince once. Titles meant nothing.

"I am in captivity. That makes everyone superior to me."

"It means I am influential and powerful," she tried again.

"And yet, you come to me to give you the things you most wish for." She completely deflated at that observation. "If you're so powerful, can you undo my bonds and release me?"

Her cheeks flamed. "No."

"Then what does your power or influence matter to me?"

"You are sharp today!"

"And you are sharp every time you visit me," I reminded her. "I do not start or end every conversation with a criticism of your appearance."

"Fair," she conceded. "Should I not visit you?"

"It depends on your intent. If your design is to add to the derision and mistreatment I must suffer at the hands of others, then I can well do without you."

"I'm sorry. I meant to tease, not to hurt."

"I suppose I will forgive you."

The corner of her mouth quirked up. "You're still ugly

though."

"So I keep being told." And I didn't disagree, but I didn't have to accept it outright. "No one has specified though — compared to what?"

"Compared to...." She furrowed her brows in thought. She set her books down on the ground and then took a seat on top of them. "That's a good question. I don't know. I suppose compared to a man."

"But I am not a man, so how can I be compared to one?"

"You are also ugly compared to a regular bird too."

"Which regular bird? If a sparrow, then yes, I must seem quite monstrous to a sparrow."

"Another firebird then?"

"Firebirds are not regular birds." I puffed out my feathers a little. "And, in the world of firebirds, I am considered an attractive specimen. Next time you are so inclined to call me ugly, I would caution you to remember your frame of reference."

"So you truly are an Otherland creature?"

I could lie to her. But I already had to lie about so much. I longed for truth since the palace and the court that surrounded me thrived on lies and manipulation. But I couldn't just tell her that I was simply the same disgraced prince in a different kind of costume. Even if the tsarina lied to me about there being a way out, I didn't want to wear the name Mikhail and bear the burden of his shame anymore. And if she knew any of that, if anyone knew any of that, I would again have no company and no respite from the mockery that would again come my way.

"I am not an immortal Kind and Fair creature, if that's what you think. But I am touched by the Otherlands," touched by its magic at least, "so I doubt you will find another of my kind easily."

"I knew it."

"So you believe in The Kind and Fair despite having

invoked the Great Holy... twice, I think, in my company?"

"Is that offensive to you?"

"Not at all. I am just curious how you can believe in both."

"Politically?" She laughed. "I don't. In Ilyichia, I do as the Ilyichians and give offerings only to The Kind and Fair." She lowered her voice. "In my homeland, I give offerings to both, The Kind and Fair as a supernatural intermediary on earth, and the Great Holy as a deity above all of us, The Kind and Fair included."

Varnasia, like Ilyichia, only acknowledged one while condemning the other. What might have been different if I didn't have to choose? I didn't know much about Altania, but I liked the sound of its open-mindedness and spiritual inclusivity.

"I have never seen a Kind and Fair though," she confessed. "Have you?"

"No."

"Even though you're an Otherland creature?"

"Currently, I am baser than the worm that freely wriggles through the dirt. No Kind and Fair would find me worthy enough to appear to me."

"They are supposedly capricious. You must always give them a great amount of respect and a healthy dose of wariness. And if you leave the proper offerings, they will decide what is worthy."

"The proper offerings?"

"It's not much different than honoring the Great Holy, truly. Food is customary, but blood is supposedly best, although I never offer blood. Maybe that's why I haven't gone home yet. But it doesn't feel right giving pieces of me away."

The tsarina used blood with the roses when she issued our game. She had invoked The Kind and Fair, and if roses were linked to magic.... Someday, I would have to go to her private rose garden and see what I could do. The Kind and Fair would probably not listen to me, but it might be worth a try. After everything else, could it hurt?

"Perhaps," I began, "when next you give The Kind and Fair an offering or you speak to the Great Holy in private, you might mention me in your prayers?"

"What is it you would have me ask?" Her face twisted in confusion. "Better food? Less attention from the tsarina? The Great Holy does not listen to prayers from animals, but—"

Her confusion over what I could possibly desire and the dismissal as an animal struck me as cruel, a testament to her casual, self-absorbed lack of empathy for anything beyond her own wish to be free.

"Nevermind," I said, turning away from her. "I'm sure no one would listen to prayers on my behalf anyway. No one ever has before."

I lay silent and still while the tsarina finished, my contributions, pitiful and unenthusiastic though they were, having long been spent, and the sound of bells long muted. I couldn't find the will to pray during the midst of my trials, so I examined the ceiling painting as I had years before when the tsarina kept me on her bed instead of the floor.

My own home — former home — had paintings on almost every ceiling too. Different themes, of course. Many of them legends of Ilyichia instead of the more commonplace pastoral allegories popular throughout the continent. And there was the Karilitsyn crest over every major doorway. I didn't miss the family seat. In my heart, it was still my forefathers' house, as any possible son of mine might have considered it more mine than his.

I would never have children now. The tsarina would not be fool enough to become pregnant. Even if the tsarina could be trusted about the Alfinian baby, that child would never know me. There would be no other life for me beyond the tsarina's menagerie, and no one else would share the tsarina's unique proclivities to bed me, even if I were amenable. Which I never thought I would be again. Not after this. The mere idea of lying beside anyone in such intimacy inspired intense nausea.

"You might at least pretend to enjoy it," the tsarina said as she rose from me. "I don't waste my time with just anyone."

"Do you not have your Allemandian lover?" I pushed myself onto my elbows. At least she had kept her word about leaving my wrists unbound when I visited her. "Why do you have need of me?"

"Why should I eat pork every night when I can have fowl on occasion?" She wandered out of the bed enclosure to begin her morning ablutions. "You are going to join me today. My ministers are going to bore me to tears if I don't have more pleasant distraction."

"They aren't going to want me in your meetings."

"What they want doesn't concern me." She wiped her hands and face on a cloth. She came over to the railing that wrapped around the bed and stared at me. "Do I need to muzzle you, or will you stay silent?"

I didn't want to be muzzled, but I also didn't know how I might be tempted to break the illusion of tsarina's pet. I had a proven record of not being able to keep my mouth shut and opening it at the worst times.

"I'll feed you from my plate today if you behave," she added as she disappeared into her dressing room.

The offer of food from her selection caused a primal betrayal from my stomach. I had lost a significant amount of weight and my muscles had wasted, both with disuse and malnourishment. I hated the physical weakness that so easily abandoned any high-minded principles I wanted to uphold.

She returned in her undergarments and stood over me. "Have you decided?"

Nothing mattered anymore, did it? In answer, I sat fully and put my wrists behind my back, waiting for her to bind them.

"Good boy," she said as she dropped a kiss on the top of my head on her way to fastening the bands.

She had reduced me to the lowest of the low, transgressed every moral and physical propriety, and yet, somehow, her kindly touch defiled me still further than even her cruelty. I yearned for the day when she lost interest in me.

"I had brackets installed on my chairs so that I can keep you with me wherever I go." She finished tying the cords together and then slid her hand down my back. "I'm going to let my ladies in now. Behave."

She stood again and went to the bedroom door. Upon opening it, the ladies swarmed in with a forced vibrancy I shrank from. Several of the women spotted me, and their boisterousness died as they edged the room. The tsarina noticed but said nothing as she led the way into her dressing room. Princess Alaina was last to follow, casting a doubtful look in my direction.

They didn't take long. The tsarina, dressed for a day of state affairs, led her ladies out of the dressing room and approached me. She unfastened the lead and tugged me to my feet. I followed, the ladies giving me a wide berth. The tsarina glared at her ladies who kept their distance, disdainful of their mousiness.

We made our way out of the tsarina's apartments. At the main section of the palace, the tsarina lost patience with my slow gait from the jesses and handed me off to the first person beside her, which should have been Ekaterina, except that she fell back when the tsarina thrust out my leash. Princess Alaina was thus left staring at the lead.

"Take it!" the tsarina snapped, and the princess took it, more startled to be called upon than at her assignment. "Meet us at the council room."

And the group, no longer confined to my limited speed, moved past us, the tsarina motivated to reach the council chamber and the rest of the ladies eager to be away from me and the princess burdened with my conveyance.

The princess stared at the end of the lead in her hands as the rest of the group, no longer confined to my shuffle, abandoned us. Her gaze traveled up the chain, to the collar, then up to my face. She had never been this close to me. At the pavilion, she always sat outside the radius of my tethers. The proximity now stunned her into silence.

"If the tsarina's morning expression didn't frighten me, yours certainly does." I glanced about, ensuring our solitude. Nonetheless, I lowered my voice. "I see what you mean about being called on for cross thoughts. Yours currently must be of the utmost annoyance."

"What?" She blinked at me several times. "Oh. I... I've never seen you standing before. I didn't realize you were so tall. She must trust in your obedience to consign you to my direction. You could probably topple me without the least effort."

"I will not cause difficulty for you, if such is your concern. I know how she preys on helpless things."

"Are you suggesting I am helpless?"

"Are not all of us helpless when it comes to her?"

"Alas."

"Just deliver me to the council room, and your odious task will be over."

"Why? Is the council discussing policy on The Kind and Fair and Otherland creatures?"

"I am to spend the day at her side so that she may feel generous when she feeds me something from her hand."

The princess scrunched her face in disgust.

"I cannot afford to be proud," I said. "She's the one who dictates if I eat at all."

"Why does she need to do this to you?"

"If she can make an Otherland creature bend to her will, no one else has a chance of standing against her."

She looked down at the lead in her hand. "This doesn't feel right."

"I can tease you to make up for it when next you visit the pavilion."

Her brows scrunched together as she redirected her gaze up at me. "Do I not already receive enough teasing?"

"Not nearly enough," I assured her. "You fail to appreciate the enormous restraint I exercise on a daily basis. I have so much to say and no one to say it to."

A small smile touched her mouth. "I can only imagine."

The faint moment of humor cleared her face of prior concerns. I appreciated the unguarded look. She could still smile without it furthering strategy or hiding ulterior motives. She still possessed a core of authenticity that was so rare, so precious, that I hoped she could leave Ilyichia before that light was put out forever. Her dark eyes sparkled with a touch of mischief as she held my gaze without any of the usual revulsion or wariness I received from others.

"Not that I am in a hurry to be a fixture at the tsarina's feet," I said, hesitant to disturb the only moment of genuine connection I had shared with another in such a long time, "but we should go. I do not want you to get into trouble on my behalf. If she should say anything, you can blame me."

"That's very noble," she said, her mouth twisting in dismay. "I think you get too much of her ire though."

"I prefer her ire to her favor since they both look the same."

"I don't know how to make any of this easier." She

gripped the chain, not as a tug but as a gesture of resolve. "We will go slowly. Just be careful." She met my eyes with a deliberate intensity. "And I do not just mean on the stairs."

XX.

After several more nights in the tsarina's room and days kept at her feet unmuzzled and quiet, unhooded and obedient, she finally permitted me to have my arms unbound. The leather bands and the ties that dangled from them remained to remind me of how tenuous my new allowance. The guards objected to my unbound wrists, but when the tsarina called them cowards and threatened them with being put to death because I sat beside her unbound for days and she did not fear, they relented.

When the caretaker noticed my new freedom, he left me a marrow bone between meals. Although I left it beside the barely-touched slab of gray meat on the plate, I recognized the attempt at kindness. The princess too noticed my complete disinterest when she later came by, a basket at her side.

"Not in the mood for typical raptor feed or treats?" She set the basket down on the bench and approached the pavilion. "Did she completely spoil your appetite with fancy court fare?"

"So it is true. You truly do not have anything better to do than waste your time with me."

"You should feel honored that I deign to give you any company at all."

"Naturally, as you are so illustrious," I added with a little bite to it, "princess."

"You're a brat!" She folded her arms over her chest. "But I suppose that is half the reason I like you."

"And the other half?" I rose from the ground and folded my arms over my chest in imitation.

"I haven't figured that out yet. But I will be sure to let you know if I have any epiphanies."

"Please do."

Her cape fluttered in the breeze. If I were able, I would have been bundled up in a fur-lined cloak and gloves. I supposed I was wearing a cloak and gloves since my birdness had been bound up in my attire, but I still shivered.

"Aren't you cold?" I asked.

"It's always cold in Ilyichia."

"You should be wearing a heavier cloak."

"You're unbound today," she said, ignoring my concern.

"Only my wrists." I unfolded my arms and held my hands out, palms up. I moved one foot forward to show her that my ankles were still connected and those still attached to the bolt in the ground. "But my shoulders are grateful."

"No other creature in the menagerie is kept as you are."

"She knows I would escape."

"Where would you go?"

It was a good question. I didn't know. Where in the wide world could I go like this?

"Anywhere," I said. "It's only a matter of principle now."

"I too would go anywhere."

"More poetry today?" I asked, gesturing to the basket.

"Not quite." She retrieved it and joined me under the shelter. She set the basket down and touched the chain that dangled from the collar. "Isn't that annoying?"

"It is not the worst thing I have worn."

"Could you bend down a bit?" When I leaned over, she gathered the chain and tied it in a cluster so that it didn't swing. "Now, sit, and I'll show you what I brought."

I obeyed and sat with my tail feathers splayed behind me and my legs crossed in front.

She sat across from me, the basket between us, her skirts fanned out on the dirt and straw. She opened one side of the basket and removed a book. Then she began pulling out things that were most definitely not books. She laid a thin floral blanket beside the basket upon which she set two lidded casserole dishes, two plates of the palace's bone china, several of the palace linen napkins unfolded and tied in parcels, and cutlery.

"You never seem to eat much of what they give you out here," the princess said, "so I've been paying attention to what you do eat." She began untying the napkins to reveal pastries, cheese wedges, cured meats, breads, and roast chicken. She lifted the lids from the covered dishes. "I also brought caviar and soup. I plan on talking to your caretaker to see if you can get food you will actually eat." She met my eyes expectantly. "Well?"

"How did you manage all this?"

"I asked for a picnic lunch and just couldn't make up my mind. So they gave me a bit of everything!"

I wouldn't cry. I wouldn't. But at a time when I thought I might never experience an ounce of thoughtfulness from anyone again, it was sorely tempting to do so.

"I don't like the idea of you not eating because she doesn't feel like feeding you."

I took a deep breath and focused on the food. I almost said thank you, but that was not how we communicated. I didn't want her to know how deeply this affected me.

"I bet you're just fattening me up so you can sacrifice me to The Kind and Fair this winter," I said when I finally could speak without my voice trembling.

"I hadn't thought of that," she admitted as she chose food for herself. "If you pester me enough, that's exactly what I'll do."

"Not if the tsarina sacrifices me first."

"She could sacrifice any of us. We all live in fear of her." The princess took a bite of the chicken, chewed, and then set it down with the arrival of another thought. "She ill-uses you."

"That implies that I have a use at all, and I do not."

"Oh, but you do — to keep me company! And that is a great honor, you know."

"So you have said."

"Does she know you're intelligent?"

"No," I lied. "She thinks me a stupid creature. It's easier that way."

"You are a conundrum," the princess declared. "You speak like the most educated among us, and yet you stay silent. You're patient to a fault at times, and then I come out to visit and you're as contrary as can be."

"No one wants to be around a creature that fails to amuse them."

"You're silent to be left alone?"

"I little enjoy most interactions."

"Do you want me to leave you alone?" she asked in a whisper.

"Please don't."

"Why not me?"

"You've been kind to me." I gestured to the spread before us. "And you're not doing it to get something from me."

"Except for our banter, which is intentionally mean-spirited, you've been pleasant to me too."

"Why, it's almost as if I have feelings."

"Absurd," she teased. "Surely not."

"Don't tell anyone."

"I wouldn't dream of it. Besides, I have no one. Who would I tell?"

"So any company, even the inferior company of something like me, will do?"

"If any company, even the subpar company of a spoiled lady, will do for you."

"That sounds sufficient to me, princess."

A scowl crossed her face as she glared at the pastries.

"What grave offense have the confections committed to earn such a condemning look?"

"What?" She blinked up at me and then smiled. "Oh, no. They're fine. I was just thinking that, maybe instead of you using my title, you could use my name?"

"Is not using Alaina quite forward?"

Her eyes doubled in size. "You know who I am then."

"I have known who you were for a while now, even when I could not see you." The conversation had gone a little serious, so I added, "I could smell your cheap perfume three leagues away."

"Oh, do hush." She shoved a piece of chicken in my direction. "I don't comment on your stench of wet grass and excrement."

"You should have told me earlier, if that's what I smell like." I took the chicken from her. "I could have borrowed some of your perfume!"

She wadded up one of the empty napkins and tossed it at me.

"And what's your name?" she asked.

I almost choked. I stared at her and froze from not having anything ready to give her. I hadn't anticipated needing to create an identity for myself. Mikhail, even without the title of prince, seemed too damning, especially so close to my supposed execution.

She added, "If you have a name."

I could always say I didn't, but then I ran the risk of the princess renaming me, probably to something vapid, infantile, and insulting like Birdie.

"*Michele*," I said at last, using the Varnasian alternative of Mikhail, the name Irena used for me exclusively.

"Mikalay," Alaina repeated, deliberate in its pronunciation. "That doesn't sound Ilyichian."

"It's not."

"Did the tsarina name you?"

"No."

"That explains it. Most of the tsarina's menagerie have more traditional names. Even the elephant is named Ivan."

"She has an elephant?"

"A gift from a visiting dignitary."

"I've never seen an elephant," I confessed. "They are the kind of animal you hear about but only half believe is real."

"If I visited Ivan and told him that I frequently converse with a firebird, he might disbelieve in you too."

That thought amused me.

"Are you smiling?" she asked.

"I don't think so." I didn't think I could with a beak.

"You were definitely smiling," she insisted. "Maybe not like others do, but I know your eyes now."

I didn't want her looking too closely at my eyes. They wept more than any bird's should.

"You do have beautiful eyes," she added.

"I bet you say that to all the birds."

"I've never said it to anyone. Ever."

And this time, it wasn't foolish flattery from someone wanting something from me. She had nothing to gain because I had nothing to offer. And she never shied away from calling me ugly, so I could only suppose that she actually meant it.

"Then," I said, taking a deep breath, "thank you, Alaina. For everything."

XXI.

"Do I at least get a blanket?"

"That's what feathers are for," she said.

I hated being cold, and I hated Ilyichia for being cold all year long. But not being provided any accommodation for the creeping chill of the seasons struck me as a type of torture beyond any she had yet inflicted.

"Feathers only do so much," I argued. "Am I to lose fingers and toes because you refuse to provide? You're not giving me the option to provide for myself."

"You are a nightmare this morning."

"The chain is cold. The collar is metal and cold. The tile you make me lie on while you warm yourself upon me is cold." I gestured to her poor accommodations. "You want your amusements, very well. But if you're going to send me back outside with nothing, I'm going to complain about it."

"You'll be brought inside before too much longer."

"But that's not now. I'm cold *now*."

"What is with you?" She pressed her fingers to a spot on her bodice and held it. "Mikhail the Jester wasn't like this."

"Mikhail the Jester was never cold like this," I snapped. "Mikhail the Jester, despite having the worst clothing in the world, still had clothing. Mikhail the Jester lived inside. Mikhail the Jester had a basket, so he didn't have to sit directly on a cold tile floor!"

"I will figure something out," she said as she sat in the nearest chair.

I didn't think she noticed how much weight I had lost. Or if she did, she didn't care. The cold seeped into my bones now.

And where it had once just been uncomfortable, now it flayed me alive.

"My dear," she said, gesturing to the chamber pot, her hand splayed flat on the front right side of her torso.

I ignored her and gathered the blankets off her bed. I settled the blankets on the floor, layering them to provide a barrier against the tile, and curled up. I didn't stir when the tsarina heaved. What could she expect me to do while I was chained?

I only bothered giving her another glance after the sixth or seventh time, since I could get no rest while she was loudly being ill. She clutched her body. Tears leaked from her eyes. No sympathy welled up inside me. She had watched me sicken after my transformation, and she had enjoyed it. I wasn't perverse enough to find pleasure, but I did not extend myself to think of anything but what her complaint might hold for my future. It was the first moment throughout this ordeal where I realized my suffering might not be eternal. What if she died? It was hard to imagine that any successor would treat me worse. No one would want me for the same purposes. Maybe Alaina could go home too.

Eventually, servants, held longer in wait than usual and concerned about the change in routine, found her. The peaceful room devolved into chaos. Between cleaning crews for the floor and the furnishings and personal servants tasked with cleaning up the tsarina, dozens of people invaded a room normally reserved for less than a handful.

Between preoccupation with the tsarina's condition and the ten other things that had now become priority to get her back in her bedroom and comfortable, I was forgotten. At least until the servants remade her bed and found new blankets, since no one wanted to come near enough to me to take the ones I had stolen.

The tsarina, cleaned up and accompanied by a flurry of

useless hovering helpers, returned to her remade bed and was brought every kind of comfort another hovering group following closely behind could imagine: pitchers of juice, comfits, jellies, flavored ices, and more. A pair of servants followed them, bringing the receiving room samovar into the bedroom so that tea might be ready at any moment. The physicians followed them and waved away most of the delicacies and concerned nobles alike.

The physicians hummed and muttered and asked delicate questions. They conferred and broke off into smaller groups to consult each other and keep their voices low. And then one of them nearly stumbled over me, and I was ordered out. By the time the guard came, the physicians had already vacated the bedroom, and the sun had retired early in accordance with the season. I therefore stumbled through the dark, disallowed to take any of the blankets with me, and returned to my enclosure to face another night puffing up my feathers and burrowing into the fetid straw.

A steak, cooked properly, awaited me, although the steam had long since disappeared, and I was still obliged to eat it with my hands. I could thank Alaina for the positive change in my diet, even if I couldn't have her ask that knife, fork, and napkin be left out for me too. I drank from the pail and shivered, the water so cold that I marveled at it not being ice yet.

I withdrew when light came around the copse of trees that kept the enclosure private. With the tsarina taken ill and the caretaker having already set out food and water for me, I did not expect any other visitors. I retreated as far into the shelter as I could, blending in with the darkest shadows just in case it was another half-drunk guard out to take revenge on some perceived slight or serve abuse that would not be tolerated toward any other creature.

"Mikalay?"

Alaina held the lantern aloft, the soft glow illuminating her face and shining off strands of her dark hair. The dramatic lighting painted her like the Varnasian masters, muted tones and stark contrasts washing her with mysterious contours and a refined beauty that could not be seen in any harsher light.

I stepped out from the shadows, relieved, almost delighted to see her after the expectation of a night spent dwelling on discomforts and dreaming of kinder, warmer days that I would never have again. Even my name, my Varnasian name, on her lips inspired a small ember of joy somewhere deep within me. I would never know the pleasure and peace of Varnasia again in my lifetime, but for a moment, I could be recalled to a place where fear did not live long, and there was love above all else.

"Here, princess."

She flashed a smile that outshone the lantern. And it was for me. Who was daft enough to smile like that for me?

"I came by earlier, but you weren't here." She set the lantern down on the bench. "And with everything going on with the tsarina, I didn't know if you…." She stopped as if not quite certain where she was heading with that thought. She approached the shelter. "If you weren't here this time, I was going to go to her apartments and get you."

"I was there most of the day."

"How is she?"

"The physicians called it 'women's complaints' and told her to rest."

"It is nothing more serious?" The princess lived too long at court to make the mistake of expressing hope that harm might befall the tsarina even in front of me, but disappointment saturated her question.

"She demonstrated a great deal of pain, more than one might consider for their assessment, but I am no physician." Her face mirrored my hope. "You share my thoughts. You might have a chance at freedom. If."

"My freedom? You're the one that's chained."

"You're a spoiled, pampered princess," I said. "Of course, I want to be rid of you."

"How silly of me to forget. Still, my lot is not as dire as yours."

"You said that you pay attention when I'm with her. I pay attention too. And you wear a collar just like mine, only no one can see it."

She blinked, likely never having thought of her title or position in such a way, even if she had recognized the confinement of them.

"How do you bear it?" she asked.

"What choice have I?"

"You could always kill yourself if it got unbearable."

"I tried. I tried twice," I snapped. "Things only got worse."

"How could it get worse?"

"Did you never wonder why she bound my arms?" I held them out in front of me, the wide leather bands still dangling their ties. "And the anklets? Have you not noticed that they keep me far enough away from the wall to discourage another crude attempt? If you choose to bring me a knife or a pistol, I am sure I would have greater success."

"That explains why your caretaker didn't want to add anything to your enclosure." She reached out and touched my forearm, just with the tips of her fingers, light and questioning, but she had not hesitated in the gesture. "If it means anything, I am very glad that you're still here."

"Who else of such wit and engagement would you find to torment with your company?"

"Precisely." She dropped her hand and moved out from under the shelter. "Do your tethers allow you this far?"

It was only a few paces, but I hadn't tried it. I hadn't tried many things, resigned to the life designed for me. That warmed me with an unexpected dose of shame. How pathetic I had become!

"You can see all the stars tonight," she said, as she sat on the ground and pulled her thin cloak around her.

"Any falling ones? I have so many wishes to make."

"Come join me," she patted the ground beside her, "and see for yourself."

"Is that a command, princess?"

"Do I need to make it one?"

I shuffled towards her and, gratified that my tethers did indeed let me go so far, took the offered seat.

"If it had been, I would have refused to obey."

"You contrary thing," she said, a smile spreading across her face.

I did not sit so very near but close enough, gazing up at the ever-optimistic stars that twinkled heedless to the suffering of the admirers below. I wrapped my arms around my body, my wings pulled tight against my back, and shivered. It could have been from cold because, as I had told the tsarina just that morning, I was cold almost all the time now. But this time, it wasn't. It was a mixture of grief and despair and hopelessness that crept into my spine and shook me like a child's toy. My view of the stars, however clear the sky, would always be framed by black feathers and a beak. I pressed the tips of my talons into my ribs. I scooted up so that my tail feathers splayed out against the ground behind me. I breathed deeply the scent of some distant fire.

In. Out. In. Out.

Alaina shivered too.

"You need to start wearing heavier cloaks," I scolded her. "How long have you been in Ilyichia? Even visiting foreigners are better prepared for the weather than you."

She tore her gaze away from the sky to look at me and shrugged.

I didn't know if it would be too forward, especially since our only point of physical contact had just occurred and that between fingertips and an arm, but I extended my wing closest to her in an offer of shelter.

"They aren't good for anything," I confessed, "but they're warm."

Her mouth opened and her eyes widened.

Her horror at my offer embarrassed me. Painfully. Like I was asking her to dance as a kindly gesture, and she reviled me for being in that chicken costume all over again. Except that this costume would never come off. I withdrew my wing, and I cast my eyes to the ground.

I couldn't blame her. Not last time. Not this time. I was the tsarina's pet, an ugly ridiculous thing. Faced by the day — the hour, the moment even — with the evidence of my degradation, how had I forgotten it?

"Was that an offer?" she asked.

"I thought—" I couldn't tell her of the comparison I drew between now and months ago, but surely, she could understand my initial interpretation. "You looked horrified by the suggestion."

"Not at all!" She scooted close beside me. "Just surprised. Does the offer still stand?"

I extended the wing out again, and she nestled herself within it. She stroked the feathers like the pelt of a fine fur.

"It's very soft," she said.

I didn't thank her since I couldn't be gracious about an anatomy I hated.

"You said that your wings aren't good for anything?" she asked.

"I can't fly."

"Flying isn't everything. If they're warm, then they are of great good, especially here in Ilyichia."

She shifted again, sitting slightly more to face me, but so very near. I had complained of being cold and had taken exception to how little Alaina wore in the night chill, but right now, I heated to a degree I could not attribute to feathers alone.

"You're warm," she said. "What need have I of a heavier cloak if I visit you?"

"Feathers will do that."

"I thought you'd be scratchier," she teased.

"I thought you would be too."

"Why?"

"Because you're so prickly in every other way."

"At court," she said, "that's called survival."

"Most survive by being false to their core."

"I see that you've spent more than enough time inside to see the truth of it."

I couldn't tell her that I spent the bulk of my life trying to escape it.

"I like that you're honest," she said after a moment. "You don't feel the need to flatter me just because I'm a princess. And the heir to Altania's throne." Then she added, a smile in her voice, "Although I might think a great deal more of you if you weren't always quite so honest."

"And if you weren't so haughty, I might think a great deal more of you too."

She laughed, no ulterior motives hidden behind it. No agendas or schemes or plans. Because I couldn't do anything for her but give her my company.

"Mikalay?"

"Yes?"

"I'm afraid that, if I tell you, you'll think me foolish."

"Not at all," I assured her. "I already think you foolish. Nothing you can say will change that."

"You're awful!"

"So you've said, many a time."

"That's true," she agreed. She twisted her hands in her lap and then, reaching out, set her hand on top of mine. "All teasing aside though...."

My breath caught with the gesture. This wasn't a stray or absent touch. This wasn't accidental or impulsive. She took a moment and decided, even with the hideous strangeness of my hands, to touch me.

"Yes?" I choked out.

She whispered, "I like this."

I nodded, not trusting my voice.

"I am very alone in Ilyichia," she admitted, "but even if I were not, I would prefer your company to anyone else's."

"You like to suffer, it seems," I teased.

"You simply give what you get. You match me with whatever orneriness I have to offer, and yet, somehow, you're still so gracious about... nearly everything! It's almost sickening, you know."

"My graciousness?"

"It still shames me to think of how cruel I was to you before you told me that you understood. How dare you be so tolerant!"

Alaina and Klessa probably would have made good friends if a world of titles did not separate them. I didn't know how I could arrange that introduction now. I didn't even know Klessa's public name, beyond "Pietrodillo's wife." I admired them both for their navigation of treacherous court life, and in a place where everyone could be an enemy, I trusted them both. The idea of them joining forces was a formidable one though that Drook or any other they opposed might regret.

"I will try not to be so gracious in the future."

"And," she continued with her list of troublesome virtues, "although everyone is afraid of you, you're kind."

"I am *not.*"

"You're currently keeping me warm."

"Purely selfish! Who else would visit me if you caught ill?"

"Pish. You're kind. Princess Alaina of Altania and Ilyichia

decrees it. I could go on," she threatened when I groaned. "You're clever. And funny. And you put up with me. And you're comforting."

"You made those up," I grumbled.

"I wish. It's annoying how much I like you."

"It's annoying how much I enjoy your company as well."

"We're friends, right?" She put her other hand on top of mine too. "Can we be friends? Is that strange?"

"Strange, yes," I agreed, "but fitting for a princess who likes spending time with a bird whose existence is disbelieved by elephants."

"But we can be friends then, even if it is strange?"

"Yes," I said. "We can be friends."

"Good. Because I like this. I really like this."

I didn't tell her, but I really liked this too.

XXII.

With the removal of the jesses, I could walk a natural gait
for the first time since the beginning of my captivity. The only
distance I needed to walk, however, consisted of five steps into
my new inside accommodation, those rendered unnecessary by
a forceful shove from one of the guards. Unbound though I
was, the cage door then swung shut behind me and the lock
engaged.

For a pair of parrots, the cage might have sufficed.
Although sizable enough for anything smaller, the bars were
too widely spaced. For anything larger — a person, for
example, even if that person looked like a bird — it offered no
space at all. I couldn't lie down without feet and legs sticking
out. I couldn't stretch my wings. Sitting, my tail feathers butted
up against the bars. And, to make my exposure worse, the cage
took a place of prominence in the middle of a public foyer. I
couldn't even keep a wall at my back.

I resumed being the most boring creature in the tsarina's
menagerie, curling up and sleeping, or pretending to sleep,
most of the time. Even when people paused by the bars, no
one remained for long. Even the offhand insult failed to reach
me nowadays, desensitized as I had become to the casual
abuse.

When Alaina visited me that first night, I asked her if she
could tie the chain up as she had at our picnic. The task was a
little more complicated through the bars, but she accomplished
it skillfully, even taking a blue ribbon from her hair to secure it
so that it would not come loose.

"I can probably get the bands off too," she said, taking

one of my hands and looking at the ties on the wrist guard.

"Maybe you could just knot up the laces?"

The bows she made were too pretty to be of my doing, but effective, so I did not say anything but thank you.

"I'm sorry I cannot visit during the day now," she said.

All four hours of day that we had left at this time of year.

"Evening visits will suffice," I assured her.

"Can I do anything else?"

"A blanket?"

"Only if you promise that you won't hurt yourself with it."

"I will be much less likely to harm myself if I'm not cold all the time."

"Then that is easily accomplished. Is there—"

Voices came from down the hall, and she froze like a child caught stealing a sweet.

"Should I run?" she asked.

I whispered, "Take several steps back."

Alaina put a respectable distance between us.

The voices grew louder upon approach, oblivious to the princess.

"Have you seen it yet?"

"Only in passing. But I tell you, there's something different about it."

"I haven't."

"I kept meaning to get outside, but it's been so cold."

"I'm glad she took it in."

"She should have brought it in weeks ago."

"Your Highness!"

Alaina forced a smile in their direction.

I turned just a little to see the newcomers, and both to my relief and my shame, Drook, Agara, and Grigga stood in the foyer. They bowed and curtsied respectively as they approached the princess, presumably all there for the same thing: me.

"I did not expect anyone about at this time," Alaina explained.

"We aren't anyone," Drook said.

"Have you seen it before, Your Highness?" Grigga asked.

"The tsarina gave me charge of it some time ago," Alaina answered, "and since then, I think it knows who I am."

"I wouldn't be surprised." Drook furrowed his brows and approached. "I keep telling anyone who will listen — I think it's intelligent."

"Birds of prey are well known for their cleverness," Alaina said to downplay Drook's implication.

"More than that," said Drook as he approached the bars. "It has human eyes."

"And it's not just a man dressed to look like a bird?" asked Grigga. "With a good mask perhaps?"

"No," Drook said a touch mournfully. "We know what a mask looks like."

"Have you seen such a mask before?" Alaina asked.

"We once had a friend with a beak," Drook said to Alaina. Then he turned to me. "Do you speak, friend?"

The temptation to reveal myself nearly overwhelmed me. This was forever, so what did it matter if I told these people who had been so dear and so good to me during my earlier trials? But Alaina was there too, and I didn't want her to know that her pathetic bird friend was the disgraced prince of months earlier. Maybe, without Alaina, I could have reclaimed them, but not with her. And so I said nothing.

"And it hasn't said anything to you, Your Highness?" Drook spoke to Alaina but never took his eyes from me. "Even though it knows you?"

"He stays quiet most of the time," Alaina said.

"I'm sure he does." Drook smiled. "Safest that way."

"Oh, I didn't mean——"

"Of course you didn't," Drook interrupted.

To a princess, such an interruption was beyond rude, but Alaina relaxed at the assurance. Grigga and Agara turned their attention to Alaina, then to me, then pointedly to Drook.

"I was wrong," Drook declared. "He doesn't speak."

"Thank you, Pietrodillo," Alaina said.

"It's nothing. And no one knows because we're no one." Drook tipped his scarlet hat at her and then gathered up his two companions. He took another long look at me, no recognition in his face but deep furrows in his craggy brows. "Glad to see he's indoors. Good night, Your Highness!"

"Good night," she said as the three of them departed.

When their voices no longer echoed through the halls, Alaina flew to the cage. "They know!"

"They guess," I said.

"I didn't mean to give anything away."

"They won't say anything," I assured her.

"Are you sure?" She looked up into my face through the bars and reached her hand into the cage to take mine. "I couldn't bear it if you came to any harm because I did something silly."

"You're a princess," I told her. "You have a propensity for doing silly things."

"That's a mean thing to say," she scolded me.

"I know a little something about princesses. And about princes too." I squeezed her hand. "Your privilege makes you all do silly things."

"You're not angry with me?"

"They aren't the first to guess."

"I hadn't heard any rumors. Who?"

"The caretaker," I admitted. "Apparently, I am built in a way that made him suspect when he first looked at me."

"And you really aren't just a man dressed as a bird?"

I released her hand. How did I answer that? Because I was. And I wasn't.

"You're not, are you?"

"Would that I were," I whispered.

"I didn't think so, but I had to ask after they suggested it. You are too stately to be the result of some tar and a bunch of feathers."

"Disappointed?"

"No, but it would have been easier if you were. Whenever I get back to Altania, I'm not sure how I'm going to explain bringing a man-sized bird with me."

"You would want me to join you in Altania?"

"Of course! If you wanted, that is."

"Is it warmer than Ilyichia?"

"My dear Kaylay, everywhere is warmer than Ilyichia."

That strange warmth spread through me. It wasn't just that little joyous ember of her using my Varnasian name either. Irena had abbreviated it once, and now Alaina had too, in a different way, partnering it with an endearment.

"True." If being a bird was my future, then at least I could be a bird somewhere other than under the rule of someone who misused me. "You would really want me with you in Altania?"

"I would miss you dreadfully," she confessed. "And I don't think I would ever rest if I knowingly left you with her."

XXIII.

Days blurred into each other. Alaina visited during the evenings when she could, although never for long. I did get my blanket, but I dearly wished that, in treating me like an abnormally large bird, someone would have decided that my cage should be curtained off during the night, both for peace and for warmth.

Nobles, both major and minor, milled about in the foyer most days with their attendants and distinguished friends, their footmen and pages occupying the space for longer durations when not permitted any farther. The engineer delegation for the ice palace construction came through several times, each time their faces more grim. And Drook and Klessa came by several times, maintaining their distance, but obviously there to see me.

I couldn't wave them over. I couldn't ask them to see me later. I couldn't tell them the truth. I didn't know that I wanted to. Mikhail was dead and had been for months. But they never came near enough for me to debate it with any seriousness. That made my decision for me.

No word on the tsarina's health reached me, although, by her visitors, she must be feeling up to resuming her obligations. Perhaps that was why the delegation returned so many times, hopeful to be seen but turned away. But before I could be grateful for her forgetfulness of me, I was ushered back to her bedroom.

"Oh, look! Someone tried to make you pretty," she said when she saw my wristband ties knotted into bows. "Who did it?"

The samovar that now lived full-time in her bedroom served as the only indication that she had been ill. I wanted to suggest that she not drink so much kvass too, but I didn't care that much, except in how her ill-health might benefit me in the long term.

"A child who didn't have the sense to be afraid," I lied.

When she was done with me, she left without further conversation.

For time interminable, that was the most variety I had in my life until an unusually busy day in the foyer. The bulk of those waiting were not the usual palace residents, and while not serfs or peasants from the city, the fashions did speak of a lower-class populace. Had I still not been able to see them, I would have smelled them even over the stench of my own excrement in the unretrieved chamber pot. Unused to seeing the tsarina's firebird, they crowded around my cage. I largely ignored them. And then someone grabbed my tail feathers and yanked.

As if torn directly from the end of my spine, I yowled. I circled to see a young woman standing at a distance from the cage holding one of my golden red feathers aloft.

"I want a feather from the firebird too!" others cried when they saw.

Dozens of arms reached in and grabbed at me, their searching fingers pulling and tearing feathers from my shoulders, wings, head, anywhere they could grasp. I lashed out. When my attackers started screaming from the wounds I inflicted, the guards stepped in to separate us. I didn't hold any illusion that the guards' intervention was for my safety.

My own wounds throbbed too much to care about the injuries I inflicted on others. I bled from the sites where hands tore indiscriminately, some rendered bald from the assault. Those patches did not reveal the truth of my origins, no human skin hidden by feathers, just wisps of down on flesh punctured by empty feather shaft sockets.

Eventually, the foyer cleared, those waiting for audience diverted to other halls and reception rooms to prevent another round of idiots from wanting their own souvenirs. And no one checked on me. I didn't expect that anyone would, but the confirmation of my own pessimistic outlook on life vindicated me in continuing to hold it. Beloved pet, my arse. Maybe the willingness to be proven wrong constituted a type of hope, but I didn't have the energy to contemplate the philosophy behind it. I hurt too much.

I slept, determined to make the most of the quiet and solitude despite the pain.

"Kaylay?"

My name on her lips pulled me from sleep. I blinked several times, banishing the lethargy so that I could be a fit companion. When I looked up, I gazed directly into her eyes. She sat beside the cage. The deep hollows in her face, pronounced beyond the shadows of evening, betrayed more than eagerness to see me.

"Princess."

I pulled the blanket over my shoulders to hide the glaring bald patches as I sat.

"I thought you stirred," she said. "I didn't mean to rouse you."

"Of course you did. You love to torment me."

"Ah, you've discovered my devious intentions. How unsubtle."

"Nothing about you is subtle, princess."

Instead of a round rejoinder, she offered a faint smile.

"Not going to pretend to affront?" Something had to be wrong. "Are you changing routine with me now? I may not know how to converse with you if so."

"I have not the vibrancy today to be witty in insult," she

confessed. "Only dull enough to bray like an ass should I attempt it. I do not wish to give you such an upper hand."

"Most strategic. Would you prefer to sit in silence then?"

She shook her head.

"No insults and no silence. You have effectively struck out our only two pastimes. Whatever do you propose we do?"

"Would you think less of me if I only wanted to talk?"

"It would be difficult to think less of you," I assured her, "as I think so little of you already."

"Mercy, please! I concede to your wit. You are the clear winner."

"Something *is* wrong. You would never give up so easily."

"I'm tired," she said. "I have not the wherewithal."

"It's more than that."

"Do stop being so perceptive. I'm peevish and out of temper, and I may cut you if pushed."

"It is far too late for that. Have you already forgotten our first days?"

She threw her hands in the air. "Kaylay, please!"

I reached between the bars and put my hand on her skirt, presumably where her knee was. "Tell me?"

"Will you be serious?"

"Life is already so unbearable. Being serious might make me more miserable. Then you would never visit me."

"I know." She put her hand on top of mine. "I'm sorry."

"An apology! Things must truly be dire. Tell me."

"You won't be derisive about it?"

"That depends. Is it a real problem, or did they not chill your vodka sufficiently?"

"So much worse," she said, smiling truly this time. "The caviar was warm."

"Oh, that *is* a problem."

"I will probably cry myself to sleep over it."

"I should never have doubted you."

She squeezed my hand. "How do you do that?"

"Do what?"

"I didn't even tell you anything, and you still managed to cheer me up."

"Now you see why the tsarina keeps me around."

"I hate her."

"All the hate in the world won't change anything," I said. "But I hate her too."

"You have cause."

"Tell me — what happened?"

"The tsarina heard petitions today."

"That's why it was so busy."

"I asked her if I could go home again. I explained how useless I am to her household and to her court, no longer fitting properly within the hierarchy since I had been left a widow. Altania would be better provisioned to look after me, maybe find me another husband, and let me start a proper family. I thought she might understand, being a widow herself and stuck in Talvia for such a long time."

"She declined your petition?"

"She left her chair and slapped me in front of all assembled for wasting her time. Then she berated me for expressing such discontent after the years she spent hosting me, and that she's ultimately doing me a favor because no one would have me again as a wife."

"That's her own fear speaking. No one wanted her, and she couldn't bear to let you get married again while she could not."

"How do you know that?"

I found myself without a way to answer that wouldn't give me away.

"I pay attention," I said, hoping that would be enough. "You hear much when everyone thinks you cannot understand."

She nodded and dropped her gaze to her lap, to our hands.

"I just want to go home, Kaylay."

"Don't we all," I said, intentionally rhetorical, but she perked up.

"Where do you call home?"

I cursed my idiocy. I did not want to have to invent a backstory, lie to her, and remember the tale I told.

"I used to live in paradise and now I live in torment," I said, that at least no lie.

"Any family?"

Alexei didn't count anymore, did he? And neither did any of the other numerous Karilitsyn aunts, uncles, and cousins. But Irena blotted out all thoughts of anyone else.

"I had a… a mate," I admitted, only barely managing not to use the term "wife" because it would give too much away.

"Like you?"

"No. Beautiful. Like an angel. And she teased me like a demon."

"That sounds apt." Alaina grinned. "Where is she?"

"Dead," and I didn't cry this time. Irena and her husband were both dead now. "You're a widow?" Although I already knew Alaina had been married, I couldn't know that in my current circumstances. And it took attention away from me.

"Of several years now."

"Were you happy with him?"

She met my eyes and then shook her head.

I reached out my other hand to put it on top of the two of ours. The blanket slid off a shoulder.

"What happened?" Alaina pointed to a featherless patch of skin on my now-exposed arm.

"Nothing." I withdrew both hands and pulled the blanket back over me.

"That's not nothing."

"I had my own incident today," I confessed, "but I didn't

want it to take precedence over yours."

She glared me down until I told her about it.

"I don't think there's any permanent damage," I assured her, "and I washed off most of the blood. There's a spot by my wing that I couldn't reach. Would you look at it?"

"Of course!" She gestured for me to put my back to her.

I shifted position, dragging my back along the bars so that the wings would have no choice but to go sideways, leaving my shoulder exposed to her view.

Her sound of disgust told me more than any description she could give me.

"I'm going to get the water." She stood, walked around the cage, and then slid the water dish around to where she tended me. She resumed her seat and began working the tip of a handkerchief into my shoulder. "Were all your wounds this bad?"

"They don't hurt anymore. I think it's just the dried blood pulling on the feathers with this one."

She rubbed, working at the crusted blood and lymph. It should have been painful, but I relaxed into her touch and settled back against the bars. Irena used to sit behind me and peel dead skin off my shoulders, scolding me all the while for basking in the sun long beyond what my fragile Ilyichian skin could handle. Alaina wasn't Irena, but I almost forgot for a moment.

"I hate that you're subject to such cruel treatment," she grumbled.

"Ilyichia little cares about its people. Why would anyone give a thought more for one of the tsarina's curiosities?"

"Kaylay," she ventured after a long stretch of deep thought, "is the tsarina done with you?"

"If only. But she does not seem to require my presence as much as she once did. Why?"

"What if I could have you come under my care?"

"I do not think she would relinquish her hold on me so easily."

"Unfortunately, I agree. But if I could have you moved up to my apartments, that might keep you safe."

She dropped her hands from my shoulder, and I turned to face her.

"I am going to have to make a perfect nuisance of myself," she said.

"That should take no effort then."

"I'm going to have to complain, often and loudly, about today with you. About how cruel it is. And about how neglected you are. And how something so ugly needs to be protected, for how could such a rabble be expected to control itself when faced with such a creature?"

"Thanks."

"If I pester her enough, maybe she'll decide that, if I'm so concerned about your upkeep, I should take responsibility for you."

"It sounds like a distant possibility — for normal people, anyway. For the tsarina? It sounds like. And she hasn't been in good health, so maybe she'll be too tired to think of anything more clever."

"No promises," Alaina said, "but I can try. And if it doesn't work, I'll come right out and tell her that I could do a better job."

"If you cannot, I will not blame you."

She reached out and touched my cheek, her thumb lightly stroking the beak.

"You deserve better," she said. "And I cannot have you getting hurt. I would miss you if anything happened."

"Ah, ha!" I teased. "Your seeming concern boils down to selfishness."

"Of course it does," she agreed without shame. "Did you forget who I am?"

"Not at all, princess." I reached up and took her hand from my face, holding it within both of mine. "You wouldn't let me."

XXIV.

The tsarina was out of temper, more than usual, and I paid
for it several times that day. That evening, in the final moments
of being dismounted for what was probably her last go of the
day before retiring, I sat up and settled my back against the
footboard of her bed, legs pulled up to my chest. I didn't care
about what had set her off, but I was probably looking at
another couple of days and nights spent at the foot of her bed,
making up for her foul mood.

"What have I done now?" I asked.

She shot me a glare over her shoulder as she went to fetch
her robe.

"You can tell me," I said, "and I can try to understand
what's going on, or you can not tell me and just be angry with
me forever."

I fully believed that she wanted reasons to be angry,
especially with me, so that she could rationalize her
mistreatment. She might never tell me, if indeed she had a
reason for her moodiness, just so she could continue with her
behavior without having to think about it.

One arm at a time through the gauzy fabric of her robe,
she stared at me. "You never asked how I was."

She had surely heard about the situation on petition day
with me, and she had seen the bald patches now growing in,
and she never asked how I was either.

"Since you've had me resume my functions," I said, "I
thought it was evident that you were doing significantly
better."

"And," she went to the samovar, "you didn't do anything

to help when I was ill. I don't think you care at all."

I cared very much in how her ill-health might affect me, but she was correct. I didn't care about her. How could I? What reason had she ever given me to do so?

"If I die, you're stuck like that," she said.

How much of an idiot did she think I was? I could see right through her lies. I was stuck like this, no matter what. Even if her assurance of a way out was true — which I didn't believe — that was an impossible requirement. Holding onto that kind of hope was exhausting in its futility, and I was already so tired. This was forever, her death or not. And it made everything easier, not looking for a way out.

"What would you have had me do?" I gestured to the chain that she kept affixed to the bed.

"Something. Anything!"

"If I had called for help, you would have been furious at me for breaking the silence you yourself imposed!" The futility of my situation was not a revelation. She would have been upset with me for anything I did or did not do. "You want me to be your Otherland pet. I did as you asked and behaved as any pet would have."

"I just want you to care," she said. "I don't think you care at all!"

I had a choice. I could tell her the truth, that I didn't. Or I could do as she did to me and lie. Maybe neither choice would make any difference, but it might.

I took a deep breath, stilled my fury, and then held her gaze.

"Of course I care!" I held my hands out to her, palms up, asking for hers. "I have been beside myself with worry. I didn't dare ask after you for fear that I might hear dreadful news, and I couldn't bear it."

I surprised myself with how convincing I sounded. And I convinced her. She hurried over to me, her own hands outstretched, taking mine as she lowered herself back to the ground beside me.

"You didn't seem like it mattered to you at all," she accused with red-rimmed eyes.

"I dare not show you my distress," I said, "when you carry the heavy responsibility of managing the empire."

She clung to my hands, squeezing them and holding them close.

"I have been so sad and so lonely," which weren't exactly lies, "but I haven't wanted to burden you with my upset." I worried about overdoing it, but I had her, and she wanted to believe it. "And then I worried that, perhaps, even knowing who I had once been, you found me too repellent to continue thinking upon me kindly. I truly think you hate me sometimes."

"Never!" She abandoned one of my hands to stroke my face. "You have always been my favorite."

The tsarina's favorite. Her favor didn't feel like favor, not when it came partnered with increasingly worse punishments.

She pulled my head down and kissed my brow. I struggled not to pull away and push her off me. I didn't want her affection, but I had honesty with Alaina now. Endurance of the tsarina's falseness sat a little easier because it meant fewer restrictions in enjoying the only authentic connection I had to anyone nowadays.

"You always seem so discontent," she said.

"I am bored," I confessed. "The conditions you've set for me ensure that I cannot read or idle my time with others. I am accustomed to more engagement and activity than currently allowed. Boredom ensures that I have no other occupation than to notice every discomfort and dwell upon every anxiety."

"Should I keep you with me more often?" She stroked my face consolingly. "You seem discontent with that too."

"With you, I must still act and behave like I do not

understand anything of my surroundings."

"I see." She dropped her hand from my face. "And what then is Princess Alaina's interest in you?"

There we were. That was what had been bothering her this whole time. Not my lack of caring.

I feigned ignorance. "What do you mean?"

"She mentioned your discontent to me."

"When I was outside, she used to come and read, often aloud. Practicing her Ilyichian, I assumed. I enjoyed listening to it."

"Is that all?"

"I would not know. Unlike the other ladies of your court, she never wanted anything to do with me when she knew who I was."

"And since?"

"You handed my lead to her once, and she was patient with me."

"Nothing else?"

I pretended to think and consider as if every one of our precious interactions were not burned on the inside of my skull.

"I am ill-adept at playing the part you've assigned to me," I said, "to the point that others have noticed. I think she realizes that I am as alone as she is. She is afraid of me though and trying not to be since you have demonstrated that you are not."

"And why would she do that?"

"Who else does she have to look up to? You have been her only example of true leadership and authority." And that, though flattery, was also true, and I hated that for Alaina. Would that she could see a sovereignty not based on bitterness and resentment! "And, from the little I have gathered, she is in much the same situation as you once were," I framed it without blaming the tsarina, "living in a foreign land after tragedy made her a widow. Surely, she sees herself in you. And she sees the heights to which you have ascended after so much hardship. Can you blame her for wishing to be all that you have become — even if it is through such poor means as overcoming her fear of me?"

"Do you really think so?" For once, her face had gone nearly blank, the lines of malice disappearing in her contemplation of an idea she had not yet entertained. "All she ever seems to do is whine to go back to her precious Altania."

"I do not know her well enough to say it with any certainty," I offered, "but how could she not long for your approval? And if she does not feel as if she will ever earn it, then perhaps that is when she most longs for her homeland. I too despair when I convince myself that you abhor the very sight of me."

"Oh, my darling." She took my hand in both of hers and squeezed it. "I could never! I cannot always be with you. And unlike her, I do have obligations on my time that I cannot keep you entertained."

"I would not expect you to sit and read to me for hours," I assured her.

"She's discontent, and you are too." She narrowed her eyes at me. "What if I charged her with reading to you an hour a day?"

"If you must." I sighed as if I hated the idea. "She might refuse. Especially if you want her to do it in public. My cage is far too accessible for her to willingly practice her Ilyichian. She hasn't done it since I've come inside, and I can only suppose that is the reason."

"She certainly has a lot to say about how you're kept for not visiting you."

Was the tsarina's suggestion that Alaina didn't visit an acknowledgment that she didn't know the princess visited, or a test to see how much I would admit to?

"She visits occasionally," I admitted, "mostly at a distance.

She just doesn't read aloud anymore." And then I pushed because I didn't want Alaina to take the brunt of the tsarina's annoyance and because the tsarina's jealousy might hold sway if she thought Alaina had any kindly intentions towards me. "Don't inflict me upon the princess. Even as a man, she couldn't stand me. Her attempts at overcoming her fear are valiant but ultimately impossible. And I do not relish the idea of being subjected to the sole company of someone who reviles me in any guise I wear." I added, "Not that anyone wants anything to do with me now, unless it's to pluck a feather. Your subjects much abused my accessibility the other day."

"So I have been told." Her face collapsed into deep furrows from brow to chin. "Which is why I need to figure out what to do with you." She stroked my hand again. "She may not be the ideal companion, but my niece-by-law has been vocal about your upkeep, and it may be good for her to see that it is more challenging than she supposes. You will at least be safe with her and, if it is not so public, perhaps she will resume reading to you."

"Are you abandoning me?" I clung to her hand. "Am I not to see you?"

"Shhh," she stroked my face. "I can retrieve you as easily from her apartments as anywhere else. Do not fear, my dear. I will never abandon you."

"You will not forget about me when you shut me away with the princess?" I asked, playing to her need to be wanted.

"Of course not."

"You're the only one who knows me," I said, repeating the sentiment she told me early on in my present circumstances. I attempted restraint in my pathetic whine, weaponizing the only tool I still had left. "It would surely break me to lose the regard of the only person who truly cares about me, even — especially — like this."

Her face radiated pure triumph.

And though I hated every word that dropped from my mouth and every action of affection I pretended to, I too rejoiced. We had done it. Alaina and I had played her. I had no regrets.

"She gave me a difficult time about the key," Alaina confided once I had been brought to her apartments and her maids and attendants left us to ourselves. Despite whatever difficult time the tsarina gave Alaina, Alaina held the key up triumphantly and set it into the door lock. "In the end, she had a duplicate made. Wise of her," she said as the door swung open, "or I was going to have to bribe someone to get it for me."

"I would not have blamed you if you could not. Up here is still a marked improvement over being in a public foyer."

She held her hands out, palms down, and wiggled her fingers, offering to help me up from the floor of the cage. I couldn't refuse the gesture, rare and welcome as it was. My hands swallowed hers even before the talons closed over them, and I didn't dare give her any weight. When I stood, she backed up, leading me out into her bedroom antechamber.

"I know it's not the grand apartments of the tsarina," Alaina said apologetically, "but I hope it's okay. I can keep the fire going, and if there is anything you want or need, I can try to get it."

A fire, that I had access to, kept going just for me, embodied the pinnacle of contentment in what I might ever reasonably expect for the rest of my life. My gratitude for her consideration could not be summed up in words.

"I appreciate all your efforts to make this happen. Thank you."

"I need you to promise me two things, Kaylay." Alaina squeezed my hands. "You cannot continue to harm yourself. And, I know how strong the temptation must be because I share it, but please, do not escape the palace while you are with me. I fear you will be subject to more severe restraint, and I will never be able to help you again."

I had not planned on either course of action once transferred to Alaina's care, so agreement did not come at a cost. Just as she couldn't leave me behind, I couldn't leave her behind now either.

"I promise. While I appreciate the access to the room and fire, what will you say if anyone should find me outside of my cage?"

"That I saw no reason to cage you! It's not like you piddle on the rugs." Her eyes widened as she stared at me. "You wouldn't, would you?"

"I should be offended by the suggestion except that you present a rather useful alternative to expressing my displeasure without having to speak to anyone. So I suppose it depends on how happy you keep me."

"For the sake of my rugs then, I must endeavor to keep you well occupied and contented."

"For the sake of your rugs," I agreed.

We fell into embarrassed silence, her cheeks warm as she cast her attention down to the floor, my gaze also directed to the same bit of knotted fringe as she continued to hold my hands.

"I'm sure the tsarina wouldn't mind it though if you told her I damaged several of your rugs," I said.

"I will be certain to relate to her all the damage and difficulty keeping you in my apartments offers, just in case she gets it into her head to be jealous." She released my hands and then wound the chain on the collar so that she could tie it up again. "I did ask about getting the collar and leather bands removed, but she resisted me on so much, I did not want to jeopardize the victory of getting you up here by making a nuisance of myself on other things. I probably should have not asked and just done it."

"I am grateful you tried," I assured her, "but I am not disappointed."

"I'll be smarter about it in the future." She took my arm then and tugged me farther into the room towards the fire that called to me like a siren to a sailor. "I didn't know what you might like for furniture. Your tailfeathers and wings won't allow for a chair which I find the most comfortable for fireside sitting. But a bench might work." Indeed, a chair flanked the hearth, and a tufted gilt bench occupied the prominent spot in front of it. "Do you want to try?"

"Would you consider me ungrateful if I preferred sitting on the cushions on the floor?"

I couldn't explain it, but I could no longer justify the luxuries of tufted benches or giltwood chaises or armchairs. They were not made for me. Perhaps I had been relegated too long to cushions and baskets to enjoy the stiff propriety of anything I might sully by proximity.

"If that is the most comfortable, then please!"

I extracted myself from her grasp and moved the bench away so that I could have the floor expanse clear. Then I moved her chair closer to the fire.

"Oh, no," she protested, "I will sit on the floor beside you."

"You just told me that you prefer the chair."

"But—!"

"I do not wish to hear it, princess. Sit. You are little enough. Though I sit on the ground, we shall still be at eye level. Please."

She harrumphed all the way to the chair, flouncing into it with a great heaving sigh. And though I exaggerated about being eye-level with her while I sat on the floor, I did not exaggerate much with the chair swallowing her up. She crossed her arms as if much put out by my request, her skirts a billowing cloud of fabric around her satin shoes, which did not reach the ground.

I sat beside her, snatching one of the pillows off a nearby chaise so that I could adjust myself comfortably.

"See?" she whined from the chair. "You're so far away!"

We were not separated to the extent she complained. She could reach over the arm of the chair and touch me if she wanted.

"I don't understand why you're being so stubborn," she lamented.

"You're a princess," I explained.

"And as you've told me, that means nothing."

"It means nothing when one speaks of something to stay warm, or having food to eat, or living in one set of apartments or another. But right now, it means you get the chair."

"Kaaaaylaaaay," she whined.

I crossed my arms on top of the chair arm and rested my chin on them. I stared up at her.

"Let me join you on the floor?" she asked again.

"No."

She reached out and brushed her hand over my forehead and back through the feathers. Her touch, gentle and appreciative, did not elicit any of my instincts to withdraw as they did with the tsarina. It was illusory, of course, but Alaina's touch promised safety and care.

"Pietrodillo is right," she said. "You do have human eyes."

That broke the illusion. I jerked back as if she had struck me.

"What was that for?" she asked.

"I'm not, you know. Not human," I said, trying not to panic or bristle and make her regret showing me any care at all.

"I am going to disappoint you if you think of me like that."

"Is that what the tsarina does?" she asked, reaching over the chair to touch my shoulder. "Tries to make you a man in feathers? I don't mean to do that."

"I know you don't. And I know that you're far too intelligent to let a man degrade you by association were he in my state."

"What do you mean?" Alaina's brows bunched up.

I didn't know what my point was, but not to address it would be akin to a lie, even if I would never be in a position to be Mikhail again to her or anyone.

"If I were just a man in feathers, you would want nothing to do with me, and rightfully so. A man does not elevate his company by wearing a collar and living in a cage."

"Is that why you won't let me join you? Because you have some notion that you aren't fit company for me?"

"Something like that," I confessed.

Alaina leaned over her lap and patted her legs through her skirts. When I shifted close enough to her, she sat back and patted her knee, guiding my head down to it. Her fingers played in the feathers, soft and deliberate.

"I do not know what I am," I said honestly, her touch freeing my tongue. "Why not just let me be an adoring, if stubborn, pet?"

"Because even if you don't know what you are, Kaylay, I do." She bent over me and kissed the top of my head. "You are my friend."

XXV

Fireside sitting became my primary pastime. I could have done a lot worse. I had done a lot worse. And now, I spent my days curled up with pillows and blankets in front of the hearth, baking myself into pleasant dreaming by convincing myself that I was in Varnasia again, enjoying chilled wine and the radiant sun. The mental gymnastics required to accomplish it in full view of a darkness that lifted just before midday and descended again barely three hours after might have astounded anyone privy to my thoughts, but I had grown desperate for peace and needed few props to set my stage.

The servants who emptied chamber pots and tended the fire adapted to my presence. No one maligned or taunted me in Alaina's apartments. It was a nice change not to have to pretend not to hear things said about me.

Although Alaina could not always be with me either, she did not suggest that she lead me about by the leash as the tsarina did. She even ordered regular bathing water for me although few others saw me now. And when the servants and the ladies who assisted Alaina with her evening preparations departed each night, Alaina would join me in her anteroom and read to me.

I almost told her that I could read so that she might give me the allowance of her books, but the complications that could spring from that kept me quiet. I therefore resigned myself to the assumption of illiteracy that predominated most of Ilyichian society.

The tsarina only had me removed to her bedroom once

over the next two fortnights, and she did not chain me to the bed.

"How is it going with the princess?" she asked me as she finished up.

I didn't know if she was actually paying attention or not, so I sighed and said, "Tolerably."

"Does she read to you?"

"Yes."

"Good. I told her that you seemed to enjoy it when I read to you," which the tsarina had never done, "and that she should continue the practice."

"She has taken your advice to heart then. Thank you for ensuring that I am so provisioned."

"I cannot have my firebird growing bored now, can I?" She stood and smoothed out her skirts as if preparing to leave.

"Are you already done?" I did not relish the idea of remaining any longer than I had to, but if I had no complaints about Alaina and showed no eagerness for the tsarina's company, my peace would be short-lived. "I have hardly spent any time with you."

"I am busy, my dear."

"I know," I said contritely. "But now that you have seen me so well-accommodated, is there anyone to look after you?"

"I am being looked after," she said.

"How are the preparations for the winter festivities going?" I asked, desperately hunting about for any topic of conversation I could, so that I appeared eager for her attention. "And, what about your wonderful palace of ice? It sounds like a marvel."

"It is. Once they had the exterior built, I had my engineers put to death so that they could never build one for another monarch," she said. "It truly is a wonder of the world. The sculptors should have the details complete in time for the planned dedication to The Kind and Fair. I considered holding the winter ball out there, but the Royal Academy has projected that this will be the coldest winter on record. They encouraged me not to host anyone out there for so long a time since it would be well below the usual freezing temperatures during the night."

"I didn't realize you planned to use it as a celebration space."

"I won't, not now, since I little enjoy the idea of my guests freezing to death, but I still plan on leaving the winter offerings there after the dedication. And, of course, after the initial consecration of it, then the public can use it to leave The Kind and Fair offerings too. I would offer to take you on my next inspection, but I know how much you hate being cold."

"I am shivering just hearing about it," I agreed.

"I will be sure to find a way to show it to you before the season is over, even if I have to bundle you in furs." She tilted her head as she furrowed her brows. "You were always so delicate of constitution. Ilyichians are usually made of stronger stuff."

Delicate of constitution? She clearly forgot that I had spent more than half my life in the Ilyichian military. I just managed not to say something stupid. I had to maintain her delusions to divert her attention from Alaina. Let her believe it if she liked, especially if it meant I could stay warm, but it showed me, yet again, how little of me she knew when it was her own fictional version of me she preferred.

Instead, I looked at her helplessly and shrugged.

That satisfied her, and she resumed her trajectory out the bedroom door. Again, I waited to hear for guards. I contemplated the merits of going down to the tsarina's rose garden to call a Kind and Fair. Stirring in the corridor decided me against it. Guards arrived moments later to usher me back to the princess' apartments.

They stuck me back in the cage upon my return, still

uncertain how to accommodate the elevation in my circumstances. So I settled down into the pillows and waited.

Alaina entered not long after, other ladies in tow. She paused when she spied me in the cage but couldn't do anything about it. The ladies were not those with whom I was well-familiar, although I had seen most of them either with Alaina or around court. They, fortunately, did not give me much notice either, and none of them stayed long.

Alaina crouched down beside the cage when we were left to ourselves.

"I have a surprise for you," she said, grinning like a girl.

I oozed up from my reclined position and sided up against the cage bars. I put my hand around a bar and waited to be told of her surprise.

Her smile dimmed, and she put her hand over mine. "How was your time with the tsarina?"

"No worse than usual."

"I'm sorry you still have to endure that."

"It's a small price for our peace."

"And I hate that you have to pay it." She took my hand from the bar. "So I thought, maybe I could do something nice for you."

"You've done more for me than anyone," I assured her.

"Nonsense." She let my hand go and then grabbed the key to open the cage door. She fit it in the lock and turned it. "I have half a mind to leave the key where you can access it, but I worry that someone else might find it and move it."

"I can be patient."

"You shouldn't have to be." She opened the door for me. "I don't suppose she would treat you any better if she knew you understood?"

I stepped out of the cage and paused at Alaina's suggestion. I hadn't prepared excuses for not revealing myself to the tsarina. I had been a bit short-sighted in that probably, but so long as I could keep everyone ignorant of how much anyone else knew, I could keep the tsarina content and Alaina safe.

"Of course she wouldn't," Alaina said in answer to her own question, sparing me from having to dig for excuses.

"She wouldn't want me around you if she thought I might speak to you too."

"She would probably just keep you muzzled all the time," Alaina said, her disgust so heavy as it dripped from her words that I half-expected to see a puddle of it beneath her. She crossed the room and went to the doors that led to her bedroom. "Come along."

I didn't follow. I trusted Alaina and did not think she had similar intentions towards me as the tsarina did, but I couldn't make myself take another step in that direction.

"I am content out here," I said. "Thank you."

"Do stop being obstinate and contrary."

I took a step backwards.

"Kaylay, come here."

My back stiffened at her command.

"No," I said, refusing to submit to a second minor, if slightly more benevolent, tsarina. "Use that tone of command with me again, and I will refuse to ever obey you. You will need to call the guards like the tsarina does."

"You are so obstinate," she grumbled. "I'm trying to do something nice for you, and you're thwarting me."

"You are being imperious with me. I get enough of that from her. I will not do it with you."

"Kaylay."

"I will go back into that cage and not come out," I said. "You decide, right now, if you want a friend or a subject."

"You're my friend," she insisted as she came over to me. "I just want to give you something. That's all. I'm really trying here."

"Yes," I agreed. "You're very trying."

"Please, Kaylay?"

"Does it have to be in there?" I glanced at her bedroom door. "Could you not bring it out here?"

"I suppose I could, but wh—" Her eyes widened. "Kaylay, you don't think that I— But I wouldn't!"

"I don't know that. Not when you speak to me like she does."

"The Great Holy forbid that I ever become like her!"

The comparison between them bore an uncomfortable closeness.

"I would never," she said. She reached out to stroke my arm twice, in the direction of the feathers. "Wait here."

She disappeared into her bedroom and returned minutes later carrying a fabric-wrapped item that one of her ladies carried in earlier. With Alaina carrying it, it threatened to swallow her up. She tossed it onto the chaise to free her hands.

I stood beside her, appraising the bundle.

"What is it?" I asked.

She pulled at the fabric wrapping, revealing slivers of blue brocade and dark fur until she managed to free the wrapping entirely and discard it on the floor. The blue shimmered in the light, and the fur absorbed it. She unrolled the item, and though she held it above her head, the bottom still trailed along the ground.

"What do you think?" she asked.

I regarded the swathes of fabric, very fine, very attractive, in something of a dress pattern but not of the style she usually wore. And much too big for her. I could not help but reach out and stroke the sable collar though, luxuriating in its softness.

"What is it?" I asked again.

"It's a new outfit — for you!"

"I have feathers," I protested, "and do not need clothing."

Alaina's arms dropped in her disappointment, the garment now a puddle of blue brocade on the ground. She hesitated a moment before turning away from me and draping it over the chaise.

"I had one of my dresses made into a robe for you," she said. "Since you're so much taller than I am, I had my seamstress cut sections of the skirt to add to the bottom and make it look less skirt-like."

My gaze traveled the length of the robe. The brocade dazzled in the lamplight, reflecting and absorbing the light according to elegant folds and alternating glossy and matte foliate patterns woven into the cloth. Gold braid and crystal bead trim hid the seams from the original skirt to the additions. The front bodice had been converted into a top of military style, bedecked in gold braid and ornate clasps. The deep brown sable fur trimmed the hem and the open collar that met just above the top golden clasp.

"I wanted to give you something green to match your eyes, but I didn't have anything that color," she explained.

I took a step toward the robe and reached out, brushing my fingertips through the fur and tracing my claws over the gold braid. I withdrew before I reached the blue brocade, afraid the rough texture of my hands would pull the shimmering threads. I had not worn anything so handsome in such a long time.

I hated the robe for the covetousness it inspired in me.

"Thank you. It is a kind thought," I admitted, "but there is no way to get a robe over my wings."

There. A practical thought. A practical reason not to accept it. I would not look ungrateful with the observation but solid and resolved. And I would not offend her.

"But I thought of that!" Alaina grabbed the robe up from the chaise and turned it around, draping it over her arm. She showed me the backside, two slits running down from the shoulder blades. "The middle section goes between your wings, and then there are clasps beneath." She pinched one of the gold braid clasps that echoed the military fastenings of the front and held it out for me to see. "Provided that the slits are at the right height, of course. I would like you to try it so that I can see. And if there's something wrong or off, it can be fixed."

Someone I cared about offered me material consideration beyond some token access to fire or a cute little picnic that would be over and done within an hour. The robe was a token of her world, of her world as a person and as a princess, that she was sharing with the creature of another. This was a gesture the likes of which she might have appreciated had our roles been reversed. This wasn't care of an animal. This was a gift, a fabulously expensive gift, from one person to another, and not just any other. This was a gift intended for someone dear.

She was dear to me. And somehow, I had become dear to her.

I took a step back, frightened a little by the import.

The glitter of her eyes dulled and her voice wavered with the evaporation of her joy. "Please try it?"

The soft request broke through my hesitance. I couldn't let myself be the cause of her unhappiness, and I couldn't bear to disappoint her after investing so much thought into her present.

"Yes," I said. "Thank you."

Alaina's radiant delight returned with my acquiescence.

"Arms in," she instructed as she held the robe up for me.

"Your sleeves won't fit me," I cautioned, "if this was one of your dresses."

"I thought of that too!" She hooked one of the openings over my arm. "A tight-fitting sleeve would certainly have prevented you from being comfortable, so I had the shoulders extended with gold braid and sleeve caps. And I had my sleeves replaced with bell sleeves so you have greater movement." She fitted the back of the robe over my wings and then pulled the other sleeve over my other arm. "I spent a lot of time figuring out how to make this work for you. That's why it took so long. I was hoping it would be ready the first week you were with me, and then I kept finding faults with the design."

The sleeves slipped down my arms, luxurious and silky. The fur trim lay gently reassuring on the backs of my hands. The fur collar warmed the back of my neck. I closed my eyes to enjoy the sensations and forget for just a moment everything that had occurred this past year that made this event so special.

"The slits look about the right height." Alaina fastened the robe under my wings and tugged on the fabric to straighten it out. "The length looks good too."

I took a deep breath and opened my eyes.

"It looks splendid on you." Alaina stood before me and began fastening the clasps up the front. "How does it feel?"

I swallowed around a lump and could not find my voice.

"Does it feel all right?" she asked again when she finished.

I nodded, unable to respond with anything more coherent.

"It suits you." She took several steps back to study her handiwork. "Truly. You look so handsome."

Unshed tears burned the corners of my eyes, and I could not tell her why. I could not tell her that I once wore elegant clothing. I could not tell her that I had once worn it beautifully and without pretense. I could not tell her that I had never worn feathers before under such fine clothes. I could not tell her that I never again expected to be called handsome, even in clothes that were objectively so.

I would not cry in front of her. I would not.

"What's wrong, Kaylay?"

I took a measured breath to hold back the tears just a few moments longer since I had no valid excuse, to her anyway, for weeping.

"I told you not to make a man of me," I choked out.

She flinched.

"What's next?" I asked insensitively. "Will you glove my hands to hide them? Or will you pluck the feathers from my face?"

"I just wanted to give you something pretty. That's all."

The slight tremor in her voice betrayed deep hurt. She turned away from me to hide her own tears. Despite the bitterness I had summoned to keep mine in check and the conviction that, after everything, I had no more to shed, I silently joined her. I had forgotten how to be gracious, and I had wounded her in the process of maintaining the most tenuous hold on my dignity.

"I'm sorry, Alaina," I whispered. "You didn't deserve that."

"The tsarina treats you shamefully. Of course, that's what you would think." She turned to face me, doing as poor a job wiping at her tears as I was doing to my own. "Truly, I didn't mean—"

"I know," I assured her. "I know."

I held my arms out for her, an offer that the beautiful, shining sleeves made acceptable. I could never have done it with feathered arms.

She walked into them, wrapped her arms around me, and buried her face against my chest. I enfolded her in my arms too, and we stood there for moments that passed like hours, bodies pressed against each other for warmth, for affection, for reassurance. We were all each other had, and I refused to let any sad semblance of pride separate us.

"You went through all that trouble for me. You thought of every practical detail to make it suitable for my strange form.

And I behaved with such ingratitude. Forgive me? Please?"

"Of course, I forgive you." She released me and stepped back, running her hands down my arms to take my hands. "I didn't think how you might perceive it."

"I was being needlessly defensive." Mostly as a cover for other vulnerabilities I couldn't own, but that was no excuse. "This took great thought and consideration. I am ill-suited for such things, but thank you."

"You are not ill-suited." She squeezed my hands. "Would you come and see?"

I didn't want to. I had done it before, and the image seared itself into my memory. I had avoided mirrors since, not needing the reminder of the nightmare I had become.

But Alaina held my hands. She stared up into my face and smiled. I wore something beautiful and elegant because of her, given a measure of dignity by it that no other had afforded. She even called me handsome. And if she had asked me to do anything right now, I did not think I could say no.

I followed her through her bedroom and into her dressing room, where she too had her golden-framed pier mirror. I stood stark against the sea of glimmering satins and pastel accessories, but part of it now by virtue of the blue brocade. Beyond the mirror being on a different wall, the circumstances aligned so closely as with the tsarina that I almost had to retreat. But I didn't. Beyond her requests of the firebird — to go home, to not be alone — she had never asked anything of me. And I had never been able to give her anything beyond my pathetic excuse for company. I could give her this.

Alaina never dropped my hand, even when I stumbled, the bells on the anklets marking every step. Instead, she clasped my hand with both of hers and stood beside me while the creature stared back at us from the glass.

And it wasn't hideous. Strange, yes. Unnatural, yes. But the black feathers shone blue-green in the muted light against the brocade, and the deep sable intensified the green of my eyes.

I raised my clawed hand to my chest and stroked down the blue brocade, every gold braid fastening a prominent bump along the way.

"The robe is beautiful," I said. "It's finer than wedding clothes, and much finer than anything I have seen worn at court."

"It suits you completely." She released one hand to smooth down the guard hairs of the sable fur on the collar. "It doesn't interfere with your tail feathers, does it?"

"No. Thank you."

She leaned her head against my arm and watched us together in the mirror, her fingers laced through mine, a small dreamy smile playing at the corners of her mouth. Was she imagining the day she could return to Altania? Or maybe of the day we could go together? Whatever her pleasant thoughts, I so longed to be part of them, even if my role consisted of nothing more than sitting silently at her feet while she read to me by the fire.

I could not imagine any future, however unpleasant all my current options seemed to be, without her there, somewhere, being part of my life. The most, and best, I could hope for would be to be her pet in Altania. My obstinate mouth would probably not let me be silent for the rest of my days, but in Altania, she would set the standards, and I may not have to watch myself so carefully. Although, since I knew almost no Altanian, I may not have much to say.

And if she couldn't have me or didn't want me there....?

I tried not to think about that. It was a real possibility that, despite talking to me of going to Altania, she would not be allowed to bring me if her brother refused. Or, worse, if my presence was so wrapped up with Ilyichia and her unpleasant time trapped here, she might wish to leave me behind, even despite her protests.

I didn't know when this pint-sized princess had wormed her way into my heart, but she was there, tucked safely away, and there was no way to extract her now. I didn't ever want to be without her. And the contemplation of separation hurt worse than I could comprehend — almost like losing Irena all over again.

"You really like it?" she asked.

"You've given me back some of my dignity." I squeezed her hand. "Thank you."

"I know clothes are somewhat superficial, but they make the point. No one else may understand how special you are, but I do. And I want everyone to see it." She hugged my arm. "And I want everyone to know how special you are to me."

XXVI.

Alaina joined me in the anteroom shortly after her maid left. Freshly powered, her dark braids wrapped about her head, and wearing a dress that could probably hide an entire herd of sheep beneath it without anyone the wiser, her expression did not convey the same careful attention as the rest of her. She twisted her fan in her hands and kept fussing with the ribbon around her decolletage.

"I fear it will be a late night," she said.

"What's tonight?" I stood from my place by the fire and crossed over to her.

"Some musicians from the south."

"Is that not to your liking?"

"It's not that," she said. "It should be a pleasant night, musically anyway."

"Then?"

"It's me. Everything feels tight or scratchy, or it doesn't lay right. I think I need new stays. I went through eight gowns, all of them just wrong for no real reason except that I didn't feel good in them." She shot me a glance. "And don't tell me that I'm fortunate to have eight gowns to try on. I know I am. And that's the problem. All these beautiful things, and I don't look or feel beautiful in them."

I didn't think Alaina expected me to compliment her. It was the right cue for any interaction between a lady and a gentleman, but so many things would never have happened between us if she had been just any lady and I still a gentleman. And however cutting our teasing could be, I would not do anything to worsen her anxieties.

"I suppose, for a human, you look beautiful," I said, maintaining an air of study. "Some plumage and respectable wings, maybe I might actually think you so."

"Alas." She smiled, dropping her hands that worried at her ribbons. "We cannot all be firebirds like you, with spectacular plumage given to us naturally."

I would never have called my plumage natural, but I couldn't say that to her.

"What is it you do not like?" I gestured with a hand that she should turn around and let me see her from all sides.

"I don't know." She twirled obediently. "I feel too fussy and ruffled most of the time. Right now, I think I feel… underdressed? This gown hardly has any ornamentation compared to the others, but it's the only one I didn't want to tear off the moment I put it on. And is it the wrong color?"

The blue was darker than it probably should have been for her complexion, but the creamy trims kept it from being unstylish. She wore small jewelry and nothing in her hair. I understood her reasoning for feeling underdressed. No doubt every other lady would attend the event dripping in jewels.

I couldn't offer her jewels or dresses or anything that I might once have been able to provide, but I should have been able to help somehow, even with just moral support. Maybe something for her hair?

"It's a matter of plumage, as I said," I decided at last. "You need more."

"That is remarkably unhelpful. What do you propose I do, sprout feathers?"

"I have enough for both of us. I have been struggling to find a way to repay you for the gift of the robe."

"You don't need to repay me for that. That was freely given."

"And so too will this be." I stretched out a wing. "Take one of the golden feathers for your hair."

"Won't that hurt you?"

"I am allowed to make my own sacrifices. Please. I want you to have it."

"If you're sure." She approached, watching me all the while as if I might change my mind. Her choice, designed to deliver the least amount of pain, was not of sufficient size for what I envisioned.

"Alaina, a little tuft isn't going to do it. One of the larger ones."

"I can't." She dropped her hands and looked at me, an admonishment resting in the furrow of her brows. "I won't. I saw how losing feathers hurt you. I won't be one of those who prefer a feather over your wellbeing."

"You're making this difficult."

"And you're making this impossible. Thank you. No."

I stared her down for a long moment. Her refusal to back down decided me. I reached to my wing, found the longest red-gold feather, and yanked it out. The pain that shot through my back rivaled the initial agony of getting wings at all, and the spot doubtless bled a little, but there it was in my hand. Alaina's feather.

I presented it to her.

"The final ornament for your hair."

"Kaylay, I can't. That hurt you."

"So, ensure my hurt was not endured in vain and take it. Please."

She stared at the feather I held between us and finally relented. She took it and twirled it around. Then she brushed it against her cheek, her eyes distant, a sweet, thoughtful look on her face. When she remembered I was still present, she stopped twirling it.

"I will treasure it always," she assured me.

"I expect you to." I took her by the shoulders and physically redirected her towards her bedroom door. "Now, go pin it in your hair with a brooch. After, you can help me with my robe."

She stopped and looked at me over her shoulder. "Your robe?"

"What's the use of having it if I cannot show it off a little?"

"You're coming with me?"

"Of course, I am. You did not invite me, but I will forgive you for the oversight just this once. What better ornament than your very own firebird?"

She rewarded me with a brilliant smile and then dashed off to her bedroom to fix the feather in her hair.

The woman who came out of the bedroom the second time was not the same as the one who had come out the first. This Alaina laughed and grinned and teased as she helped me with the robe, the brilliant, gleaming feather tucked neatly in her braids and held with a small blue jewel.

"I didn't think you would want to go," she said when she finished fastening the clasps.

"I do not savor my time among others of court, but who would I be if I did not come to my lady's aid in times of need?"

"Am I?" She blushed. "Your lady?"

"Naturally," I said, downplaying the possible import of her words because I did not know how to grapple with that in my current situation. Especially since I had to ask a question I did not want to ask. "Will you be using the lead for me tonight?"

"I hadn't thought about that." The frowning discontent princess of earlier returned. "I don't want to."

"Should I stay a few respectable paces behind you then?"

"Ugh, I hate that too." She nibbled her bottom lip. "Couldn't you just, you know, escort me properly?"

"I could, but is that realistic for a creature who is not supposed to understand what is going on?"

"Mute doesn't mean stupid or unintelligent. Who's to say that you haven't been observing proper behavior? I can direct you like I would a toddler, if I must: sit here, go there. And maybe, you can make enough noise with your ankle bells tonight that the tsarina will finally let me take them off you too."

"Not likely. She likes it when I…. When she…." How could I relate that delicately? "She likes the noise during…. You know."

"I hate them even more now."

"I endure." I did not wish to dwell on the sad reality of my time with the tsarina because I was with Alaina now, and I did not want the tsarina to taint our time together. I offered Alaina my arm instead. "Shall we?"

"Thank you, Kaylay."

She took my arm and beamed up at me. And in her delight and joy and eagerness, I didn't feel like the abomination the tsarina meant me to be. To my strange little princess, maybe I wasn't a man, but I could still be her evening hero in feathers.

As Alaina predicted, the music offered a pleasant night's entertainment. Everything else, not so pleasant. Most gave us strange looks when we entered, her on my arm, my feather in her hair. It took all my restraint not to fall into the manners I had been practicing my whole life. I couldn't guide her, seat her, or get her anything. She guided us. She pointed me to a settee and settled the cushion at her feet. I had to not stand for the tsarina when she entered, and the tsarina did not notice me until well into the entertainment.

In keeping with the role assigned to me, I hissed at one of the ladies who came too close to Alaina. My feral incivility kept everyone away from us, beyond the occasional servant compelled to offer food and drink. Alaina played her part too and petted me to ensure I behaved throughout the festivities.

The tsarina cast dagger-sharp glares in our direction once she noticed us, but I just looked at her wide-eyed and innocent. How could I refuse the princess' offer when I wasn't supposed to speak? A tantrum? Hardly. And if the tsarina interrogated me on our next encounter, I would tell her the truth of Alaina being good to me. Nothing the tsarina saw would contradict what either of us would be telling her.

This was not a game anyone but the tsarina could win, and I hoped Alaina realized that by now. We couldn't play to win our freedom or our happiness. We could play though to endure until something more effective at disrupting the tsarina's odds stepped in, like illness. And if we reassured the tsarina that she was winning, then we could also play to give ourselves moments of rest. A dangerous way to live, but we had no choice. I might have even been more reckless with how I played, but I had to think of Alaina now. While it didn't matter what happened to me anymore, I refused to let her suffer because I did something rash. Befriending her was rash enough.

When the tsarina departed the night's entertainment, her disregard and typical sour expression giving no indication if she had been dwelling on my attendance or not, others followed her lead. We remained until the performance ended. Having been deprived of amusement the bulk of the year, I did not eagerly surrender my seat. And although Alaina could not know of my prior trials, she probably guessed at my desire to enjoy being outside of her rooms without being confined to restrictive measures. As the crowd thinned, Alaina patted my shoulder, leaving her hand there to keep me seated until we were nearly the last in the room. Then she lifted her hand and stood.

She yawned, an impressive noise partnered with a shudder

that shook her entire body, although she gracefully endeavored to keep both under control. Her eyes, red-rimmed and eager to hide behind her lids, betrayed her valiant efforts at staying awake.

I stood also, taking her cue, and she wrapped herself around my arm. She did not gesture or direct me, far beyond thought of managing me in the midst of her drowsiness. Fortunately, few people were about, and fewer people cared so late into the night. I led her through the public rooms and up through the wing to her apartment. She stumbled a few times, losing her grip on her dress, and when I did not think we would pass anyone else in the halls, I gathered her into my arms, confident it would result in fewer bruises and a faster return.

She curled up like a child and buried her fingers around a gold braid fastening. She snuggled her face into the blue brocade. When I adjusted her up against my shoulder, she tucked her face as much against my neck as she could between the fur and the collar. I squeezed her, keeping her tight against my chest, better now on my taloned feet than months ago. She was as light and as fragile as a bird herself, and I wished she could fly away home before someone in Ilyichia crushed her.

My initial motives consisted only of expedience and safety, but with her tucked against me and my arms put to pleasant service, I allowed myself to enjoy the brief connection and physicality this configuration offered. No one else could see it lest I reveal too much of my understanding, but I never wanted to put her down. It had been such a long time since I had held a woman in my arms, and this was a woman I wanted there.

I didn't expect that in the lowest point of my life, my dearest and truest friends would reveal themselves, but despite all, I could be grateful for them. I loved Klessa and Drook and all my friends who made my initial fall from grace bearable. And I loved Alaina, who had made my second fall, this time from humanity, so much less lonely.

I loved Alaina.

I was an idiot Ilyichian prince who never learned his lessons, it seemed. Alaina, who the tsarina had tried to recreate in her own image, would be the last person in the world the tsarina would tolerate being the recipient of my affections. So, of course, who else would I love but Alaina? If the tsarina ever found out, she would have both our heads.

I did not love the tsarina, not because someone else took pride of place in my affections but because the tsarina had never evolved beyond the stage of conflating ownership and obedience with love. She had not been asked to step aside because I loved another. She had been bypassed by all because she made herself impossible to love. She just refused to see it.

It wouldn't matter that my love for Alaina, or anyone else, did not preclude me from loving another. I could love infinitely in infinite ways. My love for Alexei was not the same as my love for Drook. My love for Drook was not the same as my love for Klessa. My love for Klessa was not the same as my love for Alaina. And my love for Alaina was not the same as my love for Irena. It couldn't be. Yet my love for all of them coexisted peacefully within me, did not drain my supply or impede my capability, and perhaps rather enhanced them.

It wouldn't matter that Alaina didn't reciprocate. Although if I said the words first, maybe Alaina would say them in return. And if Alaina reciprocated....

If Alaina reciprocated. If she told me. If the tsarina wasn't lying about there being a way out of wearing feathers and a beak for the rest of my life....

If Alaina reciprocated and we were still in Ilyichia, the tsarina's fury would be all the greater. There had never been a promise of freedom, at least not beyond not being a bird, not for me. And no promises had ever been made regarding Alaina. And even if the tsarina made promises, they could not be trusted.

I paused just outside of the door to Alaina's apartment and gazed down into her sleeping, peaceful face. Oh, to share in a moment of that tranquility!

What if the tsarina told me the truth? What if, in her drowse, Alaina murmured the words? Would I condemn her to greater suffering at the tsarina's hands by returning to my natural state? Surely, the tsarina would have to have everyone who bore witness to my continued existence executed to preserve her lie that I was dead.

I could only think of one absolute way to ensure that Alaina would never say those words to me. I could tell her who I was.

Still convinced that the tsarina was lying to me, I could be worrying about all of this for nothing. There was no way out. There would be no physical manifestation that someone had dared to tell me they loved me as I currently was. There would never be a trace that I had once been the disgraced prince Alaina so reviled.

But if the tsarina wasn't lying to me, telling Alaina who I was would both remove any possibility of the hope of changing again, which at this juncture might be the more merciful action, and it would ensure that she could not risk greater peril on my account.

Maybe I would tell her that I was Mikhail then.

It would hurt. Oh, Great Holy, would it hurt! When my confession hit and recognition finally settled, I would be unable to look at her, unable to bear her disgust. She would put distance between us. She would relinquish my care back to the tsarina. And why wouldn't she? She never wanted anything to do with a man in a costume, especially one he could not remove.

But it would assuage my conscience. And Alaina would be safe again. Well, safer than now.

I spied the door lever and gripped Alaina more tightly to my chest, preparing to go within. I wouldn't get many more opportunities like this to hold her, to be gentle with her, or to care for her while she would allow me. I pressed my cheek to the top of her head.

I would tell her in the morning. For now, I would let her dream of her friend, the one she wanted clad in feathers and with wings.

"Even if you end up hating me, I really am trying to do the right thing," I whispered to her. But I didn't know what I was doing. I had never had to navigate a plurality of identities before. I never had to pick which choice of all possible wrong choices was the least bad. "I'm so sorry."

"Kvasnik?"

My head jerked up. My back stiffened. Alaina stirred in my arms. A shiver traveled through my spine. That the speaker did not use Mikhail pricked at my skin. A call for Mikhail could mean any Mikhail. But she used Kvasnik, and Kvasnik could only mean me.

No. There could be no way. Granted, perhaps the timing between Mikhail's execution and my appearance on the scene might have been a little close together, but one did not immediately follow the other. I had been unconscious and detained for who knew how long before I ever showed up inside the palace again. And I had shown up as a different creature.

I had been on display in the audience chamber, in the foyers, at the tsarina's feet, in council, through the halls, outside in my enclosure. Everyone had seen that my feathers were part of me. Everyone had seen that my wings were attached. Everyone could see that this wasn't another, more extreme costume forced onto a man.

How then could anyone guess? Was magic something others believed in? I had never seen it. I had never even heard of it spoken of seriously. It wasn't something people witnessed. And if it had not altered me in undeniable ways, I might still not believe in it. How then did someone else identify me when I had been so careful?

"It is you, isn't it?"

I turned to look at the speaker.

She was a plain woman, perhaps around my age, dark eyes, her posture and manner straight and upright. Dressed like most other servants with a simple dress, apron, and covered hair, I could not place her. She had not been one of the servants to guide me in the early days of my disgrace. Perhaps she attended Alaina or the tsarina when she was ill. But why then would she call me Kvasnik? That was my name among friends, and I did not know her.

Alaina stirred again. She gathered the robe in her fist, dug her fingers into my chest, and murmured something.

I glanced between the sleeping princess and the servant who used my private name.

I wanted to interrogate the servant, determine what her relation to me had been that she might still see through this disguise, discover if one of the jesters had hired her to find out if it was truly me.

But I could not do it in front of Alaina.

If Alaina knew....

But Alaina was going to know tomorrow because I was going to tell her.

"I know it's you, Mikhail."

My public name, after the private, struck me like a musket ball, and I took a step back as if it truly had weight and force behind it. This wasn't a servant slipped a few coins to prod at me. This was personal.

I shook my head and fumbled for the lever handle of the door. When it clicked open, I shouldered my way into the apartment and closed it on the woman before she could say anything else. I leaned back against it to ensure she would not follow us in.

My heart raced. My hands shook.

Why wouldn't that woman just let Mikhail be dead?

Someone in the palace knew me, and she could tell others. She could humiliate me all over again by forcing me to bear the shame that came before in addition to the shame of now. She could tell the tsarina who would blame me and kill half a dozen others to keep it quiet. Worst of all, she could tell Alaina, and Alaina would abandon me.

Hadn't that been what I was planning to do anyway?

Having my old name waved in my face showed me the painful idiocy of that impulse.

I couldn't tell Alaina. I couldn't own that life anymore because it wasn't mine. I wasn't Mikhail. Mikhail was dead. Executed in disgrace. I was Kaylay, nothing but a sad Otherland creature in captivity.

Was it truly a lie of omission if I didn't tell Alaina? Would that make me dishonorable for not being upfront about my disowned history if I expected to wear feathers the rest of my days? In the end, it didn't matter. So long as I was not Mikhail ever again, I could never burden her with my humiliation. Even if it meant I had to continue to lie about everything to everyone, I would do it. And I could live with that.

I just needed that woman not to tell anyone of what she thought she knew. Alaina hating me now would be the most painful punishment I had yet endured.

XXVII.

I had long ceased staring at the fire, opting to close my eyes and absorb her words. Like the warmth of the flames, her voice washed over me, offering comfort and safety and peace. The pressure of her leg through her skirts against my shoulder kept me grounded and mindful of her soft company.

If I could be assured that this could be the rest of my life — quiet, peaceful evenings by the fireside with Alaina reading to me and the occasional excursion outside her apartments — I might be content. It wasn't the life I wanted or expected to have, but it could be worse than this. It had been worse than this.

Alaina paused in her reading, tucked in a ribbon to mark her place, and set the book on the side table. She stood from her chair and stretched. She looked down at me and smiled.

"I need some tea. Can I get you any?"

"No, thank you."

She crossed over to the samovar.

If I still had a proper mouth and not the damned beak, I might have accepted. A warm drink sounded delightful. To partake, I envisioned having to go over to the samovar, turn the spigot, and let the tea pour directly into my mouth like a savage. My pride, reduced to ashes at this point, still would not grant me such abandon.

"Why don't you tell me a story?" Alaina asked as she returned with her teacup and resumed her seat. "I tire of my own voice."

"Because all my stories end unhappily."

"Do you only know Allemandian tales then? Those are all

dreadfully depressing.”

“Many Ilyichian tales are also dark.”

“Surely, you can think of one that isn’t.”

“In a certain tsardom, in a certain country,” I said, “there was a princess who befriended a strange creature. And they remained friends all their days. The end.”

“While I like that one very much,” Alaina grinned, “that was too brief. What about folktales and such? Fairy tales?”

“They’re called wonder tales here.” I considered for a moment. “There’s the scarlet flower, where a merchant with three daughters asks them each what they want before he sets out on a voyage. The older two ask for splendid things. The youngest asks for the most beautiful scarlet flower in the world.”

“There is a Jeanvian story that is similar.” She said something in Jeanvian, presumably the title of the story, that I could only half translate. “Except the merchant in that one loses everything. Continue.”

“Although the merchant sees many beautiful scarlet flowers on his journey, none is the most beautiful. On his return trip, he is set upon by bandits and finds shelter in a magnificent palace where he is restored to health. And there, in the courtyard, is the most beautiful scarlet flower in the world, so he takes it.”

“Does a terrible creature appear and demand that one of the daughters come to live with him?”

“I see you know this story already. What need have you of me to tell it?”

“Don’t be like that. I’ll try not to interrupt.”

“Try,” I warned her. “And so the youngest daughter goes to the palace where she is treated like a princess and given every comfort and luxury she could imagine.” I paused because this seemed like a moment when Alaina would interject. “Any commentary?”

"No." Then she asked, "What does she think of the creature in this tale?"

"He hides so that he cannot frighten her. If she knew what he was, she would not want him. And yet, despite his precautions, he is revealed to her eventually. She finds him horrific and returns home."

"Is that all?"

"No. I'm just giving you ample opportunity to contribute so that you are not speaking over me before I go on."

"How considerate. Do continue."

"At home, she is surrounded by people who treat her poorly and who wish to hurt the creature that has been looking after her. She returns to him, and when she agrees to marry him, he transforms into a prince. All very routine and maudlin."

"The Kind and Fair are in the Jeanvian one, but it ends the same."

"There's another called Finist the Falcon that starts similarly, where instead of a scarlet flower, the youngest daughter asks for a feather from the famous bird prince, Finist."

"I don't know that one." Alaina sipped her tea. "Tell me."

"Her father finds it and gives it to her. But Finist, now that the girl has possession of his feather, can begin to visit her. He comes with the aid of a magic ring each night to woo her and share her bed. But her sisters get jealous and injure him on one of his visits. And then she leaves to find him and marries him to see him healed."

"Is he a bird who bears the title of prince, or a shapeshifter, or a prince who has been transformed into a bird?"

Maybe I shouldn't have mentioned Finist the Falcon or any other tale of transformation. They suddenly all seemed a little too telling. Had others endured my fate for there to be stories about it?

"It all depends on the teller of the story," I said. "They're good for children, but princes are boring when you live at court."

Indeed, good for children. At my age, I expected to be telling wonder tales to my own. Now, I would never have any.

"The stories are just downright cruel," Alaina said. "If you're a princess and told growing up that you'll find love, especially when that's the least likely scenario possible, it sets one up for a lifetime of disappointment."

Love was definitely a precious commodity between nobles. And even if you were fortunate enough to have it, as I had been, the price could be dear, which I also found out.

"Are you a prince, Kaylay? Is that why you're so unique?"

"No," I said honestly. I hadn't been reinstated. I wasn't a prince. Not anymore. "I'm an amusement."

"So you aren't Finist the Falcon or the keeper of a scarlet flower? If you tell me that you are a prince in the Otherlands, I won't be surprised."

Like the creature of the scarlet flower, I did not want her looking at me too closely. Not that I thought she ever looked that closely at me when I was Mikhail, but if she saw me, truly saw me as that unknown woman had, Alaina would leave me too.

"I am Kaylay, not Finist," I said, "and I have no magic rings or flowers, scarlet or otherwise."

"But you gave me one of your feathers," she said. "And here you are, with me every night. Is that what I need to do, Kaylay — agree to marry you?"

"I would never ask so high a price as marriage."

"I would never be at liberty to give you such a price if you demanded it. Only the tsarina could form such a match while I am here in Ilyichia."

"Or your brother, if you were in Altania?"

"I am above the age of needing his consent."

"Then you might agree on your own behalf?" I asked, more than a little surprised. "I hope not. You should not sell yourself so cheaply."

"Well, no," she said. Then she added, "But I would still be open to being wooed."

I didn't know how to take that statement, which should have been spoken more like a confession, and yet, she said it proudly, boldly, no trace of shame.

"Are you absolutely sure you're not one of these folklore legends?" she asked again. "I think you would make a fine candidate."

"I'm supposedly the firebird. Or have you forgotten?"

"Oh yes! Tell me about the firebird?"

"The firebird doesn't have its own story. It's just a device to tell the stories of others, much like I will be when biographers write about you, if I am mentioned at all."

"You might be a little too fantastical for anyone dull enough to write a biography about me. I'm just a little princess in a country that doesn't want me but refuses to give me up."

"The tsarina was a little princess too, in Talvia, once, and now she wields more power and influence than most monarchs." I gazed up at Alaina, reassessing, and then I nodded. "There is greatness in you. I can see it plainly. I think there was greatness in her too, but she let bitterness gnaw it away."

"Maybe she wouldn't have, if she had her own Kaylay to remind her who she was in Talvia."

"You need to remember the lessons you learned here when you are queen of Altania. Don't rule as she does. There's a reason they call her The Terrible even while she lives."

Alaina blushed, betraying her knowledge of the tsarina's nickname.

"She pulled me aside today," Alaina said, her voice a

whisper. "She wanted to know why I keep bringing you to entertainments."

Had that woman who recognized me that night said something to the tsarina? Was talk circulating, enough that even the tsarina took notice?

"I told her that, ordinarily, I wouldn't, but she seemed to have made such strides in training you that I was confident you could be trusted to join me without disruption. She keeps telling me to take care of you, and yet, when I do it, I don't think she likes it."

"She wants to be the only one to command my obedience." I sighed and settled my head on Alaina's lap. "I'm sorry if I've made things more difficult between you. Maybe you shouldn't bring me anymore."

"But you enjoy it!" She stroked my head gently. "And I don't want anyone else's company but yours, even if we cannot speak in public."

"If she questioned you today, she is going to want to reassert her power over me soon, even if it's just a few hours, to remind me of my true master."

"Do you think she would take you away from me?" Alaina's hand stilled. "I couldn't bear that."

"I will not tell you that it is impossible. Like you, I don't think she wants me either, but she will not let me go. So we must tread carefully. Leave me behind the next few events, and if she asks, tell her I'm being difficult."

"I don't like it." Nonetheless, Alaina resumed petting me. "We need to leave Ilyichia soon. We need to go somewhere she can't touch us."

"Wouldn't that be nice?" I didn't see it as a realistic possibility. If the tsarina would not let Alaina leave, then she was stuck here. And if she was stuck, so was I. "Maybe someday."

Alaina finished her tea, yawned, and then guided me off

her lap. She stood and smoothed her skirts. She petted the top of my head as she passed me and disappeared into her bedroom.

I stood also and put out the candles. I rearranged the cushions and grabbed my blanket off the chaise. I settled back down in front of the hearth to wait for her to come back so that I could say good night.

She floated in like a ghost only a few minutes later, her white nightshift stark against the shadows, the chamberstick flame thin and tenuous. She crossed over to me and held out her hand palm down. As per what had become our nightly ritual, I took it and pressed the back of her hand to my temple, in deference and in affection in the absence of the kiss I could not bestow with a beak.

"Good night, princess."

Instead of her usual "good night, Kaylay," she set the chamberstick down on the side table, took a seat on the chaise, and never let go of my hand. Instead, she put her newly free hand over mine.

"Is everything all right?" The shift in routine alerted me to new stiffness in her posture and resolve in her grasp.

"Yes," she said. She smiled, the gesture absent and distracted, secondary to thoughts she had not yet given voice. "You know, Kaylay, you don't have to sleep on the floor."

"I know." I squeezed her hand, touched by her concern. "But the chair doesn't accommodate me, and the chaise is not long enough."

"I didn't mean the chair or the chaise," she whispered.

"Then?" I stared at her a moment, and she didn't elaborate. "I know you don't mean the cage," which still resided in the anteroom.

"Of course not."

"And you certainly aren't proposing that I climb into bed with you."

Alaina averted her eyes at that suggestion and nibbled her bottom lip. The implication silenced me as effectively as the muzzle. And she didn't say no. She flicked her gaze to me, a question set deeply into her brows.

"You're not serious," I gulped around my shock.

"Why shouldn't I be?" Alaina's gaze fully returned with her affront. "The tsarina keeps you in her bed."

"She keeps me on the floor."

"Even for....?"

"We don't sleep," I said, correcting Alaina. "And I never share her bed."

"I hate her!" She worried at my hand in her grasp. "You should be afforded a bed. I would like to share mine with you."

"I cannot."

"I am not a maiden," she argued.

"I did not realize you were proposing that kind of arrangement."

Not that I hadn't had silly little daydreams about being able to be freely affectionate and intimate with her. But that's all they were — daydreams, what ifs, illusions of possible joys — all devised to keep me alive for the here and the now. That was all. They were never intentions or plans for the future. She was a princess. It didn't matter what the folktales said. A princess wouldn't want a monstrous bird. I chose to ignore that the tsarina did.

"I was just reassuring you that in accepting my offer, you wouldn't be sullying my purity," she said.

Things had somehow become very serious very quickly, so I asked to keep it barbed, "What purity?"

"Then you should have nothing to worry about!"

I glanced at the doorway of her bedroom. "I cannot."

"Is this like the last time? Do you think I will hurt you like she does?"

"No, but...." I withdrew my hand from her. "I am content

out here. Good night, princess."

I settled myself in front of the hearth as usual. Alaina rose from the chaise without any additional protest and retrieved the chamberstick, taking the hint. The muffled sounds of her slippered feet against rug grew distant with her retreat into the bedroom.

I breathed more easily knowing that I had won this small test of wills. Why then did some nasty nagging little piece of me point out that I was disappointed?

A stupid, pathetic tear slipped over what had once been the bridge of my nose. I studied my talon-tipped fingers, my scaled palms, and the feathered backs of my hands and arms in the firelight. Could such hands provide warmth and intimacy in the bedroom, no matter what the arrangement? The tsarina still wanted me like this. Could Alaina?

Alaina's steps grew louder as she returned to the antechamber. I couldn't find enough voice to ask if she had come back to torment me, and by the time my voice could rise above my distressed contemplations, she had laid a pillow down behind me and joined me on the floor. She cuddled against my back, as much as she could given my wings.

"Alaina, what are you doing?"

"If you will not join me in my bed, then you leave me no choice but to join you in yours."

"Alaina." My throat tightened.

"It won't be the same," she promised. "We can just sleep. That's all. Just sleep. Just like this."

"You're a princess."

"And you're my friend."

"And your friend can sleep on the floor, especially when that friend is the court pet."

"That's an even worse objection," she scolded me. "Any pet would sleep on my bed with me. They would not fight me about it like a certain contrary creature."

I did not know how to combat that logic. Most of the nobles at court with pets babied them. And yes, they probably shared their owners' beds too.

"You are out-maneuvered, Kaylay." She ran a fingertip over the ridge of my wing. "Admit it."

"You are only thinking of yourself in this," I whispered.

"I just want to be close to you." She withdrew her hand. "Do you not want to be close to me?"

"Please." The lack of her touch stole my warmth despite the fire.

"Please stay? Or please go?"

Yes. Yes, yes, yes. Please. And I didn't know how to explain it to her.

I didn't want to tell her the truth, the shameful reality of my own weakness, and how, even misused, I could still not banish longing. It would tarnish me in her eyes still further. But there was nothing else that I could tell her to explain my conflict.

"Regardless of my form," I said, "I am not immune to wanting."

"Wanting," she repeated, her voice devoid of the judgment I was certain it would contain. She replaced her hand on my wing. "What is it you want?"

"Please, do not encourage futile desires."

"Does the tsarina not…? I thought—"

"Sex and affection are two very different things." I pulled away from Alaina, disturbed in a variety of ways, and sat up, resigned that I would not be sleeping for a long while.

"Does the tsarina not give you affection?"

"No more than your husband likely gave you."

"Don't you dare bring Pytor into this! My relationship with—"

"You understand duty, necessity, ownership," I continued, talking over her protestations. "You understand the danger of refusing. And like most noble women, you laid back, submitted, and endured. Sometimes you even considered taking a lover on the side to offer you the intimacy that your legal bedmate refused to give you."

"What does any of this have to do with—?"

"*What do you think I do?*"

Alaina stopped. She stopped touching me. She stopped speaking. She just stopped.

I hated the silence, but I could not fill it. My heart thudded like I had been running. My back ached from the stiffness. And I didn't want to say anything else to Alaina.

I bowed my head and regretted my honesty. Alaina was my only company, and she was good company, keeping me from dwelling too long on my impossible situation. But even to her, though we called each other friends, I was but another amusement. Like I was to the tsarina. But, unlike the tsarina, if Alaina lost interest in me, I would lose everything all over again.

"I hate having serious conversations with you," I confessed at long last. "They always become too serious. You're going to grow bored of me."

"I wouldn't."

"Not yet."

"I don't know that I ever could be," she said. "I enjoy tormenting you too much. Which is why I am insisting on sleeping beside you."

"A torment indeed."

"Kaylay?" She reached out and touched my arm. "I don't want to sleep on a floor."

"Then don't. You have a bed."

"It is cold and lonely, and you will not join me in it."

"It is not right that I should."

"It is my bed," she said, "and I am your social superior. I get to determine what is right or not. And I declare that it is right."

I didn't answer.

"I don't want sex," she said. "I want affection. I want *your* affection."

She released her hold on my arm and sought out my face. When she found it, she placed both hands on my cheeks and bent my head down. Her lips pressed to my brow.

"I don't know about the ladies in the wonder tales," she whispered, "but I can appreciate the magic in my life."

That almost set me to weeping again.

"Come to bed with me. Please." She stood and found my hand, tugging me up with her.

This time, I was helpless to resist. I stood and followed. The warmth from the connection of our hands radiated through me. I would have followed her anywhere to maintain it. She released my hand only when we reached the head of her bed.

Sense returned with the breakage of connection. I took a step backward. "I can't."

"Kaylay!"

"I will defile you."

There it was, the other unspoken truth I did not wish to commit to words. I would lower her. I would ruin her. And I didn't want to do it even at her request. She would never know that I had been Mikhail, but her rejection at the ball left a lasting mark. Even now, wearing a form so different from my last and bearing another name, I still feared making her ridiculous. A princess and a monster. Wasn't that ridiculous?

"The tsarina keeps you as a lover. If it does not defile her—"

"The tsarina defiles herself beyond any measure I may."

Alaina sought my hand, took one, then took the other. She led me back to the bed.

"You had the right of it when you described my marriage

to Pytor. I have not known one content moment in my bed since my arrival in Ilyichia. But I have known affection, and that has all been from you.”

“Then,” I said with great reluctance, “as a pet. At the foot of your bed.”

“Beside me. Princess Alaina commands it.”

“Then I most certainly refuse.”

“You will not join me when I command it on principle. And you will not join me when I ask it as your friend. What must I do?” She raised the backs of my hands to her mouth and kissed my knuckles. “From one lonely person who wants to be held and cuddled, who wants to feel safe and valued, to the only person she cares about in this entire country — please, Kaylay. Lie beside me. Ease my nights? Let me ease yours? Please.”

If I hadn’t been a monstrosity, the warmth of her tone might have suggested that we become lovers too. For a man, the invite was there. But for her strange friend with wings, it was a far more intriguing proposition — an offer of softness.

“Yes,” I whispered.

She climbed backwards onto the bed as she led me, releasing my hands only to draw back the blankets and tuck herself between them. She found my hand again and held it until I lied down beside her. She fit herself against me, placing her head on my shoulder, throwing her arm over my chest. She took one deep breath and then let it out, and with it, all tension and space between us as she relaxed into me.

I longed to enjoy the connection and the care, but all I could imagine was the tsarina bursting through the apartment doors on some pretext and finding us together, limbs entwined, Alaina’s face tucked against me, compromised in our closeness.

I wrapped my arms around her on instinct, as if I could protect her.

"This is dangerous, Alaina," I whispered to her in the dark. "Why?"

"Because the tsarina does not share." I stroked her back absently through the shift. "I do not have much to lose, but you do."

Alaina buried her face in my chest and mumbled something that I interpreted as "I don't care."

I wanted to tell her, "Remember, there was a prince who had everything taken from him because he told her 'no.'" But I couldn't because I wasn't supposed to know about that.

"You will need to do something about the sheets since I shed feathers," I said instead. "And we should probably lock the doors. If she should find us—"

"Kaylay, shhhh. She's never been in my apartments."

I wanted to argue, but I did not want to think of the tsarina. I did not want all the fear and worry and doubt she inflicted on both of us to ruin our time together. Instead, I referred to our earlier conversation.

"Recall the folklore. Stories are cautionary. If I visit each night and share your bed, a jealous person is bound to harm me. And then you might have to marry me to fix it."

"Mmm," she said, a smile built into the sound. "I could do worse." She stretched up and kissed the underside of my chin before returning to her place on my shoulder. "I could do so much worse."

XXVIII.

She locked the doors when the last maid left the room. She leaned back on them as if it might not be enough.

"Kaylay, they know."

In my situation, there were a lot of things that a lot of people knew. That unidentified woman knew I was Mikhail. The caretaker and Drook knew, although I had never proven their theories correct, that I spoke. The tsarina, to whom I owed my situation, knew almost everything about it.

"Who are we talking about and what do they think they know?"

Alaina came away from the doors, glancing over her shoulder at them as if the tsarina might walk in and make an official accusation. She passed her chair by the hearth and instead took a seat on a cushion beside mine. She took my nearest hand and spoke to it instead of me.

"While at the countess' salon today, one of the ladies brought up how resourceful I've been in making you my lover."

I was unsurprised. Alaina, too, had to know that was coming. With feathers on her blankets, she could not avoid such talk.

"Of course, the others joined in. And the accusation came partnered with the usual insults," she continued, "about ugly Altanians and no one wanting me. And how the only creature I could persuade to have me would be one who couldn't say no."

"They describe the tsarina, not you."

"It matters not who they describe. The tsarina will hear

238

about it.”

“What did you say when they made this accusation?”

“I laughed. They said it as a tease, of course, so that they could always say it was never truly meant if the tsarina’s ire should extend to them too for repeating such indecency. But I told them what perverted minds they had since it had never crossed mine to look at you in such a way.”

“Good.” I squeezed her hand. “That was the correct answer.”

“Was it?” She gazed up into my face. “Truly? I hate having to malign or diminish you to others. I feel like such a false friend.”

“Here, it is survival. Now, if we were in Altania, where you have the authority to raise me up or strike me down with a word, and you spoke of me with disparagement, I might then feel betrayed. Do not fret on my account here.”

“I cannot help it.”

“I have been doing my part while you’ve been gone,” I assured her. “I have made certain that the maids have found me sleeping on your bed. There are reasons for feathers on your blankets besides whatever salacious accusation sounds the most titillating at the time.”

“I just want to go home to Altania,” she said. “We would be safe there.”

“I probably shouldn’t sleep with you anymore.”

That pulled her from her consideration of Altania.

“Kaylay, no. Please.”

“I did not realize how the gossip might affect you.” Of course, she’d be horrified. A friend who was a monstrous bird was bad enough, suggestive of her desperation for any connection. But suggesting that same monstrous bird served other functions? Utterly insupportable. “You should not be subject to the rumors that have occurred because of the tsarina. Just because she has unique proclivities does not mean you share in them."

"I hate lying," she said, turning her face away from me.

"It's survi—"

"Yes, I know. But lying to you isn't survival."

"Oh." I waited, but when she did not say anything else, I pried. "What have you lied to me about?"

"About not thinking of you like that. You told me you were not immune to wanting." Her voice lowered to the barest whisper. "Neither am I. But I don't want to be her."

"You share her unique proclivities?"

"No!" She turned back to me and then cast her eyes down to our hands. "I mean, not in general? But yes, maybe?" She looked into my eyes, her brows quirked. "It's not like I've spent my entire life wanting to bed a firebird. I never even considered it before."

"Before?"

"Before you." Her cheeks flooded with color. "I trust you, Kaylay. And you're the only one I would trust like that." She squeezed my hand. "That's why the rumors bother me so, because they're true, in spirit if not in deed. And I have to deny it, even when I would rather not."

I didn't know how to respond to that.

As a man, I had been accustomed to ladies vying for me and my attention, their intentions obvious, their goals clear. I, as a person, had always been secondary to the title, the wealth, and the charm. But even in a chicken costume, divested of title and wealth, the charm still presided, swaying ladies when I thought I had nothing. As the tsarina's firebird, when I could not openly be charming or claim the reputation that had once been mine, when my physical circumstances lowered me beyond that of any degraded man, I found someone who seemed to want me as I was, even if I did not have the energy for charm and devolved too often into moodiness, sharpness, and sarcasm.

The princess was not Irena, but the similarity of earning her interest without the pretenses that attracted others shone like a beacon. *Here! Here! Safety, acceptance, and authenticity! Here, you could be loved!* False hope because I did not think anything could come of it. But her candor met me like an embrace all the same.

"I don't expect anything of you," she continued. "I would never. I don't want you to withdraw from me because you think I'm like her. Even admitting it to you feels like I've transgressed because I don't want it to alter what we have. You've been my dearest friend in Ilyichia. I am safe with you in a way I am with no one else. And maybe it would be wiser not to sleep together, but I don't want to give that up when it brings me so much comfort."

"Me too," I confessed.

She leaned her head against my shoulder and stared into the fire.

"What are we going to do?" she asked.

It was a good question. I was not much of a strategist. I hated court games. But here we were, needing strategy.

"I will maintain my innocence, of course," she said. "And I think I will loudly be upset with you for sleeping on my bed."

All wise courses of action.

"We need to get out of Ilyichia," Alaina added, "the sooner, the better."

Also wise, if it could be managed, but I did not have much hope.

"What about you?" she asked.

The tsarina hadn't summoned me yet to interrogate me about Alaina having me escort her to events. But she would at some point. And then, provided that she continued to leave me loose and did not keep me chained at the foot of her bed as had happened the last few times, maybe I could sneak off to fulfill my curiosity.

That meant playing the tsarina more daringly than Alaina had to know about.

"I am going to ask for help," I told Alaina, "from The Kind and Fair."

"It matters not what you are," the tsarina said as she entered the room. "You will always be the greatest thorn in my side."

I hadn't done anything. Not this time. Not that I could think of. Not yet. Had that woman gone to the tsarina and told her that she knew I was Mikhail? Surely not. Surely, that was madness. But maybe there were rumors if the woman had told someone who then told someone else who then told others. Then, viola! I was found out. The tsarina would have to execute a lot of people, and I would probably be muzzled for the rest of my natural life.

She stopped six steps into the room when she finally deigned to look at me. I expected her to order me off her bed, where I had settled once the guards brought me in. But she didn't say anything, not right away.

There had been talk. More talk. Alaina relayed it to me each day. Of course, the same murmurs had gone around about the tsarina when she first started sporting feathers on her undergarments, but it had not lasted because it was the tsarina. But with Alaina, the gossip would endure because she did not have the power to silence it. And the tsarina would hear about that gossip because it wasn't about her.

"I heard you've been spending time in beds," the tsarina said.

"Floors are cold."

"Is that all? The servants speak of more."

"The servants always speak of more." I flopped back onto

the bed, my wings splayed. Although Alaina and I agreed on our story for consistency, Alaina did not know that I too spoke to the tsarina. As a result, my personal course of action took a more reckless approach, if only to keep attention off the princess. "If she's not there, there's no point in wasting a perfectly good bed with a fire nearby. And it annoys her when I misbehave."

"What about when she takes you out of her apartments?" The tsarina approached her bed and sat on the edge of it. She stared down at me. "You behave for her then."

"Of course, I behave then. I'm bored otherwise." I pitched a whine in my voice. "You rarely have time for me."

"I am busy."

"And so I am entitled to get my amusements when and how I see fit. And if I must play to the princess to get my small reprieves, then what of it?" I stretched out my arm and settled my hand over hers. "So long as I am available when you are, I do not see why it should matter that I use her."

"You're using her?"

"Do you think I enjoy spending time with that horrid little Altanian?" I scoffed. "You insult me."

"And you surprise me."

"Did you think that I had forgotten how court works?"

"Sometimes," she said. The pinched creases of her mouth smoothed out and then twisted into a smile. "Are you using me, my dear?"

"I would if I could," I said, "but I don't think you could be used by me. You're the only person who knows who I am. You're the only one with whom I can truly be myself." I shifted onto my side, folding my wing under me. I propped myself up on my elbow. "I know you don't think I fully appreciate that, but I do."

She continued to stare at me. She was trying to read me, to see what my motives were, to see if she could trust my words.

But there was no obvious gain.

"How long do I have you today?" I asked.

"I do not have any obligations until tonight."

"Might I suggest a change of configuration then?" I sat up and inched over to her. I grasped her hand as it lay beneath mine and squeezed. "Let me lead?"

Her eyes narrowed, and she sat a little straighter.

"I have been in such need," I whispered like a confession. "It's been too long since last you called me to you." I raised her hand to my cheek. "Let me make you happy as I once did."

I released her hand, but she kept it on my cheek. Instead, I brushed the backs of my fingers against her face, suggestive and gentle.

"I know I am not the man you wanted, not anym—"

"I have always wanted you."

She stroked her hand down my face and neck. She stopped at the collar and traced her fingers over it. She paused when she reached the lead, tied up with Alaina's blue hair ribbon. She unclipped it from the collar and tossed it behind her.

With no additional persuasion, the tsarina surrendered to my undressing of her and my ministrations. She cooed and moaned and shook and, at length, she lay contented, spent utterly. I made sure of it.

I left her only to take a long drink of water from the pail that was left for me. Like any considerate lover, I poured tea from the samovar into a prepared cup and brought it over to her, anticipating her thirst as well. I sat on the edge of the bed and held it for her as she propped herself up to drink. She drained the cup, and I returned it to its place beside the samovar.

"Lie with me?" she asked from the bed.

I slipped between the blankets, holding my arms open for her. She pressed herself against my chest and closed her eyes. It was a matter of minutes before she slept, but I remained a while longer to ensure that the sleeping draught I had prepared in her cup before she entered the room, taken from among her medicines, set in.

I pried myself out of her arms and abandoned the bed. At the doorway to her private gardens, I attempted to borrow her wool cloak, but it wouldn't sit properly with the wings.

More incentive to be quick then.

I snuck out. My breath misted in the frosted air. Although snow had fallen, the frozen layer did not yield to my footsteps, and I breathed relief at not having left betraying tracks. I descended and followed the path the tsarina had first taken me on when I wore no feathers. When I reached the rose courtyard, I stopped just inside the doorway.

There were no roses on the bushes. There wouldn't be now in the cold, of course. I had no experience with roses, but they were like any flower, weren't they, even if they were magical? I should have known. But I wasn't thinking of flowers or seasons. I was thinking of the game I could not win and hoping I could replicate the tsarina's results in service to Alaina. Appallingly shortsighted and naive, my impulse had been well-meaning but ultimately pointless. What did I do without roses?

I may as well try anyway, after all the preparation to ensure this attempt. I hadn't been guaranteed success even with roses in full bloom. I wasn't a worthy supplicant anyway. Would a Kind and Fair with any power listen to a prince with no title, a man who wore the shape of a monster, and a convert of the Great Holy?

The basin in the middle of the bare bushes had frozen over, unreceptive and useless for an offering of blood. I addressed the nearest bush instead. I grasped a branch and pressed a fingertip into one of the thorns. It poked and sent a sharp pain through the finger, but it did not break my thickened skin. Instead, with my talons, I chose a place on the inside of my arm that would not be noticeable. The blood trickled out from the wound, and I wiped it up, transferring it to the branches. It soaked in, muted and negligible, a stark departure from the aesthetic tableau red blood on a backdrop of white snow should form.

"Please hear me," I whispered to the wind.

I waited, no sound or sign forthcoming. Nothing indicated that I had connected with the Otherlands or found a willing ear among The Kind and Fair. How long did it take? It happened for the tsarina in minutes, but presumably she left offerings frequently. If it happened for me, would it happen now? Should I wait?

I gazed up at the palace, at the line of windows that comprised the tsarina's apartments. She should be asleep for a couple hours, both from exertion and the tea. Still, I worried.

A small brown sparrow flew past me and perched on a twig of the bare rose bush. It studied me, the little head tilting and bobbing from side to side.

"Little friend," I cooed at it, "you should be south by now, enjoying the parasol pines in the Varnasian sun. If I could but fly like you, that's where I would be, not here in this miserable land."

It stared at me as if it understood what I said. I couldn't remember all the lore of The Kind and Fair, but didn't Otherland animals sometimes serve as messengers?

"If you are of the Otherlands, little friend, could you take a message for me?"

"Am I not a sufficient recipient for your message?" asked someone behind me.

I spun around. My heart beat frantically. I had been caught, found out, not just out of her apartments as if in another escape attempt, but speaking, and all would know that there was something else wrong and unnatural with me. And maybe others would figure out that I had once been Mikhail.

Alaina would abandon me, and I would again own all the shame of before in a shameful form.

But it wasn't the tsarina, and it wasn't a guard.

Someone stood off to the edge of the tsarina's garden, as pale and as brilliant as the white roses that graced the bushes in summer. The stark white hair lay coiled in a loose braid over their shoulder. They wore pale gold robes flecked with silver thread. Their mask and gloves, also pale gold, bore heavy, intricate metallic embroidery. Although nothing shimmered or glowed, the light reflected off them in a way that almost caused me to step backward. This had to be a Kind and Fair Protector. An impressive one.

The sparrow flew passed me again and took perch on The Kind and Fair's shoulder, studying me from its new vantage.

"Forgive me, my lord." I lowered myself to my knees and bowed my head. The Otherlands had answered, and this was no mere underling sent to relay a plea for help. "I did not realize that you had arrived. I have never done this before."

"Do you not find us worthy of your offerings?"

I did not look up to confirm my impression, but I could feel the assessment. My heart thudded against my ribs for a different reason than being caught by the tsarina. The tsarina could order things to be done, and people, earthly people, agreed to see her words carried out. This being, this Kind and Fair, possessed true power, the like of which needed no other to see it come to fulfillment.

"I have never needed to ask for anything until now," I said. "I never realized that I could."

"What then would you ask of me?"

I should have had my requests well-rehearsed and ready to offer. But I didn't believe that I would get this far, and I didn't have anything eloquent prepared. Words abandoned me in the presence of a being whose existence I had not believed in.

"As if I need to ask," the Otherlander continued in my

fumbling silence.

"No," I said with the surety I could not muster for anything else. I looked up at the Otherlander. "I have nothing to ask for myself."

"But you are human. Do you not wish to be again?"

"Fixing this," I held my hands out to him, "fixes nothing."

"I see." The tone grew more serious. "How came you to be this way?"

"I am not permitted to speak of it."

The Otherlander stepped forward and leaned down to get a closer look at me. He reached a gloved finger out to catch one of the leather ties on my wrist bindings. Then he withdrew.

"Who keeps you collared?" he asked.

"The empress."

"As a pet?"

"And more."

The Otherlander stiffened at that, his body poised in tense rigidity. His eyes narrowed. Waves of fury rippled off him.

I bowed my head again. Although I was not the target of his rage, I did not wish to further his frustrations and have them aimed at me.

"As you ask nothing for yourself, what is it you want?" he asked again after a long pause in which he regained his composure.

"There is a princess here at court who has become dear to me," I began. The wish sounded infantile now that I put words to it, unworthy of the power of this being who protected nations, but it was the only desire that deserved attention. "I fear for her safety here in Ilyichia. I desire her protection above all else."

"How much would you give to see her safe?"

"Everything."

"Would you die in service of her safety?"

So it would come to that.

I did not grieve. I had never deluded myself into thinking that something miraculous would give us a happily ever after. Even if Alaina brought me to Altania, we could never truly be together. Being human once more was a hope I no longer entertained. I would never kiss her. I would never see the summer sun again. I would never have children of my own.

But Alaina might if I could keep her safe.

"Yes, my lord. I will die for her."

"Loyalty is the virtue I prize above all others." The Otherlander approached me and knelt. His dark eyes stared into mine, compassionate, empathetic, kind. He raised his finger, the tip beginning to glow through the glove, and he put it to my forehead. "Even when it may cost you dearly, be true to her and she will be safe."

XXIX

Alaina noticed my distraction and ill temper before I could even put words to it, and gave me space to be temperamental at my leisure before we retired. We said little to each other as we took our respective sides.

In bed, I stared at the muted colors of the ceiling painting and the elongated dancing shadows of the molded plaster as the fire crackled in the hearth. No matter how I placed my wings, tight against me or splayed behind, I could not get comfortable.

Did the putti of the paintings and frescoes hate their wings too? They never looked as if they minded the unnatural appendages. Maybe it was because they were born with them. Were putti born though? Maybe they were created fully formed, wings and all, and did not know the difference. Or maybe they received them to indicate serving higher powers. Maybe they wouldn't resent them if the higher powers gave all their beloved messengers wings.

I was not a beloved messenger.

The collar choked me. The leather bands on my wrists and ankles pulled at small feathers. The ankle bells made hollow thunks when I shifted. The blankets bunched beneath me. I grew too warm beneath the blankets, but I was too cold if I put a leg or an arm outside of them. Everything hurt and annoyed.

"If you tell me about it, you will feel better," Alaina finally said.

What did I tell her? Everything was wrong and unfixable? Nothing was wrong because nothing had changed? Did I tell her that I expected her life to get a whole lot worse soon while I died protecting her?

My imminent death would be the last thing I could tell Alaina.

"I met a Kind and Fair Protector today," I told her, opting for the factual rather than the implications derived from the meeting.

"A Kind and Fair Protector?"

"Yes."

She scrambled to prop herself up on her elbow. She stared down at me. "How?"

"The tsarina has a private garden for her devotions. I used it."

I used the tsarina too, but that would be something I wouldn't tell Alaina either. After so long being the tsarina's unwilling lover, confessing to a willing, if exploitative, encounter might truly crystallize the impression of inconstancy.

"And you met a Kind and Fair Protector?"

"One came to hear my plea." Her next barrage of questions dangled in the air between us, most of which I did not want to answer. I cut her off. "I told you I was going to ask The Kind and Fair for help. He could not offer much."

Alaina did not settle for that. "How did you do it? How do you know he was a Kind and Fair? What did he look like? What did you ask specifically? Tell me everything!"

Not being able to tell her of the events that led up to it, the subject of my humanity, or the result of my concern for her well-being, I related a highly edited version that reduced the encounter to a pointless if awed meeting. Alaina harrumphed at the conclusion of my vague debriefing.

"I understand it is unsatisfying," I assured her lest she think I could not appreciate how underwhelming my story appeared. "I too am left grappling with the impression of great import tempered by the reality of material inconsequence. And you see too the reason for my distraction and vague annoyance at the world.”

“He could offer nothing?” Alaina flopped back onto the bed. “A Kind and Fair who could not help? What a useless being! No wonder people are converting to worshiping the Great Holy by the droves.”

“I think he means to help,” I corrected her, unwilling to let her think ill of The Kind and Fair who, for reasons beyond me, genuinely seemed to care about my plight. “I do not think he yet knows how. But,” I added, an item of hope coming to mind, “he did not seem impressed with the tsarina.”

“What do you mean?”

“He answered my call as if accustomed to responding to trivial summons.” Recalling it yet again solidified an idea that I had to verbalize. “The tsarina is the steward of an earthly domain, but I suspect she treats him as she treats us all, as a servant to her whims.”

If the tsarina had fallen out of favor with The Kind and Fair, what did that mean for us? Did it mean that her reign would be cut short? Could we wait that long? If so, what if she were replaced with someone worse?

Alaina cuddled closer to me, fitting herself under my arm and resting her head on my shoulder. Her fingers played at the edge of my throat where feather met scaled skin. Fingertips brushed under the collar. She moved her hand up to the far side of my face and gently smoothed the feathers down along my jaw and cheek.

I closed my eyes and settled into the mattress. I softened my shoulders and relaxed my hands. Her hands did not threaten me. Her touch did not possess me. Her teasing did not torment me. I allowed myself to enjoy the attention. Would that we could enjoy such simple intimacy all the rest of our days without a threat over us!

I longed to turn my face and kiss her fingertips. I wanted

to kiss her, her forehead, her brows. I wanted to tell her why her kindness and care meant so much. I wanted to confess my love for her even if, despite her own confession of physical wanting, she could never feel the same way. And I wouldn't get the chance.

I didn't mind dying. I had faced death so many times by now that it served more as a faithful companion than a threatening stranger. And despite not wanting her to know that I was Mikhail the Disgraced Prince while I lived, I dearly wanted her to know the truth about me after my death so that at least one person might not look back on my memory with shame. And my friends among the jesters too, who embraced me all the more when I could do nothing for them. I wanted them all to know that they were loved and cherished by me until my final moments. Dying was just an event that had been put off for too long.

I minded all the lies I had to tell though to stay safe. I despised all the vague misdirections I needed to provide to avert suspicions. I loathed all the omissions I needed to make to keep those around me from coming to harm. And it looked like I was going to have to keep doing all of it until I did, at last, die.

Maybe Alaina would never know the truth.

"We may not have to wait for The Kind and Fair to take pity on us," Alaina whispered.

That pulled me from contemplating my bleak short future. "What do you mean?"

"I didn't know if I should tell you," she said. Alaina's hand slipped from my face and down over my chest. She plucked at feathers on my far shoulder instead. "Indeed, I have become conflicted about it myself."

Her tone and vagueness pricked at me. Something dangerous loomed ahead.

"Alaina, tell me."

"I wrote to my brother," she admitted. "I didn't know what else to do! I am so discouraged being told I cannot leave that I decided to approach it from the other end. Maybe he could help. He's king, after all, and his word holds more weight than mine. Maybe he could put pressure on the tsarina."

I had no doubt that the tsarina had all of the princess' correspondence intercepted and read before it found its way to the intended recipient. If it found its way. My blood chilled.

"Did you send it?" was all I could ask, hoping she had not. My mind raced through every possible and terrible outcome.

"Yes. This afternoon. My maid is discreet."

All the discretion in the world was not enough for someone looking for any reason to make the lives of others miserable, especially those to whom the tsarina held special enmity. And the princess, in the tsarina's efforts to twist her as she herself had been twisted, had now exposed herself beyond repair. If that maid was in the tsarina's pay, or not as discreet as Alaina believed, or distracted for even a moment.... Or maybe the courier to whom the maid was to give the letter could not be trusted.... There were too many people involved in the transference of correspondence for it not to be compromised somewhere down the line.

"Don't be angry with me," she said, misinterpreting my silence. "I need to feel as if I am doing something, anything, to aid our plight. After I sent it, I regretted it because I should have talked to you first. But the draw of being in Altania allured me so. And to have us both safely out of Ilyichia! That was a risk I needed to take. I had to take it, if it could be achieved."

"I am not angry with you," I assured her, not angry but deeply disturbed.

I could have warned her or talked her out of such a foolhardy idea. If she had just spoken to me before she sent it.... After the chill of terror, the heat of panic took over.

Perspiration poured from my temples. How did I protect her from her own folly?

"I am sure there's something my brother can do," she said.

"Did you explicitly mention me?"

"Of course. If I go back to Altania, you go with me."

I lay there, mute in my horror, panicked in the knowledge that this would be found out, but silenced by my own unwillingness to shatter her hope before the manifest result of my certainties did it instead.

This was how I protected her, saved her, sacrificed myself for her. Surely, this would be it. I couldn't claim to have written the letter. I couldn't claim to have dictated it. But I could own that I was the reason for it, that I inspired her to write it. And surely, if I told the tsarina that I was the malcontent who manipulated his way to get the princess to pen a letter for his salvation, then surely, she could not be as angry with the princess as she was with me. If the princess was painted as nothing more than an easily swayed simpleton preyed upon by a scheming, vengeful prince, the tsarina would have to believe it, wouldn't she?

I didn't want to know what Alaina wrote about me. I could not imagine any description that would be innocuous or sufficiently understated yet realistic that would enable me to join her in any rescue. What loving, considerate, cautious brother would allow his sister's strange pet to join her if that pet caused the insane jealousy of the one she fled? I wouldn't allow any sibling of mine to bring something that would endanger the entire mission. Surely, he was not such a fool either.

"And, in Altania," I queried, willing to indulge the fantasy for the moment since cold practicality could not change anything, "what will you do with me?"

"Anything you want! We will be free of her. For good."

"You will be free," I said. "But what of me?"

"No collars or leads or bells or cages, Kaylay. I promise."

"Your brother may not trust me as you do. What if he insists on them?"

"He will trust me. And if I say you should not be kept that way, then he will oblige me."

Her hope, her expectation, veered sharply toward the wishful and naive. But then, I did not think I would truly have to worry about being in Altania because I fully expected to die here.

"Are you not happy?" she asked. "She will not be able to harm us any longer. Please. Say you are happy."

"I am happy for you," I said as diplomatically as I could. It gave her hope when it came in such short supply. "I do not think it will be the happy change in circumstance you envision for me."

"What aren't you saying? What worries you?"

That Altania would only offer me the same shameful existence Ilyichia did. That Altania's king would view me much like Ilyichia's empress: a strange addition to a menagerie and no more. There was no promise that Altania would treat me with more dignity or care than I received here. Alaina would be there, but what assurance was that? She might have more power there, but she might not.

I hoped that I would be dead before it mattered.

"Please don't keep me like she does," I whispered.

"I wouldn't." Her voice, small and questioning, added, "Would you want to leave me?"

"I don't know how I could stay with you. I am not built for court. I am not suitable for the wilds. Your brother, if he is sensible, will not want me to stay in your apartments."

"I don't have anyone else I trust as much." She rubbed her cheek against my shoulder as if her wishing could change anything. "It won't be the same. You can come and go as you please. And if you like, we will sit by the fire every evening and share stories as we do here."

"Not if your brother says otherwise. You are as subject to his wishes as you are to the tsarina's."

She buried her face against my neck and grumbled.

"Maybe it won't come to that," I said. I brushed my hand over her head, smoothing her hair. "Maybe you're right. Maybe things will be different after all."

"It will be. It has to be." She kissed my jaw. "You'll see. Life is going to be so different for us."

I didn't doubt that our future would be different. I just didn't know if it would be any better.

XXX.

"Kaylay!" Alaina embedded her fingernails into my shoulder.

I roused, the urgency in her voice and the pain of her grip pulling me from the fitful dreams that plagued my night. Crashing and raised voices punctuated the darkness. I tried to leave the bed but could not extricate myself from Alaina's hands as she held me close and lay half on my wing.

"What's happening?" I rose on an elbow and put my hand over hers, trying to pry her fingers out of my flesh.

"We locked the doors, didn't we?"

But locked doors would not withstand whatever came our way.

I fumbled, trying to get Alaina to release me. I needed to leave her bed, no matter what the situation. No good would come of staying, but she froze in terror, bound to me through horror and uncertainty. She had never been through this, but I had, and I needed her to let me go.

Boot heels clicked on the tile floors outside the bedroom.

"Alaina," I hissed as I struggled to pry her from me, "please."

But Alaina's attention fixed upon the bedroom doors, leaving her insensible to my plea. Within moments, those doors burst inward, jambs splintering when the hinges did not give. One of them lay twisted back against a wall when the force of its recoil dislodged it from its hardware.

Guards filled the room, the firelight casting dramatic glints from their weapons. Whatever they expected to discover on our side of the door, they were unprepared for the princess, down to her nightshift, entwined with the tsarina's pet. Although our tousled state suggested more than we had ever done, the guards cast doubtful glances at each other, recognizing our configuration as dangerous proximity.

Alaina clutched at the blankets, a feeble attempt at preserving her modesty, although to the eyes of all who gazed upon us, she had no modesty left to preserve as she huddled to me with the same damning ferocity. Feathers in her sheets and on her nightshift told a tale of its own, but her aggressive hold on me illustrated to all, even those who had never repeated the gossip, the likely truth of those rumors.

No one would believe our innocence now.

"By order of Her Royal Majesty, Empress of Ilyichia, Princess Alaina, you are hereby under arrest for treason against the kingdom and the crown."

Alaina's grasp stiffened, and I more easily dislodged her with the pronouncement. I pushed her behind me and set myself between her and the guards. I did not delude myself that I could change the outcome of this situation, but I could argue for her. I could remind them all that, if the tsarina thought to strip the princess of titles as had been done to me, the princess still maintained titles in Altania that required acknowledgment. She needed to be treated with more care than I had been afforded.

None of them stepped forward to enact the declaration.

Maybe the guards remembered too that the last person who harmed me lost his life because of it.

"What is she said to have done?" I asked.

Murmurs rose through the ranks, and several guards stepped backward. Those who maintained their ground looked to their compatriots. No one had anticipated my interjection. None of them knew I could speak.

The leader of this group readjusted his shoulders and resumed his prior confidence. "You, creature, are not named in the warrant. This is not your concern."

"I will not leave her," I told him.

He nodded and then gestured another of the guards over. He whispered instructions into the young man's ear. The second guard listened, gave a wary glance at me, and then departed the room.

Alaina put her hand on my back while we waited in our silent standoff. Eventually, she replaced her hand with her forehead. And though our wait was not of long duration, a lifetime of terror passed before the clicking of shoes accompanied by boots approached the bedroom.

"I charged you with a standard assignment," came the well-known voice, shrill and dour as ever.

"My apologies, Your Majesty," the head guard said before she was even in the room. "But I needed additional instruction on how you wanted us to handle your firebird."

I had considered separating from Alaina before the tsarina entered, but that would leave Alaina exposed. And behaving as if I had done anything wrong would send the wrong message. As little as I liked Alaina looking weak, especially in front of the tsarina, it served her best to let me bear the brunt of the tsarina's displeasure.

"My firebird?" But as she asked, she stepped into the room and stopped. Her gaze landed upon us, and the flickering fire revealed the rapid succession of emotions that crossed her face. When she finally regained control, her eyes narrowed. "I wondered why she mentioned you."

"I put her up to it." I slid from the bed, pushing blankets out of my way, and took several steps toward the tsarina.

"Why would you do that?"

"I want to leave." Several more steps brought me to stand directly before her. "I played upon the princess' own desire for home that I might accompany her."

"She believed you?"

"It didn't take much." I cast Alaina a glance before returning my attention to the tsarina. "A few kind words on occasion, the illusion of friendship…. All resulted in the betterment of my condition."

"You lied to me?" Alaina's voice trembled behind me.

"I didn't lie about one thing," I said, not bothering to turn around to address Alaina. "I didn't lie about how much I wished to be away from the tsarina."

"To the point of bedding her?" the tsarina asked. "You'll fuck anyone."

"I fuck you, don't I?"

The tsarina took a step back from me, too stunned to be angry. Yet. The yet brewed in the air like a storm.

"A wedding would be a fitting opening to the winter festivities." A soulless grin spread across the tsarina's face. She tilted her head at me. "You like weddings, after all, my dear. I will host it. And I have a beautiful palace all ready for you."

"Whose wedding?" Alaina asked.

"Yours," the tsarina said. "I will not harbor a whore in my court. But with you married to the monster you've been sleeping with, all is forgiven."

The tsarina intended to humiliate Alaina by making her stand beside me in public ceremony. And nothing would be forgiven.

"I will have to plan the particulars. There's always so much to do with weddings, and there's so little time! You can join the procession through the city. And then a magical wedding night at the ice palace."

The ice palace. The ice palace that the Royal Academy had warned her against using it due to freezing temperatures.

"We will surely die," I said.

"Not necessarily." She thought about it for a moment. "If you fuck all night, you might live. But probably not." She turned to the head guard. "Post guards outside the windows and outside the doors. We would not want our little love birds to be disturbed now, would we? I have wedding preparations to oversee."

The guards filed out after the tsarina departed and took their places at the doorway that led out of the apartments, closing the mangled doors behind them. Not even moments after the last guard left the bedroom did voices from other guards float up to the princess' windows.

We had been issued a shared death sentence.

"She knew you spoke."

I kept my back to Alaina. I could have lied. Lies came so easily now. But I didn't want to. All I had ever wanted was authenticity.

"You told me she didn't know," Alaina said.

"I couldn't have you slip and tell her that I spoke to you."

"I wouldn't have."

"I was trying to protect you."

"Great good that did," she snapped. "You should have just stayed out of it."

I turned around to stare at her. My hands trembled. I bit back the vitriol I wanted to unleash. I could have done it so easily. What did it matter now?

"I have only ever tried to protect you," I managed with a calm I did not feel.

"I don't need your protection!"

"Do you know what the word 'treason' means?"

"Of course, I do."

"I don't think so, or you would understand why I stepped in. I am already damned to the cruelest fate she could imagine. I did not want that for you."

"You could have just told me the truth." Alaina's voice trembled. The bed nearly swallowed her as she still clutched at blankets. "You didn't have to lie!"

I crossed back to the bed and sat on the edge of it. I

reached out for her hand, but she pulled it away.

"Yes," I said, head bowed. "I lied to you. I have lied to you about a great many things. I'm not proud of it, but I've had little choice. And I will probably lie to you again."

"I wouldn't have told her, Kaylay!"

"I couldn't risk it. If she discovered at any time that I spoke to you, that we conversed regularly, or that we had formed a connection beyond you keeping a pet, she would have had me chained again at her feet, and you would be, Great Holy forefend, debased in some way as viciously as I."

A thoughtful pause stretched between us.

"Probably," she admitted. She reached out and put her hand on top of mine. "I've seen her ruin the lives of her courtiers before."

"Every lie I've told, I've told to keep others safe." That seemed like truth to me. I couldn't recall lying purely for my own sake. Usually, my mouth just got me into trouble. "I'm not sorry I've done it. I would repeat every one of them. Maybe add a few new ones, if I could do it all over again. But I am sorry that I have had to with you."

"When did she find out," Alaina asked, "that you could speak?"

"From the beginning," which wasn't a lie. "I pleaded with her not to keep me as a pet, hoping that I might move her to mercy. Instead, she found other purpose for me."

"Not captivity," Alaina mused, "but enslavement."

I put my other hand over Alaina's.

"She's jealous," I confessed. "Being found in your bed just made it so much worse."

"How could she be jealous of us," Alaina laughed mirthlessly, "from whom she has taken everything?"

"We have something she can never have: the regard of another. As a bitter, miserable person determined to make others as unhappy as she is, it is something she will never know. Can you imagine how much she must hate it, knowing that a monster such as I may earn the affection of another when she herself cannot?"

"You have earned it because you are not a monster," Alaina insisted. "And she cannot earn it because she is."

I pulled both my legs onto the bed and knelt facing her. I took both her hands in mine. I surveyed her hands, small and slender and almost pale against my black, scaled skin. I wanted my hands, my proper hands, to be holding hers, to experience the softness and the warmth directly. But these were my hands, however strange and monstrous, and they would be the only hands of mine she would ever know.

"I'm so sorry," I whispered. "If it hadn't been for me —"

"If it hadn't been for you, I might have done something drastic these past months. You have been the one bright spot in my time in Ilyichia. Please do not be sorry for that. I could not bear it if I thought you regretted your time with me."

"Never."

"This is my fault. I should never have written home."

"It doesn't matter," I assured her.

"I always thought I would face a beheading block or sword if brought to an untimely end," she mused. "I doubt anyone has heard of death by palace of ice." She gulped and met my gaze. "We are going to die, aren't we?"

"Very likely."

Alaina squeezed my hands and then released them. She sat, quiet and thoughtful, hands resting on her lap. Then she remembered I was there and redirected her attention to me.

"I'm so sorry you're part of this, but, and this is selfish of me —"

"I would expect nothing else, princess."

A corner of her mouth quirked up. "I'm glad I won't be alone."

"You won't be alone," I promised.

She raised her hand and placed it on my cheek, stroking it with her thumb. "You're taking this all very well."

"A life in a collar is no life."

Her hand slid down my face and rested on said collar. "Kaylay, I...."

I silently pleaded with whatever forces ruled the universe that she not say it. To be unmasked now, when we needed each other so much, would be a cruelty beyond expression.

But wouldn't it be nice to hear it, just one more time, by someone I loved?

"Yes, Alaina?"

"I..." She faltered. Her hand dropped. "I'm sorry. I'm embarrassed to say it."

My heart gave a traitorous little leap in my chest.

"There's no need for embarrassment," I assured her. "What is it?"

"I want you." She leaned forward and kissed my cheek. "And you told me that you want sometimes. I want you to lie with me."

If I had not been hoping for a more maudlin sentiment to be uttered from her lips, I would have gauged her suggestion accurately. Instead, in the absence of what I wanted to hear, I blinked at her.

"But I do lie with you."

"*Lie with me* lie with me." She took a deep breath to gather her courage and nerve. "Bed me. Like the tsarina said."

A thousand excuses why that would be impossible lined up, waiting for me to verbalize them, interspecies relations and potential bestiality foremost among them. But the tsarina had also told me when I first discovered my suit of feathers that I was still a man, just in a costume I could not remove. And the man still longed for things the bird could never attain. Yet, here was Alaina, offering the bird the sweet physicality and a glimpse of paradise only the man had ever known.

"Why?" After the word had escaped me, I did not think I wanted to know the answer. "Surely not for the sake of novelty."

"I've never had that kind of intimacy with someone of my choosing. And I choose you."

"Even though the entire world, you included, has told me how ugly I am?"

"And I'm still a brown little twig."

"I like brown little twigs."

"And I like you."

We both fell into an embarrassed silence.

"You wouldn't regret it?" I asked.

"Never." She took one of my hands and kissed the back of it. "Even though we're going to be married, will you still respect me afterward?"

"I would have to respect you now first," I teased.

"Then, my dearest Kaylay," she whispered as she removed her nightshift, "fuck me like you don't respect me at all."

XXXI

Hours later, sweat and sex thick in the air, I woke to Alaina's hair in my mouth. Her arm across my chest, her head tucked under my chin, the heat of our proximity, and the effort of our activities invited me to return to languorous sleep even with our impending executions. Perhaps because of it, we pushed ourselves to the brink of passion and the edge of exhaustion, unleashing our desperate need for connection beyond the rigid roles we had to play.

We laughed and teased and touched like young lovers. And though I had been carrying the burden of grief and shame to spirit-breaking limits for almost a year, the tsarina's decree allowed me to set it aside for several perfect hours because it didn't matter now. Nothing mattered anymore. Nothing but me and Alaina and our brief happiness together before everything in our worlds came to a stunning, horrible conclusion.

Freezing to death, especially with how much I loathed the cold, might have been my least preferred punishment, perhaps second only to being made to linger for another forty years, enduring the existence I had endured these past months. And I could speak to punishment, especially of the imaginative type that undermined any sense of personal identity. How many times had I lost the things that had hitherto defined me?

But Alaina did not deserve the fate to which she had been condemned. She just wanted to go home, where she was valued, and cared for, and loved, at least loved by more than a lowly nightmarish creature.

If I had a place that I thought of as home, I would have joined her in that fervent desire. I was alone though. Every hope of family met with disappointment, tragedy, failure, and rejection. I didn't think Alexei ever thought of me now, beyond a horrifying embarrassment he would spend the rest of his life trying to erase. My isolation made it easy to relinquish this life. But Alaina....

The Kind and Fair assured me she would live with my loyalty, and yet, putting myself between the princess and the tsarina had only worsened the situation. Perhaps the tsarina could see that I would give nothing for her when I would willingly give everything for Alaina.

Alaina snuggled harder into my arms, grip fierce. She kissed the underside of my chin though to demonstrate her wakefulness.

"We should be making escape plans," Alaina mumbled into my shoulder, "but I don't see any way out."

"We are too diligently watched here to make a successful escape." I had failed several times already without the vigilance the guards were instructed to employ now. "Perhaps we can find some flaw in the ice palace itself. There were weak spots in the plans."

"Weak spots?" She perked up. "How do you know that?"

"Because I saw them." And then I realized that Mikhail the Jester had seen them, not Kaylay the Bird. I added, "It's remarkable what people say around creatures they think are beneath them."

Alaina accepted that.

"She spoke of a procession," she mused. "Surely her guards couldn't keep us defended in such a crowd. Could we appeal to the people? Might they help us?"

"With the way they have been subjugated? All the pointless public executions? That's why she arranged the winter festivities and the ice palace anyway — to distract from their discontent. They might take more delight in seeing the downfall of nobles than become inspired to rescue us." But as soon as the words were out of my mouth, the implication of them chilled me with the use of "nobles" and "us."

Alaina mercifully did not think anything of it.

"If they won't help us," she mused, "maybe we could just slip into the crowd and disappear?"

"Maybe you could, but I doubt that I would be able to blend into a crowd."

"And I'm not going anywhere without you."

"I need you to save yourself," I told her as I rubbed my temple against the top of her head in place of the kiss I would have rather bestowed, "if indeed that's what it comes to."

"I refuse."

"You have a destiny, Alaina." And she did. In Altania, she would be a magnificent ruler, just and compassionate and strong, schooled by the cruelty of her own captivity in Ilyichia and the example of rulership that would hopefully form her in a more effective way. "In Altania, you are going to have a beautiful, fulfilled life with children if you wish it, and a new husband too who will know your worth and adore you above everything. As you deserve. Eventually, your time here will seem nothing more than a distant, unpleasant dream, and you will forget all about your strange Ilyichian bird."

"I could never." She pulled herself from my arms to roll onto her back and glare at the ceiling. "I don't like how you talk."

"If I ever said something you liked, then I would know something was truly wrong."

She pushed herself up to sitting and drew her legs up to her chest. She fussed with her hair, pushing it out of her face, twisting it into a long rope, and then throwing it behind her shoulder. She stared at the blankets in front of her.

I sat up too and scooted closer beside her.

"Even if I somehow managed to make it out of Ilyichia alive — and right now that seems extremely unlikely — do you really think I could forget you, Kaylay?"

"I hope you will," I admitted. "That would mean that you would have a full and happy life, and you wouldn't be thinking about the past."

She reached out and put her hand on top of mine. She traced one of my fingers with hers.

"I had another gift for you," she admitted, "something you could have even if I couldn't be with you during the days. It seems a bit pointless now since we're about to die together." She looked up at me, her eyes red-rimmed as if she might burst into tears with the slightest provocation. "Can I still give it to you?"

"If you wish to bestow it, even if the purpose behind it is no longer necessary, then I will receive it gratefully." I did not dare tell her that I did not require or want presents lest she misconstrue it as a rejection. "I treasure the thought behind all your gifts."

The corners of her mouth lifted even if she did not smile. She squeezed my hand and then slid from the bed, taking a blanket with her that she wrapped around her shoulders. She disappeared into her dressing room for several moments and then returned. She climbed back into bed and knelt facing me, her hands cupped. She opened them like a child might reveal a secret pet, like a frog or a mouse, hidden from the adults and intent on keeping it that way. On her palm lay a golden band, the exterior design enameled in green, a thread of gold weaving through like a vine, tiny inlaid rubies serving as flowers dotted along.

"Finist the Falcon had a magic ring," she said, "and since you insist that you are not he, I wanted you to have your own ring, even if it isn't magic, embellished with scarlet flowers."

I stared at the small marvel of metalwork robbed of words.

"I've been a little scared to give it to you," she confessed.

"Why?"

"I worried that you might think I wanted something from you."

She was correct. I would have.

"I hope it's big enough," she said. "The court jewelers regarded me like a mad woman when I told them what I wanted, but I think they did it rather well."

Practicality swept in before I had finished processing the magnitude of such a present, almost as if to spare me from having to confront it.

"You don't have those kinds of funds," I said, awed and equally inclined to regard her as a mad woman.

"I had them use some of my own jewelry. And, really, does it matter now? In fact, I am more glad than ever that I did it. What use are jewels and funds and finery now? At least I can give you this. If you'll have it." She nibbled her bottom lip and then blushed. "If you'll have me?"

My heart stopped beating for the same duration as my lungs stopped taking in air.

"I know she means to embarrass us," she rushed on, "but what if we get married because it means something to us and not just because the tsarina makes us do it? I can hear all your protests without you even saying a word, Kaylay — but what about my future or my brother or my political career or any other reason this might ordinarily be an outrageous suggestion — but that would be our final act of defiance against her, don't you see?"

I saw. For a whole few moments of her suggestion, I had acquired some fragile, fleeting notion that maybe, truly, Alaina loved me too. Her suggestion that we willingly do what the tsarina imagined she was forcing us to do as resistance disintegrated all that wispy hope. It was a moral stance, a political stance, a prideful stance, meant to combat the cruelty and ridicule the tsarina would inflict. Love never entered into it.

"I am already devoted to you," I said. "You do not need to take the vows of an absurd wedding seriously for that."

"I may never have the children I always hoped to have, but I will marry again at least. Let me marry someone of my choosing?"

It didn't matter if she loved me or not because I could not say no to her.

"Are you planning on making an honest bird of me then?"

"If you will let me."

She plucked the ring from her palm and held up the perfect circle so that the light shone through it, the burnished gold like a brilliant glowing halo. She took my hand with her free one and looped the ring over my talon and pressed it past the joints. It wasn't a perfect fit, but it stayed on.

I choked out, "I'm sorry it didn't work."

Alaina's face furrowed. "What didn't?"

"We've agreed to wed. I have a ring, like the stories, and still, no handsome prince am I."

"Do not apologize." She stroked my cheek. "I am not disappointed."

She should have been. I was.

I stared at the ring again, the weight and heft on my finger a distant memory from before the tsarina's heartless theft. Its delicacy and expense clashed horribly with the gnarled finger on which it currently resided. It was the most beautiful ornament I had ever worn.

Tears broke free, and I wiped ineffectually at them. Alaina had answered the one plea I had been making for months — I had a wedding band. Maybe not Irena's, but mine nonetheless. And I would die wearing this one.

"What's wrong, Kaylay?"

What could I tell her? Last time her gift left me undone, I

covered it with prickliness and ingratitude. I would not make the same mistake now. But I still wouldn't tell her the truth, tempting though it was.

"The tsarina has deprived me of everything I might once have been able to offer you," I said. That at least was truthful. "I can give you nothing in return."

"I have things," she spread her arms out to indicate the room and her finery beyond it. "I have had things my whole life. I do not need more. What you give me is more valuable than all my things put together."

How quickly would her regard for me vanish if I told her I was the former prince she so reviled?

"I would still like to give you more than flimsy comfort and warmth." I could offer her nothing but paltry tokens of affection, but what did those matter when her life was threatened? Cuddling wouldn't keep her safe. Or.... I grabbed Alaina's arm and startled her with my action and sudden intensity. "She didn't think this through."

"The wedding?"

"Our deaths."

"The Royal Academy said that this is the coldest winter Ilyichia has ever experienced, and she is going to keep us overnight in an ice construction. What other outcome is possible?"

Maybe the Otherlander had helped us. Maybe that was why Alaina had never told me that she loved me, not even in the midst of our earlier passions. Maybe the Otherlander ensured that she wouldn't because only as a bird could I protect her. My feathers were my gift and her salvation.

"We might live," I spread my wings out, "because I can keep you warm."

XXXII.

Alexei, young though he was, stood up with me when I
wed Marfa, my mother onlooking and expectant. Marfa's
family too, onlooking and expectant. Neither Marfa nor I had
been asked if we wanted to marry. State marriages were like
that. And though not as young as she, I still shifted nervously
from foot to foot with all eyes on us. There had been no
competition for Marfa. Though well-connected and noble, I
had been the prize in that arrangement — the elder Karilitsyn
prince who would inherit the wealth and the estate. And as
such, ladies and their parents alike had vied for the place of
prominence in my family's favor. And it had not hurt that
those of court found me favorable in looks and demeanor,
even if I did not possess the ambitions of my esteemed and
lauded uncles and forefathers.

Marfa, poor Marfa, shook that day, terrified of the
attention and of her unknown groom. The beads of her
kokoshnik trembled, and she did not look up at me once
throughout the ceremony. Her voice barely reached above a
whisper when called upon to answer the questions of the
diviner. The white silk cord that bound our hands together at
the end of the ceremony formed the only point of contact she
maintained with me that day.

I found out later that she had spent the days leading up to
our marriage weeping. There were no other sweethearts or
attachments, no others that she might have preferred, but our
wedding night remained unconsummated as we navigated our
awkwardness and the empty expectations of others together.
The vodka of the celebrations had resolved us both enough to

go through with it if we had no other choice, but we remained clothed in our nightshirts as we turned to hot spiced wine to get us through the cold discomfort of transforming from strangers to spouses.

Although no love match or great sympathy of souls, Marfa and I did find our way. Almost a decade together, we had seen much and been through more. We had lost two children, a grief no title or wealth could relieve. And until the day she died, I had been faithful to her.

As the head of the family at that point, I possessed the luxury to take my time and make a careful choice when finally inspired to consider remarriage. Except that I didn't.

Irena dazzled me. Her charm, her wit, her beauty offered everything I couldn't have with Marfa. She promised a fairytale romance that I could only dream about as a young man, showing me the love that should have been, and could have been, if not for the demands of state and family. Our wedding was small, just her family in attendance, and for two perfect years, we enjoyed our relative anonymity while we desperately tried to start a family. And where I had been loyal to Marfa, no other woman existed in the world outside of Irena.

After Irena, that was it. I expected Alexei to be my successor and his children my inheritors. I expected to live out my days a wandering widower, restless, lonely, and occasionally seeking solace in the arms of someone I could pretend was Irena.

I never expected to marry yet again.

"Contemplating your nuptial bliss?"

My back stiffened with the tsarina's question. I did not turn though. I slid Alaina's ring from my finger and tucked it in the leather band on my wrist lest the tsarina take this one from me too. I pointedly watched the crowds from the window, a sea of faceless nameless people outside the gates of the palace, the promised processional path obscured by the fur-clad city inhabitants.

"Did you have the same turnout for your wedding procession?" I asked her. When she did not answer, I turned around. "Do your thoughts not turn to Frederick at such a time?"

"I have arranged a wedding just as elaborate and public as mine. I have spared no expense to give my favorite the wedding he deserves since I wasn't there to approve the last. My apologies about the bride though. Funny how someone renowned for his beauty is going to marry the ugliest woman at court."

I swallowed back the observation that the tsarina would have had to be the bride for that to be true.

"Spare the princess," I asked. "Your objection is with me. If the price of my life will content you, then have it. But you do not need hers."

"Your life is in peril, and yet you speak of her."

"What have I to gain by a pardon?" I spread my arms out to show what she had made of me. Granted, I wore the luxurious robe Alaina gifted me, which elevated me beyond the condition the tsarina kept me, but I was still as the tsarina had made me after the game she forced me to play. "Continued existence like this? Nay. I shall welcome death like a brother."

"You could always renounce her," the tsarina suggested.

"And why would I do that?"

"Because I could free you."

Her admission rang like falsehood. She had to be lying.

"You told me that you could not," I reminded her.

"As if you have never lied to me either."

"You could have undone this?" Her confession rocked me, although I still only half-believed it. More likely, this was just as everything else, simply another way to hurt me and to keep me bound to her. "You could have granted mercy at any time?"

"I still can." She took several slow steps toward me. "Renounce her and return to me. I can reinstate you. I can see that you live out the rest of your days in peace and comfort. All of this," she waved her hand loftily, "will be as if it never happened."

"What of Alaina?"

"Forget Alaina," she whispered. "Renounce her. Be mine and be free."

The offer of release from my shame tempted me far more than I wanted to admit. But I was weak and desperate, and it settled like sweet poison in my ears. I longed for it. And it would have been easy enough to see if she lied.

"I can raise you up again," she tempted. "I can give you back your titles. I can reunite you with your family. You can live fully once more." She lowered her voice to a breath. "You can be a man again, Mikhail."

The use of my old name pulled me from the spell of her offer. I wasn't Mikhail. I was Kaylay, as my beloved had named me. And there was no abandoning Alaina now. What I wanted didn't matter. And if embracing my changed form meant keeping her safe, then I would cling to it until death separated me from it.

"What do you say?" she asked.

The tsarina may not have been old in years, but she was old in manipulation. Her tired, sagging face and swathes of graying hair spoke of malice far beyond her age. Her desperation in wanting something she could never have etched weary lines along her eyes and mouth. Even when she took it by force, she could not possess it.

I recalled her in earlier days when I had lain with her, when I could not find the strength to refuse. Life had knocked her about like a ship in a storm even then, and she had struggled to find safe harbor. Though no beauty or wit, I had admired her strength and resilience then. I appreciated her will. She had smiled then at times, laughed too without motive, and if not cared about me, pretended to care convincingly enough that I had never considered she would turn on me with such hatred. She rarely smiled now and almost never laughed, both touched with bitterness and mockery when she indulged in either. Once vibrant and hopeful, her shine had abandoned her. Cruelty dulled whatever was left. Her finery, all glitter and sparkle, drowned the woman out.

I had become a monster, and I learned the harsh lesson of my worthlessness with it. But I had still managed to hold onto my soul. When had the tsarina become the real monster?

I could do nothing but pity her. Alaina would never declare her love for me now, but she would willingly hold my hand through death itself. Even human, the tsarina would never have that.

"That is a generous offer," I said. "But I would rather die a monster in her arms than live as a man in yours."

Several months prior, I would have caused as much havoc and mayhem as I could manage. I would have fought and struggled and made the guards regret every decision that led to them being the ones keeping me in custody. I would have broken their bones, torn their uniforms, and given them reason for sufficient wariness without revealing any of my higher faculties.

Instead, today, I assured them I would not offer any opposition. My voice and my docility unnerved them more than any disobedience ever could. Though charged with ensuring my compliance, they withdrew to some small distance once in the ceremonial hall where the wedding would occur.

Nearly as dense as the crowds out in the cold, the courtiers packed into the expansive room to witness the strange amusement the tsarina had arranged for them. While my appearance offered no novelty of amusement, the wedding of such an ill-favored creature to one of their own ranks promised the cruel titillation my own divestment of titles had provided. Their voices raised with tension and excitement, no spectator paused to acknowledge my arrival unless to point it out to their companions.

"The wedding of a maiden to a monster," said a voice behind me. A moment later, Drook stood at my side. "It seems worthy of a poem."

"Neither of us is a maiden," I responded reflexively.

He laughed and grinned up at me. "I knew it."

I glanced down at him. "That I wasn't a maiden?"

"That you were more intelligent than you let on."

"I'm not. I'm getting married again, aren't I?"

I had not meant to say it, but I fell into easy conversational stride with Drook. I had never been able to keep my mouth in check.

His grin faltered. His dark-eyed intensity took in my full measure before a flicker of recognition crossed his face.

"Kvasnik?" He didn't wait for my reply before he grabbed his hat and threw it on the floor. He unleashed a string of profanities in Varnasian. "Klessa was right. Klessa is always right. And now I'll have to tell her."

I crouched down. "Klessa guessed?"

"I told her it was impossible." He studied me again and grabbed my shoulders. "But how? This is no costume."

"She has means of permanence outside of a seamstress' needle." I could have called it magic. I could have described her reliance on The Kind and Fair. I could have said a hundred different things more direct. But even to me, who had worn the effects of it, it sounded fantastical. "Forgive me. I could not safely tell you sooner."

He grabbed me into his arms and held me with a grip I

could not dislodge had I been inclined. I embraced him in
return, content now that I had set down the burden of
deceiving my friends.

"The princess cannot know," I said.

"Why not?" he asked as he released me.

"I have my reasons. Please."

Drook's face did not validate my assessment, but he
nodded in agreement.

"Where are the others?" I asked.

"Part of the processional."

"Will you please tell Klessa?"

"You can tell her yourself." Drook glanced over to the
other side of the hall. "As I am the one to stand up with you,
Klessa is the princess' bridal party."

As if choreographed, two women, followed by their own
detachment of guards, emerged from the doorway on the far
side of the hall, one tall and stately, the other short and stately.
Their measured steps held no hesitation. Alaina's face held no
uncertainty. Klessa, although usually self-assured, wore a light
veil that obscured her face and any expression she may have
been making.

Alaina would, as the tsarina intended, feel the insult of our
chosen attendants, but for me, I could not think of any other I
preferred if this situation must play out. I could not find two
finer people in all the world to bear witness to my wedding and
share the final hours of my life.

I stood, prepared to meet the princess I was to wed.

Alaina dressed as any traditional Ilyichian bride. Her satin
gown reflected the soft candlelight that illuminated the
ceremonial space. The gold chain woven through her braids
sparkled against her dark hair. Velvet burgundy ribbons with
strands of seed pearls tied her hair back and up. Her pearl and
satin kokoshnik, stark against dark hair and skin, framed her
face most becomingly. A necklace in a cascade of teardrop

pearls hung from her throat. For all the cruelty and insults about her Altanian features from the court, even for all the teasing I had done about her unimpressive size, her radiance and serenity stunned me into dumbstruck admiration.

I bowed so that I could hide my embarrassment. Even in the blue brocade and sable robe, I still wore feathers and had nothing but what she herself had given me. I vowed to keep her alive tonight since that was the only thing I could offer.

"Rise, dearest Kaylay."

I swallowed back my insecurities before I did as she instructed.

"You might have at least dressed up for our wedding," I said, afraid that if I did not fall back on teasing, I would indeed become an emotional fool. I made a show of looking her over. "You didn't even try, did you?"

"I tried more than you," she said, her stoicism disintegrating as she tried not to smile.

"Nonsense. I wore my finest feathers."

"Hmm." Alaina took her turn to size me up. "So you did."

"Shall we get this over with?"

"You are a most unwilling groom."

Drook crossed behind us to speak to his wife.

"It is like any state marriage," I assured Alaina. "They are rarely conducted between willing participants."

"How relieving then, that we are like every other couple." She reached out and took my hand, squeezing my fingers in reassurance. "Regardless of how this came about, I will take my vows seriously."

"As will I." Even if I only had hours in which to honor her.

"I KNEW IT!" Klessa pushed past both her husband and Alaina and threw her arms around me. "I knew it," she mumbled into my shoulder.

Alaina released my hand in her surprise.

When Klessa withdrew, she lifted the veil so that she could allow me to appreciate her scolding look. The hair on her face had thinned and was shorter than last I had seen, enabling a better view of her facial features. And then it struck me. That maid who recognized me… had been Klessa!

"Why?" I reached up to touch her cheek. "Why would you shave your beautiful hair?"

"To get near you, you idiot." She glanced over her shoulder at Drook and gestured to me. "Do you believe this?"

"I suppose." Drook shrugged. "He was never the sharpest among us."

"I told you," Klessa said pointedly, "you shine. No matter what."

"But like this?"

"So pretty. So dumb." Klessa patted my cheek. "Yes. Like this. Like anything. I would know you."

A woman true and fair, indeed. And I loved her very much.

"Alaina," I interjected, content to be affectionately ridiculed but aware of how left out my bride must feel, "these are my friends. My truest friends."

Alaina glanced at Drook, then Klessa, and then back to me. I could not mistake the question in her eyes.

"I will tell you all about how that came to be," I assured the princess, "tomorrow."

No one responded to that, all eyes cast down to the floor, knowing the likelihood of our survival.

The crowd hushed behind us, and I gazed up in the direction of most turned heads. The tsarina had entered, taking her place in her balcony box, as if attending a theatrical event and not the forced wedding of nobles she had condemned to death. Her Allemandian lover took position beside her.

Rumors abounded about the Baron and the nature of his relationship with the tsarina, many citing him as the one who wielded the power because the tsarina was too caught up in her own pet interests. But not having seen him in her presence, I suspected that many of those rumors might have come from the man himself, looking to bolster his own reputation at court. The tsarina only seemed to tolerate him now due to the point she wanted to make to me: if I had just said yes, then I would have been up there beside her instead, titles, wealth, and reputation intact.

The tsarina's personal diviner shambled out moments later with help from several younger members of the religious order. His sparse hair and black robes made the wizened face resemble a skull, an ill omen to anyone with eyes to see it, even to a follower of the Great Holy.

Klessa and Drook took their respective places beside Alaina and me, all of us falling automatically into the roles we were required to play in this farce. And farce though it may be, punishment as might have been intended, I could not have wished to have anyone else beside me at such a time than the three people I held nearest and dearest to my heart in this era of trial.

The diviner's shaky voice rose and fell in unbalanced cadence as he announced the purpose of the festivities: to honor The Kind and Fair.

All sat in rapt attention, less on his words and more on the princess who was being forced to marry the court pet. No one announced that Alaina was losing her titles, but the occasion certainly implied that her titles had been reduced to nothing.

An acolyte carried out the usual blood sacrifice, this time a hare, at the basin. The diviner droned on, heedless to the act and the couple he had been charged to bless for the festivities.

"The tsarina, in her continued devotion to The Kind and Fair, has offered her best," the diviner finally looked up from the book in front of him to gaze at Alaina, "and her favorite," at which point he looked at me. The untamed brows did a wild dance upon realizing the strange tableau Alaina and I created with court entertainers as our attendants. "May this union between the representatives of Ilyichia and the Otherlands ensure our mutual prosperity for the years to come."

The younger helpers guided the diviner out to where we stood. Another followed with the traditional white satin cord stretched between his hands.

"Do you, Princess Alaina," the diviner continued, "offer the one beside you a share of your position and your life?"

"I do."

"And will you take it to husband for the prosperity of Ilyichia?"

Klessa added in a whisper, loud enough for me to hear but likely not loud enough for the diviner, "Even though he is a stubborn fool who will constantly frustrate you?"

Alaina's brows shot up as she dampened a smile. "I will."

"And do you — er...." The diviner stuttered and stumbled, figuring out how to address me.

"Prince of birds," Drook supplied and then stared the diviner down in challenge.

"Er, do you, prince of birds, offer the one beside you a share of your position and your life?"

"I can give you nothing," I told Alaina.

"You have given me everything." She took my hand and squeezed it. "Everything that matters. I don't need anything else. Go on."

I returned my attention to the diviner. "I do."

"And will you take her to wife for the prosperity of Ilyichia?"

"Even though she be but an ordinary human and as small as me?" Drook asked.

"I will." I cast him a glance but kept my attention on our officiant. "With all my heart."

The cord bearer stepped forward and began wrapping our

hands with the satin. After several loops and passes, he tied the ends together, binding us before all assembled.

"I offer to Ilyichia this formal union. May their sacrifice please The Kind and Fair."

I didn't look up to see how the tsarina reacted to our marriage. I didn't look behind us to see how the courtiers behaved in the wake of Alaina's quiet disgrace. I didn't even look to Klessa or Drook for their support and approval. I had no thought for anyone but my wife.

My wife.

She gazed up at me, thoughtful and sincere, perhaps having the same moment of incredulity as I. For she now had a husband again.

"I am sorry, my lady," I told her.

"Kaylay, whatever for?"

"Even in marriage, I still cannot give you a happy ending."

"I don't need a wonder tale to be happy." She reached out with her unbound hand and tugged me down to her. She kissed my brow and then released me. "I just need you."

XXXIII.

The guards split the crowds for us, holding back the nobles as they made way for our small wedding party. Although the binding of my hand to Alaina's ensured that we would not separate in the crowd, she clung to my arm. Her serenity, so perfect and unshakable at the head of the room, crumbled when faced with the harsher reality of our situation. Even Drook and Klessa, bearing the brunt of the staring as they made the way for us, did not loosen Alaina's hold on me.

While I had spent nearly a year becoming accustomed to derision and humiliation from those around me, Alaina had not done this before. I patted her hand on my arm, told her to breathe as Drook had once instructed me, and promised she was not alone. Klessa even fell back to let Drook lead alone while she took up position on Alaina's other side, shielding her from the crowd physically during that long march to the hall's main doors.

The blast of freezing air from the courtyard when the doors were thrown open gave Alaina another moment of collection. She released her death-grip on my arm, glanced up to Klessa and smiled, a show of gratitude she had not yet found a way to verbalize.

Outside, more guards greeted us, although they were our sole reception with the courtiers still within the ceremonial space and the common throng outside the courtyard gate. The processional line-up itself, just inside the gate and waiting to be ushered out into the city, offered no reassurance. The participants had no thought for us, although Alaina and I were to be a hilarious focal point for the tsarina's subjects.

A guard came over and unbound our hands. Several others, loaded with furs and coats, followed behind, handing cloaks and coats to Drook, Klessa, and Alaina, followed by hats and gloves. Nothing was offered to me.

"He will be out in the cold like the rest of us," Klessa pointed out to one of the soldiers when she realized the oversight. "He needs something too."

"It has feathers," was the reply from the disinterested guard who walked off so that he would no longer be subject to complaints.

"It matters not," I assured her. "Nothing fits over the wings."

The negligence about garments to keep me warm served only to remind me of the malice behind this entire situation. The tsarina understood my objection to being cold, so what better way to ensure my discomfort until it finally killed me? I did not doubt that it had been intentional.

"You need gloves at least," Klessa insisted. But of the three of them, no one had hands my size, and none of the guards would voluntarily give up theirs. She switched her hunt to a muff and could not find anyone in ready distance who possessed one. "I worry about frostbite."

I might have been more worried about frostbite too, if I had any hope of surviving through the night. My feet, even more than my hands, burned in the cold. But I only needed to keep Alaina alive, and I could do that even with frostbitten extremities.

"I will keep him warm," Alaina assured her.

Another detachment of guards approached from the end of the processional, and I gave Klessa and Drook another round of embraces. They did not willingly release me, even when the guards stood at my back.

"Tell the others," I charged them. I let go and stepped back so that they would not be subject to any physical redirection the guards might inflict due to my delay. "And pray for us."

The guards separated us, guiding us to our respective places: Drook and Klessa toward the rear of the processional, Alaina and me toward the front. Alaina wrapped herself around my arm as if I had any idea more than she did about where we were to go. I followed our guards, glancing behind us when the sounds of others began filling the frozen air. Alaina glanced over too and then buried her face against my arm.

I understood her shame and embarrassment and fear. I no longer shared in it, but I hated not being able to shield her from it.

The guards marched us to a rolling staircase, several people holding the base beside an elephant.

"Look." I directed Alaina's attention to it. "Is that Ivan? Should I introduce myself?"

She lifted her face away from my arm to see what I pointed out. She brightened a little at the recollection of earlier conversations, before everything had gone horribly wrong.

"Up," said a guard behind us, likely wanting his portion of his duties to be over so that he could get out of the cold.

Alaina went first, reaching for my hand so that she could be assured I was not far behind her. I followed her up the staircase. At the top, she backed into me. A golden cage, fitted with braces and blankets and belts to keep it atop the elephant, awaited us. Outfitted like a carriage with two small stools, the door hung wide open.

"I can't," Alaina said.

"It's traditional to carry a bride across the threshold, is it not?"

I scooped Alaina up, unwilling to let the guard have an excuse to touch or mistreat her, and carried her through the cage door. He shut it behind us. The lock engaged.

Alaina still wrapped up in my arms, I sat on one of the stools, a detail deliberately considered since there was enough space for wings and tail.

"They locked us in," she whispered.

"I am accustomed to this," I reminded her. "I'm sorry."

"How?" she murmured, prying herself slightly more from my arms so that she could look at me. "How do you bear it?"

"I didn't think I would at first." I released her lower half so that she could better sit, although she seemed disinclined to release me fully. "Drook and Klessa reminded me that, no matter my circumstances, I was not alone. And then, when deprived of their company, a princess came my way."

"This princess," Alaina said, curling up against my chest, "did she make life better for you?"

"She tormented me to the point of distracting me from my troubles."

"Hmm. Surely, no princess I know then."

Ivan shifted beneath us, alerting me to the commencement of our procession. I cast a glance down to the elephant's attendants, also bundled in fur coats and accessories, who were leading the creature. No one had much thought for us. Doubtless, they too thought this a ridiculous demonstration and longed to be inside and in front of a fire.

Alaina grabbed my right hand, free from holding her, and tucked it into her coat. I appreciated the gesture, but I did not think a little momentary warmth would help much with the trial ahead of us.

"Do you want my hat?" she asked, gesturing to the white fur that sat atop her head. "I know how much you hate being cold."

"You keep it." She needed it more than I did, and all of this would be for naught if anything happened to her. "Having my wife tucked up against me is keeping me sufficiently cozy."

"Your wife," she repeated as if she forgot that we had just

been married.

Ivan lurched, and the cage rocked on his back. Through the gates and into the crowd, the shouts and cheering and noise flooded us as if the courtyard walls held back a tide.

Alaina took a glance around at our audience and returned her attention to me.

"Kaylay?"

"I'm here." I squeezed her. "I have you."

"I couldn't do this alone."

"If you had to, you could." I put my cheek on top of her head. "We learn things about ourselves in trial. You're so much stronger than you think."

"I don't feel strong," she admitted. "I feel pathetic and weak."

"You're not. You and the tsarina have been through the same trials, the same exile, and the same court derision. In her elevation, she has let her bitterness rule. You will not surrender to the petty cruelties that have twisted her. You do not have that in you. Not now. Not when you have your throne."

"If I get my throne. I am so afraid," she confessed. "I know I have reason to be afraid, but that is not what bothers me most."

"What then?"

"I hate that they're all staring. I hate feeling so ashamed, especially when I'm not ashamed of anything I've done."

"They're staring at me," I told her. "None of these people have seen a firebird before, remember? They probably haven't seen Ivan before either. Can you imagine how fantastical this must be to all of them?"

"I still feel their stares."

"True," I agreed. "They may never have seen a real-life princess before either, but — and I apologize — I feel like a princess pales in comparison to an elephant and a firebird."

"You're probably right, as much as I hate to admit it," she

said, giving me a smile although she mustered it up from the depths. "Is there a plan, or is the plan just to survive?"

"From here to the palace, we are under lock and guard, and will not have an opportunity to escape into the crowd. From there, I know not what is in store."

The wind howled around the bars, and I spread my wings to keep it from reaching us. I couldn't feel my feet by now, and I tucked my right leg up behind my left. My left hand too, still holding Alaina and exposed, began to lose sensation as I buried it in the folds of her coat.

"We will have to escape the palace then," she mused. "Even with guards, there will be no crowds tonight. No one will wish to be out in such chill."

"If we wait until the small hours, our guards will also not be at their best."

"So, morning, we make our escape?" She gazed out over the heads of the onlookers, getting her bearings. "Fortunate for us that the palace sits along the river. We can follow it to port."

What kind of captain would give fare to a bedraggled princess and her strange pet? Surely, no sane one. Perhaps, I contented myself, she would not have a strange pet in tow because I would have fulfilled my purpose by then.

"Alaina, if I should die—"

"No," she said. "No. I won't hear of it. I'm going to live, and so are you. Do you understand me?"

"Yes. We will both live," I repeated. "But, if I should not—"

"Stop. Please."

"Alaina." I waited a few moments to see if she would speak over me again. "I need to ask a favor of you. And as you say, I will not need it. But still, please listen to me?"

She glared at me, but she remained quiet.

"When we escape," when, not if, because if it came to my

last wish or her survival, I needed her to choose her survival, "and when we make it to safety, if I should take ill or it looks like I may not make it, I want two things. I would like you to have my collar removed, and I would like to be wearing my wedding band."

She shifted out of my grasp, took her place on the opposite stool, and grabbed at me so that she could see my left hand. My bare left hand.

"Oh, Kaylay, did she take it?"

"I didn't trust her not to. I have it tied into my wristband." I pulled out the ties with a talon to show her the glint of gold. "See that it finds its way onto my finger if I cannot do it myself."

"I understand, and I will see that it is done," she assured me, "but it will not come to that."

Alaina's face set so sternly and so resolutely that I almost believed her. If will alone could ensure our survival, then I would have had no doubt.

I reached out and took her hands in mine.

"Of course it won't," I lied.

XXXIV.

The key in the lock inspired Alaina to hold onto my arm yet again. The guard led, and I followed, Alaina clinging to me from behind. Down the mobile staircase, we ended our descent inside a courtyard of ice that led to the tsarina's palace.

I appreciated the construction as the site of my impending death, but beyond that, I found the moniker of "palace" misleading more than anything. Ornate and masterfully accomplished, yes. I could not deny the care and attention to detail the carvers and engineers had devoted to the project. It shone like a frosted mirror in the twilight. But despite all its flamboyancy and aesthetic precision, it did not impress upon me the grandeur of a palace. Indeed, it was little more than the size of a carriage house for an up-and-coming merchant. Even the steward of my former estate lived in something that rivaled its size.

Alas, even my tomb would be a disappointment at the end of things.

"Your coat," a guard demanded of Alaina.

I attempted to put myself between them, but someone grabbed the sable collar of my robe from behind and pulled me away. They tore the robe down the seam and yanked it over my wings, snapping several joints. The pain tore through my back and sent me to a knee.

I struggled to my feet, now devoid of any covering beyond the collar, leather bands, and ankle bells, none of which would provide warmth.

Alaina, treated more gently if not with more mercy, had

surrendered her hat, gloves, coat, and satin dress. The guards allowed her to keep her stays, undergarments, and satin slippers. They had apparently drawn the line at stripping her naked, even though their confiscation of garments left her as good as.

Seeing me struggle, she came to my side and clung to my hand.

I scanned the crowd, faces peering over the line of guards at the courtyard ice walls. Too many guards, too many people creating a barrier that we could not slip into, too many people watching. Even Ivan, who might have offered some pretense at diversion, had been ushered away during our undressing. A single gaudy carriage still in the courtyard served as the last remaining vestige of the wedding processional.

Our move would have to be later.

"Your bridal bower awaits," one of the guards said, pointing to the doors of the construct.

Others in his unit who overheard the comment sneered.

"That's disgusting," said one of them.

No one laughed.

"Go on," said the initial guard, gesturing for us to head into the building of ice, hand on the hilt of his sword in case we did not comply.

Alaina took the lead, our hands still clasped. Together, we entered the building. We turned to look upon the crowd one last time.

The carriage, now at the gates ready to leave, had the curtains drawn back. I met the tsarina's empty gaze. Never breaking the stare, I pressed Alaina's hand to my chest and put my other hand over it.

The tsarina's Allemandian companion looked out over her shoulder.

Guards swung the double doors shut. A bolt fell moments after.

"At least we're out of the wind," Alaina said, releasing me, her breath fogging the air. "Are your wings all right?"

They hurt beyond expression, and my back cried out with shooting pain, but the sensations would be temporary. The cold, however, burned my feet and my fingers. I puffed up as much as I could and stuffed my hands under my arms to keep them functional.

"They will manage," I assured her.

Alaina surveyed the palace interior with a scowl. She crossed the room and disappeared into a doorway. A few moments later, she came back through the foyer, crossed to the other side, and again disappeared into the other doorway.

"Some palace!" she cried when she returned to me. "There are three rooms."

"Any windows?"

"None."

I stamped my feet to maintain circulation.

Alaina glared at the entry hall table, also carefully carved from ice, with three playing cards frozen into the table top.

"I hate her," she said. She grabbed the table and threw it against the wall with all the rage her little frame had bottled up. "I hate her! I hate her so much!"

Alaina then went off and proceeded to smash ice chairs, ice birds, ice console tables, ice curtains, and every other decoration that came into view until the foyer was littered with ice debris from once carefully sculpted ornaments.

I did not discourage her. Her fury and activity would help keep her warm. I hoped her rage would last all night, although if it did, she would run out of things to destroy before much longer.

"There's a bedroom," she spat as she came toward me, pointing in the direction of a doorway. "She thought of everything. Even little ice caps and ice nightshirts and ice quilts. Ice everything." She grabbed my hand and tugged me in that direction. "You need to see it. You need to see what she thinks of us."

I didn't need more proof of the tsarina's resentment, but I let Alaina bring me into the room designated as the bedroom. When I just stood there and gazed upon the artifacts Alaina pointed out, she screamed and threw another side table against the wall.

"See?" she shouted.

"She hates us. I know."

"Why are you so calm?" Alaina crossed back over to me. "This is a nightmare."

"This is a wonder tale."

"An Allemandian one, maybe," she grumbled. "How can you be so calm?"

"I'm not calm. I hate her more than you could know."

Alaina grabbed one of the ice nightcaps and thrust it at me.

"Throw it," she instructed. "It will make you feel better."

It didn't even though the dramatic smash against the wall should have been satisfying.

Several more pieces from Alaina followed, and though her breath came out in puffs, her cheeks reddened with exertion. Her manic, raging glee offered me a measure of hope I did not have prior. In encouragement, I pointed out other decorative elements for her to destroy. By the time she was finished, nothing but what had been built into the walls had survived. And those not for lack of trying.

She screamed at the walls several more times for good measure, and then, drained of all her furious energy, she came back to me and buried herself against my chest. I wrapped her up in my arms and rubbed her back and shoulders. She gazed up at me after several long moments.

"I'm so tired," she said.

I gathered her up in my arms again and headed back to the demolished bedroom. The alcove in the wall where the sculptors had placed the ice garments upon the ice bed offered the only pretense of shelter. I carried her into it and arranged my wing and tail feathers so that she would not have to sit or lean directly against the ice. I surrounded us both with the other wing, containing the heat of our breaths and our bodies in the confined space. I barely registered the pain of their injuries, half-numb with cold and insensible to any discomfort that might impede my ability to protect Alaina.

She tucked her hands into my feathers under my arms and kept her slippered feet beneath my legs. She shivered and pressed herself into me. She nestled her face against my neck.

"I don't know why I'm so tired," she lamented.

"Sleep if you need," I told her. "I'm here. I'll keep you warm."

Eventually, her grip loosened and her breathing evened. I shifted her so that I could get my damaged wings in a more comfortable position. The bells on my ankles echoed in the empty room.

This was it.

I dug into the leather band on my wrist, pulled out the wedding ring, and slipped it back onto my finger.

I was tired too. So tired. I would sleep like her. I just did not know if I would wake back up.

"Kaylay?"

I might have dreamed my name, whispered and light, the connection to wakefulness as fragile as crystalized breath. I sank back again into the welcoming darkness, no awareness of my physical being. I longed to put distance between us again. That's where pain and emotions lived, where I had to have an identity and a purpose, where hardships awaited. Why would I want to go back?

"Kaylay," she repeated, this time imbuing her invocation with urgency. She coupled the word with action, pressing her hands to my chest and shaking me. "Kaylay!"

Despite my desire to remain blissfully unaware of my state, her voice reminded me that she was still alive and well and, if she still needed me, then I should be present for her. I blinked frost from my lashes and groaned.

"Thank the Great Holy," she murmured as she moved back from me to let me shift my position.

Moving proved more difficult than merely assuring her I was still alive. My left cheek had been pressed against the ice wall of the bed enclosure, and I could not feel it. My left hand too had been folded under me, and I could not move my fingers. My legs shifted, and pain shot up through my left knee. And the wings screamed with every small adjustment, their injuries now more apparent in the fullness of time rather than in the after moments of stunned horror.

"I thought...." She stopped speaking and shook her head.

Frozen channels of tears stained her cheeks, and I reached out for her with my right hand to rub them with my thumb.

"You're not alone," I assured her.

"It's not about being alone." She pushed my hand aside as she wiped at her eyes. "Don't you understand? I don't want to be without you."

That certainly complicated my plans.

"You will feel differently when you're back in Altania," I said. "You have people who love and care for you there, and you won't need me anymore."

"I would rather die, here, with you, than face a future without you in it."

Her sentiment silenced me. No one had ever given me such a gift as that.

I crushed her to my chest because I was beyond words. It

spoiled my expectation of dying, but she needed to live. And if her will to survive depended on mine, then I would have to rally for that. It wouldn't have to be long, just long enough to get her somewhere she would be safe.

"I love you, Kaylay," she murmured into my neck. "Separation from you now would seem a crueler fate than any I can imagine."

She said it.

She loved me.

I closed my eyes. I did not lament when nothing happened. The tsarina lied to me constantly, and it was no surprise that she had about this too. Or maybe I had thwarted whatever magics she invoked either by speaking and revealing myself as more than just some Otherland bird or by confessing to who I had been with Drook and Klessa. But it did not matter anymore. And Alaina loved me anyway.

"Kaylay?"

I opened my eyes again when I heard her confusion.

Alaina sat up and held her hands out in front of her, palms full of feathers.

Alaina loved me. And it was the worst possible time for her to declare it.

"We have to leave now," I told her, projecting an air of calmness in the midst of my panic.

"Why now?"

The wing that separated her from the ice melted into a flurry of feathers. My shoulder slid down the wall, no longer supported by the other wing. I struggled against the bunched-up summer cloak beneath me, fumbling with the leather gloves as I tried to unclasp it so that I could straighten myself out. I couldn't feel my toes in the boots.

Alaina screamed and shoved me back. She launched herself off me, fleeing out into the demolished ice bedroom. She waited in the corner like prey, deciding if she needed to prepare another attack or if she could safely run away.

I couldn't blame her. I probably looked a mess.

I slid myself off the ice bed and stood on numb legs, no longer accustomed to how my old body moved and still accommodating wings and talons and tail feathers that were no longer there.

"I cannot keep you warm anymore, Alaina," I said, holding out a gloved hand in her direction.

She stared at me for hours, days, lifetimes. Precious moments, perhaps life-saving moments, slipped by as she stared at me in my thin black clothing.

I couldn't wait for her. I grabbed the cloak and approached her, throwing it over her when I was close enough.

"You're Finist the Falcon?" she asked, only now beginning to put it together.

"No." I knelt to clasp it for her. "Just Kaylay."

The cloak dragged on the ground, but it would have to serve.

"We need to leave," I said again, this time my voice more confident, command built into the suggestion, so that I could override any of her lingering stupefaction. I stood and moved toward the doorway, stumbling several times on the ice debris, the frozen bells around my boots silent even in my missteps. I held my hand out to her again, pleading with her to join me, glad it was gloved and more like what she expected than a naked human hand. "Alaina, please."

She took a deep breath, hiked up the cloak, and then joined me as we crossed into the entry.

"What's the plan?" she asked, clearly over her moment of disbelief.

"I need you to lie convincingly," I told her. "Scream at the door. Cry. Plead. Beg. Whatever you need to do to get the guards to listen. Tell them I'm dead. Tell them anything. Just get them to open the door."

She nodded, her face set, hard, and determined. She gathered herself up and released my hand. She flew at the doors. She threw herself bodily against them multiple times, wailing and screaming for help.

I took position beside the doors, shivering when the ice wall touched my back. I did not tell her my part in the escape. I did not think she would approve. But I had grown vicious in my captivity, and survival, her survival anyway, meant that I could retain no scruples or high-handedness. If I had to kill to keep her safe, so be it.

"The creature is dead," she cried out, "and I am not far behind. Please!" She clawed at the door and pounded her fists. "I'll give you my pearls," she shouted. "I'll give you anything! Anything!" She gave one last burst of pounding before she sank into a pile on the floor and wept. Loudly.

If I had not told her to put on an act, I would have certainly mistaken it for sincerity. Such emotions were likely not far from the surface though. She had managed stoicism so far with grace.

Nothing happened. No sounds from the other side, no answers in return. Were the guards debating the wisdom of opening the doors? Were they loyal to the tsarina to the point of turning down the princess' jewelry? Had they fallen asleep? Were there even any guards out there?

Alaina's gaze met mine. Unspoken fear and doubt passed between us. After a moment, she made a move to rise, but I held up a hand.

The doors shuddered as the bolt slid out of position.

Alaina perked and then melted back into her position of abject defeat.

A single door swung outward. A guard, backlit by a fire from without, stood in the opening.

"He's dead," Alaina repeated, pointing towards the doorway opposite the bedroom. She lifted her chin, her face tragic and pale in the dim light. "Spare me, I beg."

Another guard joined him at the doorway and looked her over.

"Please," she fumbled at the teardrop pearl necklace at her throat. "It was my mother's. A coat is all I ask."

In their avarice, the guards entered without checking their surroundings, believing Alaina's tale of my death.

I grabbed the nearest one from behind and smashed his head against the ice wall. He slid down, a streak of blood left behind. Alaina kneed the guard who allowed his attention to be caught up with his companion's fate. He doubled over with the violence of her placement. In his incapacity, I relieved him of his sword and concussed him with the hilt.

Together, Alaina and I stripped the guards. I donned the hat and coat from the first one, pulling the collar up around my face. She had the second guard's coat on under the cloak and a fur collar wrapped around her neck by the time I rejoined her. I could barely see her eyes beneath her own hat. I offered her the first guard's wool-lined boots and bear-skin gloves. She stuck her feet, slippers and all, into the boots and drew the gloves on, although they ill-fitted to such a degree that it might have seemed comical if we were not desperate.

We stopped just outside the ice building to ensure there were no other guards we needed to disarm. The silence and isolation, especially when our last view had been of a crowded entry, weighed upon me. Fortunate, of course, but so desolate and empty that I could not help but worry over our obviousness. We pulled the doors shut and bolted them again so that the guards could not pursue us, and no one would suspect what had happened until someone came in the morning.

We took a moment in front of the fire. I gave her the sausages the guards had been cooking as I warmed my hands through the gloves.

"It's bad when toes burn, isn't it?" she asked.

"It's worse when you cannot feel them at all," I assured her, although I did not tell her that I had stopped feeling my toes and the fingers on my left hand some time ago. "Wiggle them, if you can." Mine were completely unresponsive, but that was a problem I couldn't think about now.

"To port?" she asked after a few moments.

"To port," I agreed.

She set out in that direction, and within several strides, I caught up with her. She glanced up at me briefly but then returned her attention to our path, effectively preventing any discussion between us. Wise of her to conserve our energies as we trudged through the freshly fallen snow in silence. The original slickness of the roads and the heavy accumulation eventually slowed us to a crawl as we fought to maintain our pace.

Even with our new barriers against the cold, the biting wind tore through them, and my will to continue waned in the painful, numbing, frozen air. I winded before she did and slowed my pace still further, trying to catch my breath and still only managing the most shallow gasps as the breath-dewed fur clung to my lips.

I took another several steps and stopped. My lungs burned. My chest heaved. I willed myself to take just a few more steps, just a few more, but my legs did not respond to any directive.

"It's not much farther," she encouraged when she noticed I had stopped completely.

I gulped and pulled the coat collar away from my face, certain I could breathe again if only I could get enough air. I took another staggering step, and my boot slid on the ice. My leg went out from under me, and I fell to my knees. Pain spread through my body like a bolt of lightning. I was burning. Even the collar around my throat clung to my skin by frozen fiery sweat.

"Leave me," I rasped.

"No!" She grabbed at my arm. "You are NOT giving up now. I forbid it!"

I struggled to rise, not eager to continue, but recognizing she would give me less of a fight if I could manage. My legs, numb to everything, fumbled beneath me, and I fell again.

"Get up!" she screamed. She pulled at my shoulders to help me rise. "You need to get up!"

I had never considered that it might end like this, that I might die out in the cold, struggling to keep another alive, disgraced, collared, and mostly nameless. But I could not keep up, and I could not let her throw away her chance at escape and a new life because of me.

"I have never been able to save anyone that I've loved," I told her. "So I need you to be safe now. Please. That's all that matters to me."

She tried to haul me up and slipped. I fell even deeper into the snow and closed my eyes. Nearly frozen shut anyway, giving into the inclination came too easily.

In the darkness, she called my name, my Varnasian name, my Varnasian name made sweet by her abbreviation of it. I wanted to answer her, to promise her it would all be well, to tell her I would be at peace, that my suffering was over, at long last. I couldn't. My lips wouldn't work. My voice didn't come. I hoped she understood that I hadn't wanted to leave her, but my purpose was fulfilled.

The Otherlander's promise ushered me into tranquil welcome oblivion.

XXXV.

Someone moaned.

All was darkness. Had someone put a hood back on me? If they bound my hands behind my back again, that would explain why my back and shoulders ached so much.

But hadn't I died? Out in the snow, saving Alaina. I had frozen to death. But surely, death should be less painful.

I hoped Alaina was safe.

Someone moaned again.

"Great Holy," came a breathless whisper. "You're awake."

Clearly, they meant someone other than me because I was dead. And I couldn't be awake when I was dead, could I?

I managed to say, although it came out raspy and hesitant, "Someone is in pain."

"Yes," said my unseen companion, her voice stronger now. "That someone is you."

"I'm dead," I told her, still half-certain that I was.

"No, but you gave it a good effort." Fingertips, warm and gentle, touched a place on my collarbone. "I thought I lost you several times."

"I'll try harder next time then."

"There better never be a next time," she scolded me in that commanding tone. "I've barely slept for worry."

"I told you to leave me, princess."

"And I told you that I wouldn't. Are you thirsty?"

I nodded. Or I thought I nodded. I couldn't tell with my head throbbing.

Something hard and cold met my bottom lip. Then it tilted

upward. Water flowed slowly and in spurts as the rim
seesawed. I licked my lower lip when the cup withdrew. I
couldn't remember the last time I had drunk from a cup.

"Are we safe?" I asked. "Are you well?"

"We are safe and I am well, all because of you."

"Have I been rendered blind by the cold?" My question
came out more bravely than I thought it would. Although I
had become accustomed to the hood and the sightlessness it
inflicted, light still peeked around the fastenings. And yet, now,
no light had greeted me. If that had been the price I had to
pay, although a hefty one, then so be it.

She did not respond. I registered her intense stillness more
than anything else.

"I befriended you sight unseen," I reminded her. "I can
live with that if you promise still to talk to me occasionally."

"It's not that," she said. "I mean, I don't think so anyway.
You've been in and out of fever for so long that you'll have to
tell me if anything else is amiss. I have few candles lit and
you're bandaged, which is likely why all is darkness to you."

Bandages implied injury, but I could live with injury.

"I had to shave your face for the physician. I didn't do a
very good job." Her fingers stroked my right cheek. "You have
dreadfully uneven stubble now."

I asked without time to think better of it, "Would you
prefer feathers?"

She pulled her hand away.

"I wanted to tell you," I confessed. "So many times I went
to and then thought, why burden you with it?"

"No, of course," she said. "Why would I have expected
you to tell me the truth?"

"I did not foresee any reversal of my fate."

In our first days, I waited on her in silence and in the dark.
Her words were balms, her presence a comfort. But for her,
she had been with her bird friend, and I was now but a

stranger. Her silence suffocated me.

"You should have just let me die," I told her more bitterly than I intended.

She put her hand on my shoulder, and I pulled away from her grasp. I could not bear her touch even though I craved it. She didn't want me, not like this, not anymore. And maybe she never truly had. Our coupling had been her defiance, her demonstration of autonomy in the face of one who would have seen her spirit broken, not a statement of true desire.

But for me....

If the last year of my life had not numbed me to grief and heartache, I might have given in to the infantile urge to weep.

Alaina might have told me that she loved me, but I was still someone else to her then, and we were facing death. I couldn't believe it now.

She tried to touch me again. "I know you're upset—"

"Damn right, I'm upset!" Anger served me better than tears. "That was supposed to be the end. I was supposed to die. And then I would never again have to worry about disappointing anyone. But I'm alive. And I am still found wanting by the only person I give a shit about."

"That's not true, Kaylay."

"I'm not your Kaylay!" Didn't she see that was the point? "I'm a complete stranger to you."

"You're not a stranger."

"You screamed when you saw me."

"I was being held by a magnificent bird one moment, and in the next, I'm being held by a man. Screaming was a perfectly reasonable reaction!"

She wasn't wrong.

"You're not a stranger," she repeated. "When I got to Ilyichia, everyone spoke of the tsarina's favorite lover."

Blyat.

The chill of her knowledge combatted the heat of my

shame. A fallen prince reduced to servitude and subjugation owned more humiliation than some pretty, anonymous servant the tsarina plucked off the street and made her slave.

"You know who I am."

"I know you were a respected soldier. I know you worked tirelessly to earn back the honor of a powerful and influential family that your forefathers jeopardized. I know you were considered one of the most eligible bachelors in the royal households of the continent."

I could not dispute any of it.

"You were also said to be the most handsome man in Ilyichia," she added.

"Maybe fifteen years ago."

"I saw you the other day," she asserted, "and there was no lie."

"You know too then that I am disgraced," I reminded her lest she get caught up in her own fanciful and romanticized idea of me.

"No one could miss what she did to you."

No indeed. How could anyone miss that? Not Alaina, who had been both kind and painfully honest through my initial ordeal.

"I believed her when she told everyone that she had you put to death," Alaina added. "It seemed highly plausible that she had had her fun and then tired of you. I didn't put it together that you were him until just a few days ago."

"But you've seen me before—"

"I've never seen you without a beak!"

We both fell into silence with the strangeness of that observation.

"I can see why she was so taken with you." She put her hand on my shoulder again, and I didn't pull away. "Even as a bird."

"And what about you? Would you still prefer me with

feathers and wings?”

“Kaylay.”

“That means yes.” It hurt more than I expected, even though I anticipated no other answer. “I have spent my life trying to do the right thing, the honorable thing, and she still took everything from me. Everything. And the only thing I had any personal ability to regain was my humanity. And even then—”

I broke off, unable to complete my thought. My voice already cracked on the words. I wasn’t enough. And I would never be enough.

“You don’t understand,” she insisted. “I didn’t love the beautiful man in the bird costume. I didn’t know him. But the bird in her menagerie was safe and kind even when I was a horrid little brat. And I did know him. And I did care about him. And it turns out that my friend, *my love*, really was just a beautiful man in a bird costume after all.”

“Your love,” I repeated, testing its veracity.

“My love,” she assured me.

My right hand fumbled with the blanket as it sought her out. I wanted her hand. I wanted her to touch me and ground me and remind me what I had tried to die for. But I could not find her, and I gave up when she did not breach the distance. Instead, I reached up and touched the linen shirt and then the featherless skin beneath it. I expanded my explorations to my neck and found it bare.

“I thought I was going to lose you,” she said when she noticed my discovery. “How dare you have the audacity to try and die on me after everything we’ve been through!”

“Alaina, be honest,” I pleaded. “Something is terribly wrong, and you are keeping it from me.”

“You had severe frostbite.” She found my hand and held it between both of hers. “The ship surgeon saved as much as he could.”

"Do I still have...?" I didn't know how to describe my initial concern delicately. "Am I intact?"

"How like a man!" She choke-laughed, betraying the possibility that she had been crying. "Yes, you're intact."

That was a relief. But then other concerns followed. My left hand had been unresponsive in the cold, and I had not tested it since wakefulness. I freed my hand from her grasp and threw the blanket off me, hunting for my left arm. I found my elbow and traveled down the rest of my forearm. I met bandages at my wrist. I still had a wrist, and I could feel the base of my palm below that, no stump indicating a complete amputation.

"The surgeon took most of three fingers and the tip of a fourth."

I took a deep breath. It could have been worse.

"Anything else?" I didn't want to know the answer, but I had to know.

"Four toes on your left foot and the smallest two on your right."

I could live without toes, even without fingers. But I also had bandages on my face.

"Alaina," I marveled at my calm, "what do I look like?"

She didn't answer.

Alaina loved me as a bird, and now she would have preferred me that way. I had to be ugly. A different kind of ugly.

"Please tell me?"

"Kaylay—"

I lost all pretense of patience. I struggled to find my way out of the sick bed on the opposite side of where Alaina sat by me. I stumbled when I rose, my left leg stiff and subject to stabbing pains that radiated through my foot. I tore at the bandages that covered my face and freed myself from them.

As Alaina had told me, the few candles still lit around the

room offered little light. It was a sumptuous room, decorated and outfitted like any well-appointed bedroom at court. I wanted to see if perhaps she had given me her room while I convalesced, but I refused to turn around, certain now that my face was unbandaged, I would offer her nothing but a hideous disfigurement that was all too humanly repulsive.

"You're still unwell," she scolded.

It didn't matter. I needed to know, and I needed to know now. But no mirrors hung on the walls. No vanities occupied the gilt bedroom. No reflective sconces offered enough surface to see the damage. Just before I resorted to emptying drawers, I found a hand mirror on a dresser top and turned it over.

The facial hair I had worn from my time in prison had likely minimized the damage, as the lower half of my face sported nothing but a few minor cuts from shaving. Wounds on my forehead and cheek scabbed over on the right side of my face, still raw, still angry, but healing. Eventually, with time and salves, those would make a full recovery.

But the left side of my face....

I had already endured so many lowering experiences, but there had always been the possibility of restoration and reinstatement. Even as a bird, I had been given the tenuous possibility of being human again. But there was no remedy for being an ugly and ridiculous man. This was permanent, and I could do nothing about it.

If Alaina had been open to accepting me as a man, then surely this was what had prevented the continuation of her affections. No wonder Alaina had withdrawn from me.

I lowered the mirror.

"The surgeon said you would die from infection if he didn't...." She could not verbalize the description of the procedure that took a significant portion of the left side of my nose, scarred my cheek, temple, and forehead, and deprived me of most of my left ear. "I couldn't let you die."

She would just see that I lived out the rest of my days in a different isolation and shame. Even though I had been ugly as a bird, I had still been whole. Maybe being blind in addition would have been preferable so that I would never have to fully know this reality.

"What did you have in mind for my future?" If she wanted to see me live, I was determined to find out why she thought this fate might be preferable to dying. "Do you need a disfigured jester for the Altanian court? I have experience. My suffering has entertained many."

My left leg trembled with exertion and pain. I could not risk returning to the bed because I would have to turn around and face Alaina. Instead, I sank to the rug. I began laughing, afraid that if I did not find some hideous humor in it, I would devolve into weeping in earnest. And then I might never stop.

I didn't even have my face for more than a few hours. And, sentimental fool that I was, I had allowed myself to hope in that brief time that Alaina might want me with her in Altania, not as some reclusive pet, but something more. As a man, albeit a foreign man without any connections and a past he would not disclose, I could have found reason to live among others and be at her side. How could she want me with her now?

She approached me from behind and joined me on the floor. She put her hand on my shoulder and rubbed it through the linen shirt.

"You can be whoever or whatever you want to be here," she whispered.

"I should never have left Varnasia."

"I'm sorry," she said, "but I'm selfish. And I give thanks both to the Great Holy and The Kind and Fair that you were in Ilyichia when I needed you most."

"I don't believe in fated purpose, higher or otherwise. If not me, someone else would have stepped forward to help you through.”

“Not likely. I needed someone who wasn’t like the rest of them. I needed you.”

“But you don’t need me here in Altania.”

“No, I don’t need you here in Altania.” She inched closer and rested her cheek against my back. “I want you here in Altania.”

“Why? So that all your acquaintances can mock your foreign oddity?”

“They would not dare mock my husband.”

Husband.

“No one sane would hold you to that,” I assured her, “not once they knew the circumstances and the inferiority of the groom.”

She tugged on a lock of hair at the nape of my neck in chastisement. “I will thank you not to speak so ill of my husband.”

“You are your brother’s heir,” I insisted. “You cannot be wedded to a disfigured foreign nobody.”

“I can be wedded to a noble man who earned grievous wounds by keeping me safe.”

“Gratitude is not enough. You deserve more, better.”

“There is no one better, not for me.” At my silence, she rose and kissed the spot behind my right ear. “I meant it when I said it. I love you.”

“I don’t see how you can.”

Alaina stood and swept her skirts around me. She arranged them and then sat on the floor again, this time in front of me, fluffing up the pink satin layer of skirt like a flower unfurling its petals. Her long dark hair, loose and silky, draped her shoulders like an exquisite shawl.

I turned the left side of my face away from her.

“Kaylay,” she said in her haughty princess voice, “do you know how insulting it is to think that I only care about you for your looks?"

"You should care." I was unrepentant. I certainly cared about them. "I will not ruin the rest of your life by holding you to a marriage that was arranged out of malice and cruelty. You do not owe me that. And if I saved your life, then you must share it with someone worthy, someone who will be a credit to you. That is the extent of your debt."

Selflessness was not my intention. I wanted to be her husband, to live in ecstatic bliss together in Altania and make up for every indignity we had suffered. I wanted to drown her in kisses and adoration. I wanted to worship her in every way I could. I wanted to beg her to love me as I loved her, wholly and completely.

But I knew the world. I knew her world. Her reputation, her future, and her throne would surely suffer if she honored a marriage to a man who had lost everything that might have made him suitable.

She took my left hand, bandaged as it was, and raised it to her mouth. She kissed it. "You are someone worthy."

"I have been reduced to an ornament, a curiosity, an amusement. I have no value."

Did she know how it hurt or what it cost me to verbalize my greatest insecurity?

She grabbed my chin as she had once done with a beak and forced me to look at her. I did not pull away. If she wanted to view the ruin of my face, then so be it. Maybe she would come to her senses if she looked long enough upon the truth.

"You are more than what the tsarina would have you believe," Alaina insisted. "Did the last year teach you nothing?"

"It taught me that I am disposable." I stared straight back at her. "It taught me that I can work hard, do all the right things, and still end up with nothing. It taught me that the things I have always wanted most in this world are not meant for me."

"If you still had feathers, I would pluck one out for such a defeatist answer."

"Alaina, please, look at me. Truly look at me. This," I gestured to my face, "won't get better."

"Yes," she said thoughtfully after a good long moment of looking. "You are as ugly as I expected. My opinion hasn't changed on that."

"And you," I said, realizing her game and surrendering to it, "are still the size of a twig." An amusing thought pulled up one side of my mouth. "No. I've thought better of it. You are more the size of a fifth nested doll in a matryoshka."

She dropped my chin and cupped her hands around my face. She bent my head down and kissed my brow as she had done so many times before.

"I love you. All of you." She pressed her lips to my forehead. "Your wounds are honorable." She pressed her lips to my temple. "And noble." She pressed her lips to my cheek. "And beautiful." She kissed the bridge of my nose, where it healed after being broken.

She had never kissed me with a real face before, and now she never would.

"Why don't you want to be my husband?"

"I cannot face court again," I admitted. "I've had my fill of being the brunt of every joke and the subject of every insult. If I had my wish, I would fade into obscurity somewhere and never have to be in the public eye. I'm not strong enough to withstand the Altanian court finding fault with me at every turn."

"Unfortunately, being my husband does mean being at court." She fiddled with her hair for a moment before sweeping a large section behind her shoulder. "But Altania is different than Ilyichia. It's warmer," she said, knowing how much weight I put in that. "And I will not tolerate anyone treating you as less than."

"But I am less th—" I broke off, my attention caught by a bandage on her chest, visible now with her hair brushed aside. "You told me you were well," I accused.

"And I am!"

"That's a wound, princess."

"Yes. And," she said, brushing her hand over the bandage, "it's probably going to scar."

My throat constricted.

"Don't you dare blame yourself for it," she threatened. "I went through that ordeal too. And I'm going to wear my scar proudly. I earned it. After all, I couldn't let you get all the glory."

She had an odd notion of glory.

"I plan on wearing daring decolletage for the rest of my life so I can show it off," she said.

If only I could feel that way about mine.

"We should tell your brother that you're alive," Alaina said.

"He won't want me back."

"Then you leave me no choice." Alaina took my hand again. "Prince Mikhail—"

"Former prince," I corrected. "I haven't been reinstated."

"No. Not yet." Alaina smiled. "My brother, however, is king, and you are now a prince of Altania. I don't remember what district he's given you, but it was a good one. You'll have to talk to him about that. And he's made you a member of the Order of the Falcon for saving me. It's the highest honor you can be given in Altania." She shot me a glance through her eyelashes. "Now, Prince Mikhail—"

I held my tongue this time.

"Good." She took a deep breath, content with my submission. "I, Princess Alaina of Altania and heir to the throne, have heard your arguments against acknowledging a wedding that took place in Ilyichia not long ago under stressful circumstances. Being your social superior, I have answered them all to my satisfaction and have determined that your reasons are insufficient to merit an annulment. So I only have one more question to ask to determine if indeed I should let it stand." She dropped the act and reached out to take my hands. "Do you love me, not just as a companion through difficult times but enough to spend the rest of your life with me?"

"Yes." It was the easiest answer in the world.

"Then it is decided. I will have none other." She lowered her voice. "Although I think perhaps we should also get married in the sight of the Great Holy too. What do you say? Be my husband? Remember, if you say no, you doom Altania to an heirless throne. The hopes and expectations of an entire country, and more importantly, me, rest on you."

"What do we do about my face?"

"Perhaps a small mask if it so concerns you."

"No feathers," I stipulated.

"I suppose if you insist. Hammered gold and jewels then? To match your ring?"

I probed the bandages on my left hand. Though I had nothing beyond the second knuckle, the wedding band remained.

"You really want me, after everything?" I asked.

"I wanted you as a bird too," she admitted, reaching into her bodice and retrieving the red-gold feather I had once given her as an ornament for her hair, "but I couldn't figure out how to make that work. This is so much easier."

Nothing would be easy. I didn't know Altanian well. I would have to learn a whole new set of cultural expectations and norms. I would have to become acquainted with a whole new set of people who would look at me as a suspicious foreigner. But I would have Alaina there beside me, and no one else had to know my true history.

"Then, my wife, let our marriage stand."

And for the first time, she leaned over and pressed her lips to mine.

XXXVI.

I paused in my tale, uncertain what else there was to tell.

"I think that's all of it," I said, "at least until something new and eventful happens here, but I am hoping for plain, boring peace."

"You have earned peace," the pale masked Otherlander agreed.

We sat on the marble bench in the garden, in my alcove dedicated to The Kind and Fair. The offering bowl, serving as a bath for birds and other creatures when not in use, sat atop a granite pedestal currently holding the pale pink water of my devotional.

Newly planted rose bushes around the alcove had yet to bloom, save for one. Finding roses proved a challenge, but word got out of a Rivani couple selling rose bush cuttings just north of the capital. Alaina sent a special envoy to procure them on my behalf. Although the Rivani couple relayed that their cuttings only spawned red roses, the Otherlander pricked his fingertip on one of the thorns. That bush immediately overflowed with white.

After his display of magic, the Otherlander draped his bronze robes over the bench as he sat, retrieved a squirrel that caught its claw on the embroidery of the Otherlander's robe, and then gestured for me to sit beside him. He asked me to recount my full tale now that I was no longer under constraint. We gazed not at each other but outward as we spoke, or rather, as I spoke to him. It made the storytelling easier, not having to face him while I detailed my sordid experiences.

"Tell me," the Otherlander said, "what is the anniversary day of your birth?"

An odd question, but this was a Kind and Fair Protector of Ilyichia and my unlikely benefactor, so I told him.

"I give you the tsarina's death as a present then," he said. "The day after, Ilyichia will be free of her."

"I do not require such a gift," I demurred, not wishing to offend him, but also not sorry for secretly coveting it.

"She no longer has my support, and I need to make way for her successor. I will also ensure that you are reinstated. Will your brother pose any obstacle?"

After our second wedding, this time in a chapel dedicated to the Great Holy so that no one could dispute our marriage, Alaina insisted that I write to Alexei despite my misgivings. To my surprise, he answered my correspondence. His letter, filled with warmth and heartfelt apologies, assured me of his genuine relief to learn that I had not perished and reaffirmed his continued affection. He promised me, whenever the political tide turned again, that he would gladly surrender the family estates, funds, and titles to my care once more. Although I never intended to return to Ilyichia, the assurance of uncontested reinstatement eased the guilt of having come to Altania with nothing.

"I think that my brother dislikes the attention it puts on him."

"Then you are fortunate," said the Otherlander.

I debated saying anything else, but this Otherlander had come to my aid when no one else would. And as one person in a mask to another, he might understand.

"I am afraid that this and this alone will be my legacy," I confided. "I fear that I will never be remembered for anything else but my time at the hands of the tsarina."

"Often that is the way of it," the Otherlander agreed.

"Tell me if you can, my lord," I asked humbly, "how is it

that one year of a human life can be so dramatic that it obliterates everything that came before?" My question came out like one from a child, but compared to the presumed age of the Otherlander, I probably was to him. "I have lived upon this earth for over four decades, and yet, this will be all that anyone recalls of me, as if I had no life prior."

"I have lived many ages more than you, and yet a recent incident in my life has consumed and obliterated all else that I have ever been." After a long pause, he asked, "Do you know why that is so?"

Likely because it was the most delicious gossip to tell. I bit my tongue though and shook my head, unwilling to be my sharp self with this powerful creature.

"Those incidents determine our strength. They allow us to prove who we are beneath the pretense of our given societies. My situation, your hardship. We are still here. We still endure. We have proven ourselves more than what others thought of us. Be proud of your struggle. It is not your year of torment that is the moral of your story, but your triumph over it. It forged you into something better and stronger than you were before."

The chipmunk sleeping in the Otherlander's sleeve woke and poked its head out, sniffing the air before deciding that the sleeve offered more warmth and comfort than anything outside of it. Maybe I was just another little creature seeking warmth and comfort to this Otherlander since he offered sympathy no one else around me could provide.

I grieved the loss of my fingers, my glove stuffed where I could not fill it, my boots too where there were no toes. I resented the mask that kept my scars out of sight. Too frequently, I roused from slumber or could not sleep at all for the irrational fear that I would have to return to the tsarina. I dreamed of those I loved turning from me. I dreamed that I was trapped in a costume I could not remove. I dreamed of being blinded and bound again. I dreamed of the cold. I did not know what to do with those wounds.

Speaking with the Otherlander helped, even if I did not feel better or stronger. I just felt tired. So tired.

"Better and stronger." I turned to face him, mask to mask. "Is that the lie you tell yourself, my lord?"

A soft laugh emanated from behind his beaded silk. "What else would you have me say?"

"That 'better' and 'stronger' are just temporary balms we put on wounds that will never heal."

"So they are," he conceded.

"I will never heal, will I?"

"Not fully. Never fully. But there is a new life awaiting you, a fresh start, where it sounds as if you will be honored for your trials. You have all the makings of a happily ever after."

"I do not believe that there is such a thing. There's just life, and more life, and it isn't a matter of if I will have another struggle, but when, and to what magnitude. In essence," I concluded, "life is shit."

"Life *is* shit," the Otherlander agreed. "But your friend is right. As long as you live, there is hope, and that makes it worth enduring."

"Oh!" I could barely contain my grin as I recalled an important detail I had forgotten to relate to the Otherlander. "Alaina is pregnant." That was hope, tangible, immediate hope. "Granted, I have already lost three children, so I fear to hope," I confided. "And the baby was conceived while I was a bird, so we will have to see if there are any feathers involved. But still, it is already much loved."

"Many felicitations. Take my assurance — your child will survive. And if there are feathers, I am sure they will be most comely."

The sparrow that nestled in the Otherlander's hair spotted something tasty on the ground and left its perch on his shoulder. The Kind and Fair's gaze followed it.

"Invite me to the naming ceremony," he said, "and I shall grant your child a gift."

"You have given me a chance at a new life. You have made me worthy of it and of those who love me. I cannot ask anything more of you."

"Invite me nonetheless."

"As you wish, my lord."

The Otherlander stood, and I stood with him, deferentially and at attention.

He glanced toward the doorway leading into the antechamber of our bedroom and gestured with his head. "I believe your lady wife has come to fetch you."

I turned my attention to the doorway. Alaina stood there, hair in a loose braid over her shoulder, dressed in her morning robes.

A vision. My whole world.

I turned back to the Otherlander, expecting to make introductions despite not knowing his name. But he had gone, silent as ever.

Alaina took several steps out into the garden. "Was that....?"

"Our benefactor, yes."

She stared at the spot where he had been, silent and awed.

I broke the spell. "Finally decided to join the wakeful, did you?"

"We cannot all be early birds like you," she said, reaching out to beckon me back inside.

I breached the distance and took her hand with my good one.

The magnitude of all that had happened constantly overwhelmed me. It likely would for a long time. But I was here, in Altania, with my wife, looking forward to an unexpected and exciting future even with open wounds.

I rubbed her fingers to ensure that she was real.

"I love you, Alaina."

"And despite my best efforts," she said as she pulled me down towards her, threw her arms around my neck, and drowned me in little kisses, "I love you too."

When I was living in Italy in 2006, I wrote a nice little Italian-centric Beauty and the (bird) Beast that went like this:

In 1740, Prince Michele (Michael in Italian), whose appearance I based on a violinist I saw in Russia the year before, travels to Italy and converts to Catholicism to marry Alaina. His queen, furious at his conversion and marriage (because she wanted him for herself), turns him into a bird.

I wrote 45k+ words on it before putting it away.

In 2022, I was listening to a historical podcast on my commute to work. The episode was on the Russian Empress Anna Ivanovna and included a story about a courtier. Prince Mikhail (Michael in Russian) traveled to Italy, converted to Catholicism, married a woman there, and was then punished by the empress. She made him a jester, and her favorite punishment? Dressing him up like a bird. And when she built her ice palace, she forced him to marry anew and spend his wedding night in that palace… in 1740.

I had to pull over on the highway because my hands were shaking.

And it only got weirder.

When I started looking into the history, I discovered Prince Mikhail's Italian wife was named Irena and his eldest daughter was named Elena. Princess Irena/ Elena/ Alaina. Prince Mikhail and I also share a birthdate. Although his is listed on genealogy sites as 27 October, Russia used the Julian calendar in 1687, not the Gregorian. His actual birth record lists his birthday as 17 October, just like mine. And though not confirmed with 100% confidence due to my inability to cross-reference, given the limitations of the genealogy site, I am very likely related to him.

I reached out to several experts and institutions that specialize in Russian history to further my knowledge without success. So I began learning Russian so that I could deep-dive into primary sources on my own. I have begun compiling a respectable bibliography of Prince Mikhail's life. Because I am limited in my abilities and I will likely never be able to return to Russia, I am always looking for other avenues of research, and I welcome anyone to contact me who might have those leads, skills, or archival access.

While *Tsarina's Favorite* isn't strictly adherent to the facts, I used much of my research in the novel. And when I strayed, I attempted to stay as close to the spirit of the history as possible, even in the fantastic elements. Prince Mikhail was a man who accomplished much and earned everything he accomplished despite the historical burden of his title. And still, he has only ever been undeservedly remembered by history as the tsarina's jester and the bridegroom of the ice palace. Indeed, the only image of him during his lifetime that I have been able to find is an engraving of him in a cage!

Although I am but a little author and a specious relation, I have a duty to tell his story, not the story of a tsarina with a prince she persecuted, but the story of a man who endured much just to find the peace he so desperately desired. And so, as a gift to him, I released *The Tsarina's Favorite* on our birthday, hoping to reframe the narrative of his life and give him the dignity history has not been kind enough to afford.

My best,

Valt

P.S. Nowadays, kvass is sold as a soft drink. But historically, it was a low-alcohol-content ale: bitter, sour, and often mixed with things like horseradish to be used as a hangover restorative. Mikhail strongly advises against trying it.

ABOUT THE AUTHOR

Little is known about this writer. Complaints made to city hall about a nude humanoid figure wandering the grounds of his 1871 fortress residence have largely been ignored due to the typical inclusion of horns in witness descriptions. Although he gives operatic performances on occasion, paparazzi have been unable to catch him vacating his lair with some sources implying that he possesses shape-shifting abilities. Internet statements positively attributed to this writer claim a birth year of 1638, intensive training in Liberace Fashion Principles, and the discovery of a sixth-dimensional cube in his cereal in 2002. Within the last year, sightings have spiked with independent investigators suggesting that he has come out of seclusion to vindicate an ancestral Russian prince.

www.valtinen.com